In Loving Memory

of

Dianne Price

(1933 – 2013)

The
Promise
of
Dawn

Dianne Price

BOOK THREE OF
THE THISTLE SERIES

Ashberry Lane

© 2014
Ashberry Lane
P.O. Box 665, Gaston, OR 97119
www.ashberrylane.com

Published in association with Terry Burns of Hartline Literary Agency, LLC.

ISBN 978-1-941720-02-8

Cover design by Miller Media Solutions
Cover images by Ashlee Murr Photography and iStock.com

Use of the Gaelic Biblical Texts by kind permission of the Scottish Bible Society.

Scripture used in this book, whether quoted or paraphrased by the characters, is taken from the English Revised Version of the Bible, Oxford Press, 1885. Used by permission.

Map © 2013 Mary Elizabeth Hall

Other Ashberry Lane Books
by Dianne Price

Broken Wings, Book One in the Thistle Series
Wing and a Prayer, Book Two in the Thistle Series

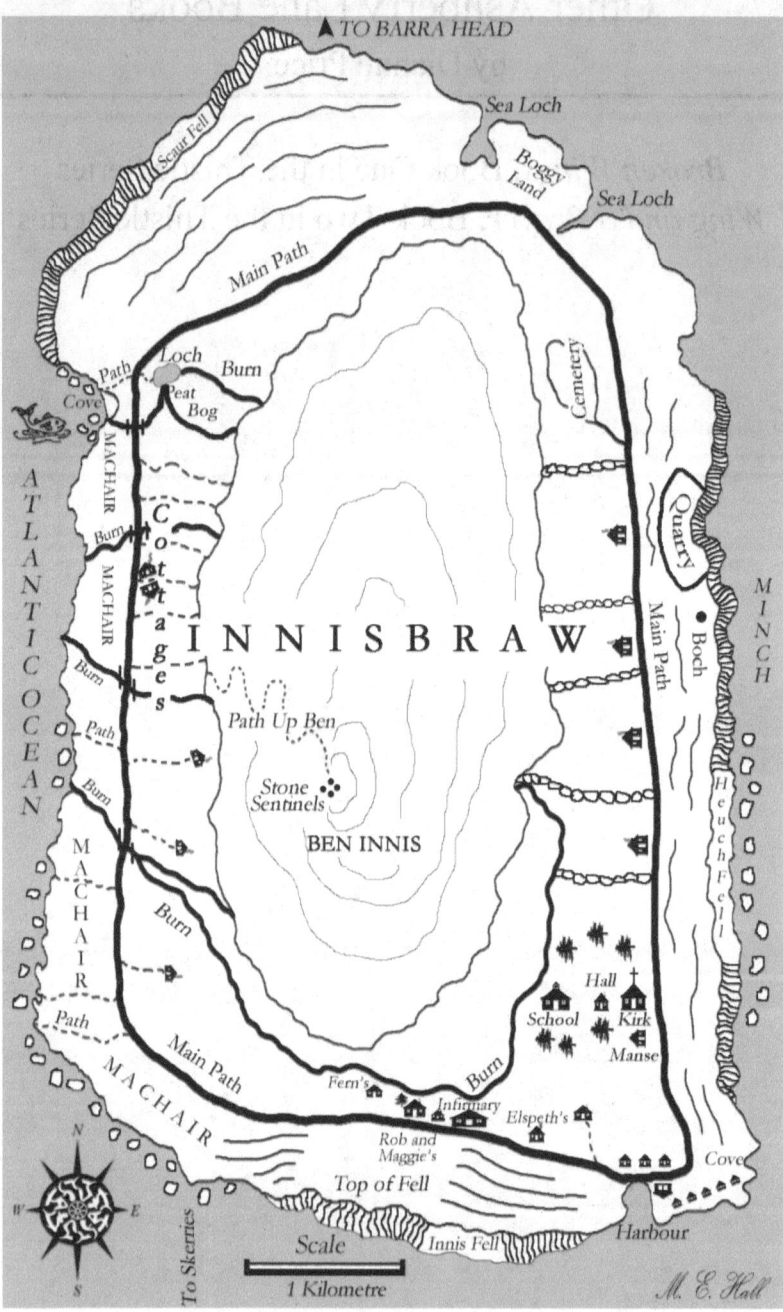

Written with some British spelling, this book also includes a
Scottish Gaelic glossary.

Philipianach/Philippians 4:13

Is urrainn mi na h-uile nithe a
I can do all things in
dheanamh tre Chriosd a neartaicheas mi.
him that strengtheneth me.

Never give in, never give in, never; never; never; never—
in nothing, great or small, large or petty—never give in
except to convictions of honor and good sense.
~Sir Winston Churchill, 1864-1965

And O! be sure to fear the Lord always, and mind your duty,
duly, morn and night;
lest in temptation's path ye gang astray,
implore His counsel and assisting might:
they never sought in vain that sought the Lord aright.
~Robert Burns, national poet of Scotland, 1759-1796

Dedication

For the glory of my Lord, Jesus Christ.
And, as always, for my True, who
lived up to his name in every way.

In Loving Memory

Dianne joined her beloved Savior and
her husband in heaven one week
before her first book released. She is
probably dancing a Scots reel even as
you read this.

No more screams from the wounded or dying. No more Pathé news films with horrifying pictures of sinking ships, burning dockyards. No more families picking through the rubble of their bombed-out flats, hoping to find a precious fragment from their past.

And on the Isle of Innisbraw, no more worrying about the fate of their lads in uniform.

WWII is finally over.

Chapter One

Isle of Innisbraw, Outer Hebrides, Scotland
August, 1945

I'll never fly again.

The glow of peat embers glinted off the silver colonel's eagle Rob Savage held in his palm.

Heaving a ragged sigh, Rob re-pinned it to the shoulder of his American Air Forces blouse and ran his hand over rows of ribbons below the wings.

Nine hours ago he'd worn that blouse with his uniform for the last time—to the special service held at the kirk when word reached the island that the war with Japan was over.

Rob closed his eyes. Would he ever overcome his grief at receiving a medical discharge? A graduate of West Point, career officer, full bird colonel in charge of the 396th Heavy Bomber Group ... and now he couldn't fly. The ache to return to his days piloting a B-17 bomber brought a yearning so profound he fought tears.

Aye, Innisbraw was his home now—a wee, green island peopled by all the folk he considered family. But to fly again, to chase the clouds, to fling off earthly fetters and lose himself in a sky so blue it seared itself into the deepest recesses of his brain ...

His dog, Shep, pressed a cold nose into Rob's palm.

"Want a run, lad?" He pushed himself to his feet. "'Tis verra early, but I'm thinking we both could use the exercise." He laid the blouse over the back of his rocker, padded over to the large window in the kitchen, and lifted a corner of the lace curtain.

A bruised, dusky-grey sky.

"'Tis light enough to see the path." He bent and rubbed the

1

Australian shepherd's silken ears. "On you come, then." He let the dog out and eased the door closed so as not to awaken his wife.

Maggie, biggen with their second bairn, was a light sleeper and didn't deserve to be awoken before their laddie, Robbie, called for her.

Footsteps muffled in the heavy pre-dawn air, Rob walked along the stone-flagged path through Maggie's garden to the front gate set in the drystone dyke surrounding their home. His slow trot soon became a long, loping run as he and Shep covered the path down the slope of Innis Fell toward the harbour below. The chilly early morning air brought hen's flesh coursing up his arms beneath his light, long-sleeved Jacobite shirt.

The waters of the Minch beyond the harbour shone inky-black with glimmers of white splintering the tops of the waves. Above the horizon, an occasional star blinked a faint protest before being swallowed by the slowly brightening sky.

The path was deserted. At a bit gone 0400, even the fishermen, always the first to be up and about, were still abed or savouring their first cup of tea.

Shep and Rob ran past the infirmary, Elspeth NicAllister's cottage, the path to the MacPhee croft, and the stone buildings housing the post office, howff, and weaving shop on the inland side. Past the piers, the old herring-packing shed, and five tiny, thatched, stone cottages lining the harbour. He turned the wide corner where the path followed the contour of the island and headed west toward the Atlantic shore.

As he ran, Rob fought to blank out any negative thoughts. This was a time to renew his body and mind. The kirk to his left was unlit, but a soft light shone from one of the windows in the manse. Surely Hugh MacEwan, the island's minister, also found sleep difficult after such an emotional day.

For most of the islanders, the war had ended with the surrender of Germany the previous May, bringing an end to the guards walking the shore at night, to fears of being shelled from the Atlantic, to dreading the fate of their uniformed lads.

But Hugh was one of the few who recognized the high cost of American lives in the Pacific Theatre. Most likely, he was deep in the Word at this time of the morning.

The sheep and the coo gangs of the large crofts Rob passed were hushed, nature holding her chilled breath until the first rays of sun flooded land and sky with warmth. Only a friendly bowf from one of Alec MacDonald's herding dogs and the throaty *pruk-pruk* of a raven broke the silent dawn. But when the path turned south, the muted roar of the Atlantic breaking against the western shore gave voice to one of God's masterpieces.

The sweet scent of heather spilled down the slopes of nearby Ben Innis. The same fragrance had drawn him to his Maggie more than three years ago. He didn't have to close his eyes to remember how she looked that night in the officer's club at Edenoaks Air Base. He stood a little over six-five, but she was so tiny the top of her head didn't even reach his shoulder. Her luxurious black hair in a regulation bun above her RAF Nurses' Corps uniform collar ... startling violet-blue eyes seldom meeting his gaze ... petite body stiff with obvious embarrassment that the commander of the base had asked her—a Scots nurse loaned to the base hospital—to dance. All of those traits attractive, but the provocative, warm-honey scent of heather clinging to her skin and hair captured his heart with the first breath. If he lived to be a hundred, that meeting would still be burned into his memory.

His brogans juddered on the wooden planks as long strides took him across a bridge. The wide burn, its pebbled bottom hidden beneath dark, peaty water, ran toward the sea. Twa mute swans glided silently across the near-black surface of Loch Domhnall, hurrying their seven grey cygnets to the safety of the far shore.

Shep still ran at his side.

"Looks like they've been taking herding lessons from you, lad." Rob upped his pace.

There were no macadam or even gravel roads, only a wide, sandy path leading around the island. And no automobiles or trucks, just wooden cairts pulled by small, shaggy horses the Scots called "cuddies."

At first, he'd been horrified by that. What a difference three years made. Now walking or running everywhere, he reveled as his senses were overwhelmed by the smells of heather, salty sea, and peaty bogs. Amid emerald green girse, brilliant wildflowers waved for attention between the ever-present grey rocks. Sheep and coos grazed voraciously or lay in groups, chewing their cuds. And the sounds: pewlie and black-headed gulls keening on high, the barking of the seals lounging on the large, flat rocks cluttering the shoreline, and the constant hollow boom of waves crashing against the steep, craggy cliffs of the fells. The taste of salted sea air brought saliva to his mouth.

This was why he ran before sunup every other day. Not only did it strengthen his legs, but it was a time to concentrate on all his blessings from God. At last, the war was over. His body was almost as strong as ever after innumerable surgeries and months of therapy to repair the broken bones and torn muscles suffered in his last B-17 crash. He had a new life with his love, his Maggie. And though he couldn't fly, he could focus on building a rescue boat for those who encountered trouble at sea.

Och, why did his bonnie lass put up with his impatience to build the boat? To blow through the constant impediments life put in his way?

He crossed another bridge and gazed over the machair. Vast stretches of wildflowers competed with the green girse while smaller areas, separated by low drystone dykes, rippled in varying shades of green and yellow as oats and barley stretched their slim stalks toward rain and sun.

Should he become a crofter, toiling in the soil or raising sheep or coos, instead of opening the Innisbraw Boatworks? Or even a fisherman, spending his days at sea on a trawler?

Och, Faither, give me Your peace, please. I know You brought me to Innisbraw to build the rescue boat so our fishermen could have help in time of need and to provide work for our island lads, but right now, I'm so whummled I don't ken what to do. I need that lumber from the States, Lord, and with rationing still tight, I don't ken where I'm going to find all the necessary fittings and hardware.

Shep cut in front of him, turned up a tiny path heading over Ben Innis, and veered off through the yellow gorse and purple heather in pursuit of a rabbit.

4

Instead of whistling the dog back, Rob gave chase. He hadn't been over the ben for several weeks and the view from the top always sent his blood racing. Fifteen minutes later he reached the summit, placed twa fingers in his mouth, and gave a shrill whistle.

Within seconds, Shep appeared out of the underbrush, flanks heaving, blue eyes begging for praise.

"Well done, ... you," Rob panted as he rubbed the dog's furry ruff.

Shep nosed around for a soft spot to lie down.

Rob leaned against one of the four ancient stone megaliths towering above them. When breathing came easy, he walked around the stones, trailing his fingers over weathered inscriptions, faint and rendered undecipherable by hundreds or perhaps thousands of years of wind and rain.

Below, a few lazy drifts of smoke from peat fireplaces and stoves curled around thatched cottage roofs. Burns, wide and narrow, fed from underground springs, tumbled in wild abandon toward level ground. The sea surrounding the island pulsed in never-ending waves against the rocky shore. And all around, heather bushes rustled as birds and other small creatures stirred at the dawning of another day.

If the Lord had called him home to heaven during the war, this was where he would have been buried—the bonniest place on earth.

The vast, endless sky grew a luminescent, pearly grey as the sun inched toward birth over the Atlantic on the Minch side, wild and unfettered from horizon to horizon. To the south lay Ireland, only a soft smudge of purple floating on an inky sea. A rising wind played a haunting song around the ben's stone sentinels. So familiar, that song. The same melody that had played through the wing-wires of his Stearman PT-17 bi-plane when he was learning to fly. Tears choked his throat.

It was bad enough giving up his flying career, but if his fears about the rescue boat sinking when she was launched came true … He fisted his hands. *Please help me, Lord. 'Tis Your plan. Don't let me believe the De'il's sly whispers in the night. Help me believe she'll float.*

Chapter Two

"Guard Robbie from the flames, Shep." Maggie Savage set her laddie on the fireplace rug. She poured a cup of tea, added milk and heather honey, and sat at the kitchen table across from her husband as he attacked his breakfast. Thank the guid Lord island living provided an ample, unrationed supply of meat and eggs or, despite Rob's hearty appetite, she'd never be able to add weight to his tall, lanky frame.

The sun's rays, shining through the window, highlighted his brown hair and green flecks shone in his almost-translucent hazel-brown eyes beneath heavy brows. The therapy on his shoulder had added so much muscle, the shirt she'd made less than a year before fit too tightly over his broad torso. *Such a braw man, both inside and oot.*

He was bright, able to design a rescue boat by studying books and questioning local fishermen. And quick to pick up the Gaelic, the only language of the aulder folk, and the Scots commonly spoken by everyone else on Innisbraw.

Och, a native of Innisbraw, she spoke the Gaelic and Scots and had learned English at the boarding academy on Harris Island, but Rob was also fluent in German, French, and Italian. How had God considered her worthy of such a man?

Lost in her musings, she flinched when he tapped the tip of her nose.

"You're quiet as nesting creatures at the gloaming."

"Just enjoying the bonnie view."

"You've been staring at me, no' ootside."

A tease tickled her tongue. "That's what I said, enjoying the bonnie view."

6

He rubbed the long scar above his right eyebrow, then spread tinned beans onto a slice of fried bread.

That scar again. Would Rob Savage never tolerate a compliment on his braw looks? "How is Graham working oot then?"

"Och, verra well. He's a changed lad since he's become my partner. Mebbe 'tis because his leg is doing so well after all the therapy."

"Changed how? You've always said he's bright and seldom takes time to fauld his fit."

Rob chewed a mouthful of minced sausage dipped in egg yolk and stared out the window at the Minch. "I suppose time has put some distance between taking that Jerry bullet in the leg and all the death he saw that day, unlike so many of the de-mobbed lads from Innisbraw who can't give up memories of the horrors they've seen and done. He's more focused, as if he's put the past behind and is ready for the future. I'm thinking he'll be a lot of help when we start building the rescue boat."

"Which will be soon, knowing you." Maggie ran a hand through her hair, working out a few tangles.

He wiped a smear of egg yolk from his plate with his last bite of fried bread and drained his coffee mug. "That's the way you should always wear your hair, luve." A smile deepened the dimples beside his lips. "It looks black as storm clouds tossed on a blowsterie wind, all loose and spilling down your back."

"I haven't even brushed it yet, and I need a barrette to keep it off my face so it doesn't tangle so much." She wrinkled her nose, unable to resist another bit of devilment. "Besides, I'm thinking I may need to cut it, what with being biggen again. You know how 'twas always in the way after I birthed Robbie."

Panic flashed in his eyes. He snagged her chin between his fingers. "Don't even think it."

"I was only having you on, luve. I'd never cut it, though I do have to trim the ends when they get too far below my waist." She got up, perched on his lap, and nestled close. "You're wound tighter than a wet mooring rope this mornin. What has you in such a fankle?"

He buried his face in her hair. "Och, 'tis all this waiting to start the rescue boat. But wound up or no', I mean it, Maggie. If I see you with a pair of scissors in your hand, I'll throw them over the side of the fell."

⁂

A sudden squeal drew his attention from Maggie.

Their lad toddled toward them, arms outstretched for balance, fingers waving, blue eyes sparkling, and mouth wide open.

Maggie slid from Rob's lap. "Don't say owt," she whispered.

Rob went down on one knee and held out his arms.

Robbie teetered for a moment before he took a few more steps. He smiled at his father and squealed again.

It was all Rob could do to stay still instead of scooping up his lad and kissing him on that sweet-tasting place at the back of his neck, beneath those soft, black curls.

The lad waved his hands wildly and teetered on the brink of a fall, regained his balance, and toddled into Rob's arms.

"Well done, you! You walked all by yourself." Rob passed their son to Maggie, who showered his face with kisses until he arched his back and squealed in protest. "He wants to do it again. He's had a taste of it and he'll no' be satisfied till he's running."

Maggie laughed, violet-blue eyes dancing a jig. "Och, he's just like his faither." She stood Robbie at a chair and moved back.

This time the lad's objective was Shep, who cowered, eyes anxious, tail tucked tightly between his hind legs.

"Shep doesn't like this one bit," Rob said. "He'll have to work even harder to keep the lad oot of danger."

Robbie wobbled toward the dog, tiny fists opening and closing. Again he teetered on his bare feet and righted himself. When he reached Shep, he pounded the dog's back with both hands and buried his face in the soft, blue-merle coat.

Rob groaned. "I'm thinking I've lost my dog. Nowt will separate those twa now."

"He'll still have to go with you when you run. A herding dog needs exercise."

"We both do." He patted his waistline. "I'm getting fat."

8

Maggie stepped back, hands on hips. "Rob Savage, stop that talk. You still don't weigh as much as you did when we met, and you were shilpit then." She patted her own tummy. "Now, if you want to see someone getting fat—"

"You're barely showing, and if I've told you once, I've told you a hundred times, your body's perfect."

They looked at one another for a long moment, then broke into laughter.

He gathered her into his arms, rocking her back and forth. "Listen to us. We sound like a couple of auld merrit folk."

She cuddled closer. "We are auld merrit folk, luve—and you're no' fat."

"You keep teasing me with that saucy smile and neither of us is going to get owt done the day."

"Are you threatening me?"

"For biddy certain." He kissed her again. "You'd best rescue Shep. Your lad has his fingers in that poor dog's mouth."

Maggie tried to lead Robbie away, but he plonked down on his bottom. She picked him up and he hugged her neck, burying his face against her shoulder. "This one's already worn oot." She headed for the bairn's bedroom. "And his hippen's soaked again."

Rob called Shep over and scratched his ears. "There's a guid dog," he said in the soft, deep voice Shep loved. "A verra, verra guid dog." He grabbed his thermos and walked into Robbie's bedroom. "I'm away, then."

"Don't disremember your scones. I added extra for Graham. They're in a napkin on the kitchen table."

"Thank ye, lass." He patted her bottom. "And you're no' fat." He grinned as he dashed out the door.

Not often did he have the last word with that cannie lass.

He jogged down to the shed, enjoying the warm morning air. There were few days like this left in the year.

The flat rocks at the base of Innis Fell were deserted, the seals at sea, gorging on fish to store up fat for the coming winter. The sheep and coos at Angus MacPhee's croft browsed the girse or lay in the sun chewing their cuds, while pewlie and black-headed gulls

9

circled the harbour, drifting in lazy circles.

He opened the shed door and stepped inside.

Graham MacDonald sat on one of their wooden folding chairs, chewing a pencil as he perused a sheet of paper. The lad looked guid, ruddy-cheeked like all the island's young natives, short black hair combed back from a widow's peak. Blue eyes flashed a hint of mischief when he looked up. "You're late. I was about to send out a rescue party. Have a long lie-in?"

Rob chuckled as he opened the thermos. "Have a guid reason for being late." He poured them each a mug of coffee and pulled up another chair. "Robbie took his first steps this mornin. Walked all over the living room."

"Congratulations." Graham swigged his coffee and reached for a scone. "Or maybe I should offer my condolences. If he's owt like you, there'll be no stopping him now."

"What lad doesn't like to run?" Rob ate half a scone in one bite.

"Aye." Graham stood and held out his hands. "In case you hadn't noticed, there's another lad on his own twa legs."

Rob glanced around. "Where's your walking stick?"

"In the infirmary supply room, where it can remain till Nevermass, if I have any say."

What grand news. "It shouldn't be long before I've a new running companion."

"That's right. In fact, John radioed and said to take my instructions from you from now on. Just no running or climbing rocks for at least a month."

"You mean he trusts me to keep you in line? That doesn't sound like John."

"He said to tell you he'll be back on the island in a few weeks and if I'm doing too much, he'll have your skin."

"You'd better listen to me then. I don't want to tangle with Doctor John McGrath, father-in-law or no'."

"I'll listen. But right now, I've some news that could make your day."

Rob leaned forward. "And what might that be?"

"Mither's auldest sister and her husband were both killed when the Krauts bombed Clydebank, just ootside of Glasgow. Their youngest lass was already merrit and biding on Harris Island. Her husband took over a boatyard from his faither and ran it till he went off to war in forty-twa. He was killed helping the Underground fight in France."

"Another family torn apart ... but how is that good news to me?"

"My regiment was in Italy then and Mither wrote me that Fern took it hard. She's been trying to run the yard herself, but the lack of a need for sma' boats during the war ate up her reserves. She's selling everything."

The good news! "Everything? The tools, equipment?"

"And the inventory. She has twa diesel engines and boxes of fittings, plus a large pile of lumber."

Rob whistled. "This could be the break we've been looking for." He got up and paced. "Do you know how much she wants for it all?"

"She's got it priced to sell piecemeal. Don't think she thought anybody had enough silver to buy it ootright."

"I'll need a list of everything she has, so I can make her an offer."

Graham drained his coffee mug. "I'm thinking you should go to Harris and look it over. You must have all the prices memorized since you've been pouring over auld catalogues as long as I've known you."

Rob's hands shook as he picked up the long list of items they needed. "I'll take this along and see how many of these she has."

"I seem to recall you saying you'd no' take another trip without Maggie and Robbie going along."

That stopped Rob short. "Right. Either they go or I don't."

"I'm sure Fern could put you up. She has the room and I'm thinking she's most likely lonely."

"No bairns?"

"One, a lass about three. Her name's Katie."

"How can I contact Fern and set a date?"

"I'll get hold of her this een. Any particular time guid for

11

you—and don't say yesterday."

"You took the word right oot of my mouth." Rob grinned. "Today? Seriously, as soon as possible." He punched a fist into his palm. "Does she have a radio, or only a telephone?"

"Radio. Harris was set to be connected to Scotland by telephone when the war broke oot. And since they didn't have any air or naval bases and weren't considered important, they're still waiting."

"Sounds familiar."

"Aye, it does that."

Maggie acted pleased when Rob told her the news. Of course he was eager to get started on the rescue boat, but that meant fears for his safety would soon become an unpleasant part of her daily life. Commanding a rescue boat could be so dangerous in high seas. During all the bombing missions he had flown, she had prayed and prayed for the faith that the Lord would bring him back. And He had, even that last time when Rob had been so terribly injured. She tried to fight off the mounting panic but failed miserably and ducked her head to hide the tears filling her eyes.

Rob gathered her into his arms. "What's this? I thought you'd be kittled up. Is the trip too much with you being biggen?" When she didn't answer, he palmed her chin and forced her head up. "What's the matter, Maggie? What have I done to cause you a fash this time?"

She felt sick—and ashamed. When would he realize she wasn't perfect? And why did he always take the blame whenever she was upset? The closer he got to building and launching the rescue boat, the more he reverted back to the insecurities of his tragic, lonely childhood.

But now was no time to tell him her fears for his safety had returned. It would only burden him further. Why had she promised never to lie to him?

Please help me, Faither. I can't do this to him again. She bit back tears and hugged his waist, forcing herself to meet his gaze. The bleak look in his eyes tore at her heart. "I ... don't know what to ... to do with Robbie while we're gone," she stammered, voicing a

12

small part of the truth. "He's still suckling." Her shame deepened when his body relaxed.

"Surely you didn't expect us to leave him behind. I know 'twill be hard spending so much time on a trawler with a bairn, but I'll do all I can to help. Fern lives near Leverburgh on the southern tip of Harris, so the trip shouldn't take any longer than sailing to Oban."

"Then 'tis settled." *But only if I get some spiritual help from Hugh before we go.*

His long fingers kneaded her tight shoulders. "I've already contacted the mill in New Hampshire. The lumber I ordered will be sent on the first available merchant ship. If I can pick up the tools and equipment I need, plus some inventory, it'll speed things up considerably."

"'Tis coming together, luve."

"Aye, finally, thank the Lord."

The moment Rob left for the shed the next morning, Maggie radioed Hugh and asked him to come to their home. "I'd walk down to the manse, but Robbie's too heavy to carry and he's only started walking."

"You sound like you're in a fair fash."

She wiped impatiently at the tears welling in her eyes. "I am, and it's gone on too long. I desperately need your help."

"Consider me already on my way."

Maggie hovered in the doorway a short time later as Hugh unlocked the gate and walked up the path. Of average height and carrying an extra stone or twa that evidenced his love of food, he and his round, cherubic cheeks and elfin smile always lifted her spirits. Climbing the steps to their stone-flagged entry, he opened his arms wide.

Just the sight of his dear, kind face and the rough texture of his tweed jacket against her cheek when he hugged her eased the tightness in her throat. She handed him a mug of coffee and seated him at the kitchen table, putting a finger to her lips. "Robbie's taking an early nap, so we'll have to be quiet."

13

Hugh sat unmoving while Maggie poured out her fears and her inability to put them aside even after hours and hours of reading the Word and praying. "I'm so ashamed. I can't let Rob know how I feel. The closer he gets to building the boat, the more afraid I become."

Hugh took off his eyeglasses and polished them on his handkerchief. Maggie's fears were understandable considering Rob's lingering so near death only twa years before. *Help me, Faither. Give me the words to show her once again how to rest in Your perfect will.* "So you're afraid Rob will drown?"

Tears slipped down her cheeks. She nodded, head bowed.

"How many times does God have to pull that lad back from the brink of death before you see He has a special plan for Rob's life?"

"But why does His plan have to be so dangerous? Doesn't He know what Rob means to me—how I can't face life without him?"

"Of course He knows." *Your words, Faither, no' mine.* He steepled his hands on the table. "After all, it was our Lord who brought you together in the first place, knowing the needs in both your hearts and meeting those needs perfectly." He pulled a worn Bible from his jacket pocket and paged through it.

Maggie groped for her handkerchief.

He gave her time to dry her eyes. "You will find this in First John 4:18: 'There is no fear in love: but perfect love casteth out fear, because fear hath punishment; and he that feareth is not made perfect in love.'" He leaned back in his chair. "We all have times in our lives when we doubt God's ability to take care of our problems and fears, but those of us who have learned the promises of God— as you have, Maggie, lass—have hold of the greatest power in the world. God's power. And His power is divine. Just think, no' human power, but divine! Moses and David and Abraham and Isaiah all drew upon that power when circumstances made them weak and faint. Remember David's words when he stood before Goliath? 'The battle is the Lord's.' That was no longer David's battle to fight. It was God's."

She met his gaze warily.

"The hardest thing a Christian faces is to wait on the Lord." A

14

chuckle rumbled in his chest. "As impatient as that lad is, I'm thinking our Rob would agree with that."

She nodded, a tight smile showing her agreement.

Opening one's mouth and allowing the Holy Spirit to speak—so hard to learn, yet so easy to do. "But waiting on the Lord doesn't mean to sit back and do nowt. It means letting go of your fears and remembering one of His greatest promises: 'He offers strength to the weak.' No' the strong, nor those trying to solve their problems by their own efforts, but to the helpless. Is the God who created the universe suddenly so weak He cannot pluck Rob from the waves when something goes wrong during a rescue? Is the Lord who gave Himself on the cross for all of our sins suddenly so uncaring He wants you to be tortured by fear?"

Her cheeks flushed. "Of course no'."

Hugh returned the Bible to his pocket, rose, and pulled Maggie to her feet. "Every time you fear for Rob's life, I want you to picture our Lord creating the stars and flinging them into the universe. Sometimes we disremember the power at our Lord's fingertips."

She dipped her head. "I will try to remember."

Chapter Three

Thomas Campbell steered his old fishing trawler out of the harbour and into the Minch.

Rob turned for a last glimpse of the marram grasses far back on the shore, golden spikes standing tall and proud. Though chilly this morning, the wind seemed to be holding its breath as the sun thrust a sliver of yellow above the horizon.

The old captain professed to knowing only Gaelic. The other old-timers with no schooling, like Thomas, prided themselves in their refusal to learn Scots—or even worse, English. Of course, the man had picked up some English in order to barter with the buyers that lined the dock when he landed in Oban with a fish hold filled with salmon, haddock, cod, skate, and, in summer and autumn, mackerel. And though he pretended not to understand a word of Scots, who could live on a small island where it was the common language, without learning what he heard?

Maggie added another sweater to the twa Robbie wore, but when she tried to place a hap over his shoulders, he screamed and stomped his feet. She folded and dropped it into the large basket at her feet with a sigh. "Are you certain you're no' going to be cold?" she asked Rob.

His right eyebrow rose. "I'm wearing my gansey sweater and A-2 jacket. If the wind doesn't pick up soon, I'll be sweating like a cuddy pulling a cairtload of flagging stones."

Without Shep to keep him out of trouble, Robbie never stopped moving, and Rob soon found himself at a dead run trying to keep the lad away from the trawling machinery on deck. The bairn's busy fingers prodded and poked into everything. Rob could ask Thomas for a length of rope to tie around the lad's waist, but tethering his

16

own flesh like a wild, young bull was too horrible to contemplate. If only Robbie hadn't learned to walk so soon.

The light sea chop turned to heavy swells as they neared Barra Head, a tall, rocky promontory north of Innisbraw. The trawler rolled from side to side and Maggie, who was telling Rob about the lighthouse perched high at the top, suddenly turned white and leaned over the side railing, retching.

Rob picked up Robbie. "Och, luve, I'm so sorry," he said when she wiped her mouth with her handkerchief.

Perspiration beaded her forehead. "I feel terrible." She moaned.

"Would you rather go into the wheelhouse?"

"Och, no, I need the fresh air."

"But the smell of the diesel ..."

"'Tis worse in the wheelhouse."

How could he help? Maggie had never suffered a moment's physical discomfort since he met her, other than giving birth and having a sore throat. "There's tea in your thermos."

She pulled away, face blanching. "Please just keep an eye on Robbie. I'll be fine."

He spent the next few hours keeping Robbie entertained, pointing out a pod of bottlenose dolphins stitching their way south and rare schools of herring so thick they looked like wide ribbons of molten silver.

Maggie sat on an overturned crate and suckled their lad while Rob guiltily wolfed down three bacon butteries in the wheelhouse and finished off a thermos of coffee. After he took Robbie again, she returned to the bow and turned her face to the brisk, salted breeze.

Rob talked to the lad until his voice turned hoarse. He shared old tales Elspeth NicAllister, island elder and dear friend, had told him about the fabled "wee people" who used to inhabit the caves so prevalent along the shore, and made up stories about the tall bens and large rocks on the islands they passed. He wanted to tell the tale of the Selkie, the magical seal which turned into a beautiful, black-haired, blue-eyed woman when she touched shore, but Robbie was too young to understand a love that could last forever and ever and ever.

Rob's gaze was pulled to Maggie, the urge as strong as a magnet attracting iron. The tale might be considered ancient lore to most folk, but Maggie was his Selkie. And their love would last through eternity.

Though the lad never fell into sleep, he did quiet, seeming content to be held close to his father's chest … as long as that deep, familiar voice didn't fall silent.

By late afternoon, Thomas threaded the trawler into the harbour at the southern tip of Harris. The island little resembled wee Innisbraw. Dark, mysterious bens loomed high in the distance, casting deepening shadows over hillocks and braes. A large complex of dilapidated docks and abandoned sheds hugged the treeless, rocky shore. Empty mooring buoys, covered with gull-droppings, bobbed on the calm water.

Maggie appeared at Rob's side.

"'Tis so guid to see you with some colour in your face." He rubbed his cheek against her hair, realizing this was just a small taste of how she must have felt when he was injured and in so much pain. How had she stood it? Being helpless was agonizing.

"I'm sorry I couldn't help you with our lad." She hugged his waist. "This has been a tedisome voyage for you."

"Nowt matters as long as you're feeling guid now."

"I'm fine." She nibbled Robbie's fingers. "I've missed holding you, laddie."

Robbie arched away from Rob and struggled to reach his mother.

"You're too heavy for your mither to carry, lad." Rob held him firmly. "Watch closely now and in a tick we'll be ashore and I'll put you down so you can walk."

Maggie leaned closer. "I'm thinking I should remind you Fern speaks only English and the Gaelic. They don't speak Scots on Harris."

The trawler bumped against the old tyres cushioning the dock, where Fern MacNeill waved. She looked so much like Graham, Rob couldn't help staring. Same black hair, same blue eyes and naturally rosy cheeks, and same dimpled chin.

Katie had her mother's large blue eyes, but her hair was the colour of a newly minted ha'penny and a sprinkling of freckles covered the bridge of her delicate nose. Rob felt an instant bonding with the winsome redheaded lass and she appeared taken with him, calling him "Uncle Rob" and hugging his legs immediately.

They all squeezed into the front seat of Fern's battered old Bedford truck, Robbie in Maggie's lap and Katie in Rob's.

"I had no idea you'd be so tall," Fern said to Rob, unsuccessfully hiding a smile as he crammed his legs between the seat and dashboard and ducked his head to fit inside the cab. "But we don't live as far away as Leverburgh, so we'll be home in a few minutes."

"I'm used to tight fits." He hoped he didn't scare her off with his tortured grin.

Maggie grew animated when she learned that Fern was also a nurse and had graduated from the Royal Infirmary's Nursing School in 1937, only three years before she received her own degree. The twa talked nonstop until Fern pulled off the road and onto a short lane leading to a crushed cockleshell driveway shared by three detached cottages. The buildings leaned toward one another like frail, doddering auld women huddling for protection from the cold wind ripping in off the sea.

Rob lifted Katie out of the truck, straightened, and rubbed his aching neck.

Across the lane lay the blackened ruins of a large cottage, a form which appeared to be a roofless, soot-streaked sheep fauld, and several other decaying sheds surrounded by collapsing drystone dykes.

"What happened there?" he asked Fern as he took Robbie from Maggie and set him on his feet. "Must have been quite a fire to burn cottage and fauld."

"Oh, that happened many years ago and it was a tragedy that affected this area for years. In you come, I'll make some tea."

"You've sparked my curiosity," Rob said. "I'd like to hear more about that fire."

Fern sighed and turned to Maggie. "Why don't you take Katie

and your laddie inside out of the wind while I tell Rob about it? It isn't a tale for tender ears. Won't be long."

Once the front door closed, Rob followed Fern across the lane.

She gestured at the ruins. "This was once a very large, profitable sheep croft owned by the Grant family for generations. My cottage and the ones beside it were for the families of the men who helped the last owner, Michael Grant, run the croft. From what I've heard, they were very busy—until the owners of the abandoned islands south of Barra, like Mingulay, decided to go into the sheep business. When the glut of sheep caused the price of wool and mutton to plummet, Michael couldn't hold onto his business and he started drinking."

Why had he asked? This couldn't have a happy ending.

"After a year of putting up with his drunken silences, his wife left him, taking their lad and two lasses with her." Fern plucked a strand of windblown hair from her cheek and held it away from her face. "Then, one summer night, after the bank threatened to foreclose on his loan, he either drank himself into madness with whisky or went truly daft. He set fire to everything."

"Everything?"

"It's said he herded over a quarter of his ewes into that large shearing fold, then closed and barred the door. And he set fire to some paraffin-soaked rags he'd thrown on the dirt floor."

"He ... he burned his own animals?" It seemed unbelievable.

"All but the lambs and those ewes and rams in the outer pastures—and the four herding dogs and family milk cow."

"How could a man live with himself after doing something like that?"

"No one will ever know. He drove his dogs away, went into his cottage, and set fire to it too."

"He killed himself?"

"It is thought that was his idea all along—that he couldn't face losing the croft his great-grandfather, grandfather, and father worked so hard to improve."

Rob's fists clenched. How frail, the human spirit.

"The men who worked for him didn't know about the fire until the noise of the sheep bleating woke them. By the time they ran across the lane, there was little they could do. They told the leader of the fire brigade that Michael staggered from the cottage and ran toward the fold, his clothes on fire, but the heat from the roaring flames kept them from getting close enough to help. When the fire finally burned itself out, they found his charred body at the door of the fold, his hand caught in the drop bar, as though trying to lift it."

"So he changed his mind but waited too long?"

"That's what was decided at the inquest into his death."

"And his wife and children?" He could only manage a hoarse whisper.

"It's said his wife was in a hospital for days after she found out what he'd done. She and the children moved away to someplace on Lewis after that. Nobody blamed them for trying to escape such horrible memories."

Rob closed his eyes to blot out the frantic bleats and the nauseating smell of roasting flesh the sight of the ruined buildings conjured up. Losing his parents so young was a tragedy, but this was one of the most horrifying stories he had ever heard. That it was true was almost more than he could bear. "I can't imagine any man doing that to innocent animals, let alone, himself."

Fern ground her toe into the crushed shells. "You can see why I didn't want Katie or Robbie hearing this." She sighed deeply. "It's just another true story of what can happen when men get so caught up in their tragedies they turn a blind eye to the welfare of those around them."

Rob turned his back and walked toward her cottage. *Faither, please cleanse my mind of all this evil. Keep me focused on the welfare of others.* "What happened to his men and their families?"

"They lost their cottages and had to find other work. The bank that held Michael's loan sold to a buyer from London, but with the mutton market so glutted, he let it fall to ruin—never even visited. After years, they put the cottages up for sale. Edward and I had a hard time even considering it, for we'd heard the stories, but we were desperate for a place of our own so we bought the middle cottage."

"And the others?"

21

"The one on the left is owned by the manager of the bank who uses it for holiday, and Jane and Kenneth Frazier own the other. He works at the docks and she watches Katie when I'm at the boatyard. She's a dear soul with three children of her own, as you can see from all the washing on her line." She led the way to the porch. "I'm sorry to upset you, Rob, but you did ask."

"Aye, fool that I am, I did that."

"Come away in, then."

The flagged steps had been recently swept, but the paint on the windowsills and front door buckled and peeled. The tiny, neglected yard showed no girse, only weeds, bent and shriveled by the cold wind. At least she didn't apologize for the condition of the truck or the run-down appearance of her cottage. She'd worn twa hats for several years, one of mother and another of boatyard manager. It took a lot of tenacity to hold on so long under the most adverse conditions.

She showed him into a clean room crowded with well-used furniture. Maggie had already put the kettle to boil and three cups of tea waited on a small table.

Though he hated tea, Rob grabbed a cup and gulped it down, burning the inside of his mouth, ridding himself of the bad taste lingering at the back of his throat.

※

While Rob went out to the truck to retrieve their baskets, Maggie finished her tea, holding Robbie on her lap as he eyed the unfamiliar surroundings.

When he jabbered and squirmed to get down, Fern led the way into a small bedroom. "I've put a cot at the foot of your bed for Robbie. It was Katie's until she outgrew it."

"It's perfect." Maggie removed the last of her heavy sweaters. "If you don't mind, I could use a wash-up. For the first time in my life, I got seasick today."

Fern eyed her rounded belly. "I got an upset stomach when I was expecting Katie. I guess it is just another thing we have to put up with."

Maggie gave a weary smile. "I expect so."

Fern fixed a simple tea of toasted cheese and coddled eggs. Though he'd thought himself starving, Rob could barely swallow. Not only had Fern's story upset him, but he was anxious to see what she had for sale. He fingered the list in his back pocket. If she had the right equipment, this long, exhausting day had been well worth it.

The twa of them alone in the bedroom, Maggie laughed when she heard the main reason why he had eaten so little. She paused changing a yawning Robbie and smiled at him. "You're like a wee lad waiting for Faither Christmas."

"That's exactly how I feel." He took her into his arms. "Are you biddy certain you don't want to go along to the yard?"

"I'm sleeperie so I'll have a lay-down with Robbie. 'Twas guid he ate twa eggs and a few bites of toast dipped in tea since I was sick all the day."

He kissed her and Robbie and put on his A-2 jacket. "We'll be back as soon as we can."

"Och, we'll be fine. On you go and have a guid time."

Grinning, he closed the door softly behind him. He didn't look across the lane as they walked to the truck.

"Do you want to drive?" Fern dangled a key from her fingertips.

"I haven't driven in years. Besides, it's been too long since I drove on the wrong side of the road."

Her pert smile reminded him of Maggie. "It may be the wrong side to you Americans, but it's the right side to us."

He laughed and scrunched into the passenger's seat, Katie curled up between them. Despite his usual discomfort around strangers, he'd taken an instant liking to Fern. Warm and unaffected, she spoke perfect English and her voice fell soft and pleasing to the ear. It was a good opportunity for him to brush up on his mother tongue.

After a short trip, they found Thomas pacing the road in front of the shed. "My cousin brought me over," he explained in the Gaelic. "He said he has already been by, and one of the diesels is just what I need. He also said the price is more than fair."

"I would be happy to sell it to you." Fern looked back and forth from the twa men. "But Rob has first pick."

"It's fine with me," Rob said. "I've already told Thomas he should get the engine if it's what he needs."

"Then that's the way it shall be." She walked across a fenced yard surrounding a huge shed. A few skeletons of old, rotting boats rose from the weeds like bleached bones in an ancient, neglected graveyard. "Come away in and I'll show you around," she said to Rob in English.

Katie grabbed Rob's hand as they entered the building.

He squeezed her fingers and she smiled up at him, dimples deepening in her cheeks.

Thomas went immediately to the twa engines, kneeling and prodding with a grubby finger, the tip of his tongue peeking out from between his chapped lips.

The equipment in the shed had seen hard use but had been well-maintained. Oiled hand tools lined the tops of the workbenches. Bins of fittings and small hardware hung above the benches. Saws and other power tools stood in silent rows as if waiting to be used. A very large pile of lumber, including three heavy beams, lay stacked against the far wall.

Rob made an inventory, ticking it off against his list. Though there were a few duplicates since he had already purchased some equipment, it wouldn't hurt to have a few spares when it came time to open his boat-building business.

His excitement mounted as he and Fern began talking about a figure to purchase everything she owned. It was only a wee bit higher than he would have to pay if he bought each piece individually, and he would save weeks of looking and then waiting for everything to be shipped to Innisbraw.

Thomas insisted on paying in full for the engine he had chosen. "I will pick it up in one week," he told Fern, "since I need to arrange for help getting it down to the dock and loaded aboard my boat."

She pocketed the worn notes and hand-printed him a receipt. "I am happy you could use it."

Rob made arrangements to meet Thomas at the dock at 0400

the following morning, then lifted Katie into the truck and climbed in beside her.

When Fern got in and started the engine, her hands shook on the steering wheel.

Time to put her mind at ease. "I'd like to buy everything you have, and your asking price seems fair."

She glanced over at him, tears shining in her eyes. "Are you certain?"

"I'm certain. You've done your homework. The price you quoted was about what I would have had to pay anywhere else."

"It's obvious you're not Scots. I was surprised when Thomas paid what I asked so readily. Most Scotsmen would have bargained for hours and never settled for the asking price."

He switched to the Gaelic. "Indeed, I'm not Scots-born, but thriftiness can be carried to extremes."

A throaty laugh. "You may not be a Scotsman, but you speak the Gaelic like you are." She reached over and took his hand, shaking it gravely. "I like you, Rob Savage," she added in English, "and I like your Maggie. I'd luve an opportunity to know you better."

"Then come and visit us," he said as she eased the truck into gear. "We've extra bedrooms for both you and Katie."

"I may do that. I've been working so long, we've had no chance to visit Uncle Alec and Aunt Morag and I've been dying to see Graham."

"He's a fine lad."

"I don't think you could have made a better choice of a partner." She smiled over at him, blue eyes misty, most likely from happy memories. "When we were bairns, Graham had to climb higher, run faster, and win every game. I've never seen a lad so motivated to be at the very top."

"Then he hasn't changed; only his goals have."

The old truck's gears ground a throaty protest as she shifted down at a sharp curve. "Aunt Morag radioed me a few months ago when he was injured, asking me to pray. I understand he's doing well now, though."

25

"He's doing grand. He was on crutches, then a walking stick, but he's walking unaided now. It won't be long until he loses his limp and is back to living a normal life."

A radiant smile. "You know, I haven't seen him since just before he went off to war. He was always my favourite cousin."

"Then all the more reason you should come for a visit." He tapped the tip of Katie's nose. "This wee lassie should get to know her kin. There's nowt more important than family."

Fern pulled the truck into her driveway and sat for a moment, staring off into space. "My parents were killed in the war and my only sister lives in Glasgow. She's so much older, we've never been close. Edward, my husband, was an only child and his parents emigrated to America in 1938, just before the war started." Tears glazed her eyes, blurring Rob's face. "I think I'll take you up on that visit. Who knows, we may even decide to move to Innisbraw. There's nothing to keep us here now."

Katie hugged her mother, then Rob. "Would we live with Uncle Rob and Aunt Maggie?"

"Oh, no, lass. They have their own family. If we do decide to move there, we'll have our own cottage."

"But close so I can play with Robbie?"

Rob hugged Katie. "It will have to be close, as I've a feeling a certain bonnie, wee lassie has taken a very large place in my heart." He opened the door and Katie raced him to the front of the house.

Fern remained in the truck, heart thudding painfully. Could she really hope to sell the cottage and boatyard? After all, she wasn't the legal owner.

Chapter Four

Fern and her guests enjoyed a companionable supper of gammon, tinned pineapple slices, shortbread, tea, and coffee, then took their chairs into the tiny backyard where the cottage protected them from the constant onshore wind. Once he learned the Tilly lamp was off limits, Robbie ran around, Katie at his heels making sure he stayed nearby in the gloaming and didn't put anything he picked up from the ground into his mouth.

"I'm hoping this one will be a lass." Maggie patted her belly. "They're so different from lads."

"I suppose so, though the only experience I've ever had with lads was with my cousins. All boys." Fern laughed as Robbie ran from Katie's hovering. "Your little one never seems to stop. How do you manage to keep up with him?"

"I've had lots of practice with this one." Maggie squeezed Rob's hand. "If he's no' moving, he's either asleep or thinking about what has to be done next."

He leaned over and kissed her cheek. "You're no better, lass. The only difference is, when you're sitting, you're either knitting or sewing something. It's a bit hard for me to find owt I can do sitting down."

"I see why you and Graham get along so well," Fern said.

Later, Fern lay staring up at the ceiling of her bedroom, but it wasn't sharing a bed with Katie that kept sleep at bay. The love between Rob and Maggie … she ached to have Edward's warm, strong body next to hers. How she missed him—his twinkling blue eyes and unruly mop of red hair—and his optimistic outlook that always made the future exciting. Did she dare try to sell the business?

Tears trickled down her cheeks, wetting her pillow. All the years of hard work, of trying so desperately—and failing—to hold on during the war. *Help me, Lord, please. I want to start a new life, away from all my failures. Give me Your strength when I falter. I'm so afraid.*

She rose early, fatigue suffocating her mind and body like a heavy blanket of onshore fog.

The front door closed. Most likely Rob coming in from the outside privy.

She dashed into the kitchen and placed a large cauldron of water to boil on the peat-burning stove so they could have a quick wash-up before leaving.

The festive duties of cooking a large fry-up for breakfast and filling their food basket with cheese and pickle butteries and sweets diverted her thoughts from her fears. And, after all, Rob had promised to post a check for the equipment the minute he arrived back home. By the time everyone loaded into the Bedford and she took her place behind the wheel, she had talked herself into thinking nothing but positive thoughts.

When they reached the dock, Katie was inconsolable until her mother promised they would be going to Innisbraw very soon, if only for a visit.

"Tomorrow?"

"Not tomorrow, but Uncle Rob wants all of the equipment he bought shipped right away. As soon as it's all gone, we'll go."

"You promise?"

"I promise."

Maggie hugged Fern. "If you could, we'd luve to have you there on the twenty-fourth. 'Tis wee Robbie's first birthday and we're having a ceilidh at our home to celebrate."

Positive thoughts, Fern MacNeill. "Count on us being there then. I haven't been to a ceilidh in years."

To Rob's relief, the breeze was light as a whisper, and with only a slight chop, Maggie did not get seasick. She told him about the islands they passed, but skipped one.

"But isn't Benbecula there between North and South Uist?"

"Yes, but 'tis only rocks and shore you can see from here. Most of the cottages are in the center of the island."

"They vectored our planes when we bombed the sub pens on the shores of Norway. I'm sorry we can't have a keek."

"Aye, they had a large RAF base there during the war."

His knotted muscles relaxed when she ate heartily and laughed frequently, violet-blue eyes sparkling as bright as the sunlight on the waves. She also drained her thermos of tea before they reached the shores of Eriskay and even accepted the last of the shortbread without an argument.

Robbie, worn out from all the new sights and experiences, laid his head on Rob's shoulder and slept the rest of the way home, cradled in his father's arms.

Graham met them at the dock, accompanied by Shep.

Robbie woke, squealed, and hugged the dog's neck, babbling nonstop while Shep whined and whipped his plumed tail from side to side.

"Thanks for watching him," Rob said. "I hope he wasn't too much trouble."

"Och, he's a guid dog." Graham patted Shep's head. "He was dreariful most of yesterday, but we went for a walk this mornin and he finally decided to eat."

Maggie called to Shep and took Robbie's hand, leading them down the pier.

"Well?" Graham asked Rob. "Did you buy any of it?"

"I bought it all. Now we just have to figure how to get it here."

Graham, a true son of Innisbraw, ducked his head. "'Tis all taken care of. I've lined up twa of the larger trawlers and their crews to help."

"Well done, you." Rob clapped him on the back. "I'm thinking in about a month we'll be in business. All we need now is that shipment of lumber from the States."

"I've got Faither's cairt and cuddy waiting. Figured you'd like a ride up the hill after your long trip."

"I could get used to this real fast. Having a partner, especially such a smart one, has some definite advantages."

Cheeks blotched red, Graham toed the rough dock planking. "Since I didn't have any silver to sweeten the pot, the least I can do is take some of the load off your shoulders."

"You're definitely doing that, lad."

⚜

Exhausted from the long journey, they went to bed early. Rob spooned close to his Maggie and fell into a deep sleep, only to be awakened by someone pounding on the front door.

"Och, who can that be this time of night?" he grumbled. He untangled his fingers from Maggie's hair, rolled off the bed, and pulled on his denims. "They'll wake our lad," he muttered as he made his way through the living room.

There was a muffled shout before more pounding. "Rob! Wake up, Rob!"

Shep barked as Rob threw open the front door and stared at Angus MacPhee, whose knuckles were raised for another knock. "What's happened, man?" Rob asked.

The crofter sidled in the doorway and grabbed Rob's arm. "You're needed at the howff. We've had a fair riot down there."

Maggie, wearing her robe and carrying a fussing Robbie in her arms, joined them. "What's the fash? You've got everybody awake."

Rob grabbed Shep's collar and pulled him inside. "No bowf," he ordered sternly as he looked at his watch. "What's the howff doing open past the turn o' the night?"

Angus ran fingers through his wild red hair. "Och, no' the howff itself, but the path in front. Tormad's cottage is nearby and the sound of shouting and glass breaking pulled him from his bed. When he got there, he tried to separate the lads, but he's only one man and there were four of them. My lad Edert heard the shouting when he was ootside sneaking a puff o' tobacco from my cuttie. 'Tis bad, Rob. Blood's been spilled!"

Chapter Five

"Blood!" Rob raced into the bedroom and pulled on a shirt and shoes. "You might be needed at the infirmary, Maggie." He took his torch and A-2 jacket out of the front closet. "I'm sorry, lass." He kissed her cheek before dashing out the door after Angus.

"Be careful!" she called.

Torch on, Rob quickly outpaced the shorter-legged Angus who was already winded from his run up the fell. Blood? Had someone used a knife? Och, surely no' on Innisbraw. He passed Elspeth's cottage, the lamp she always left lit at night since Germany's surrender glowing in the front window. Though he strained to hear shouts ahead, or even voices, the roar of the surf pounding on the rocks at the base of Innis Fell swallowed all other sounds.

When he reached the post office, Alice Ross, the postie, stood on the top step in her dressing gown. "What's wrong?" she cried.

"Don't ken!" he shouted over his shoulder. "Radio Alec and Hugh!" Nearing the front of the howff, Rob skidded to a stop as his probing light revealed forms on the ground.

Three motionless bodies lay in the middle of the path, Tormad MacKinnon on his knees beside one.

Rob shone his torch around the front of the howff.

Kenny Grant slumped against the door, a daft grin on his face, waving a whisky bottle through the air like he was conducting an imaginary orchestra. A young lad, not even auld enough for fuzz on his cheeks.

Rob checked for pulses on twa of the prone figures before kneeling beside Tormad. He shone his light on the battered, bloody face of another young lad. "What happened?" he asked the fisherman.

"Och, they must have been trying to break into Paddy's. Their shouts and the sound of breaking glass woke me from a dead sleep. 'Tis a wonder I heard owt what with the tide incoming. Got here in a tick—though too late for this poor laddie."

Rob probed for a pulse. "He's still alive, but his face is such a midden I don't recognize him."

"'Tis Iaian Boyd, Bridget's lad." Tormad's voice trembled.

Rob flashed his light over him.

Tormad shivered violently. A trickle of blood ran down his forehead. He wore only breeks and rubber boots, and his arms and chest were near blue with cold.

Rob removed his A-2 jacket, placed it over Tormad's chest and shoulders, and pushed him onto his back. "Lie still. Your head's bleeding."

Angus fell to his knees at Rob's side, his breath coming in wheezes and gasps. "What can I do?"

Rob swept the torch around and ground his teeth.

Kenny still curled around a bottle in front of the howff door and the other twa lads appeared to be asleep.

He'd had some first-aid training, so he shouldn't leave Iaian and Tormad. Angus was near spent, but Rob could ask him one last errand. "If you've any breath left, go back to Alice's quarters and bring bed covers and haps. As many as you can carry."

The crofter grasped Rob's shoulder, pushed himself upright, and took off at a fast walk, throat whistling.

Rob stared down at Iaian Boyd's face.

The lad's nose was smashed to one side. The sandy outline of a boot heel marked his battered cheek. Both eyes were swollen closed and a welt large as a duck's egg crowned his forehead.

Rob moved over to Tormad. "Stay on your back, but tell me all you can."

"Och, all I ken is when I got here, twa of the other lads were kicking and hitting Iaian, shouting over and over he'd best no' tell on them or they'd kill him. I pulled them off, but one had a rock in his hand and duntit my head, then the other lad chappit my face." He winced as he fingered a livid bruise on his cheek. "I saw stars, Rob, I really did, but it got my dander up. I grabbed both lads and

32

clapped their heads together. They dropped like stones and haven't moved since."

"They're reeking of whisky but their pulses are strong. Most likely sleeping it off." ·

Angus collapsed to his knees beside Rob, his arms laded with bed covers.

Rob grabbed the top one and covered Tormad, then spread twa over Iaian and another three over the blootered lads. "Did Alice call Alec and Hugh?"

"Aye. They're on their way."

"Tormad!" Anna MacKinnon's agonized cry shot across the path. In seconds, she was at her husband's side, holding him close to her woolen dressing gown, rocking him back and forth, wailing.

"Unhand me, wife." The fisherman tried to untangle himself from her clutching hands. "I'm fine."

"You're no' fine. There's blood on your head and your face is all swollen up."

Poor woman. Always fearful for owt happening to Tormad. And she had cause this time.

Alec MacDonald's cairt drew up. "What's happened?" He and Hugh jumped down.

"A drunken brawl. I'll tell you about it later, but we need to get Iaian up to the infirmary. His nose is broken and only the guid Lord knows what else."

"Iaian Boyd!" Hugh grasped the side of the cairt. "But he's a guid lad."

"We'll get this straightened oot later." Rob scrambled to his feet. "Put one of these bed covers into the bottom of the cairt so I can lay the lad on it and you come with me, Tormad. Maggie needs a keek at your head. I'm sure some of the other fishermen are coming soon. They can stay with Hugh and guard these skellums. From the looks and reek of them, they're fair blootered."

It took precious minutes for Tormad to convince Anna she could not leave their wee lass, Kaitlin, alone in the cottage. By then, others had arrived to watch the boys.

On the way at last, Rob rode in the back with Iaian, cushioning the lad's body against the rough ride.

The infirmary was ablaze with lights and Maggie waited at the open door.

Rob carried Iaian inside. "Where to?"

"The OR—and Alec, help Tormad into an examining room. I'll be there as soon as I can."

"Where's Robbie?" Rob helped Maggie undress Iaian.

"Flora's with him." She started an IV and checked the lad's eyes. "'Tis most likely a concussion. His pupils are equal."

This was only the second time Rob had seen Maggie use her nursing skills on anyone other than himself. Impressive.

She ran hands over Iaian's chest, arms, and legs, spending a great deal of time examining his ribs. "At least twa are broken, as well as his nose. His body is covered with contusions." She straightened and looked into Rob's eyes. "I'm going to have to sedate him a wee bit before I set his nose. You can monitor his breathing and blood pressure for me. Go wash your hands while I get the cuff on his arm and have a quick keek at Tormad."

An hour later, Tormad was on his way home with a small plaster over the cut on his head. Iaian slept off the nitrous oxide in one of the patient rooms, his nose set and splinted, nostrils filled with cotton batting, cuts treated, and an IV dripping saline into his arm.

"Has anyone thought to go for Bridget?" Maggie asked.

Rob knuckled his burning eyes. "Och, I don't know, luve, though I'm certain Hugh's seen to it."

"Somebody should radio the polis in Oban." She snapped off her gloves. "Whoever did this could have killed him."

"Alec said on the way up the fell he was going to wait till he talked to the rest of the Island Council. It looked to me like all the lads involved were upper primary students, which means they're only twelve or thirteen at the auldest."

"Tormad told me they had been drinking, but there's no reek of whisky on Iaian."

"I noticed that. But he must have been with them. Tormad heard them threatening to kill him if he told on them."

Tears glistened in her eyes as she went into his open arms.

"Och, Rob, what's happened to our island? I've heard of ranting neds in Glasgow or Edinburgh doing something like this, but never here, never on Innisbraw."

Hugh opened the door and slipped in. "How's the lad?" he whispered.

"I'm thinking he'll be all right, but he's going to be covered with bruises the morra," Maggie said. "I'll keep him here for at least three days. That nose and those ribs will be painful."

Hugh sighed. "Bridget's ootside in the foyer. Should I let her in or do you want to talk to her first?"

"I'd best prepare her. Poor woman, she's been through enough already what with losing her Gregor and twa auldest lads only three years ago. Iaian's all she has left."

Rob ducked out of the room and into a vacant patient room across the hall. Just thinking about the trawler wreck that had claimed not only the skipper's life and his twa lads, but twa other fishermen as well, made his stomach cramp. He had been there when their lifeless bodies were dragged from the sea just off the southern shore of Innisbraw.

It wasn't Gregor's face or his lads' that Rob saw, for they were already beyond saving, but Dougal MacLeod's. Maggie and he had laboured over the thirteen-year-old lad so long, only to have him take his last breath after an hour of saline infusions and frantic artificial respiration.

The lads involved in the fracas spent the rest of that night and next day locked in John's cooling shed so they could sober up and contemplate what they had done. But after another day of talking to the lads, no one was certain what had sparked the violent brawl in front of the howff. They voiced only remorse for how they had treated Iaian.

Iaian refused to reveal anything, even when his mother pleaded with him. "I've nowt to say," he repeated again and again.

Rob asked Tormad to speak to the lad. After all, he was the first to come to Iaian's aid.

Tormad sidled up to Iaian's infirmary bed. Poor lad, with his nose full of waddin', and face all swollen up. How did Rob expect him to make Iaian talk? The fisherman knew what other folk said about him: so close-mouthed his teeth squeaked. But that wasn't true. He always answered important questions, and any conversation about fishing or boats hooked him in. He just couldn't abide idle blether, especially gossip. Aye, he'd questioned new boathands about how well they could bait a line, but this was different.

Too much like invading another skipper's secret fishing spot.

He pulled up a chair and sat, bunnet clasped between his knees. He'd promised Rob he'd try. "'Tis Tormad, lad. I was the one what found you on the path."

No' a word. Was the lad asleep?

Tormad cleared his throat and leaned closer. "Care to tell me what happened?"

A sma' shake of the head, so no' asleep.

Och, this was so hard. But Gregor Boyd had been his friend and Bridget, poor soul, didn't need any more grief. 'Twas time to put sound to his thoughts. He groped for Iaian's hand. "You need to listen close, lad. Your faither was my best friend and a finer, more honest man never lived."

"I ken that." A bare whisper, but at least the lad was listening.

Tormad's callused fingers tightened around the limp hand. "Gregor would never keep silence to cover a wrong done by others. Is protecting those lads all you care about? Or does your faither's guidness still speak to your heart?"

Iaian's fingers clutched his. "This has been coming for a long time," the lad muttered through clenched teeth. "And I can't fault them." He turned his face to the wall. "Though they shouldn't have taken it oot on you."

"What were they upset about? They're only primary school lads."

"That's just it." Iaian winced, clutching his ribs. "What do any of us have to look forward to? I've ... I've been doing odd turns to help Mither, but no' a one of us have the silver for academy. I've tried my best in school, but the other lads gave up long ago." He turned his head and opened his eyes enough to meet Tormad's gaze. "There's no turns here on Innisbraw. What do we have to look forward to—nipping a hen or some neeps from a field to help our mithers?" He squeezed his swollen eyes shut, tears trailing down his bruised cheeks.

The Island Council called an emergency meeting at the manse and asked Rob and all the lads and their parents to attend. It was an uncomfortable meeting, made even more so by Fergus MacCrae and Alistaire MacIver, twa irascible old-timers who launched verbal barbs at every opportunity.

"This is the very reason I want to start a boatworks here on Innisbraw," Rob said in the Gaelic, interrupting the latest of Sandy's tirades. "You lads involved the other night are too young to benefit from that right away, but I've an idea I'd like to put forth for the Council's consideration which could cover that."

"Have your say." Elspeth, the one-hundred-one-year-old head of the Council, tapped her walking stick on the floor. "That's why we asked you to attend this meeting."

Rob's gaze swept the group. "Our Bridget's Iaian isn't the only widow's lad at this meeting. Barabel's Martin lost his life at sea in '42, just like Bridget's Gregor. And Rachel lost her husband to that same sea when her lad was only a small bairnie. Only Julia's Jock is still living, but after he broke his back in that fall at the quarry, he's unable to work, or even walk without difficulty." He took a deep breath, weighing his next words carefully. What he revealed would hopefully give weight to his proposition. "I ... I know what it's like to grow up without a faither to look up to and to keep you on the right path. But unlike these four lads, I had no mither, either."

Everyone stared.

Rob lowered his eyes, face flushing. Only Elspeth and Hugh knew he had grown up in an orphanage. He cleared his throat and raised his eyes, unable to bear the shocked silence. "I know everyone on Innisbraw helps keep our widows and Jock's family provided with peat, food, and other needs. But now that their lads are not small, but nearing manhood, we must do more."

Fergus MacCrae leaped to his feet. "With what? Most of us don't have twa coins to rub together."

Rob reined in his impatience.

Fergus had reason to be testy. The sole caregiver for his older sister, who had been terribly crippled in an accident when she was a lass, he was surely exhausted and worried about another expense he could ill afford.

"I know that, Fergus, but if you'll sit down for a minute and let me have my say, you'll understand."

One tap of Elspeth's stick and a reproving look from her dissolved the old man's starch.

Rob paced the chaumer. "I'm not talking about silver. I'm suggesting we find a way to put these lads to work after school or on their holidays—give them a trade they can be proud of—and someday, a way to earn their own silver."

Fergus and Sandy leaned forward in their chairs.

"All of us know someone who's skilled in something. Dougal Stewart's a fine electrician. Gordon MacLeod can scribe and cut a stone into impossible shapes. You—Fergus and Sandy—you can thatch a roof that will hold even in a hurricane. I know you can't climb ladders any longer, but you still know how to prepare and bundle the thatch and see it's placed and weighted properly. And there are some skilled carpenters on the island—and twa or three plumbers." He met each inquisitive gaze.

A lot of responsibility rested in their positions on the island council—hours of meetings and the well-being of over twa hundred folk weighed on their decisions.

"Until Iaian's nose and ribs are healed, I'd also like to suggest that the first job these lads are given is repairing the rotting thatch on Bridget's cottage, fetching her water from the burn, peats from her peat pile, and any other task Iaian usually does. And then they need to help Paddy to make up for the cost of replacing his broken windows." He stopped pacing and gave each of the lads a broad smile.

A spark of interest replaced the sullen resentment on faces.

"If each lad chooses which job he's interested in and is paired with somebody with a skill in that job, their families will be spared years of heartache. And the lads will be saved from a life of whisky, brawling, and the government dole."

Chapter Six

"Morag and Alec's cottage only has twa bedrooms. With Graham living at home, there's no room for Fern and Katie. Would it bother you having them use our upstairs bedrooms for their visit?" Maggie eyed Rob. If he agreed to her plan, it would be grand having the company.

He reached for another buttery. "Why should it? That's why I added those twa rooms upstairs."

"But what if she decides to stay on Innisbraw? 'Twould take a long time to build her cottage."

His eyebrow rose. Not a good sign. "Are you hoping to use me for a way oot of a fankle?"

Thick-headed man. "Of course no'. I'd luve having them here. I just don't want to hear you complaining about no privacy if they stay on for several months."

"You mean we'll have to lock our bedroom door at night?" He laughed and grabbed her hand, running his lips over her knuckles. "I luve those blushing cheeks, lass. You've mentioned the only negative I can think of. Let's hear all the reasons you're sitting on heckle-pins for my answer."

No' thick-headed. Sly, that's what he was. "Whatsomever do you mean?" She pulled her hand away and poked his chest. "Is it wrong to want a little blethering with another female?"

No reply. Just those dancing dimples beside his lips.

"And we can share the cleaning and such. And Robbie and Katie get along well. And Fern's a nurse. She could help me at the infirmary if somebody needs care. And ..." She jumped up from her chair and plonked down in his lap, throwing her arms around his neck. "And you're letting me blether on like an eejit, knowing you're having me on."

Soft lips nuzzled her cheek. "Feel better?" Smooth as butter, that voice.

"Aye. I do."

"Then, since our lad's abed, let's go enjoy some of that privacy while we can."

Graham helped Rob build twa box-bed frames for the Savage guest rooms in anticipation of Fern and Katie's visit. Rob gave Malcolm MacNeill, owner and skipper of the *Sea Rouk* trawler, some pound notes for twa used mattresses.

When Malcolm returned from Oban on his every-other-day postal run twa evenings later, the burly skipper removed his seaman's cap and greeted Rob with a shrug, blue eyes downcast. "I'm sorra, Rob, but I couldna find even one mattress." He stuffed the notes into Rob's jacket pocket. "Business is picking up, what with all the de-mobbed lads returning home, but there's still no' enough merchandise. The auld sot what runs my local looked at me like I was blootered, and me with only my usual pint of ale in my hand. 'Have ye no' heard?' he said, leaning over the bar like he was telling me something from the King's lips to my ears. 'Even the *Scotsman*'s saying rationing winna end for years.'"

"But I still owe you for all that time and effort. Someday, I'm hoping you'll let me pay for all you've done."

"Och, and me letting you down this time." Malcolm kept his eyes lowered. "When that rescue boat's built, consider us more than even. Just being able to go oot and ken help's at hand will be a blessing."

"Then I'll just have to wait till rationing ends to repay Angus for all the times he's loaned me his cairt and cuddy. I was thinking of getting another used digester and installing it for the MacPhees since Angus won't take any silver for all he's done. A bit like you, now I think on it."

Malcolm grinned and clapped Rob's shoulder. "That's what friends are for—but how's Iaian? And what's happened to those skellums who thrashed him?"

41

"Iaian's doing grand. His eyes are open, but he has the best set of keekers I've ever seen. Looks like a white dog I once saw with black circles around both eyes, but that lad's are yellow, green, *and* black. The other lads have been busy redding up Bridget's cottage and replacing Paddy's windows. They've all chosen what they want to learn so they can do a turn when they've finished school this year. I've paired them up with those men who said they'd be willing to teach their skills." Rob stared out at the harbour. "I suppose only time will tell, but I'm hoping something guid can come from that black night."

"Weel, they've been given a chance." Malcolm turned as if to go.

Rob laid a hand on his arm. "I've an idea about the rescue boat I want to run by you."

"You've already sooked my brains empty with all of your questions when you were putting the designs on paper. Surely you don't think I could help now."

"You ken how I was considering building the boat myself, with Graham helping when his leg gets stronger? Now, I'm wondering if it isn't time to hire some of the lads who've gone off to work on the Mainland or Scotland."

Malcolm stroked his grizzled chin. "'Twould speed things up for certain."

"That's what I'm hoping. That way the boat should be ready by next winter, if no' before."

"That's a grand idea. I know of at least three local lads who were working at naval boatyards during the war—twa at Stornoway on Lewis and another in Oban. They're most likely oot of work and ready to come home now."

"Give me their names and I'll see if I can get hold of them."

"I'll go you one better. Let me talk to the lad in Oban, and then I'll have the others radioed by their folk living here. They can use my shortwave." He slapped his thigh. "Och, Rob, you're finally ready to do it."

Rob grinned. "Tell them I'll pay them what they were earning and a healthy bonus once the boat's finished."

"Sounds more than fair to me. And I know there are three

families here on Innisbraw who'll think verra highly of an offer like that."

"'Twill only be fair. I intend to work their tails off."

"Knowing you, they won't be working any harder than yerself. What does Graham think about it?"

"He's all for it."

"Guid. I'll get on it first thing on the morra."

Maggie made up the twa guest beds with linens that were handsel gifts from their wedding, the mattresses gifted by Hugh after finding them in the manse attic. She confirmed there were enough wooden hangers for the closets and newly ironed newspaper lining the shelves. Putting out jars of fresh wildflowers would have to wait until just before Fern and Katie arrived.

When Rob shared his idea of bringing some of the lads home to work on the rescue boat, she hugged his waist. "That will be three families reunited. What a blessing."

"And, don't disremember, the silver will stay on Innisbraw instead of being spent on cramped quarters and food elsewhere. I'm hoping 'twill help the families, too."

"Och, 'twill that. Now we have to find a way to bring our lasses home. If we can, we'll be insuring new families stay on Innisbraw, and begging for a whole new generation of bairns."

He patted her belly and waggled his eyebrows. "We're doing our share."

"Aye, we are that." His teasing smile, the flecks of green dancing in his hazel eyes, made her body hum and tingle. She buried her face against his chest. "Luve, how do you feel about working wives?"

"Whatsomever do you mean? You never stop working."

"I'm no' talking about that." Her cheeks felt hot. "I've had an idea for several weeks, but I've been a bit afraid to tell you."

He sat in his rocker and pulled her into his lap. "You know I'll always listen to you, luve."

"'Tis just that I'm no' sure 'tis a guid idea. It would take a lot of work and I'm no' certain it would be a success."

His arms tightened. "Don't keep me on heckle-pins. What have you been thinking?"

She pulled back and looked at him. *In for a penny, in for a pound.* "I'm thinking there might be a place here on Innisbraw to start a weaving business."

A broad smile. "Sounds promising. Tell me more."

"Every lass on the island learns weaving from an early age. It wouldn't take much time for them to sharpen their skills again. I'm just fretful there might no' be a market for goods woven on a small island in the Hebrides."

"No' a market?" He stared at her, eyes wide. "If my kilt and dress jacket are examples of what the women here can weave, there's certain to be a market. Just think what such a business would do for the local sheep crofters. They could sell a heap o' their wool on Innisbraw instead of shipping it to the mills in Scotland."

She worried her lower lip. "I don't even ken where to start. I have no education in marketing."

"Then we'll find someone to help with that end of it." He tapped the end of her nose. "You could handle the weaving end, getting it organized, that sort of thing."

"Then you think 'tis a guid idea?"

"No, I think 'tis a grand idea." He kissed her soundly. "The only tickler will be finding a place to do the work. I know a lot of women have their own looms, but no' all do. It will take a verra large building if your loom is any example."

"There's Mary MacCrae's place next to the howff. It will handle several looms, and there's room galore to add on to her building."

"But she's the island's weaver. Will she welcome the competition?"

"We could always pay her to oversee the operation and the use of her place. She barely ekes oot a living now, mainly weaving patches for worn tweeds."

Rob kissed her again. "No' only did I marry the bonniest lass alive, I merit the smartest. Go for it. I'll support you all the way."

"It'll mean I won't always be home, you ken." Uneasiness floated in her belly.

"We'll be just across the path from each other when at work. Yet you can't do too much while you're biggen."

She wrinkled her nose. "But I'll be biggen forever. Isn't that what you said when I told you I wanted eight bairns?"

"Aye, that's what I said." He cupped her chin in his palm and looked deeply into her eyes. "We'll make it all work somehow."

The moment Rob left for the shed the next morning, Maggie radioed her father at the Royal Infirmary in Edinburgh, first telling him all that Rob had accomplished.

His voice rose with excitement. "All Rob's talk about wanting a boatyard on the island and it's about to happen."

"Aye, 'tis his dream coming true. Now, I'm thinking there's a way to bring back some of our lasses. With the war over, and all the turns that went with it—cleaning other folk's flats and tending tables in howffs so far from home—that's no' how we want our lasses to make a living."

He listened quietly while she outlined her idea to start an Innisbraw cottage industry that focused on weaving.

When she finished, he was silent so long, she feared he thought her plan unsound. She reached out to flip the switch to broadcast an apology for wasting his time.

"Actually ..."

Her hand stayed.

"One of our young doctors has a wife in textile marketing. I'm going to have her contact you. You may be onto something."

"Then you think it could work?"

"That's for biddy certain. With the war done, there'll be a need for guid wool clothes the world over, no' just in Scotland. This could be the start of something verra big. I'll try to get you twa together on the radio as soon as possible. Of course, she'll want to see examples of what you can produce."

Her heart pounded. "We have examples all over the island. I'll begin gathering up what I can."

"You do that. I'll get back with you the minute I have owt to report."

45

"Thank ye, Faither, from the bottom of my heart."

"No thanks needed. What you and Rob are attempting could save our island. I should be thanking you twa."

"Are you still coming before the twenty-fourth? Remember, we're planning a ceilidh for Robbie's first birthday."

"I'll be there on the evening of the twenty-first. I can't wait to see your new home, but what I'm really wanting is to see that grandbairn of mine."

She laughed. "He's walking all over now."

"Och, I've missed his first steps. I'm definitely going to have to think seriously about retiring and opening our infirmary on Innisbraw permanently. I'm missing too much."

Those same words had been spoken too many times to actually mean he would leave either of his positions. As head of Orthopaedic Surgery at the Royal Infirmary and Chair of Orthopaedics at the University of Edinburgh's Medical School, his expertise had garnered him world-wide fame. He often traveled to London or, now that the war was over, even Paris and Brussels, to lecture on surgical techniques he had developed. He would be giving up a great deal when he finally did retire.

"That would be nice. I miss you terribly."

"And I miss you. Och, I almost disremembered to tell you, Calum will be coming with me. The lad's signing on with a new boat the end of the month. He has a few weeks between turns."

Tears flooded Maggie's eyes. She hadn't seen her younger brother for so long. "Wonderful. What a joy it will be to have our family together again."

"Indeed it will. I luve you, lass. Kiss wee Robbie for me and tell Rob I couldn't be any prouder."

Maggie left the shortwave on Receive and sat back, chewing her knuckle. Could she really do it? Start a weaving business? Such a large responsibility, that. But it would keep her thoughts from those dreadful images of her precious Rob battling the waves and losing—always losing.

Chapter Seven

The first shipment of equipment to arrive from Harris included Thomas Campbell's diesel engine, saving the fisherman twa days of sailing. With the help of several crofters and a hand-pulled sledge Rob had fashioned for the larger power tools, the move from boat to shed went smoothly.

After Rob paid the crofters for their help, he and Graham toiled for hours, bolting large saws, planes, and a drill press to the wooden floor, then sorting hardware and fittings into the bins they had built above benches crafted from driftwood and used lumber.

As they worked, Graham amused Rob by singing silly Scots ditties in a surprisingly fine tenor voice. "Come on," the lad urged. "I'm certain you know some of these songs. Join in."

Rob grunted and tossed a handful of wooden pegs into a bin. "You don't know what you're asking. I'm what they call in the States 'tone deaf,' sort of like a musical 'Johnny One Note.'"

"Johnny One Note? Weel, I'm thinking it can't be high C, no', with your deep voice." Graham's lips curved in a devilish grin. "You sure it isn't Johnny bullfrog?" He batted his lashes and raised his foot, wriggling it provocatively. "If you're no' a bass, I'm a yella-haired lass wi' ribbons roond ma toes," he crooned in a high falsetto.

"Ribbons ... roond your ..." Rob threw back his head and laughed. When he regained control, he wiped his eyes and nudged aside the remaining box. "We need coffee. We're both so spent, we're acting blootered." He poked Graham's shoulder. "Especially you." He grabbed Graham's arm and marched him across the path to the howff, stopping when they reached the front door. "And don't start batting those lashes in Paddy's. I don't want you ruining my

47

reputation."

They collapsed against the stone building, laughing until their eyes teared.

The door popped open and Paddy McDonald roared, "What's goin' on out here? You two been tippin' a flask of Auld Goldie in that shed over there?"

Rob tucked his shirttail into his denims and flashed the young Irisher a bemused grin. "Och, Paddy lad, you're looking at twa tired men. Have pity and take a pottle of strong coffee to that table in the front corner."

An entire pot of coffee, six scones fresh out of the oven, and resting for half an hour rejuvenated their exhausted bodies and they returned to the shed to unpack the remaining box. When it was empty they stood back and gazed at the hand tools lined up in neat rows on twa benches.

Rob kneaded his left shoulder. "I didn't think it possible. We may have to change things around a wee bit when everything else arrives, but so far it looks guid." He forced down a laugh and grinned at Graham. "What? No grand aria to show your pleasure?"

"I'm aria-ed oot." Graham leaned against the wall, a smile creasing his braw face. "So the lumber from Fern and the rest of the larger tools should be here in twa days?"

"Aye, and that should do it. We can use some of the lumber to partition off office space and a place for the rescue service radio operator. From what I can remember, her lumber wasn't nearly as guid as what we'll receive from that mill in New Hampshire—too many knots, for one thing." Rob joined Graham, resting his aching back against the rough wood. "I can't thank ye enough for lining up all the transportation. And it didn't cost as much as hiring a shipping company."

"The twa fishermen only needed to be compensated for no' having a catch for four days, though I'm thinking they were a bit on the low side when they estimated how much it would cost them."

That didn't sound right. "Then we'll have to add more silver. I'll no' cheat them—they work too hard for the sma' bit of silver they take in."

"Och, I don't think they feel cheated and I wouldn't insult them

48

by trying to pay more. They want this rescue boat more than you do, if that's possible. Remember, they're back to fishing the Atlantic, which means taking their chances around the skerries south of us. 'Twill give them the security they've never had."

"Well, I don't like it, but I ken they're prideful." Rob rubbed the side of his nose. "If you're certain ..."

"I'm biddy certain. Let them contribute too."

As promised, the final shipment from Harris arrived twa days later—with a surprise on board. Fern and Katie stood on deck, all of their personal possessions in boxes stacked high at the bow of the *Anna*, Tormad MacKinnon's large trawler.

Rob lifted Katie into his arms and wrapped the other arm around Fern's shoulder. "I couldn't be happier you've come."

Graham greeted his cousin with a hug and kiss. "Welcome home, for home it will be from now on."

"I wasn't sure I was doing the right thing ..." Fern's voice broke. "But now I know I am."

"We'll have your home built as soon as possible." Graham patted her arm. "Mither and Faither's croft is large, but with Faither expanding his herd ..." He shrugged. "We've all agreed a spot near Rob's would put you close to Maggie and your Katie can have somebody to play with."

Fern pulled a handkerchief from her sweater pocket and wiped her eyes.

"Have we overstepped, then?"

She shook her head. "I'd luve living near Maggie and Rob, but I don't know if I can afford a new home right now. The banker I use bought my cottage, using a wee bit of chicanery to get around the legal ownership, but he's not sure about the boatyard since it's so much more costly and isn't in my name. We didn't have time to add me to the deed before Edward shipped out."

"But surely you have papers from the Army about his—" Katie's breath warmed Rob's cheek and he swallowed the word. "Everything he owned should rightfully be yours."

"I've submitted everything I received from the Army and a

copy of our marriage certificate from the Harris Free Church in Leverburgh. With the war over, a man with a large boatworks on Lewis has voiced an interest. Now it's all in the hands of the solicitors. All I can do is hope—and pray."

Rob hugged Katie tightly. "Then pray we shall. And it will all come out fine."

She shot him a brilliant smile. "How did you know we'd stay?"

Saucy lass, just like his Maggie. "I didn't. But I intended to convince you 'twas the right thing to do if you were wavering. Graham, Alec, and Morag were planning to add their own arguments in favour of it."

"Katie, lass, I think your Uncle Rob's a schemer."

"He is not." Katie's dimples deepened. "He's my uncle, and I luve him."

That earned her a kiss.

"If you don't mind, could you supervise the unloading while I take Fern and Katie up to the house?" Rob asked Graham. "I know your folks don't have room and Maggie already has their bedrooms ready."

Humour danced in Graham's eyes. "You just don't want to let loose of wee Katie, here. No' that I blame you. She's a bonnie lass."

Katie blushed and buried her face against Rob's shoulder. "I want to see Robbie," she whispered in his ear.

"And you shall." He nuzzled the lass's cheek before turning to Fern. "Have you marked which boxes have your clothes and other things you'll need till your new home is built?"

"Four boxes with large Xs on the fronts."

"Have the lads bring those boxes up to our house and take the rest to the infirmary," Rob told Graham. "We'll store them in the attic storeroom till her home is ready." He nodded to Fern. "We can use the cairt if you want, but it's a pleasant walk up the hill."

"We've been cooped up all day on the boat. I'd luve the walk." Her eyes misted again. "I don't want to put you and Maggie out. Perhaps there's a small cottage we could rent for a while, though I didn't bring much furniture."

"This is the verra reason we built such a large house. With Maggie being biggen, Robbie's running her ragged. She's counting on Katie's help distracting him—and you to give her the only adult conversation she'll hear most days. She can't wait to see you again."

"But with a new baby coming ..."

Rob, who had been speaking English to Fern, lapsed into the Gaelic with its richer nuances of meaning. "Oh, Fern, you cannot believe how much room we have. Our home is your home for as long as you want." He stopped walking and looked her in the eyes. "I think there is something you do not know about our small island, but it is something you will soon learn. Our people are warm hearted and loving. As far as they are concerned, there can never be enough folk here to share all this island has to offer. Welcoming family home to Innisbraw is something to be celebrated, and celebrate we shall."

～☆～

Fern soon became an indispensable member of the Savage household. She watched Robbie for hours while Maggie scoured the island for examples of Innisbraw weaving. Maggie's job was made much harder when Elizabeth MacGruder, the marketing specialist her faither had recommended, put a very unexpected impediment in her way. "You can't compete with the mills on weaving the clan tartans. They're already set up and can do it much more cheaply."

Choking back a groan, Maggie asked, "Then what are you looking for?"

"A weave of some sort that will set you apart."

"Have you any idea what might sell best?"

"Anything that can be sewn into men's suiting or women's wear, or even both. There's an immediate need for woolens right now. You just have to come up with something unique and your market is assured."

Maggie called an emergency meeting of the Women's Aid Society and insisted that Fern accompany her.

Fern frowned. "But I haven't had time to weave in years."

"That doesn't matter. You lived on Harris a long time. We don't want to duplicate what they weave, like the Harris Tweed, but you may be able to tell us if one of our patterns looks familiar."

"Well, if you're certain ..."

"I'm biddy—och, very certain. Besides, I want you to meet the women in the Society. You're one of us now so, over time, some of them will become close friends."

"Won't it cause a problem that I don't speak Scots?" That troubled look was back in Fern's eyes.

"No' when they learn you're taking lessons from Elspeth. She's a charter member of the Society. Besides, you do speak the Gaelic."

⚶

Flora MacPhee, Angus's wife and the Savage's neighbor, picked them up for the ride to the meeting. Elspeth already sat on the front bench of the cairt. After Maggie had introduced Flora and Fern, the four were soon talking excitedly in the Gaelic about how much a weaving enterprise would improve their island.

Elspeth pulled her shawl up over the white braids wrapped around her head like a shining halo. "I'm surprised nobody came up with it long ago, though I suppose the war kept us too busy to even think about coming up with new ideas to better our island." She patted Maggie's knee with her tiny, gnarled hand. "I'm not surprised it was you who came up with the idea. Between you and Rob, our island is truly blessed."

Maggie lowered her eyes. She didn't deserve such praise. "Oh, Elspeth, this can't compare to what Rob is planning."

"It is not only the lads who need to be brought home." Elspeth's stern gaze reminded Maggie of her childhood.

With so many women gathered, the meeting had to be moved from the manse to the kirk hall. Morag MacDonald, the society's current president, called the meeting to order and immediately turned the proceedings over to Maggie.

She got right to the point. "We need a way to get our young lasses back to Innisbraw," she said in the Gaelic to accommodate not only Fern, but a number of the older women who spoke no Scots, "and what better way than to offer them self-employment weaving cloth that would be sold in Scotland, perhaps even London or America?"

Everyone started talking at once.

Maggie waited for the hubbub to die down. "I've been in touch

52

with a textile marketing expert. She assures me if we can come up with a weave unique to our island, we will have an instant market for our goods."

Katag MacLeod, one of the poorer sheep crofter's wives, waved her hand. "But what could that be? We don't know what's already out there."

"That's a good question but I can assure you, from the time I spent in London during the war, there are many weaves our women do that I never saw in clothing there." Maggie looked out at the crowd, catching as many eyes as she could. "I propose that every woman on the island who does weaving and wants to take part submit her own design in a sample swatch. It doesn't have to be large—just big enough to show its characteristics. If you already have your loom warped for something you are working on, submit an article of clothing you wove earlier. We'll look them over, cull out those that are duplicates or too common already, and vote on the others."

Susan Ferguson's hand shot up. "Who does the voting?"

Maggie smiled at her childhood friend. Since Mark, Susan's husband, used his long-buried father's auld trawler for fishing, added income would be much appreciated in that cottage. "The women who weave. That's only right."

The women all nodded, talking excitedly.

Maggie raised her voice over the chatter. "And, to sweeten the pot, my husband is going to offer a prize to the winner."

"A new cottage?" shouted Sheila MacNab, the kirk organist.

Maggie laughed along with everyone. "Nothing quite that grand, but he is willing to convert every window in the winner's cottage to ones that open and close."

The meeting broke into pandemonium.

After several minutes of hilarity, Morag took control. "We will now take a vote. Those who are willing to go along with Maggie's proposal, raise your hands."

Arms shot up all over the room.

"All opposed, raise your hands."

Maggie held her breath.

Not a single hand was raised.

Morag waved her arm. "Then let's get the word out. Our young girls have been gone long enough. Let's bring them home."

Maggie and Fern talked excitedly with Flora and Elspeth on the ride home. "There are several patterns I can think of that I haven't seen anyplace else," Elspeth said, "though I've only been to Oban, Stirling, and Edinburgh, not London."

Flora grasped Maggie's arm. "I'm thinking of that pattern Rinait used on the skirt she wove me for the Hogmanay ceilidh. I'd not seen it before, and she said she just made it up."

Maggie had admired the skirt too. "She should submit it. I know everybody will still have to do their own weaving for their families. But by bringing our lasses home and including all those women already here who could use the extra, we should have enough weavers to gain us a place in the market."

Elspeth nodded. "That was kind of Rob to make an offer to reward the winner, but knowing the lad, it doesn't surprise me."

"I thought he was going to start on the rescue boat," Flora said. "When will he find time for windows?"

Maggie turned in her seat. "I asked him the same thing. He said he was still waiting for all the lads to get here from Oban and the mainland and for the lumber to arrive from America."

Och, will we never return to our eens of quiet blethering?
Yet this was all my idea.

Chapter Eight

Maggie and Fern cleaned and aired out the McGrath cottage to get it ready for John and Calum's arrival the next evening. Bright chatter and girlish laughter, interspersed with shrieks when Robbie and Shep dashed between legs, stretched a normally short chore into a day-long effort.

"I don't know what I would have done without Fern's help." Maggie confided in Rob as they undressed for bed. "She's like having the sister I never had. 'Tis almost frightful how many times we think the same thoughts."

"I'm happy you get along so well." Rob tossed her sweater on the bed and massaged her stiff neck muscles. "But I'm still thinking you did too much."

"I'm no' the one putting in twelve to eighteen hours a day." She closed her eyes and leaned into his probing fingers.

"You do that every day, luve, without even thinking about it."

Och, what nonsense. How could he compare house-tending to the manual labour that raised calluses and cramped exhausted muscles?

She pulled away and faced him. "One of these days you're going to admit to the long hours you work and when you do, I'm either going to drop dead from surprise or be long in my grave."

⚜

Hovering grey clouds pressed the louring sky as Maggie turned eager eyes to the *Sea Rouk* bumping against the dock.

There he was, standing on the deck. Calum!

Luve flooded her, warm as a rare summer sun. How much he had grown—no longer a bony, awkward lad, but a tall, mature young man.

Rob kissed her cheek and picked up Robbie, moving to one side.

Fidgeting while the boat was tied off, she allowed her mind to wander back to the bitter-sweet day Calum was born. She was only eight when her mither—her precious, loving, bonnie mither—died giving birth to the new brother she had wanted for such a long time.

For the first twa days, resentment kept her from even looking at him, but when Elspeth sat Maggie in her mither's rocker and placed the tiny bairnie in her lap and she looked down at his wee face with its long, black lashes and hazy, dark blue eyes, she ran trembling fingers over his soft black hair and something melted inside her heart. Tears of joy mingled with those of grief and spilled down her cheeks. She bowed her head and promised the Lord that her mither's sacrifice would not be wasted. She would raise this bairnie as her own.

And she had fulfilled that vow to the best of her ability. With Elspeth's help, she had learned how to feed him goat's milk from a bottle, burp him gently over her shoulder, change his hippens and gowns, and bathe him in the kitchen jawbox.

Robbie's squeal jolted her from the past. At last, lines secure and gangplank in place, she dashed forward, throwing herself into Calum's arms the moment he stepped to the dock. She kissed his cheek and he hers. "Welcome home," she whispered. "You'll never ken what this means to me."

His arms tightened. "I luve you, too."

John eyed Maggie's rounded belly and held out his arms, pulling her close. "You're looking a bit thin, but guid." Och, he was a sentimental auld fool, unable to keep a hint of tears from his voice. He reached over to clap Rob's shoulder. "And so are you. 'Tis obvious you're still doing those exercises I sent to build muscle."

"I am that. But you're spending a lot of time ignoring a certain grandbairn." Rob pointed at Robbie, who had a finger in his mouth.

"I'm trying not to scare him off."

Rob grinned. "That's me sorted, then."

John hugged Fern next. "I remember stitching up your knee when you were just a wee lass. Graham pushed you off Alec and

Morag's dyke when you were here for a day's visit."

Her eyes widened. "How could you remember that?"

"It was Graham's contrite tears. That lad cried harder from the stitches than you did." John pulled Calum to his side. "Lad, I'd like you to meet Fern MacNeill, Morag's niece. Fern, this is my son, Calum. You may remember him."

Fern smiled and shook Calum's hand. "I'm afraid you've forgotten I'm even older than Maggie. But I do remember a wee lad toddling around, making a pest of himself."

Calum ducked his head. "Must have been me."

John chuckled and knelt to greet Katie. "And who is this bonnie lass?"

"I'm Katie, and I never want to have stitches because it would hurt."

Resisting a smile, he said, "I hope you don't ever need stitches either, but if you do, I promise I'll make sure it doesn't hurt."

She studied him for a moment, eyes probing, face solemn. Apparently satisfied, she smiled, dimples dancing. "I like you."

⚜

Rob threw his arm across Calum's shoulder. The lad resembled Maggie so much—same face shape, same black hair. Though his eyes did not have flecks of violet in them, they were that same shade of startling blue. "It's about time you came home for a spell, though I swear I hardly recognized you. You've grown over ten centimetres."

"I'm still not as tall as you, but I'm working on it." Gone were the downcast eyes and flushed cheeks. Though still slim, Calum was much taller than his faither. His hard work on a trawler had padded his lean arms and shoulders with muscle.

How grand he had come home at last. Maggie, tender lass that she was, needed her brother. Like an unfledged chick needed its nest mates, she needed her family to feel complete.

Hopefully Robbie would feel the same toward his siblings one day.

⚜

John patted the wee lad's back and turned to Rob. "I didn't

want to come on too strong, but I can't wait another minute. Can Robbie really walk?"

"He no' only walks, he runs." Rob set Robbie on his feet and held onto the back of his sweater. "Problem is there's no telling which direction he'll choose."

Robbie looked at the gangplank and then the water on either side of the dock. His eyes lit up when he spied Shep waiting patiently at the end of the pier. In a flash, he was off, his faither trotting behind him.

The bairn's delighted giggles brought a chuckle to John's throat. "Rob's finally getting his wish. At last he has someone who loves to run as much as he does."

"Amen to that." Maggie sighed. "Between the twa of them, we'll spend all our silver just keeping them in shoes."

They all made their way down the pier. When they reached the cairt, Robbie squirmed in Rob's arms, hands grasping to reach the shaggy cuddy.

"He wants to ride," Rob said with a grin. "I thought getting close to a large animal might scare him, but all he's done is reach for Jack and bounce up and down in my arms."

Maggie hugged her faither's arm. "This is another reason you need to retire. If this lad's as much like his faither as I fear he is, he won't be afraid of anything. I see at least one broken bone in his future."

"Och, I hope not."

Calum and John tossed their bags into the back of the cairt and Maggie, Calum, and John climbed in. Rob handed Robbie to Maggie.

The lad howled with indignation.

John pulled his watch from its pocket. "Maybe he'd be interested in this."

"It will go in his mouth."

"Of course. You cut your teeth on it."

Robbie soon gummed the pocket watch, saliva running down his chin.

Rob helped Katie and Fern onto the bench, climbed up, and

took the reins, clucking to Jack.

Katie clung to Rob as the cairt moved up the path. "Is Grandfather John going to sleep in my room?" she asked in a loud whisper.

"He and Calum will stay at their own cottage." He winked at her. "Though they will be taking supper with us, along with Graham, Rinait, Aunt Morag, and Uncle Alec."

"But is Grandfather John really my grandfather? Mother's never told me stories about him."

Rob glanced at Fern. *Help*, he mouthed.

"Grandfather John isn't really your kin, like Rob isn't really your uncle. We just call them that because they're like family."

"But you said I should call him 'Uncle Rob.'"

Fern shook her head and looked heavenward as though for inspiration. "Yes, I did, and that's because he's special. And Aunt Maggie's special. We call special people special names."

Katie appeared to digest this for a moment before smiling and reaching over to hug her mother. "Just like 'Mother' is special."

John looked around and sighed.

Their home.

The soft white walls glowed in the light coming in from the large windows. Maggie's hutch stood against the longest wall, waxed wood gleaming, shelves filled with Elizabeth's prized china.

Och, his heart still clenched when he even thought her name.

His gaze swept on. A picture of Rob and Maggie in their uniforms stood on a table beside a large lamp. Light glanced off their smiling faces and puddled on the surface of the shining wood. Twa rockers, stitched cushions softening their seats and backs, faced a large stone fireplace with a driftwood mantle cluttered with candles, seashells, and a stack of books. All the room lacked was a comfortable sofa.

When rationing ended, he'd gift them one.

The large table Rob had made was piled high with food. Alec and Morag had brought a beef roast and extra chairs. Rinait MacPhee, Graham's fiancée, had contributed a large platter of crème cookies.

The meal began with partan bree, followed by the beef joint, mashed neeps and tatties, home-canned green beans, and pan bread. There was coffee for Rob and Graham and tea for everyone else.

Katie wriggled in her chair and stared intently across the table at John. Every time she opened her mouth to say something, somebody else talked.

He held up a hand to quiet the conversation. "I believe the wee lass would like to say something."

Her red curls bounced. "I just wanted to say I know why Uncle Rob and Calum eat so much."

"It's not polite to say that," Fern corrected quietly.

"But I know the reason," Katie insisted. She reached her hands above her head, wriggling her fingers. "They are both very, very high so it takes more to get to their tummies."

Rob choked and had to be pounded on the back before he could catch his breath. "I do believe you're right, Katie, lass," he rasped. "And you're smart to notice it."

Robbie sat on John's lap, smacking his lips every time Maggie spooned mashed neeps and tatties into his wide-open mouth.

"He's just started eating food from the table," Maggie explained to her faither. "I had to do something. I just can't make enough milk to fill him up anymore."

"You've been feeding him brose—och, oatmeal porridge—for a while, haven't you? Surely that helps."

"I do for breakfast and sometimes again for tea but we eat supper so late he's ravenous again, even though he's nursed all day."

"Then, by all means, feed him table food." John eyed her critically. "You're looking a bit too thin, lass. You can't expect to nurse him much longer. He's almost half again the size of any bairn his age."

A grin flashed across Rob's face. "Say that part about her being too thin again. I've been telling her that for weeks."

"You're one to talk, young man. You've lost weight since I was here last. I thought I told you to run less."

The grin evaporated. "I'm hardly running at all. I've just been

60

working a few more hours. Besides, you told me I looked guid."

✽

Maggie knew where this conversation was headed and wanted no part of it. She rose and nodded to Fern. "Rob? Graham? More coffee?"

Hands shot up around the table.

Including Calum's.

What? "Since when do you drink coffee?"

The lad's eyebrow rose. "Since I discovered how guid it tastes. You served it with supper and you know I never liked tea."

Och, no' another one with a talented eyebrow. She rested her hands on her hips and stared him down. "Mebbe no' tea—just milk by the jugful." Ignoring his ringing laugh, she stomped into the kitchen for the tea and coffee pots.

Fern gathered the empty plates. "Those crème cookies look delicious, Rinait. I'll have to get your recipe. They're Katie's favourites."

Rinait leaped up to help clear the table, cheeks abloom. "I'll write it oot for you. You'll find I use Caledonian Cream, usually flavored with marmalade."

Rob thanked Maggie for filling his coffee cup. "Sit you down, luve. 'Tis a rare evening we have family together."

Leaning across the table, Graham pointed at Rinait. "Yon lass is so good at baking, I'm the one who's going to have to watch my weight."

"Your limp's almost gone," John said. "Have you been getting in plenty of walking?"

"Every day. I'm living at home now, so I'm walking to the shed every morning and back home every evening. That's over six kilometres, plus what I get working around the shed all day."

"You're not attempting to run yet, I hope?"

"Rob said he'd have my skin if I did."

Alec gripped his son's shoulder. "I'll vouch for the lad. He's no' run when I've been aroond, and Rob's no' the only one who threatened to skin him. I told him the same thing."

Morag beamed at her son. "And I told him I'd skite his lug if I saw him running."

"See?" Graham said with a grimace. "Your island polis are everywhere. I can't get away with owt."

With dessert a pleasant memory and the bairns tucked into bed, Rob said good-bye to their guests as they departed.

John lingered on the front entry with Calum and Rob. "I can't tell you how impressed I am with this home. It's verra large, yet it feels warm and welcoming. And your ceiling in what you call the 'living room' is a marvel, the way you stopped it part way and put in those twa bedrooms. After looking at the finish work, I'm thinking you could have been a builder. You're a real craftsman."

Rob squirmed. He wanted desperately to give credit to all the others who had helped, but Maggie was always telling him he had to start accepting compliments. "Thank ye." He couldn't help himself from adding, "But I'm thinking Maggie's way with decorating brings out the best of the design."

"You twa make a guid team. The lass has always had a way with colour, even as a wee one." John laughed. "'Tis a guid thing, for I had to trust her to make sure she and Calum wore the right colour sweaters with their skirts or breeks. If it had been up to me, they'd have borne the brunt of a lot of teasing at school."

Calum joined in the laughter. "That's the truth. Maggie once took an entire hour explaining to Faither why he couldn't wear brown socks with his guid blue suit."

"It wasn't an hour."

"It was. By the time we got to kirk, it was almost time for the Benediction."

Rob cringed. That sounded too much like him. "I'm no' much better than you, John. If I hadn't been in the military where I had only twa colour choices—the dark khaki or the 'pinks'—I'd have been in a muddle all of the time."

"Well, God knew we men needed women, didn't He? And for more reasons than that."

"Many more reasons." Rob said fervently.

Calum elbowed him in the ribs.

Chapter Nine

The thin notepad in Maggie's lap weighed heavy as a flagstone, though it had only a few precious pages remaining, and those needing to be hoarded until the end of rationing. Would Robbie's birthday ceilidh prove too difficult for Rob? Would it remind him of his own childhood, suck him back into a painful past peopled with caring but harried orphanage aides and spiteful village folk?

Rob interrupted her thoughts by plucking up the notepad and waving it through the air like a captured trophy. "You've been studying this list like your life depends on it. Let's have a keek."

No sign of hesitation. No air of despondency. Just a hint of a tease in his deep voice.

The planning had gone on too long to share her fears now. "There were ever so many more I wanted to invite, but the house isn't large enough, so I decided to invite those who spend time with the laddie."

If he noticed the slight tremble in her voice, he ignored it. "I wondered how you were going to make your choices."

She sat back in her rocker. "I couldn't ask Malcolm and exclude Sim, or Graham without including Rinait, or Angus and Flora without Edert, so I listed the whole MacPhee family. Help me, Rob. I know I've disremembered somebody important."

He ran his finger down the page. "Let's see … Malcolm, the MacDonalds, all the MacPhees, the MacKinnons—why Tormad and Anna? Have they been visiting?"

"No, but Tormad's helped you so much when you designed your boat, and Katie needs to make friends with their Kaitlin. They're almost of an age."

A huge hand engulfed hers. "Guid thinking. But Mark helped

as much as Tormad."

"I asked Susan at kirk last Sabbath, but she said Mark would be oot fishing so she declined."

"But you've been friends since you were wee lasses."

"I wouldn't go to a celebration if you couldn't, luve. Besides, she feels 'tis too long a walk up the fell in her condition. She miscarried the first year they were merrit so she's being verra careful no' to lose this bairnie."

"She's biggen?" He squeezed her fingers. "Why didn't you tell me before now?"

"She wanted to be sure she wouldn't lose this one. She'll deliver sometime the last of May."

His pleasured smile warmed her heart, banishing her fears to the dark recesses of her mind. She tapped the list. "You're no' finished. Read on."

He scanned the rest of the names. "Hugh and Elspeth, John, Calum, Fern and Katie. Looks guid to me. Of course there'll be Paddy and his lads playing the music."

Her nose crinkled with delight at the thought of rollicking music filling their home. "Fern's going to help me with the baking and we'll let Katie stir the tablet."

"Tablet." His tongue slicked his lips. There was nothing like the thought of vanilla fudge to set her man's taste buds salivating.

A sudden thought brought her upright. "Did you ask Graham to help you stock the cooling shed with ale and lemon skoosh—and Alec to bring some chairs from the kirk hall?"

He pulled her into his arms. "I did, and I've finished building Robbie's cairt. I added a seat and wooden sides to keep him from falling oot." His fingers brushed her cheek. "Now you won't have to carry him on your hip, as you're wont to do."

The evening of the ceilidh, Maggie and Rob greeted their guests on the front entry, Robbie chortling with delight. Once everyone was inside and removed their coats and jackets, Maggie smiled at all their guests clad in their best clothes.

Katie wore a kilt and ruffled blouse.

"The lass is planning a surprise for Rob," Fern whispered in her ear. "She's been practicing for hours in the bedroom upstairs while he was at the shed."

"That wouldn't have anything to do with the sounds of footsteps overhead, would it?"

Fern put a finger to her lips. "She'll be heartbroken if he learns of it beforehand. It's meant as a thank ye for all the stories he's been telling her before bed."

"He enjoys it as much as the lass. There's something in his heart that responds to wee ones. I suppose it has to do with his lonely childhood."

"I can't believe what he had to endure, but it made him who he is today, so I suppose some guid came of it."

Maggie's gaze sought out Rob, who was in the midst of a lively blether with Malcolm and Tormad. "A lot of good, actually, though he still has moments of doubting his worth."

⁓⋇⁓

Elspeth touched Robbie's hair as he toddled past.

The lad had a rapt audience and made the most of it, going from person to person, begging to be held, before sliding off one lap in order to beg the next guest for attention.

"That one's going to break some hearts someday," she said to John. "With his looks and personality, he'll go far."

"It's a good thing he has a tender heart, or his drive always to be moving would impel him right through life, regardless of others' feelings." John excused himself to help the men clear the center of the living room of furniture while Paddy and his lads put down their empty ale bottles and picked up their musical instruments.

Robbie, his audience scattered, pulled at Elspeth's skirt, struggling to climb into her lap.

Fern lifted the laddie up and signaled Katie to stand back and give room for the dancers.

Rob and Maggie joined some of the other couples in an Eightsome Reel.

Robbie, excited by the lively music, squealed and bounced up and down on Elspeth's knees so hard she winced.

Stupit auld knees, always complaining about time spent in

prayer, and now this.

Ever vigilant, Fern plucked Robbie up and carried him over to a corner where Shep had taken refuge.

The laddie embraced the dog and attempted to pull the animal to his feet, but Shep ignored the grasping hands and curled up into a ball, burying his nose beneath his tail.

Elspeth chuckled as Robbie stared at Shep a moment, then lay down beside him, his fingers laced in the dog's thick fur.

There's a cannie laddie.

❧

The dance ended. Rob wiped his sweaty forehead and seated Maggie in her rocker. "Fauld yer fit, lass," he whispered, brushing his lips across her rosy cheek.

Maggie fanned herself. "I'm thinking we'd better let the lad have his presents. It's past twenty-hundred hours. He's not going to last much longer."

"We'll have the lads play one more tune while I bring the gifts in from the entry. An Open Bob—that way everybody can dance."

As soon as the music started, Rob stepped outside.

The sunset washed the sky with wide swirls of blue and purple. Orange and yellow splashed across a dark red background.

When had he ever felt so contented? He'd even been too busy to think about flying. He smiled as he turned and looked out at the fine, drystone dyke Angus had erected around the croft. He had his Maggie and Robbie and another bairnie on the way, their home was comfortable and spacious, and he had more friends than he had ever dreamed possible. It would soon be time to build the rescue boat and he was healthy and strong enough for the task. He closed his eyes and breathed a heartfelt prayer of gratitude—and another quick one that the boat would not sink when she was launched.

The last notes of the song inside faded.

He opened the door and pulled the loaded cairt inside.

Paddy signaled his lads, who played a fanfare as John picked up a sleeperie Robbie and carried him to the center of the room.

The lad eyed twa large bright balls in the wagon, reached for them. Once on his feet, he pulled them out, squealing with glee as they bounced across the floor. One stopped just inches from the open fireplace.

Before Rob could react, Shep was between the bairn and the ball. Though Robbie tried to push him away, the dog refused to move.

Edert MacPhee retrieved the ball and slid it across the floor and Robbie ran after it.

Maggie winked at Angus and Flora, acknowledging their gift of one ball, and sidled over to thank Morag and Alec for the other.

Rob scooped Robbie up and returned him to the cairt. The lad picked out a toy airieplane Malcolm had brought from Oban, eyeing it for a moment before putting the tip of one wing in his mouth.

"I'm thinking he needs a little flight training," Graham said with a laugh.

"He does that. Thank ye, Malcolm."

Rob pulled out a large wooden truck and put it down on the floor.

Robbie dropped the airieplane and plonked down on the truck, legs pumping. He moved it several feet before he got up and returned to the cairt, apparently realizing that exciting things kept emerging from its depths.

Waving for everyone's attention, Rob said, "I want you all to know that Hugh designed the truck after one he remembers seeing in Edinburgh. He's so guid, I may ask his help with my next boat."

Robbie ignored the laughter and pulled out a soft stuffed rabbit, planted a wet kiss on its black nose, and tucked it beneath his arm.

Maggie embraced her faither. "'Tis perfect. Just what he needed for bedtime."

Four small balls bounced across the floor, followed by an excited laddie.

Rob thanked the MacKinnons and Fern and Katie. Their gifts would bring many hours of pleasure to his lad—and Shep.

The last gift, an off-white fisherman's sweater replete with cable and seed stitches, didn't attract much attention from Robbie, but it did from his parents.

Rob studied the intricate stitches, tears in his eyes. Elspeth's gift. How could she knit with her fingers so stiff?

Maggie hugged Elspeth. "He'll be so proud when he sees how it matches his faither's."

Robbie struggled to climb into the cairt.

Rob lifted him in, settled him on the seat, and picked up the tongue so he could pull the lad around the room.

Robbie's eyes opened wide, a smile broadening his scarlet-red cheeks.

Calum stopped Rob in midstride and clapped his shoulder. "You've got a winner. That's a fine cairt you've made—and the well-designed truck."

Handing the tongue to four-year-old Kaitlin MacKinnon, Rob stood back and grinned at his laddie.

Robbie's squeals turned to shrieks as he bounced the rabbit on his knees.

Shep followed, tail tucked, fur standing up on the back of his neck.

Rob caught the dog and scratched his back. "It's all right, lad."

Shep nosed his master's hand and retired back to his corner where he lay down with a heavy sigh.

⁂

Robbie's shrieks became louder and louder and Maggie recognized the impending signs of what Rob called a "melt-doon." She scooped Robbie from the cairt.

The bairn squealed and arched his back, shaking his head from side to side when she tried to ease the rabbit from his arms. He was so tired he was about to stage a full-blown tantrum. She allowed him to keep the rabbit and seated herself in her rocker, hugging him tightly. "I'm thinking this lad needs some milk and then bed. If we wait much longer, he'll go too far and we'll be up all night with him."

Rob kissed her cheek. "Yes, and while you nurse him, it's a perfect time for one of Elspeth's stories." He helped Elspeth to her feet and positioned her chair by the fireplace.

Everyone drew their chairs close as a story by Elspeth was a treat to be treasured.

Maggie threw a shawl over her shoulder and settled Robbie at her breast while Katie and Kaitlin, hands clasped, conspiratorial

68

smiles on their faces, sat on the floor at her feet.

Elspeth related the story of Innisbraw's first known settlers and the broch, or common house and fort, they had once inhabited. The experts dated the stones back to the Iron Age. Though the broch probably started to disintegrate sometime in the fifth century, the remains were still visible on the top of Heuch Fell for all to see. They had all picked their way through the stacked stones and rubble and examined the remains of what had once been a hearth. She wove a story of a day in the life of the early settlers, stressing the feeling of community spirit which had governed their lives.

"Like the towering stones atop Ben Innis, we must take care to preserve such an important part of island history—of *our* history." She gazed at the rapt faces.

Even the youngest bairns were paying attention.

Lowering her voice and wagging a finger, she concluded, "Do not disturb the stones. To do so would be a travesty."

After Elspeth's story, refreshments were served and Robbie, who had fallen fast asleep, was changed into his night clothes and put to bed.

Rob tucked the soft rabbit next to his boy, piled the toys into the cairt, and pulled it into the lad's bedroom where it would be the first thing he saw when he awakened in the morning.

When it was time for the music to resume, Fern approached Paddy and made a request.

He grinned and nodded.

Katie went to Rob and hugged his legs. "This is for you." She smiled up at him, a dimple deep in each cheek. "For the bedtime stories."

Rob sat next to Maggie and took her hand as Katie positioned herself in the center of the floor, hands high above her head. She nodded and Graham MacKay, the piper, launched into the Highland Fling. The child's form was astonishing for one so young. Her small legs flashed and her toes pointed as she performed the intricate legwork, her arms never seeming to tire as around and around she went, her style unwavering. When the bagpipe wheezed its last note, Katie bowed low before making a curtsy to Rob.

Everyone clapped and whistled their approval as Rob leaped from his chair and pulled her up into his arms. "You're a marvel," he whispered in her ear. "Someday, when we've enough people living on Innisbraw for our own Hieland Games, I'm going to watch you place first in the fling." He held her close. "You'll always be my Katie lass."

She put her arms around his neck and kissed him soundly on the cheek. "And you'll always be my special uncle."

The dancing continued far into the night. Katie and Kaitlin finally tired and were tucked into Katie's bed. Sim, Edert, Calum, and Graham performed the Bull Reel, a dance for young lads only, and there was a lot of hilarity over their wild antics and loud whoops.

Maggie smiled at her faither's stern face.

Always the doctor, he wore well the look of dealing with an unruly patient.

As 0200 approached, Paddy and his lads departed and the partygoers collected their coats and wraps. When they had all gathered at the door, Hugh said a short blessing, and they were all on their way with "haste ye backs" ringing in their ears.

The ceilidh had been a smashing success.

Fern retired immediately after promising Maggie she would be up bright and early to help with the redding-up.

"Not too early, I hope." Maggie yawned. "I'm thinking we'll all have a bit of a lie-in this mornin."

After Fern disappeared up the stairs, Rob let Shep out for a few minutes. While the dog nosed around the garden, Rob pulled Maggie's coat around her shoulders and led her out onto the entry where he held her close as they gazed up at the gibbous moon and the stars winking impishly between layers of high clouds.

"You Scots really know how to throw a party, Missus Savage. I don't know when I've had a better time."

She nestled her back against his chest. "It was your party, too.

You may have been born in America, but you're a Scot through and through."

He nuzzled her ear. "That's the nicest compliment I've ever received."

Chapter Ten

As weaving patterns came in from all over the island, Maggie sorted them into piles in her weaving room. The largest stack by far was those which were fresh and original. The weavers were in for a rough time trying to pick a winning pattern. Many women, rather than weave a new swatch, submitted a garment. There were jackets, coats, skirts, and many pairs of men's pants.

Rob looked over the selection, shaking his head. "I didn't know it was possible to get so many variations on a loom. Which one is yours?"

"I've been weaving since I was a lass, and I never imagined there could be so many patterns, but you won't find one from me. It would be unethical and I've no' the time to be always at my loom."

He nodded. "You're going to be in a muddle picking just one. Mebbe your marketing consultant should help you choose the winner."

"I've thought of that, but I promised the womenfolk the weavers would make the choice and I can't change my mind now. Though, of course, Elizabeth will have the final say on what's marketable."

"Don't fash yourself. It'll all work oot in the end."

She poked his chest. "It will, will it?"

"Aye." He caught her finger and kissed it. "There's always only one choice that's right, luve. You'll see."

"You make it sound so simple."

"Simple, no. But in the end, one pattern will stand out from the rest."

"And what makes you such an expert on textiles?"

"No' an expert on textiles, only on choices. You'll go for the one that's the least likely to be common and easiest to duplicate using the workforce you've assembled. That's a simplified explanation of the way Wing used to pick targets to bomb. Choose the one least expected that will cause the fewest casualties to your squadrons."

"How can you compare weaving cloth with bombing targets?" She watched his eyes, waiting for them to lose their green flecks as a reminder of his inability to fly took hold.

"Very simple. Choice, my bonnie Maggie. In the end, it all comes down to the right choice." He sat down on a chair, pulled her into his lap, and picked up a woven coat. "Take this, for instance. It might be the perfect choice as far as being different and unexpected, but if your weavers have a hard time duplicating it, the casualties— or costs, in this case—are too high. See what I mean?" Those green flecks still shone in his eyes.

"Aye, I do see. What guid would a unique pattern be if it were too time-consuming to weave?"

"Exactly."

A kiss on the chin was his reward. "I always knew your experience at Edenoaks helped in your work, but it never occurred to me it would help solve my problem."

He laughed and hugged her. "'Tis only a suggestion. I'm sure it's much more complicated than I make it sound."

"But it isn't. You voiced what should be the twa main concerns in picking a pattern: originality and ease of duplication. Thank ye. You've just made this so much easier."

If only he could solve his own problem so easily. Four lads would report to work on the fifteenth of October and he had no idea when the lumber would arrive from New Hampshire.

He outlined some work to keep the lads busy for a while. They could build the cradle which would be needed for the keel and, using a large piece of timber included in the shipment from Harris, could lay the keel itself. But if the lumber from the States didn't arrive soon, he would have to meet payroll for lads who had nothing to do. Sending a letter by post and waiting for a reply would take far too long. Once again, he fumed about the lack of telephone service on Innisbraw. Surely they would lay the cable soon.

Mebbe he could send Graham to Oban on the *Sea Rouk* where he could contact the lumber mill in New Hampshire by telephone and get some idea of where they stood.

When he approached his partner with the plan, Graham acted excited about the idea of a trip to Scotland, even if only for a one night stay.

"Malcolm has offered you a cot in the bed sit he and Sim overnight in, but I've used it and 'tis hard as a rock," Rob said. "I'll give you some silver so you can rent a hotel room. Just be sure and be hard-nosed when you talk to the supervisor at the mill. Tell him Bill Pointer, the owner, personally told me our shipment would get top priority."

Graham grinned. "In other words, wear my 'captain's cap.'"

"Guid thinking."

"Will do. Nowt in the army gave me more pleasure than pulling rank occasionally. Kind of keeps the juices flowing, if you know what I mean."

"I know exactly what you mean."

When Graham arrived back on Innisbraw, he debarked with a smart salute. "Mission accomplished, sir. The shipment's long gone Boston Harbor. ETA is twa weeks from the day."

The tight band of anxiety around Rob's chest eased. "That's perfect. Well done, you."

With the largest problem now solved, Rob set about making priorities for himself. It looked like choosing a weaving pattern for the island was going to take longer than anticipated, so he could not begin the new windows for the winner yet.

Also, he wanted to make a chest for Maggie's bed-quilts and knitted haps to give to her on her birthday in December. Once the shed was being used to build the rescue boat, it would be almost impossible to do any personal projects there. He decided to use the week remaining before his crew arrived to build the chest.

Graham studied the design Rob had sketched. "This is grand. I'd like to make something like this for Rinait."

"Twa are just as easy to build as one. We'll use some of the lumber I bought from Fern, but you'll have to change the carving on the top. That's just for my Maggie."

"That's me told. I'll see what I can come up with."

Rob had been concerned that Graham would be in the way, but instead, he proved to be a big help. While Rob enjoyed the planing, sanding, and finish work, Graham took to the construction. They made a good team.

They arrived at the shed at dawn's light and often worked straight through to suppertime. At the end of the week, twa chests stood at the front of the shed, needing only several coats of wax.

Rob had carved a Gaelic saying on the top of Maggie's chest—Anam-charaid, or *soul mate*. Graham had chosen to make the top in a marquetry design using several grained woods. Both were beautiful, yet they looked very different.

Graham's cheeks flushed with excitement. "I've never made anything like this. What a sense of accomplishment."

"I'm just sorry we had to be in such a hurry," Rob said. "Half the satisfaction in building something comes from taking your time with the wood."

Rob's work schedule had gotten out of hand. He wouldn't allow her into the shed, so she couldn't even bring him dinner. When she suggested that Fern deliver his meal, he gave some ridiculous excuse about how dangerous the shed was now that all the equipment was set up, ignoring how long Fern had been around that same equipment for years when she ran her boat-building business. And he told her he got a bite to eat every noon at the howff but was so hungry at suppertime she was sure it wasn't enough.

The turn in the weather didn't help. It rained steadily for five days, with heavy gusts of wind driving the sea high onto the fell. Though Rob brought in armloads of peat every day to dry by the fire, the peats still smoked more than usual. Calum had left. Her father was back at the university. And Robbie was teething. His fussing wasn't easy to take when he couldn't be distracted by a trip outside to run and play.

By the end of the week Maggie could barely speak to Rob. Judging by his looks of concern, he knew he was in trouble. But he couldn't even imagine how much.

Chapter Eleven

On the evening of October twelfth, Rob and Graham pulled the completed chests into the office section of the shed and covered them with an old sheet.

Rob shrugged into his A-2 jacket. "I'd best be getting home. Maggie's no' too happy about the long hours I've been putting in."

"Tell me about it." Graham donned his waxed jacket. "Rinait will barely speak to me."

"So you're in trouble too?"

"Big trouble. And the worst of it is, I can't tell her why I've been here so late every een instead of spending time with her."

"I ken what you mean. I'm thinking I'm going to have to tell Maggie just enough to take the heat off."

"But what could you say?"

"That I've been working on something for her. She doesn't have to ken any more than that."

"But won't she keep nattering on about it every day?"

"Put on your captain's cap, lad. This falls under one of those need-to-know headings."

Graham exhaled loudly. "That might work with a woman like Maggie, but Rinait's younger and she has a bit of a temper."

Rob's right eyebrow rose. "Surely, you're no' afraid of her." Though the lad didn't reply, Rob read the answer in the way he ducked his head and studied the floor. "Maybe the captain's cap isn't the best approach. It sounds to me like you'll need to sweet-talk her into understanding."

Hopeful blue eyes met his. "You think so?"

Rob opened the shed door with an exasperated grunt. "I can't be there to hold your hand. You know the lass a lot better than I do.

Just feel your way slowly." He pulled up his collar against the driving rain. "And be ready to duck."

Rob pushed the food around on his plate. The tension surrounding the supper table had built to a brittle edge, inhibiting conversation and muting laughter. He'd sat through uncomfortable meals on air bases, but it was dread of the next morning's bombing mission that fueled the unease, not someone's cold stare. He shoved his plate away. If Maggie wanted to treat him like an uninvited stranger, so be it.

Fern leaped up and scooped Robbie from Maggie's lap. "I'm going to take this wee one upstairs with us. Katie can tell him a bedtime story. She needs the practice."

Maggie cleared the dirty dishes off the table and ran the jawbox full of hot water.

Rob covered the bowls of uneaten food and tossed them into the screened cooler in the kitchen wall, an ember of peevishness threatening to ignite into flame. Never had Maggie acted so upset about something so paltry. When she started to wash the dishes, he pulled her away from the sink and handed her a towel for her hands. "We need to talk."

"Why now? I've work to do." She turned to him, face impassive.

He took her by the shoulders and looked into her eyes. "What have I done that's so bad you won't even talk to me?"

"I could ask you the same question." A flicker of heat crossed her features. Like lightning, it was, threatening an approaching storm.

"I know I've been working late every day, but that's only going to get worse once we start the rescue boat, and it doesn't mean I don't miss you."

Chin high, she stared into his eyes. "You've a strange way of showing it." Voice cold as a snell wind.

The flame in his belly erupted. "Now just you wait a minute. I've been working all day every day." His eyes narrowed. "Or do you think I'm just sitting around, blethering with Graham, or mebbe over at the howff, drinking ale so I don't have to listen to Robbie

78

yell all day?"

She smirked nastily. "So his yelling has you in a fash?"

"I didn't say that—you did—and you didn't answer my question."

She pushed him aside, dropping the towel, and returned to the sink, lips clamped tight as she slammed a dirty pot into the soapy water.

He grabbed the towel from the floor, threw it on the bunker, and stomped to the coat closet. "We've been through a lot of hard times, but I didn't realize until this minute I merit a shrew." He pulled out his leather jacket. "For years, you've nattered on and on about me never telling you things. Well, for your information, you're no better." His hands shook as he zipped his jacket and opened the door.

"Where are you going in this plomping rain?" A throaty whisper.

"Back to the shed. I might as well be alone, talking to myself. I could enjoy the conversation. I had a lot of practice growing up."

"Please don't leave." She grabbed his arm as he walked across the entry. "You're right, I am acting like a shrew and I'm sorry. I don't know what came over me."

He glanced back at her.

Tears filled her eyes and her body shook.

Dear Lord, what am I doing? Why am I in such a bile?

The answer came in a flash and he staggered from the force of the memories storming through his mind. Rejection. Never good enough to be adopted. Alone. Always alone. Years of emptiness with no one to love, no one to share his thoughts, no one to reach out to during the long nights.

Anger dissolved, he sighed and gathered her close, stroking her hair. "I'm the one who's sorry. I should never have called you a shrew, for it's no' true. Is it the long hours I've spent at the shed?"

She shook her head.

"Then what?" He held her away again so he could look into her eyes. "Tell me what I've done to hurt you so badly, Maggie. Please."

Tears spilled down her cheeks. "You promised ... never to shut me oot of your life," she choked.

"Shut you oot? What do you mean?"

Her head bowed.

Picking her up, he carried her inside, nudging the door closed behind them. He took her into their bedroom and laid her on the bed, toeing off his shoes so he could lie beside her, cradling her in his arms. "I've no' shut you oot a'purpose, Maggie. I would never, ever do that again. I gave you a promise and I meant it."

She trembled.

He kissed her face and stroked her hair.

"You don't share your day with me anymore." A cry of pain. "All week I've waited for you to tell me about your work but you've said nowt. You've never done that before."

He closed his eyes and heaved a deep sigh. "I couldn't. I was working on a surprise for you and I didn't want to spoil it." He nuzzled her cheek and leaned up on one elbow so he could see her face. "You've a birthday coming and I had to finish your present before we start the rescue boat."

Her eyes were dark blue as she gazed up at him. "Why didn't you tell me? Would that have been so hard?"

"Och, Maggie, it never occurred to me you'd be this fashed." He buried his face in her hair.

"You went from sharing everything to sharing nowt. What was I to think?"

He groaned and laid back, arm over his face. He was an eejit. His wife was over six months biggen and he had completely forgotten how emotional she had been when she was carrying Robbie. What could he say to make things better? Anger was easier to take than bearing the pain he knew she was feeling. He rolled off the bed and stood beside her. "I don't know what to say. I've hurt you and I don't know how to undo it."

She clutched at him. "Hold me, Rob. Please hold me."

Lying back down, he wrapped his arms around her. She sobbed against his chest for a long time while he lay there. When she quieted, he covered her face with kisses, tasting the salt from her tears. "I'm so sorry, lass. I'd die before I'd ever hurt you a'purpose and it wasn't till you stopped me on the entry that I realized why I got so biling mad."

She pressed against him. "I know why. 'Twas because of all you suffered when you were in that orphanage. I should have said something before it came to this."

"I wish you had."

"So do I. Were you really making me a birthday present?"

"I was."

"But why wouldn't you at least let Fern bring you dinner?"

"Because I didn't want her to see what I was making. You said yourself you often share the same thoughts. I wasn't about to take any chances."

A tentative smile. "Och, how daft. We can't read each other's minds."

"Well, how was I to know? The female mind is beyond my ken." Outside pressure hit his stomach. "Our bairnie just kicked me."

"It must be a lass, then. She's giving her faither a cuff."

"Her faither deserves it."

She caressed his cheek. "No, her faither deserves an apology. I'm sorry, for I've done it again. After all this, you're no' going to want eight bairns."

"I wouldn't go that far. But you've got to give me a promise."

"What?"

"That you won't carry your hurt inside. We aren't so different after all. You've said yourself it's hard for me to talk about important things, but you have a bit of a problem with that yourself. Remember when you had to report back to duty before me and couldn't talk about how fashed you were?"

She sighed, pulling her handkerchief from her sweater sleeve. "I'm thinking you're right," she said, wiping her face.

"Am I forgiven, then?"

"Aye. Am I?"

"Of course." His lips claimed hers, heart swelling with love as he tasted her sweetness. This was his lass and she still loved him. All was right with his world again.

When Fern tiptoed downstairs later that night with Robbie in her arms, she eyed the closed bedroom door and smiled. She'd just tuck the bairn into bed herself. Parents deserved a little time to themselves and it appeared that whatever the problem was, it had been taken care of.

Her smile faded. She still hadn't heard from her solicitors. If only her problems could be taken care of as well.

Chapter Twelve

Hugh drew quite the gasp from his congregation with an announcement that Sabbath. There was to be a double wedding at the kirk the following Saturday afternoon. Elam Taylor, one of the Army lads who had guarded their shores, and Anna MacLeod—Gordon and Katag's lass—would be taking their vows. So would Betty Stewart, Ruth and Colin's lass, who had finally brought home to Innisbraw James MacGinnis, the Borderland's sheep crofter she had met while serving in the Woman's Land Army outside of Dumfries.

Though everyone applauded, there were a few looks of concern, especially among the women. Six days left almost no time to make handsel gifts to present to the newly merrit couples.

Hugh raised his hands and smiled. "You can put your worries to rest. Both young couples will be making a home with the lasses' families until they have the silver and time to renovate twa of the old, empty cottages. You will have ample time to make your handsel gifts. However, the MacLeods have asked that any MacLeod with enough plaid for a kilt see Katag after the service. Anna's Elam may be from the Peaks District of England, but he's most anxious to become one of us by adhering to our custom of wearing a kilt when he recites his vows."

Rob's four lads showed up for work early on Monday, the fifteenth of October. He had spent hours trying to decide how to handle the one issue that could undermine his authority—they all had experience building boats and he had none. Perhaps he could handle it much the way he had conducted a briefing before a mission.

Graham leaned against the office wall while Rob positioned himself in front of his desk. Shoulders erect, eyes narrowed, he studied the four lads standing before him. He wanted to smile, to establish a friendly rapport, but this was not the time. He cleared his throat and introduced himself. "Though I've never built a boat, I'm no' ignorant of how to go about it. I designed this boat and she'll be built following those plans to the letter." He caught each lad's eye before continuing. "This is no' a trawler. She will be verra different in one important aspect." He took a piece of doweling off his desk and, using it as a pointer, indicated the detailed plan he had tacked to the wall. "Notice these air chambers. They're the backbone of the design. With these chambers, we'll have a boat that no' only will no' capsize easily, but if she should take an errant wave and capsize, she'll right herself almost immediately without any help from those aboard."

A few raised eyebrows, but no one voiced any doubts.

"Each of you may be able to offer experience on how to do a certain task more easily. Such suggestions will always be welcomed, providing you remember one thing: I am in charge. Don't ever change owt, even the smallest detail, without running it by me first. If I'm no' available, check with Graham. He's my second-in-command." He put the pointer down. "Any questions?"

Silence.

"Then let's get to work. First, I want each of you to walk to the side of the shed and study the plans I've lofted on the floor. Take your time. When you've finished with that, we'll be ready to tackle building the cradle, so pay attention to the boat's design. In order to accommodate the air chambers, she'll draw more water than you're accustomed to, and the cradle must be built deeper and wider to accommodate the difference." He stopped himself from saying a curt "dismissed." Instead, he sat on the edge of his desk and said briskly, "On you go, then."

The lads made their way toward the side of the shed. No one slouched or held back and they appeared eager to get to work.

They'd better have the skills necessary. So much depended on it.

Graham leaned on the desk beside him. "Sounds like you've

had a lot of experience directing and motivating people. I think this lot will work out fine."

"Do you know all of them?"

"Some I haven't seen for years, but they come from hardworking families. There isn't a shirker among them. And they told me it would be grand working on something new instead of refitting reeky auld trawlers into merchant ships for the Navy."

"They all got guid recommendations from their last employers. Owt I should know about how they work or what they're like?"

Graham appeared to consider the question with care. "Colin MacCrae and Alan MacKinnon are kin on their mither's side. They went all through school together so they'll do well as part of the team."

"What about the others?"

"Norman MacDougal is the auldest of the lot. He went to academy one form behind me. He's got a guid head on his shoulders and he's grand at numbers. Danny MacIntosh is the youngest. His family moved here from Skye. They own that wee sheep croft on the western shore. He's no stranger to hard work."

Rob poured them both a mug of coffee. "Thank ye. I'm thinking it'll take them time to warm up to me. After all, I'm an incomer."

Graham blew on his coffee. "I don't think you have to worry about that. Each of those lads knows what you had to overcome just to stay alive and you've brought them back to guid jobs. They all admire you for it."

Squirming, Rob took a swig of coffee. "Everything all right on the home front?"

Graham grinned. "You were right. A little sweet talk goes a long way."

Rob didn't share any of the heartbreaking evening he'd spent with Maggie. Sweet talk indeed. Who did he think he was, offering advice to Graham when he'd made such a muddle of things himself?

The lads spent the rest of the morning studying the lofted plans. They talked quietly amongst themselves and when they finished they all gathered back in Rob's office.

"Any questions after seeing the lofted plans?"

The oldest, Norman, stepped forward. "We've just one thing to say, and it's no' a question." His prominent Adam's apple bobbed nervously.

"Well?"

"'Twill be a pleasure to build her, sir. Those were some of the most complete plans we've ever seen lofted."

That was an unexpected surprise. "Then let's break for dinner." Rob checked his watch. "Be back here at 1300 hours and get right to work on that cradle." As they started to file out the door, Rob called them back. "One more thing. You may have been asked to call your previous employers 'sir,' but I'd rather be called 'Rob.' I may be aulder than you, but I'm no' ancient." He smiled wryly.

They laughed as they crowded through the doorway.

Rob whistled as he made his way home for supper. The lads had done good work that afternoon. He grabbed an armload of peats and stomped the mud off his shoes outside the washroom at the side of the kitchen, his mouth watering at the aroma of food.

Maggie stood at the stove, flipping pieces of breaded haddock in the frying pan.

He took off his shoes and hung his jacket over a bucket in the wash room so it wouldn't drip rain onto the floor, then picked up the peats and broke them into small pieces before putting them into the basket beside the stove.

Maggie was so bonnie his heart thrummed. Her face flushed from the heat of the stove and tendrils of hair curled around her forehead. He washed his hands before putting one arm around her waist from behind and, with the other, lifting the hair off her nape so he could nibble on her soft neck.

Turning, she smiled. "Your lips are so cold. Go sit by the fire and warm up."

"No' till I've had a proper kiss."

She put the fork down and hugged him. "Hurry, the haddie will burn."

He kissed her soundly, then patted her bottom. "Mmm. I'm thinking I'm hungrier for Maggie than I am for haddie."

"Go entertain your lad." She laughed and swatted his arm. "Another tooth broke through the day. He needs some playtime."

In the living room, Fern set the table and Katie and Robbie rolled a ball back and forth.

Robbie looked up, got to his feet, and ran as fast as he could. He grabbed Rob's legs and grinned up at him.

Rob picked him up and nuzzled his neck.

Robbie giggled and planted a wet kiss on his faither's chin.

"Where's my kiss, lass?" Rob asked Katie with a look of mock dismay.

She scrambled to her feet and launched herself at him.

He scooped her up in his other arm.

She put her arms around his neck and kissed his cheek.

"That's better." He carried both children to his rocker. When he sat down, Robbie began to protest. "What's this? Your poor, auld faither can't even fauld his fit?"

The lad bounced up and down on his lap, babbling, saliva slicking his chin.

Fern signaled Katie to get down, but Rob shook his head. "It's guid for the lad to learn to share. The auldest of eight bairns, he's in for a lot of it down the road."

Maggie carried heaping platters of fish and chips to the table. "Your new lads worked out well, then?"

"Better than well. I've a fine crew, Maggie. I couldn't be happier with the lot of them."

Fern poured the tea and coffee. "You're cannie to start off with young lads," she said to Rob, using a Scots word she had learned from Elspeth. She poured glasses of milk for Katie and Robbie and fetched a bowl of boiled cabbage. "The worst trouble I ever had with my crew was from one stubborn auld-timer. He always thought things should be done the auld—no' the better—way."

He pulled out Maggie and Fern's chairs. "How did you handle discipline problems?"

"Through the paycheck," she said with a chagrined smile. "But my crew wasn't accustomed to taking orders from a woman. I'm sure you won't have the problems—och, ticklers—I had."

Rob swooped Katie into her chair. "I don't see how you did it, Fern." He lifted Robbie into his highchair. "You're a verra strong woman to tackle such a turn."

"I didn't do it, remember?" She lowered her eyes.

He touched her shoulder. "You held oot almost four years and a lot of that time you were raising a bairn. Don't be so hard on yourself. You've much to be proud of."

Tears glazed her eyes when she looked up at him. "Thank ye for that. Sometimes I feel like such a failure."

Maggie smiled at her across the table. "I think you should tell Rob what we've been talking about. I know Faither will be verra pleased with the idea. And you've some news to share from your solicitor."

Rob held up his hand. "Let's bless the food, and then I want to hear all about it." He grinned at Maggie. "You twa been keeping secrets from me, have you?"

She shrugged her shoulders and gave him a saucy smile.

They bowed their heads for grace.

"Bless this food to the nourishment of our bodies," Rob prayed, "and thank Ye for the hands which prepared it, as well as the fine boat-building crew You provided for us. May we be ever mindful of Your gracious blessings upon this home and all who bide within it. In Christ's name, amen."

Robbie grabbed a spoon and pounded it on the table, squealing and gesturing wildly.

Maggie took it from him and offered him a spoonful of mashed tatties and carrots.

He smacked his lips and popped his mouth open for another.

"So tell me." Rob passed the food around the table. "I'm all ears."

Fern boned Katie's haddock. "It's nowt grand. I've just been thinking that Innisbraw could use a wellness clinic."

"A wellness clinic? What's that?"

She leaned forward in her chair, blue eyes flashing with excitement. "That's where the folk here can come to keep up on their inoculations and get advice on how to stay healthy. I know there aren't many wee bairnies around now, but there are a lot of aulder bairns and they all need boosters against childhood diseases without having to contact Maggie and have her radio John to send the serum with Malcolm every time it's needed—or even worse, make a trip to doctors on Barra or in Oban. It would save their parents a lot of trouble and expense, which I'm certain they avoid now by ignoring the need."

"What else would it entail?"

"A kind of clinic where common, everyday ailments could be treated, like sore throats or colds. I know Maggie's already been treating some of the folk for those things, but it would mean keeping the infirmary open during set hours. Also, classes could be taught in the proper way to lift heavy things, or what to do for a strained muscle."

"Don't the folk already ken that?"

"I'm no' sure. Medicine is changing every day as new drugs and treatments are discovered. Sometimes our auld grannie's remedies work well and other times they make things worse, like putting butter on burns."

Eyebrow raised, Rob helped himself to a large helping of haddock. "How do you treat a burn if no' with butter?"

"They learned during the war the worst thing you can do is cover a minor burn with something heavy and salty like butter. Now, they recommend using burn ointment and covering it loosely with sterile gauze."

He turned to Maggie. "I suppose you'd be involved in this too?"

"At times, though Fern would be in charge. We can use the infirmary since I don't know if or when Faither's ever going to retire. It's about time it was put to guid use."

Rob nodded at Fern. "'Tis an excellent idea. I can't think of a better use for your nurse's training. Run it by John as soon as you can." He sat back and reached for his coffee. "Now, about that news from your solicitor?"

"Nothing's set in stone yet, but since 'tis technical, I don't want to bore the bairns. I'll tell you about it later."

After story time and prayers, Katie and Robbie were tucked

into bed and the adults moved into the entry. The clouds took stars hostage behind grey prison walls, only to release them moments later.

Maggie settled into a rocker while Rob stood next to Fern at the railing.

"What did you mean by no' written in stone yet'?" Rob asked Fern. "Have they at least given you hope?"

"Aye. The Army located one of the Frenchmen who witnessed Edward's ... death." She shivered and pulled her shawl tighter. "'Tis somewhat of a miracle, that, since he was the only survivor of the betrayal."

"Betrayal?" Rob turned his back to the sea.

Maggie rose and clasped Fern's hand. "Just tell us. 'Tis time to put it into words. Every time you do, 'twill heal part of your grief."

Fern ducked her head and nodded. "One of the members of the French Underground Edward was assisting must have been a German spy, or even an agent of the Vichy Government—you know how they often sided with the Germans. Edward was setting a bomb on the train tracks used to transport German troops when the enemy suddenly surrounded the men. No one knows why the bomb exploded ... only that it did. Two Frenchmen were injured in the explosion and pretended to be dead to avoid being shot, but one died later from his injuries."

Rob closed his eyes. Over twa years since the war ended, yet it still shredded hearts. "Och, Fern, don't dwell on such horror. Your Edward didn't suffer. In one instant, he was transported from the hell of war into heaven."

Night shadows hid her face when she raised her head, but the agony in her voice spoke volumes. "I hoped they could ship his ... his body home so he could have a proper Christian burial. But that seems impossible now, so the solicitor said the moment he receives a signed affidavit from the Frenchman, they should have the proof they need that he died."

Maggie slipped her free hand into Rob's and squeezed his fingers.

"A hero, Fern," he said. "Write that on your heart. 'My Edward died a hero.'"

John sounded impressed with Fern's idea of a wellness clinic. "I'll ship you the latest vaccines, medicaments, and all the latest medical information I have that will enlighten you on some of the knowledge that's come from treating our war-wounded. Medicine is seeing a resurgence of new technology. I couldn't be happier that our folk on Innisbraw can benefit from it."

Fern and Maggie stocked the shelves in the infirmary's three examining rooms, brought in chairs to line the walls in the foyer, and filled the pharmacy refrigerator and shelves with the vaccines and new medicaments John sent by way of Malcolm's boat.

Maggie and Rob, both so busy with their separate endeavours, seldom saw each other except at mealtime and when they finally fell into bed late each night.

Maggie received samples from all of the women on the island who were interested in contributing a design. She and Flora bundled the cloth into boxes which Angus transported to the kirk hall in his cairt. The twa women laid the samples out on the tables randomly, so as not to prejudice the judging. When the task was finished, Maggie asked Hugh to announce at kirk services that a meeting of all weavers would take place the following Wednesday. Then she went home and collapsed into her rocker, exhausted.

Rob's shipment of lumber came in on schedule. The off-loading by crane attracted a large crowd of folk, especially bairns whose eyes were wide with wonder as each strapped bundle was lifted from the deck, swung out over the dock, and carefully manoeuvred into place. Once the lumber was on the dock, Rob and his lads worked all day loading it onto hand carts which they trundled down the pier and over to the shed where Rob put Graham in charge of sizing it into piles. He didn't want the lad to put any added weight on his leg by doing any of the heavy lifting.

Rob checked the lumber, occasionally selecting a plank and extending it, turning it to check for warping. By the end of the day, he had not found a single piece of the air-dried lumber he couldn't use.

The lads appeared as pleased as he was with the quality and lack of knots. Aye, a knot could be reamed out and plugged, but it was a time-consuming and messy task.

※

Maggie chided Rob that night for the blisters on his hands. "Why didn't you wear gloves?" She searched through her sewing basket for a sharp needle.

"I did, but they were so auld they wore through before we finished. Besides, Mither Savage, I'm a grown man. I don't need to be reminded like a wee lad with holes in his breeks and jeely on his chin."

"You're no' as grown up as you think." She dipped the needle into a bottle of surgical spirits and reached for his hand. "This might sting a bit so don't jump."

She slanted the needle into the blister from the side and pressed on it with a piece of sterile gauze until it lay flat.

"I've never seen that done before," he said as she worked on the second blister. "Any blister I ever had just broke and was sore for a while till it scabbed over."

"'Tis a wonder you didn't get an infection."

He stole a quick kiss. "I never had a bonnie lass with a nursing degree around to take care of my blisters."

She laughed as she wound gauze around his hand and taped it down. "There. Now the other hand."

His teasing smile warmed her. "How long do you think this bandage is going to last with all I have to do? And I'll have to shower on the morra and—"

"Haud your wheesht," she scolded, pressing his hand down on the table. "And stay still."

"Aye, Mither."

"Aye, Miver," Robbie parroted.

She glanced behind her. "You're supposed to be abed," Maggie said sternly, averting her face so the lad wouldn't see her smile. She pointed to his open bedroom door. "On you go now, back to bed."

Robbie shook his head and inched closer. His lower lip trembled and twa tears rolled down his rosy cheeks. He pulled on

92

Rob's denims, trying to climb into his lap, eyes wide as he stared at his faither's bandaged hand.

"You're a skellum." Rob scooped him up with his free arm. "You can watch Mither if you sit still."

The lad watched intently as Maggie worked on Rob's right hand. When she finished with the tape, he held out his own hand, waving it in front of her face.

Five minutes later, Rob tucked his son into bed, leaving the gauze-wrapped knuckles free of the covers. "Now, you've got your hurts all bandaged like Faither's, but you mustn't pull them off till Mither says 'tis all right."

Robbie grabbed his faither, planted a wet kiss on his chin, and patted his cheek before pushing his own face into the soft belly of his bedraggled stuffed rabbit and closing his eyes with a satisfied smile.

"Well, I'm dumfoondert!" Maggie exclaimed when Rob joined her in front of the fire. "He put twa words together."

Rob pulled her into his arms. "That's no' all. Our lad no' only kissed my chin, but he patted my cheek. I'm thinking our wee bairn is turning into a braw lad overnight."

Chapter Thirteen

By Saturday, Rob was so exhausted from his busy week he dreaded having to get dressed up to spend several hours at the double wedding and the ceilidh which would follow. He closed the shed at dinnertime and sent his crew home so they could eat and bathe before the service started at 1400 hours. At home, he found Maggie in the bedroom, struggling to fasten her long blue and green Cameron plaid skirt around her waist.

"Och, I'm in a fankle!" she exclaimed, cheeks apple red. "I'm no' verra large yet but it won't reach."

Rob headed for the bathing room. "Let me have a cat's lick and I'll help."

She followed, muttering to herself.

Every idea offered by Rob was quickly vetoed, especially the notion of taping the skirt in place with Sellotape. But Fern, who had been upstairs laying out her own clothing, came up with the solution of pinning the skirt below the button and covering the pin with Maggie's sash, which would hide the small gap and pin completely.

By the time they reached the kirk, Rob was so tired from all it had taken to get ready, he was tempted to turn around and head for home.

Of course, Robbie had wet through his trews and Katie had fallen on the stone-flagged entry and torn a hole in her tights which had to be changed at the last minute, causing them all to walk much faster than usual to make it to the kirk in time.

Rob looked down at the kilt he hadn't worn since he and his Maggie were merrit. He pulled on the pleats, covering the scars on his knees, then spent several minutes on those same knees praying for peace of mind while Sheila MacNab played hymns on the pump-organ softly in the background. It wasn't until he took his seat beside Maggie, pulled Robbie into his lap, and looked up at the stained glass window of the Risen Christ towering above the altar that he realized his breathing had slowed and the irritation plaguing him most of the day had been replaced by a feeling of peace.

＊＊＊

Music and dancing filled the kirk hall. With sugar rationing even more stringent than during the war, the usual cakes, scones, and shortbread had to be augmented with bramble jelly sandwiches. Several women—including Susan and Maggie—had split their plain oat scones and filled them with a combination of heather honey and fresh-plunged butter whipped together.

Rob pulled Maggie aside. "What are the auld women doing over in that corner? Their blethering sounds like hens cackling."

"Discussing James MacGinnis's mither, I'd imagine. Didn't you see her?"

Women and their gossip. "I disremember."

"She's wearing a hat covered with red roses and a dress with ruffles." Maggie's eyes danced with mischief. "But I'm sure 'tis her frizzed hair and lip paint has them so kittled up. I doubt they've ever seen such a sight."

He raised his hands in defeat. "That's all beyond my ken. Catch up with you later, luve." Kissing her cheek, he escaped to where Colin and Gordon were introducing their new sons-in-law to some of the menfolk.

Both young men were above average height and heavily muscled from years of labouring on their faither's sheep crofts. Elam Taylor's was a familiar face since he had been one of the British soldiers based on Innisbraw just before the war with Germany ended. James had a broad, pleasant face with deep laugh lines and work-roughened hands below thick wrists.

When it was Rob's turn to be introduced, he found James's handshake hearty.

"I'm happy to finally meet you," James said in halting Gaelic. "Colin's told me about all the hours you spent together guarding the coast against the U-boats."

Rob leaned close to be heard over the noise. "You'll never find a finer man than Colin to cover your rear when it's needed," he said slowly in Gaelic.

"He says the same about you."

"'Tis grand Gordon's going to have some help," Rob said in English after shaking the lad's hand.

Elam's weathered face crinkled into a grin as he pushed an errant lock of dark blond hair off his forehead. "We're already making plans for getting more glimmers ... uh, ewe lambs," he said in his broad Yorkshire accent. "I've saved some of my pay to cover the cost and the Island Council's gunna gi' us more land for grazing so we won't be so crowded up."

Elspeth held Robbie as Rob and Maggie danced a couple of strathspeys and one slow song but it was obvious the old woman was getting tired.

"Why don't I see if Angus can run you home in his cairt?" Rob said.

"Och, no' until the newly merrit take their leave. 'Tis no' fitting."

Thankfully, the twa couples chose that moment to slip out the door with exaggerated nonchalance.

Rob chuckled. "There went your excuse." He plucked Robbie from Elspeth's lap and hugged Maggie's shoulder. "And we'll be going with you. This has been a grand but verra long day."

At the kirk service the following morning, Hugh walked to the center of the dais at the end of silent prayer. "I have twa announcements to make before we begin the lesson." His gaze swept the crowded sanctuary. "And both will affect the future of Innisbraw profoundly."

Excited whispers took a moment to die down.

"First, there will be a meeting of the Women's Aid Society on Wednesday to decide upon the winner for the best weaving pattern." He removed his glasses and polished them with his handkerchief, prolonging the suspense. "Second, tomorrow morning a wellness clinic will open at the infirmary. Those with minor injuries or illness or bairns needing inoculations are encouraged to visit any time during the day on Mondays, Wednesdays, and Fridays." His broad smile and uplifted hands welcomed a hearty "amen" from the congregation. "Fern MacNeill has assured me that if the need arises, more days will be added."

Rob tuned an ear to the babble of excited conversation after the service. Innisbraw appeared to be moving forward and everyone welcomed it. Maggie and Fern received many handshakes and hugs from grateful islanders as Maggie made it clear that the idea and most of the hard work had come from Fern.

Alec pulled him to one side. "Graham told us you've started laying the rescue boat's keel. I haven't seen the lad so kittled up in years."

"By next fall the sea trials should be over and we'll finally be able to respond to emergency calls from our waters."

Tormad MacKinnon pumped Rob's hand. "I know you've a crew now, but if you ever need any help lifting anything heavy, let me know. I'll be more than willing to lend a hand."

"I will, and I can almost guarantee there'll come a time when we can use extra help."

As Tormad and Alec rejoined their families, Rob looked up at the sky. The rain had stopped and sunshine warmed his face. A golden eagle soared on a thermal high overhead. A sudden stab of grief pierced his chest. There was a good chance he would never be able to afford to buy a floatplane, never spend his time scanning that vast blue expanse from the cockpit of an airieplane.

As he dropped his gaze to the folk clustered in groups, exchanging news and enjoying the opportunity to see one another, he had a sudden thought—his horizons had lowered, that was all. From now on, his life would not be concerned with the sky overhead, but with those he had come to love like family. When he looked at it that way, it seemed like a trade he might be able to live with over time. He found Maggie and put his arm around her.

The pain in his heart eased when she nestled close, smiling up at him.

Chapter Fourteen

Instead of the bone-chilling freezes of the previous year, this November ushered in a season of dreich weather with spells of heavy rain and gusty winds that drove the surf up to the edge of the path at high tide—gardens pummeled flat, burns overflowing, moods black. Everyone dug run-off trenches around cabbage, potato, and other root-crop pits so the deluges would not damage the precious contents. The dangerous, high-running seas did not keep the fishermen in port. They risked their lives every time they left the harbour, causing great anxiety among the families left at home.

The swollen seas and raging waves tested Maggie's faith. She often spent hours lying awake, praying for the strength to believe the Lord would save Rob from drowning once the rescue boat was launched.

The mood at the weaver's meeting was much more subdued than the previous month's. Hugh opened the meeting with a prayer for all those in peril on the sea, and all the women offered comfort and promises of vigilant prayer support to the fishermen's wives and daughters.

Morag called the meeting to order and asked each woman to place her name on the patterns she thought were the most original and the easiest to duplicate in large quantities. She handed out scraps of ironed paper, stubs of tightly-rationed pencils, and straight pins to each woman before they began the herculean task of examining every sample submitted. "We know every woman will vote for her own, 'tis only human nature," she told Maggie. "We'll take the three highest and then narrow it down by a final vote."

The women milled about, foreheads furled, as they studied

sample after sample.

Maggie wrung her hands. "I hope there aren't too many to choose from. The only ones I eliminated out of hand were those too common and a few far too complicated to be practical."

"You had to start someplace," Flora said. "I'm thinking there will be some hurt feelings but it can't be helped."

"I've already talked to those I had to eliminate. They all seemed to understand. At least they said they did."

It took over three hours for the voting. Maggie kneaded her aching back, relieved by Fern's offer to take Robbie home for a late nap so she could sit and rest. Morag, Alice, and Bridget MacNab, who had not submitted samples, volunteered to tally the results.

Voting revealed three clear finalists: Rinait MacPhee, Katag MacLeod, and Danny MacIntosh's mother, Eileen. Although Rinait's pattern received the most initial votes, the three finalists were given equal footing in a new vote to choose the best sample submitted.

This vote went quickly. Half an hour after the fresh slips of paper were handed out, everyone had picked her favourite.

"Our winner is Rinait MacPhee," Maggie announced.

The lass's face seemed to drop in open-mouthed disbelief, which dissolved into tears and then a radiant smile. She was obviously overwhelmed to have beaten many women who had twa to three times her age and experience.

"I hope Flora doesn't mind, but the skirt will now be sent to our marketing specialist who will give the final okay," Maggie said before making her way through the crowd of congratulating lasses and women surrounding Rinait. She embraced the lass and handed her a handkerchief.

"I don't mind at all," Flora said loudly, pride in her daughter straining the buttons on her sweater. "Just make biddy certain I get it back."

On the ride home in Flora's cairt, Maggie asked Elspeth what she thought of the outcome.

"Rinait's pattern was the clear winner. I voted for it. The lass has a rare talent."

Maggie nodded. "I didn't vote at all because I thought I shouldn't, but if I had, she'd have had my vote also."

Elspeth's gaze pierced her. "Do you suppose there could be some place for Katag and Eileen's patterns later? I'm thinking we should keep them in mind."

"I intend to do exactly that," Maggie said. "I'll send only Rinait's initially, but if the opportunity arises, I'll submit the other twa also. Who knows? There could be a market for different patterns later."

"Why didn't Rinait come home with you?" Elspeth asked Flora. "It would have saved her a long walk."

"Why else? She had to run to the shed and tell Graham the guid news."

The old woman smiled. "I thought it looked serious between those twa. For my part, I think they're a fine match. Has Graham said anything to Angus yet?"

Flora's cheeks flushed. "Aye, and we told the lass they'll have our blessing but they have to bide a wee while. After all, she only turned sixteen last month. What do you think, Maggie? Are we being too hard on them?"

Maggie remembered the temptations she and Rob had faced. "I know it was verra hard for Rob and me to wait, but in the end it only strengthened our relationship. I'm sure Graham loves the lass too much to hurt her by rushing things—if you know what I mean."

"We've talked about that. I told her before they sinned against their souls they should speak to us, though I can remember how hard it is to behave when you're so much in luve you act like a daftie." Flora ducked her head, cheeks aflame.

As they pulled up in front of Elspeth's cottage, the old woman raised a finger. "Just don't make them wait too long. Even though she didn't go on to academy, Rinait's verra mature for sixteen. Keep that in mind."

"You have no idea what a fankle that caused." Flora sighed. "First Sim, then Rinait, both refusing to further their schooling."

Elspeth patted her hand. "But she did well in Primary, didn't she?"

"Aye, verra well, unlike Sim, who just wanted to work with his hands. She finally admitted she wanted to learn everything it takes to be a guid home-maker and mither and that didn't include more book learning. You all ken how stubborn that lass can be."

Elspeth nodded, grasped Maggie's elbow, and hobbled up her entry steps. "Tell Rob I miss seeing him run by with Shep early every other mornin, but I suppose the rescue boat's taking all his time now."

"'Tis all he thinks about. The high seas this year only compel him to work harder and longer."

"And you? Are you feeling well, lass?"

"Verra well. I'm no' nearly as large as I was with Robbie. I'm thinking 'tis either a lass or a verra small lad."

"Then let's pray 'tis a lass." Elspeth kissed her on the cheek. "On you go then, 'tis threatening rain again."

Though Rinait's appearance interrupted work on the boat, Rob couldn't fault the lass for wanting to share her news with Graham. All of the lads gathered around, offering their congratulations. Graham kissed Rinait's cheek and hugged her, grinning with obvious pride.

"Now, you're going to have to tell me when you want your windows done," Rob said, "or are you choosing to wait a while until you have your own cottage?"

Rinait's cheeks flushed bright red. "There's no need to wait. Graham's already promised our home will be built with windows that open. Mither and Faither's cottage will be the one getting the new windows."

"Sounds guid to me."

"But no' until the rescue boat's finished," Rinait added. "None of the family wants to take you away from that."

"I'll get together with Angus for a natter. I have a few hours open every Sabbath afternoon."

Rinait tossed her heavy red braid over her shoulder. "Och, no! Maggie needs you at home sometime and that wouldn't be fair to your family. We've already talked over what we would do if I won the voting and there's no changing our minds. 'Tis after the boat's finished or no' at all."

After Rinait left and the lads were back at work, Rob took Graham aside. "So, you're planning on building your own home?"

"Aye. Nothing as large or fancy as yours, but I am going to borrow a few of your ideas, if you don't mind."

"Of course I don't mind. Where are you thinking of building, or have you gotten that far yet?"

"Next to Flora and Angus's croft. We won't need much space and that will be closer to the shed than if we built oot by my folks. Besides, I'm thinking a young lass should be close to her mither."

Rob clapped him on the back. "Guid thinking. Now, we'd best get back to work. I want to double-check the curve on those next boards we're using."

John knocked on the door the following evening and laughed at the look of surprise on Rob's face. "I didn't radio ahead since I only decided last een," he said as Rob welcomed him into the house. "I want to be here Monday when the clinic opens." He greeted all of the adults.

Robbie clutched his pant leg, begging for attention.

He picked him up. "Och, what are you feeding this lad? He has to weigh well over twa stone."

Maggie wrinkled her nose. "Ask my aching back and it'll agree. I no longer have to lift him into his bed. Now, he climbs up there all by himself. 'Tis much easier with him oot of the cradle."

"Guid. You shouldn't be lifting him, lass." John pulled Robbie's fingers from his eyeglasses and eyed her critically. "How are you feeling then?"

She patted her belly. "Wonderful, but definitely biggen."

Rob hugged her from behind and put his hand over hers. "Fern here is a great help when I'm at the shed and I try to keep the lass out of trouble when I'm home." He nuzzled the back of Maggie's neck.

"He'd like me to sit in my rocker all day, while he's down at the shed working nonstop for sixteen to eighteen hours."

John threw up his free hand and laughed. "Leave me oot of this. I don't want to be the start of any trouble." He put a loudly protesting Robbie down and knelt before Katie. "How's the little dancer doing?"

Robbie tried to push her away so Rob grabbed him up and held him out, flying him through the air.

The lad giggled and made a buzzing sound with his mouth.

Katie threw her arms around John's neck. "I'm still practicing. Uncle Rob says someday I'm going to win the Hieland Fling when we get enough folk to have our own games."

John returned her hug. "I wouldn't be a bit surprised, lass. You're already that guid." He got to his feet and turned to Fern. "You're looking bonnie. Living on Innisbraw seems to agree with you."

"I was happy to see the back of Harris. It's like I've been reborn. I've never been surrounded by so much luve."

"You deserve it," Maggie said, "for you give so much of it yourself."

John's heart swelled, threatening to crowd the breath from his lungs. This was what he missed so desperately. Though there was always work to do in Edinburgh and his efforts were appreciated, he missed having his family around him. It was time to seriously start the process of retirement from both his University Chair and his position at the Royal Infirmary. It would be hard to leave it all behind, but if Rob could give up his lifelong dream of being a pilot and move on with his life into other ventures, so could a much older man who had already earned far more accolades than he had ever dreamed possible.

***

John accompanied Rob to the shed the following morning, greeting the lads as they reported to work, admiring what they had accomplished. The breadth of the work astonished. Though he had grown up around boats, he had never given any thought to their construction.

The nearly completed framework of the keel begged to be studied, as did the plans lofted onto the shed floor.

He followed Rob to his office, out of the way of the building crew. "I had no idea of the work involved. I'm amazed you could do this with no formal education in Naval Architecture or Engineering."

"'Tis only a matter of studying and learning, and a lot of long hours an architect or engineer wouldn't need to spend, checking and rechecking specifications."

"Well, I'm impressed."

Rob squirmed.

John sought out Graham. "I see the limp is gone. How does the leg feel?"

"As guid as new. Once in a while, there's an ache in my thigh by evening, but it's always gone the next mornin."

"'Tis where the rod sits that we inserted into the bone ends. Your body's building new bone around that site but the ache shouldn't last much longer than a year."

"Are you ready to declare me fit to return to duty? I'll need to plan for a few days in London so I can formally resign my commission."

"You're certain then?"

No missing the set lips and furled brow. "Biddy certain."

"I'll get on the paperwork the minute I return to Edinburgh."

Sunday brought some much-awaited sunshine. The entire family walked to kirk, Robbie riding on his faither's shoulders. The lad bounced up and down and kicked his legs, but Rob only responded with a good-natured grin.

Love for his son-in-law overwhelmed John. Initially, he'd had misgivings about Rob. He'd thought the American colonel would only toy with Maggie's affections and then leave her heartbroken— or, perhaps worse, take her away to America. The lad had overcome so many physical ordeals and given up everything he had ever aspired to be, yet here he was, happy, working long, hard hours to build a rescue boat for the island's fishermen, and deeply involved in bringing about an opportunity to boost the failing economy.

That Rob loved Maggie completely was obvious to anyone who ever saw them together and he whole-heartedly embraced his new role as a faither. Their entire family—indeed all the folk of Innisbraw—had been blessed when this very tall, very loving Yank landed on their shores.

⚶

Graham and Rinait caught up to Rob and the rest on the path.

"Mither and Faither already took Elspeth to the kirk," Rinait said. "She wanted to put oot new candles since there were no fresh flowers to decorate the sanctuary."

"Want a wee break?" Graham asked Rob, pointing up at Robbie. "I haven't given anyone a shoulderie in a long time."

Rob wiped his forehead with his sleeve. "You sure you know what you're getting into? The lad seems to think I'm as strong as auld Jack."

"I'm hoping you're stronger. That cuddy is definitely getting long in the tooth." He reached for Robbie. "I'm game. On you come."

Once the transfer was complete, Robbie bounced up and down, twisting his fingers through Graham's hair.

"I told you to get a haircut," Rob said. "There's a lot to be said for keeping your hair in a military style when you've a lad like ours."

Graham winced. "I see what you mean." He looked at Rinait. "How are you at cutting hair, lass? My mither butchers Faither's hair every month's end whether it needs it or no'."

Rinait tossed her head. "Mither's been teaching me but she still does a much better turn." She frowned, shooting a glance at Rob's hair. "Are you certain you want it that short, then?"

Graham nodded. "Biddy certain. I can't go to London in uniform with my hair over my collar."

"Flora gave me a grand military haircut before I reported to duty," Rob said, "and my hair was a lot longer than yours is now."

"Longer than mine?" Graham eyed Rob. "I can't picture you with long hair."

"I was a wee bit busy."

"Too busy to get a haircut?"

"I figured learning to walk again was more important." Rob chided himself for sounding so sarcastic. He rubbed the side of his nose. "Sorry, Graham. I don't like remembering those times."

105

Katie reached for Rob's hand. "I think you walk real guid, Uncle Rob. Only a wee bit too fast."

He slowed down. "Sorry, lass. Your Aunt Maggie's always telling me the same thing."

"I've been skipping to keep up, but we're way ahead of everybody else."

Rob stopped and looked back. Katie was right. He took Robbie from Graham and put him up over his shoulder.

The lad's eyes were half closed and he rested his cheek against his faither's shoulder, yawning deeply.

"Sleeperie, are you, lad?" Rob crooned. He patted his son's back. "Go see Willie Winkie. Mither's coming and we're almost to kirk."

Chapter Fifteen

When John opened the infirmary door early Monday morning, patients already waited in the yard.

Och, there was no lock on the door. Why had they stood outside in the pishing rain?

"In, in," he urged. "I've a fire to warm you." He stood aside.

They hurried into the foyer, shed coats and jackets, and crowded in front of the glowing peats, hands outstretched.

Fern dashed inside last, water beading on her long lashes, a wide smile on her bonnie face. The lass looked pleased, and well she should.

Charts prepared, names taken, and complaints noted, John followed Fern as she ushered Anna MacKinnon and her lass Kaitlin into an examining room.

"She has the rash on her chest," Anna said. "I've tried everything from poultices of dandelion tea to hen's fat, but 'tis still there."

"Let's take a keek." Fern removed Kaitlin's twa heavy sweaters, a blouse, and a woolen undershirt and examined the rash. "Do you always dress her so warmly?" she asked Anna.

"Why, 'tis near winter, of course I do. Don't want her getting the pneumonie, do I?"

John stroked his beard, hiding a smile. Typical Anna, always looking for something to fret about—and worrying it to death until she found it.

Kaitlin tugged at Fern's sleeve. "It itches something fierce."

Her mother frowned at her. "You'll not be complaining."

Anna squirmed, wet shoes squeaking on the waxed floor.

"Does she get that often, the pneumonie?" Fern tucked damp

strands of the lass's hair back into her braid.

"Never! What kind of mither do you think I am?"

"A verra careful one, but I'm thinking you need to be told about prickly heat and what causes it."

Anna recoiled. "Prickly heat? She's dying? I knew it!"

John nodded to Fern. "Take off that lass's woolen undergarment and replace only her blouse and one sweater. Anna and I are stepping oot for a wee blether." He grasped Anna's arm and led the protesting mother into the hall.

Och, he should have complimented Fern on her excellent diagnosis. But that could wait. Right now he had to convince a frantic mither no' to smother her lass 'neath layers of heavy wool.

Fern didn't appear flummoxed by the strange opening to her wellness clinic. She treated twa crofters with infected cuts, applied silver sulfadiazine ointment, and administered tetanus shots. She did, however, raise her eyebrows when the last crofter pulled eggs from a basket and offered them to John as payment.

"Sorry there's only six," he said. "Hens are a bit broody. I'll have more in a few days."

The moment the door closed behind his back, Fern burst into laughter. "Six eggs. Well, you can't deposit them in the bank, but at least you won't starve."

"Och, it's a fine trade. I once had a much more unusual offer—a sheep's stomach stuffed with a tongue, heart, and liver. They were at least a week auld and so reeky they had to be buried a foot deep oot on the fell." He tapped her arm. "Let me post a note on the door telling anyone who comes in to give a shout. 'Tis time for us to get better acquainted and I prefer the comfort of my office."

A few minutes later, note posted, John pulled out a chair for her and sat behind his desk, lacing his fingers across his vest. "First, I want to congratulate you on your skillful diagnosis of wee Kaitlin's rash."

That delightful laugh again. "'Tis only because I did the same thing—smothering Katie in wool so she wouldn't get a chill, then panicking when she broke oot. It took my neighbor explaining about prickly heat to remind me of my training. Och, for a year, my cheeks burned every time she asked my advice about a cold or sore throat."

A smart young woman who could laugh at herself. Guid combination. "Maggie tells me you took additional training in Critical Care and Operating Room Procedures. Is that where your interests lie?"

"To tell the truth, I enjoy it all. I took those courses because there was a need at the time, but I suppose if I really had to name my favourite, it would be the OR, though I find working in Trauma almost as rewarding."

He settled further into his chair. Fern was a bonnie, feminine woman, but like his Maggie, when put in a professional environment, she exuded confidence in herself and in her knowledge. Should he tell her his plans? He stroked his beard as he mentally ticked off the pros and cons. Deciding, he leaned forward, eager to hear her opinion. "I'll be retiring to Innisbraw—perhaps as early as spring—to open the infirmary on a permanent basis."

Fern's eyes widened. "You'll no longer be teaching at University or practicing at the Royal Infirmary?"

"'Tis time to come home." He walked to the window and pulled the lace curtain aside. "Ben Innis. Her top's covered with a cloud but if you close your eyes, you can still see her the way she looks in summer, the heather spilling down her slopes. Even Edinburgh's historic walls and ancient streets can't compete with such a sight." He turned to face her. "And there's my family. I've neglected them far too long. I don't want to miss any more of my grandbairns' first teeth or steps. Do you ken what I'm saying?"

"Of course. There comes a time in every person's life when his or her priorities change. Edward was killed when Katie was so young he never even saw her, yet I still clung to the auld, safe ways." Tears gathered in her eyes. "When I saw what Rob and Maggie have, the completeness of it all, I knew I was living in the past. It was time to begin a new life with my daughter."

"Was it hard to do? To step oot into an unknown future?"

She twisted a button on her sweater. "In some ways, but no' on the whole. I got enough from the sale of the house and truck to live on for a while, but I'm still waiting to hear from the solicitors if I can sell the boatyard since it was deeded to Edward by his family. He was called up before we could have my name added to the deed."

"He served in the war?"

"In the Army. He was killed helping the French Underground plant a bomb on rail tracks. Someone betrayed them and the Germans somehow detonated the bomb prematurely. I never would have known how Edward died but the army tracked down a French survivor several weeks ago." She pulled out a handkerchief and wiped her eyes. "Now I know why ... there wasn't a body to bury, but even more importantly, that he didn't suffer."

A familiar ache cramped his heart. Och, that horrible war. So much suffering, so much pain. He chose his next words carefully. "Surely his property would automatically revert to you."

"It should. But he was on a secret mission. The Army sent me a cablegram saying he had been killed, but that was based on hearsay from the Underground, no' on witnesses." She offered a tremulous smile. "I sent the solicitors everything I had, including the cablegram, and I'm waiting for their decision. But even if they rule against me, I have enough silver to rent a small cottage on Innisbraw and pay off a few debts." She wadded her handkerchief into a tight ball. "But back to your question about stepping oot on my own. Perhaps the only hard thing to give up was the auld habits—work all day until you're ready to drop, try to raise your daughter with what's left of you and only twenty-four hours in a day. For the first time, I enjoy being a mither. I'm only sorry it took me so long to realize what I really wanted."

He hid his disappointment behind an impassive face. Not so hard to do—he'd had lots of practice. "So you don't want to work."

"That's no' what I meant. I just don't want to own a business that consumes me, that takes every waking moment of my life. I luve nursing."

From what he'd seen so far, she had the skills to do it well. "I'd like to hire you as my assistant. You'll get a bit of every kind of nursing, from cradle to grave and everything in between."

Fern clenched her hands. "But what about Maggie?"

"There'll always be a place for my lass, but she doesn't want to work full time. She says she wants eight bairns. Knowing Maggie, she means it. There'll be occasions when surgery requires twa nurses or an unusually heavy caseload requires extra help. She'll step in gladly, but her family will always come first. And she's also involved with the Cottage Weaving Industry. I don't think Rob will want her working verra many more hours."

"And the wellness clinic?"

"It will stay open when I return. 'Tis an excellent idea."

Emotions flitted across her face. Disbelief, apprehension, joy.

"What say you? Are you interested?"

She didn't hesitate. "How could I no' be interested? I'd be honored to work for you, John."

"No' *for* me, lass," he corrected with a heartfelt smile. "With me."

Rob and Maggie cuddled in bed as rain, which came down heavier and heavier, pounded on the slate roof and talked about John's unexpected, dinner table announcement.

"Do you think he'll really retire?" Rob asked. "He'd be giving up a lot of prestige and travelling."

"He's never said it with such determination before." She fingered the hair on his chest. "And as far as the travelling goes, he's never enjoyed it."

"Did you see Fern's face when he told us she was going to be his assistant? I've never seen her so happy."

"Aye, it's exactly what she needs, a new start in life with a promising future—and a way to support herself and Katie if the solicitors rule against her selling the boatyard."

"You're no' upset he didn't approach you first?"

"I'm glad he didn't." She placed her leg over his and snuggled closer. "I'd have hated turning him down. I have more than enough to keep me busy."

"Och, 'tis true, you do. I wouldn't have liked it."

"Of course, they may need a little help now and then."

"That's different." He brushed a curl of her hair across his cheek. "'Tis only natural you wanting to keep up with your nursing skills. I wouldn't have it otherwise." He pulled her closer. "Can you keep a secret?"

"A secret? And what would that be?"

"First you have to promise."

"Promise what?"

"That you won't tell."

"Tell what?"

He put his hands on either side of her face and brought her lips to his. So soft, those lips, so filled with promise. "Och, Maggie, you drive me crazy."

"Is that the secret?"

He grinned. "The secret is how much I luve you."

"That's no' a secret."

"Maybe no' the luve itself, but surely the depth of it. It amazes even me sometimes."

Soft fingertips caressed his face. "I'm thinking there's another who knows how much you luve me."

"Mmm, and who would that be?"

She placed his hand on her swollen belly. "This wee bairnie."

"I suppose it must. After all, it was conceived from that luve and—"

A muffled roar of wind buffeted the house.

Rob sat up and raised a hand. "Quiet."

The windowpane rattled beneath lashes of rain. The roar grew louder—and louder.

A dim memory of being shaken awake and dragged downstairs. Of rain coming so hard it drowned all sound but the shrieking wind. Of sobbing children, clutching hands, eyes wide with terror. His gut clenched.

He leaped out of bed, tossed Maggie her dressing gown, and pulled on his denims. "Cover the inside of the windows with bed covers and lay oot candles in case you lose power. And close the fireplace damper so the peat doesn't smoke." He stepped into his shoes barefooted and reached for his shirt. "And rouse Fern. She can keep Robbie oot of your hair."

Maggie tied her dressing gown and stepped into her baffies. "But it's just a storm. Why are you—?"

The pounding rain and howling wind drowned out her words.

He caught her by the shoulders and stared into her eyes. "There may be casualties, but don't try to make it to the infirmary." His palm cupped her belly. "Stay in the house." A vision of his Maggie being blown off the fell, of lying broken and bleeding on the rocks below, flashed across his mind. He pressed his lips against her throat, her beating pulse. "Under no circumstances set a foot ootside. I don't want to leave you, but you'll be safe inside. I have to see to Elspeth. Those are hurricane-force winds."

Chapter Sixteen

Robbie rolled over in his sleep, fingers gripping his cloth rabbit's ear.

Maggie glanced at the hap she'd pinned over his window.

Still secure.

She pulled the bairn's bed-plaid higher and sat at his side, thinking back to Rob's warning. How had he known it was hurricane-force winds? He'd never experienced such raging storms on Innisbraw.

But she had. Terrifying, they were, lifting thatched roofs, shattering windows, sinking boats, disrupting lives already teetering on the edge of poverty.

A cold nose brushed her hand. Shep stood beside her, eyes beseeching, tail tucked.

"Och, you act like an aulder brother, no' a dog." She rested a hand on his head. "Stay, then, but keep off the bed." She quit the bedroom, leaving the door ajar, wanting to weep, to cover her ears against the shrieking wind, to drop to her knees in prayer, but there was too much to do.

You don't have to be on your knees to pray. One of Hugh's lessons.

She opened her blanket chest and pulled out haps and bed-quilts, piling them on the floor at her feet. Why had Rob left her and Robbie in the mids of a storm? Was Elspeth's safety more important?

Och, wicked and untrue. Rob had built their home to stand unscathed through any storm. It was his burning need to protect others, even at the risk of his own life, that propelled him outside into the teeth of a gale—just like it drove him to fly lead on the most

114

dangerous bombing missions during the war.

She hugged a quilt and buried her face in its softness. *Forgive me, Lord. I've allowed evil thoughts to colour my mind. Protect my Rob, keep him safe in the palm of Your hand. Please, please, Faither, keep him safe. And be with all our folk, especially those auld and alone, like Elspeth.*

The bed-quilt dropped from her hands as warm arms encircled her shoulders.

"Rob will be fine." Fern's voice. "He's strong and fit and young. And our Saviour has a plan for his life, remember?"

A nod was all Maggie could muster.

"Katie's tucked into your rocker. She'll let us know if Robbie wakens."

"Thank ye."

"Now tell me what you're doing with all these bed covers. There's still embers in the fireplace."

Maggie held up a quilt. "This is large enough for the kitchen window. Help me pin it over the curtain rod. We'll do the downstairs first."

⁓⁂⁓

Rob clutched the stone dyke to keep from being blown off his feet. Wind battered his back and shoulders, tore at his drenched clothes. Sheets of blinding rain threatened to choke the breath from his heaving chest.

The storm came from the warmer southwest, but the moisture it had plucked from the Atlantic chilled him to the bone.

John hadn't been at his cottage or the infirmary. He must be on his way to Elspeth's.

Be with him, Faither. He's no' as strong as me and I can barely stand. His hand groped for another hold but fanned empty air.

The end of the dyke. No way to stay on his feet without hanging onto something solid. He gripped the stones with one hand and swiped a palm over his eyes. If only he could see a light from Elspeth's window, he'd know he was going in the right direction.

But wait. The dyke around the front of the infirmary ran

northeast. If he kept the wind at his back, he'd reach her cottage.

And find what? Her thatch roof blown away? Her windows imploded, shards of glass impaled in furniture, walls ... soft flesh? No! The God he worshiped would not allow a faithful servant such a fate.

He imagined the de'il laughing at such naïveté. *What about missionaries, sent by your so-called loving God and slaughtered by the very people they came to save?* The sly voice mocked him. Why? To keep him from praying.

Be with me, Heavenly Faither. Guide my steps, like the saints of auld.

Stepping out on renewed faith, he leaned his back into the wind, locked his knees, and dug in his heels to keep from being blown over. He slid through slippery girse and sucking sand, paying little heed to the cold wind and stinging rain.

An eternity later, he stumbled and fell to his knees. He forced himself to his feet and continued on, repeating one of his Lord's promises over and over, "I can do all things with Him that strengtheneth me. I can do all things—"

His toe caught. He sprawled forward and his right hand landed on something soft. He pushed himself to his knees and groped in the darkness.

Och, no' something—someone! John—or Elspeth?

His fingers grasped a thatch of hair. Short hair. "John, is that you?"

Hands clutched him. Icy flesh pressed against his cheek. "Rob, thank the Lord you've come. I've no' the strength to get up."

"Are you hurt?"

"Just spent. Can you help me to my feet?"

He leaned closer. "Do you know where we are?"

No response.

His heart slammed against his ribs. He repeated the question.

"At Elspeth's gate. I ... I've been lying here, trying to gather the strength ... to pull myself up."

Rob's fingers brushed wood. "Take my hand and get to your knees. I'll open the gate and pull you through. We'll have to crawl to her steps." He struggled to reach the hasp.

The latch released and the gate was torn from his grasp.

He shook his stinging fingers. Another small victory.

Minutes later, knees battered from the stone flags, Rob hugged John's shoulder. "I'll try to open her door. I may need your help closing it against the wind."

"Hurry."

Help me, Lord, we're so close. He groped for the latch, clasped it with both hands, and pulled himself up. His hands slipped and the door flew open, crashing against the wall. He caught a glimpse of light before the rain blinded him. He reached for John's hand, and pulled him inside. "Hang onto the wall and pull yourself up. We have to close that door."

Once erect, John added his weight to the door.

Rob grunted and shoved, claiming strength from each inch gained.

The door closed. And held. Though the howl of the wind outside still made normal talking difficult, they were out of the rain.

Rob palmed the rain from his eyes. His gaze swept the room.

Twa lamps lit. Sodden, smoking peat in the fireplace, empty rocker.

No Elspeth.

He stumbled toward the kitchen. "Elspeth, where are you? Elspeth!"

⚜

Knees pressed to the floor, Maggie unclasped her hands and raised her head.

Fern knelt beside her, lips moving in prayer. Robbie's door remained ajar.

Katie turned in the rocker to face them. She stared at her mother. "I want to play our game."

Fern stirred. "Did you say something, lass? You'll have to talk louder so we can hear you above the wind."

"I said I want to play our game. Sitting in this rocker is wearisome."

Maggie rose and pulled Fern up beside her. Rob was somewhere out in that gale, perhaps blown face-down in a ditch—a rain-filled ditch. How could she play a game at a time like this?

Fern returned her daughter's stare. "Which game, lass? We play so many."

No lassie rolled their eyes with more panache than Katie MacNeill. "The game we always play when 'tis storming. The Thank-Ye-Jesus game."

"Och, that game." Fern bumped her hip against Maggie's. "What do you think, Aunt Maggie, are you willing?"

Eyes sweeping the windows to make sure the covers were still secure, teeth worrying her lip, Maggie gave in. Anything to take her mind from imagining the worst. "You'll have to show me how. I've never played it."

Katie's face reflected a summer sun. "'Tis easy. You just think of something you want to thank Jesus for, then say it." She hugged herself. "I'll go first."

"No' so fast, lassie." Fern strode into the kitchen and returned with twa cups of tea. "Oot of the rocker. Pull a chair over here, sit on it, and then you can go first."

Pouting, Katie pulled herself from the rocker and stomped across the room, hap trailing behind her. She dragged a dining room chair across the floor and threw herself into it. "I want some milk."

Fern's smile could have attracted flies with its sweetness. "You know where the milk is—and just yesterday you showed me you're tall enough to reach the glasses."

"Forget it."

Maggie whispered to Fern, "I'm thinking yon lassie needed more sleep."

"Och, I think you're right." She hurried to the kitchen and returned with a glass of milk and a plate of shortbread.

A tiny smile tugged at Katie's lips. "For me?"

"The milk, aye. The shortbread, we can share."

Maggie settled into her rocker.

Mouth full of shortbread, Katie said, "Thank Ye, Jesus, for Aunt Maggie's guid baking."

Silence.

"You're next, Aunt Maggie."

"Och, I am? Thank Ye, Jesus, for Fern's friendship."

"Thank Ye, Jesus, for my Katie lass." Was there a hint of sarcasm in Fern's tone?

Katie wiped her mouth on her sleeve. "Thank Ye, Jesus, for my mither." Like honey, that voice, and just as sticky.

Her turn again. Maggie felt her control slip. She kneaded her hands in her lap. "Thank Ye, Jesus, for my Rob." *My precious, luving Rob. Please be with him, Faither, and with our Elspeth.*

Rob bumped into John, who dogged his steps. "She's no' in the kitchen. I'll check her bedroom."

John caught his sleeve. "Slow down, lad. Elspeth knows better than to leave the safety of her cottage during a gale."

Jerking away, Rob growled over his shoulder. "That's why I'm checking her bedroom." He threw open the door.

Light from a flickering candle illuminated the bed. It was rumpled. And empty.

"Where is she? Och, John, where has she gone?"

Pushing Rob aside, John pointed.

A wee, white hand waved from beneath the bed. They dropped to their knees.

"Pull me oot, you eejits. I'm stuck fast."

The muffled command spurred Rob to action. Tears of relief mingled with the rain on his face as he dropped to his knees. He reached one arm beneath Elspeth's shoulders and the other under her knees and gently eased her from the storage cupboard beneath the bed. He lifted her into his arms and suppressed a daft urge to laugh. "Are you hurt? Can you move your legs? What were you doing un—"

"Rob—and John. I should have known you'd come." Faded blue eyes sparked in the candlelight. Frail fingers trailed over Rob's cheek and down his chest. "You're dripping wet and near frozen. Haud yer wheest and help me stand. And stop shaking your head, John. There's nowt wrong with me a strong cup of hot tea won't cure."

John braced his legs and helped Rob to his feet.

Elspeth waved at the walking stick leaning against the foot of the bed. "Hand me that stick and put me down, you big lout. The Lord's had me on my knees all the day. I need to walk out the stiffness."

Daft or no', Rob laughed as he eased her down. Elspeth was alive and as full of spit as ever.

She clung to his arm for a minute, then grabbed her walking stick and hobbled into the chaumer, nattering about wet clothes and them catching their deaths.

Soon Rob balanced a coffee cup on his knee and pulled the bed-quilt around his shoulders, reveling in the warmth of thick eiderdown.

John, wrapped in a similar quilt, sat on the sofa beside him, nursing a cup of tea, beard twitching. "Are you certain you're having no chest pain?"

Elspeth waved a dismissive hand. "Biddy certain." She rocked and fingered the hap over her legs. "Now tell me what brings you twa here in the mids of a gale."

As though to punctuate her use of the word "gale," the wind shook the thatching over their heads and the window rattled behind its pinned sheet.

"To check on you, of course," Rob said. "We feared your thatch might blow off, leaving you to the mercy of the rain and wind."

"Och, it's weathered many a gale over the years. When Fergus MacCrae thatches a roof, it stays fast, even in a storm such as this." She rocked, keen gaze traveling over their faces.

"But what were you doing 'neath your bed?" Rob asked.

She set her empty teacup on the floor. "As I told you, the Lord had me praying most diligently all the day. Of course, once the winds started their banshee howling and the rain came pounding on the thatch, I prayed even harder, knowing why my prayers were needed. You're certain Maggie, Fern, and the bairns are safe?"

"What Rob Savage builds, stays fast—even in a storm such as this," John said, a broad smile tilting his beard.

Elspeth waggled a finger. "I expect a lad like Rob to forget his manners, but you're a grown man who should know better."

Rob swallowed a grin. "You were explaining why we found

120

you 'neath your bed."

"Of course I was. Someday that impertinent tongue will bring you a dunt on the head, lad." Her stern gaze softened. "Anyway, I closed the flue too late and the smoke from the wet peat drove me from the chaumer into my bedroom. I closed the door and returned to my praying beside the bed." She grimaced and rubbed her knees. "A feeling of peace came over me, like the Lord was assuring me He was in charge—of the winds, the rain, the island, and every soul on it. I was basking in that peace when a most dreadful bang came from the chaumer, and the wind came under the door, flapping my dressing gown 'round my legs and near snuffing the candle. No' wanting to chance and keek lest I'd lost my thatch, I wriggled into the cupboard 'neath my bed." A smile toyed with her lips. "No' the best decision I ever made, but at least I could continue praying without worrying my knees."

Rob looked around the room at the puddles on the floor, a framed picture and book from her table blown into a corner, a basket of sodden wool with knitting needles scattered across the floor, a lampshade tilted to one side and stained with rain. "We'll help you clean this midden, Elspeth. The door blew in when my wet hands slipped on the knob. That must have been the bang you heard."

"Och, 'tis easily set to rights." Her smile came, full blown. "And I'd say 'tis a small price to pay for our Lord seeing the both of you safely through the storm."

Something woke Maggie from a troubled sleep. She stretched her stiff back and looked around. She'd sent Fern and Katie up to bed when the sound of wind and rain dropped, so she sat alone in her rocker. She listened for approaching footsteps.

Silence. That's what had awakened her. The storm had blown over.

But where was Rob? Why hadn't he returned home? She closed her eyes and bowed her head. *Bring him home, Faither, and no' injured. I can't bear to see him in pain again. Please*—She looked up at the sound of running footfalls.

Rob burst through the door, stubble on his chin, clothes wrinkled, arms opened wide. And no blood.

She threw herself into his arms.

He picked her up and held her close. "Maggie, my Maggie, my luve."

"You're home. Och, luve, you're home."

His lips devoured hers. The scent of the sea and peat smoke perfumed his skin as he spoke his luve with more fervor than mere words. Her heart sang at his taste, his strong arms, his soft lips. *Thank Ye, Lord. You've brought my Rob home.*

She felt his breath on her cheek as he breathed a long sigh. "Elspeth's safe, lass. And before it was even light, Alec and Angus went around the island, checking for injuries and damage."

Fear weakened her legs. "And? How bad was it?"

He picked her up and carried her to his rocker.

She buried her face against his chest, fighting panic. Why didn't he answer? Who was injured? How many cottages destroyed? "Tell me, Rob. I need to know."

Another long sigh. "A few folk suffered cuts from flying glass and Dolly MacSween's cottage lost its roof. They found her, wet and near frozen, wandering around ootside in her nightclothes, searching for her hens." His arms tightened. "You have to be brave, luve, at what I have to tell you."

She closed her eyes and bit her lip until she tasted blood. It was her faither, it had to be. A sob tore at her throat. "Faither!" The keening cry erupted from her soul.

"No! No' your faither, Maggie." Rob pressed his cheek to hers. "He's at the infirmary, tending to the injured."

Relief unleashed a fountain of tears, relief so intense, each breath was a struggle. Her faither was safe. She clung to Rob. She needed to feel the warmth of his body, the throb of his heart, the rumble in his chest as he murmured words of comfort. Tears spent, she looked into his eyes—no green flecks, just dark pools of pain. "Tell me. I'm ready."

His lips trembled as they brushed her forehead. "Susan lost her bairnie."

Sweet, luving Susan, who longed for a croftful of bairnies as much as Maggie did. For hours they'd lain side by side on the girse as lasses, holding hands and looking up into the cloudless sky, planning perfect lives with perfect husbands and perfect bairns romping about.

"She's at the infirmary. Mark said she's asking for you."

She nodded. The tears for this loss would come later. "I'll dress and be on my way."

Her Rob knew why she couldn't weep. He'd stood beside his airieplane, shoulders stiff, face impassive, and watched as stretchers bearing the dead, blankets over their faces, were unloaded.

One tear would lead to so many more. Perhaps they would cry together. Later.

Rob sank into his rocker and knuckled his eyes. So tired. Rinait had taken Robbie and Katie to the MacPhee's cottage. Maggie was on her way to the infirmary, Fern at her side. He turned when the door latch clicked.

Elspeth hobbled in, walking stick thumping on the wood floor.

He jumped up and stood before her, back stiff as a schoolboy about to receive a caning.

"Is that any way to greet a decrepit but well-meaning auld friend?"

Her smile drew him into her arms. So frail, those arms, yet so filled with luve.

"I know about Susan's loss, lad." She stepped back.

He felt bereft, deprived of a comfort he needed. Had to have.

"Let's take a burden off our tired legs and sit a spell. I want to hear all about how our folk and island fared."

"But ... but surely Flora and Morag told you."

She thumped her way to Maggie's rocker and sat with a sigh. "Och, that's better. Now, stop looming over me and fauld yer fit. I'm ready for a guid blether with a man, no' twa nattering females bemoaning a wee bit of water on the floor." Her eyes glittered in the weak sun streaming through the window. "That fire feels guid." She prodded his arm. "Now talk, and no holding back to spare my feelings. My body may be weak, but my heart isn't."

A burden lifted from his chest. This was what he needed, to share the guid news. "Twas a miracle, Elspeth, a miracle like no other. No serious injuries ..."

Only Susan, pale and weeping on her infirmary bed, Mark kneeling beside her, shoulders shaking.

A sharp rap on his knee brought him back to the present.

"Get on with it. I told you I know about Susan's loss. I want to hear about this miracle."

Her deep, throaty laugh wrapped its healing balm around his heart.

"After all, those of us who wear oot our knees praying need all the encouragement we can get."

Thoughts jumbled together in his mind, all fighting to be voiced first. "Apart from Dolly MacSween losing her thatch, only a few roofs need repair. But some folk with hens will be looking all over the island for the flighty creatures. And Colin was afraid he'd lost a flock of ewes but found them sheltered on the leeward side of a dyke, chewing their cuds, looking down their noses like he was a daftie. And all the coos and cuddies survived, wet and hang-doggit, but no worse for the soaking they took." A laugh built and he let it free. "Now I think on it, on the way to your cottage, I kept my back to the wind, just like those beasties always do."

Her hand settled on his arm. "The kirk? What about the windows?"

"No' even a crack, though Hugh said he expected to find the bell on the ground, it was ringing so hard in the wind. A few of the trawlers snapped their mooring ropes and drifted into the harbour, but none ended battered on the rocks, and no' a one sank—a miracle in itself. A crew of men is working to bring them alongside as we speak."

Her fingers tightened. "And your shed? How did it fare?"

"With the new roof, and sturdy as it is, it came through in guid shape."

"Very good then." Elspeth pulled herself to her feet and picked up her walking stick. "'Tis time to take my leave. I hear Angus's cairt on the path."

"Och, your hearing's better than mine—or mebbe the sound

was lost in my blethering."

No softness in that stern look. "Sometimes blethering's needed, lad. It lightens a burdened soul."

She knew him well. "I'm for a shower. Then I'll add my back to those repairing the main path. A few places washed oot in the heavy sea surge."

Again, that throaty laugh. "No rest for the wicked, isn't that what they say?" She squeezed his hand. "Or for those who treasure this wee island we all call home."

Chapter Seventeen

Days later, a brisk wind blew in from the sea, salting the air. Maggie hastened up the western slope of the fell, toward a hot cup of tea and a cuddle with her laddie. The folks she'd visited the day no longer looked like refugees from a war-torn land, eyes dark and staring, heads and shoulders bowed with all the labour that lay ahead. Cuts healed, crofts raked free of debris, windows replaced, and roofs mended, their lives returned to the difficult but familiar daily struggle to feed and clothe their families.

She stood at the dyke and studied her garden. Pummeled flat by the gale's savage wind and rain. Och, it would spring back when summer brought warmer winds and an occasional day of sun. She glanced up at the louring clouds and shivered, then stepped inside and hung up her coat.

No one greeted her.

Where was everybody?

"Is that you, Maggie?" Fern's voice.

"Aye. Sorry I'm so late."

"I'll be right oot. I'm changing Robbie's breeks. He upset Shep's water bowl and had a grand time splashing about in the puddle."

Wild babbles and shrieks of joy assaulted her ears.

Seconds later, the bairn dashed from his bedroom, Shep at his heels. He threw himself at her legs. "Oop, oop!" he shouted, hands clutching at her skirt.

She grabbed a hand and kissed it. "No' yet. Mither wants some tea."

"'Tis steeping 'neath the cozy." Fern smiled and scooped Robbie up, pointing to Maggie's rocker. "Fauld yer fit while I pour you a cup. I've been on heckle-pins waiting to hear how your day went."

Too tired to argue, Maggie plonked down in her rocker and accepted Robbie into her lap. She rocked, cuddling him. "I'd say the folk and the island looked the same as it always has, if no' better."

Fern placed twa cups of tea on the table and handed Robbie a rusk before she collapsed into Rob's rocker. "Whatsomever do you mean by better?"

"Cleaner, for one thing. You know what a midden some cottages had in their yards." She sipped her tea. Every bit as delicious as she'd imagined. "Well, 'tis all raked up."

"And Dolly? Her roof?"

"No' only thatched, but she's moved back in. Lachlan and some of the lads Fergus and Sandy trained in thatching finished her roof twa days ago." She put down her cup and looked over her shoulder. "Where's Katie?"

"At Anna and Tormad's, playing with Kaitlin."

"Surely you didn't walk her down there. Pulling Robbie in his cairt is exhausting."

"Of course no'. Angus came by with some fresh butter and took her in his cairt. He'll bring her home in a few hours."

Robbie slid from Maggie's lap and ran around the living room, arms outstretched, mouth buzzing as he imitated an airieplane.

Fern squeezed her arm. "Did you see Susan?"

A soft smile played with Maggie's lips. "Aye. We had a grand blether. She said they're talking about trying for another bairnie."

The *Sea Rouk* bumped against the dock.

Rob, who had taken to meeting the trawler every other day, nodded to Alice after Malcolm tossed her the post bag.

She shuffled through the envelopes, shaking her head until she reached the bottom of the bag. "Here it is at last." She handed a fat envelope to Rob.

"Thank ye a heap," he shouted over his shoulder as he raced off the dock and down the pier. At last Fern's waiting should be over. Too late to pray it was the answer she needed, but he did thank the

Lord for the long-awaited information.

Cold raindrops pelted his cheeks. He tucked the envelope beneath his A-2 jacket and zipped it to his neck. He should have stopped at the shed to tell Graham, but the lad surely knew he wouldn't be gone long.

His feet flew over the path. Once home, he didn't open the gate but vaulted the dyke and rushed to the entry, taking the steps in one giant leap.

Maggie stood at the stove while Fern set the table, Katie at her side, laughing and blethering something about what a grand time she'd had.

"It's here, Fern. Your waiting is over!"

Fern's hand flew to her mouth.

He unzipped his jacket and pulled out the envelope.

Maggie hurried to Fern's side. "Did Alice deliver it to you at the shed?"

"No' exactly, but come on, Fern. Open it."

Fern couldn't move—could scarcely breathe. Maggie's embrace held her up until Rob pushed a chair against her legs and she sat, staring at the envelope on the table in front of her. Her future—and Katie's—lay sealed inside.

Maggie thrust a cup of tea into her trembling hands. "Drink this. And remember with each sip that our Lord's perfect will has already been accomplished, just as we've all been praying."

Our Lord's perfect will. Her scrambled thoughts tumbled into place. Who could ask for more? She took a deep breath. Ignoring the tea, she reached for the envelope.

"Faither! Oop!"

Even Robbie's excited shout and Rob's following admonition to be quiet did not fash her. *God's perfect will.* Hands steady, breathing controlled, she ripped open the envelope and pulled out a thick packet of documents and another smaller envelope from her banker. Och, did he want his silver back? But he couldn't. She'd already spent so much of it.

She put the small envelope aside and read the top paper. Halfway into the first paragraph, tears spilled down her cheeks.

Rob jogged slowly down the path. No reason to rush now. He'd been gone so long, the crew had surely gone home for the day, but better to make certain.

Not only had Fern been recognized as the legal owner of the boatshed, she already had a buyer, or to be exact, several buyers who were forming a partnership. While Fern and Maggie comforted Robbie, who'd burst into tears at everyone else's joyous outcry, he had read the letter and contracts Fern handed him. Several men who had served with Edward and recently been de-mobbed had pooled their silver and made an offer for the boatyard. Their offer of cash had taken precedence over a bid from a boat builder on Lewis. All Fern needed to do was sign the papers included in the envelope and return them as quickly as possible.

The letter from her banker was another surprise. He had resold the cottage and decided that Fern should have a portion of his profit. The envelope contained a check in the amount of three hundred pounds. Some businessmen still retained their honour.

Thank Ye, gracious Faither, for Your perfect plan, and forgive me for no' trusting You enough. Now I pray for the time to design and build her home. I'm away from my family too much as it is. He walked into the shed.

The whole crew was still hard at work.

Och, these lads had laboured long and hard to help the folk clean up their cottages and yards, with no' a yammer. Now, here they were, working overtime on the boat, to regain the time lost.

Rob and Maggie took no chances with the birth of their second bairnie. During the first week of the New Year, they brought the cradle out of Robbie's room, put it into their bedroom, and prepared it with fresh bedding. Maggie covered it all with a sheet to keep it clean.

Rob put the scissors and a roll of string on a shelf in the closet next to a rubber sheet Maggie had borrowed from the infirmary. "There's no reason to have to wash all the bedding like we did last time," she had told Rob.

He insisted they also place a stack of towels on the shelf, just in case.

Maggie's belly was still so tiny. Rob prayed constantly she would deliver a healthy bairnie and that he would be home when she went into labour, but there was no way he was going to help her deliver such a wee bairnie. Maybe she'd made a mistake with the expected delivery date because she wasn't even half as large as she had been with Robbie. This wee one would probably come into the world toward the end of February instead of near the first.

So Maggie could signal him at the shed that her time had come, he dug a shortwave radio out of the Harris Isle inventory and had it hooked up in his office well in advance of her due date.

At least Fern lived with them. If the bairnie decided to be born at night, she would be there, and even if it was during a clinic day, the infirmary was almost next door.

A warmer and wetter winter continued with high seas and gusts of wind that almost swept one off one's feet if caught outside. Though the house remained cozy and draft free, trying to keep Robbie occupied inside was a challenge. Several times a day, he tried to open the door to play outside. Poor Shep was kept in a frenzy preventing the lad from approaching the fireplace, stove, and both outside doors. Though Katie was a big help, she too was bored and tired of trying to entertain the lad.

Maggie stayed up later and later at night, attempting to catch up with the chores she had to neglect during the day. Rob's long days of hard physical labour brought him home much too late to devote any attention to the bairns, who were usually abed. He often just showered, wolfed down his warmed-over supper, and fell into bed.

Toward the end of January, at the end of another wet, nasty day, Maggie met Rob at the door with her face swollen and eyes red from crying.

He picked her up and carried her to their bedroom, kissing her forehead. "I'll help you into your nightgown."

Fresh tears welled up in her eyes. "You're more tired than I am," she protested as he undressed her. "Besides, I have things to do."

He buttoned her gown and sat on the bed with her on his lap. "Your turns are finished for the day. I'll tuck you in, take a quick shower, and eat." He wiped her tears away with his fingers. "I mean it, luve. You're going to bed."

She nodded.

He tucked her in with another kiss, brushing wisps of hair back from her face. "I'll bring you a cup of tea in a few minutes. Don't get up." He closed the bedroom door softly behind him, forehead creased with worry. His lass tried to do too much and he was no help at all. He went into the bathroom and splashed cold water on his face.

As exhausted as he was, there was no way he'd allow Maggie to know how tiring his day had been. His crew, along with the help of Mark and Tormad, had winched the keel up in the cradle so they could begin work on the stern post. They had worked for hours, and Rob's left shoulder ached and his hands burned from pulling on the ropes. He took twa APCs before returning to the living room.

Fern sat in front of the fire doing some mending.

"Are the bairns abed, then?" He put the kettle on to boil.

"'Tis almost the turn of the night, Rob."

"'Tis that late?" Rob checked his watch. "Och, I had no idea. Maggie's all tucked into bed, and I promised her a cup of tea. She must have had a verra hard day."

"I was at the clinic until late and had Katie with me, so I don't know what happened. When I came home, she was sitting at the table with her head on a pile of unfolded hippens, crying like a bairnie."

Rob's stomach cramped. "Do you think she's sick, then?"

"More like sick of being inside. You know how she luves being outside and it's been blowing and plomping rain most every day."

"Should I cut back on my hours?"

"I don't think so. This rain has to stop sometime and when it does, you'll see a new Maggie." She got up and spooned loose tea into the pot before pouring in the boiling water. "Why don't you take a keek while this steeps? As exhausted as she was, she could be asleep."

Rob tiptoed into the bedroom.

Maggie lay curled on her side, fast asleep.

He stood, looking down at her for a moment, heart heavy. How hard it must be for a biggen woman to be trapped inside all day with an active toddler. He pulled the bed-quilt up around her shoulders and walked out, easing the door closed. "She's asleep," he said.

"On you go then. Have your shower. Your supper's on the warming shelf and I'm off to bed with a cup of this tea."

Rob showered, spending a long time with the hot water directed toward his throbbing shoulder. He pulled his denims back on in case Fern came back downstairs. After eating his supper, he rinsed the plate and stepped into Robbie's room.

The lad lay sprawled flat on his back with his arms thrown out, fingers clasping that bedraggled rabbit's ear.

Rob pulled the bed-plaid higher and sat beside the slumbering bairn.

The lad's long black lashes lay against his chubby cheeks and soft black curls framed his round face.

He leaned over and kissed Robbie's forehead. This was his lad, the second great love of his life. Someday soon he needed to spend more time with the laddie before it was too late and he no longer looked to his faither for attention. He sighed and rubbed his aching shoulder. Perhaps in the spring he'd have more time.

Shep nosed his hand.

He left the lad to his dreams, turned off all the lamps but one, and led the dog outside. The wind had died to a brisk breeze as he looked out toward the sea. *Och, I'm in another fankle, Faither. I'm no help to Maggie now and I don't ken what to do about it.* He walked to the railing and leaned against it. *I'd like to talk to her about it on the mornin, so please give me Your words or I'll make a rare midden of it.* He raised his face to the sky, the stars hidden behind clouds and his eyelids dropped. *Thank Ye for the day and all that was accomplished. And for keeping the bad dreams away. In Jesus's name, amen.*

Maggie slept through the night without stirring.

Rob got up early, shrugged into his dressing gown, poured out the old tea, and set the kettle to boil for fresh. He added peats to the fireplace and stove, then brushed his teeth and shaved in the bathing room. His shoulder was a little tender, but the ache was gone.

When he went back into the bedroom to dress, Maggie stretched and held out her arms.

He lay down beside her, holding her close. "How do you feel, luve?"

She burrowed closer. "Wonderful. What time is it?"

"'Tis early—only a bit gone 0500. Are you certain you've had enough sleep?"

She turned his wrist and looked at his watch. "I'm thinking almost six hours should be enough, don't you?"

"Depends." He kissed her temple. "You were verra tired last night. I don't think I've ever seen you like that. Care to tell me what happened?"

"One minute I was folding hippens and the next I was bawling and couldn't stop."

"You haven't been getting enough sleep. Now you've stopped suckling Robbie, you have to stop working so late at night and take advantage of having some guid, uninterrupted sleep before the new bairnie comes."

She pulled away and sat up, her eyes wide. "Och, I didn't bake any bread last night. And I was going to finish the blanket for the new bairnie."

He pulled her back down and sent up a silent prayer for help. After a moment's thought, he said, "Let me tell you a story. It's about what happened to me when I tried to do too much."

"Which time?" She arched her brow.

"Just listen and you'll see."

She settled back in his arms with a sigh. "All right, but I can't imagine anything happening to you that would help me."

He closed his eyes for a moment and spoke, voice soft with memories. "I'd been fighting with Wing for more airieplanes while

133

trying to find enough men to crew the planes and working my ground crews day and night to keep those planes in the air. The weather was guid and I was organizing, plus leading, almost daily strikes deep into German-occupied air space." He opened his eyes and paused for a moment, caught up in remembering what it felt like to be so busy he was lucky to have four hours of uninterrupted sleep a night. "We were turning back from a strike over the Saint-Nazaire sub pens. The flak was unbelievable. I watched twa of my planes take direct hits and go down, no chutes visible, and both of my waist gunners and ball turret gunner were killed when the Fw 190s hit us after our bomb run. It was a slaughter."

She nuzzled into him.

He shook his head and his voice dropped to a ragged whisper. "Something happened on the way back to base. I stopped feeling. I had just lost three of my own crew, men I considered family, and I didn't feel owt—no pain, no grief—nowt. I was just numb."

Her fingertips brushed his cheek. "Don't say more. 'Tis too hard to remember such terrible days."

He caught her hand and held it tightly while he looked out the window at the grey dawn. "I don't even remember attending Interrogation after the flight. I just remember a visit from General Wells that een. Somebody must have called him, probably Hank Hirsch." He met her gaze. "He walked into my office and ordered me to take a leave. I couldn't believe it. Here I was, organizing the next mornin's strike, and that pompous, sorry excuse for a general had the nerve to order me to leave the base for a week. No matter how hard I argued, he wouldn't back down."

"What did you do?"

"The only thing I could. Took the train to a small village in Wales. Don't even remember its name, only that it was almost a kilometer long and I couldn't pronounce it. I think I slept straight through the first twa days, and then spent the rest hiking through the mountains around the village. It felt like another world. No strikes to plan and fly, no bandits or flak. Just clean, crisp air, tumbling burns, and green trees. There didn't even seem to be a war on. I went back to Edenoaks a new man. I could feel again."

"Och, Rob, that has nowt to do with me. How can you compare

dirty hippens and fixing meals with flak and ... and death?"

"I was worn out, Maggie, don't you see? No' enough sleep, too much to do, always driving myself to stay on top of things." He rested his head against hers. "The reasons don't matter, for the outcome is the same. You have to go easier on yourself ... let things go undone. That episode I told you about made me see myself in an entirely different light. I was a human being, no' a machine. I needed sleep and some time away from it all, or I couldn't give my best anymore. That's when I started having an occasional een out with some of my crew."

She looked into his eyes. "I don't know what to leave undone," she said in a small voice. "It's all important."

"Having fresh bread at every meal isn't important. And the new bairnie will do with using the blankets you made for Robbie. The floor doesn't have to be mopped every single day, nor all the furniture dusted. Don't you see? Make priorities and do just the things that have to be done."

"I want a clean house, Rob. For you. For all of us."

"I'd rather come home to a lass who can smile than a shiny floor any day."

She ducked her head. "I don't want you thinking you merit a slaisterin woman."

"Slaisterin woman? Och, Maggie, that's that last thing I'd ever think of you." He held her at arm's length and stared into her eyes. "Give me back the lass I merit, the one who can laugh with me and take time to sit on my lap and share her day. I don't care about how the house looks. I care about you. Can you do that?"

"As long as you realize why the house looks like a midden."

"You'll give it a try?"

A reluctant nod.

"On you come then." He rolled off the bed and held out her dressing gown. "If the kettle hasn't boiled dry, you can have your tea. I'll brew some coffee and dress so we'll have a wee bit of time together before our lad and everybody else stirs."

Maggie tried very hard to lighten her workload. She stopped

dusting the furniture every day, though the constantly burning peat fires deposited a fine, oily film on every surface. She also doubled up on her baking so she would have every other day to do something else. If Rob noticed the scones and bread were often a day old, he didn't say.

As February rolled around, Rob noticed a change in Maggie. Though still frazzled after a day trapped inside with Robbie, she didn't seem as exhausted. She took more interest in what was happening at the shed, often asking him to explain what he had done that day. He hadn't realized how much her fatigue had affected him. He once again looked forward to coming home instead of feeling guilty he was unable to ease her load.

Until Elizabeth MacGruder radioed Maggie.

Rinait's pattern was exactly what the market needed. When his lass wanted to organize the women into a workforce, Rob put his foot down. "Our bairnie is due any day. You can't start something now that will take up so much of your time. Remember what I said about priorities?"

"But the stormy season is perfect for weaving. There's no gardening or ootside chores to do."

"Then have Rinait take over, with Mary MacCrae supervising at her shop. The lass has to show the women how to wrap their looms anyway."

She wrinkled her nose. "Warp the looms, Rob, no' wrap." She was quiet for a moment. "You're right. Tell Graham to have Rinait come by on the morra's mornin. I'll tell her what she needs to do."

Rob grinned and kissed her forehead. "There's my lass."

Spirits higher than they'd been for months, Maggie put Robbie into his highchair—another gift from Hugh's attic—and sat at the table. Sunday morning and the sun shone, bathing the island in a lemon-yellow glow.

"'Tis only fitting, since 'tis the Sabbath," Rob said. "I'll take Robbie ootside this afternoon for a romp and you can sit in your rocker on the entry and watch us."

She smiled and stretched. "Och, that sounds glorious." She

spooned more brose into Robbie's wide-open mouth. "It's been plomping or skailing rain so long I've almost disremembered what clear skies look like."

"When Fern comes down, why don't we see if she'd be willing to take Robbie to kirk with her and Katie? That way, you and I can stay home and have twa whole hours alone together."

"Do you think we could? It would be heavenly to have some private time, just the twa of us."

When Fern appeared downstairs, she readily agreed. "Katie and I'll eat our brose and leave early enough to walk to kirk. It'll do us all guid to stretch our legs now the rain's stopped."

"Take the cairt," Rob said. "That way you won't have that wee skellum stomping about in every puddle he comes to."

An hour later, Maggie and Rob stood on the entry and watched the three take off down the path, Katie skipping alongside the cairt while Shep brought up the rear, performing his herding duties with determination.

Rob put his arms around Maggie from behind and rested his chin on her head. "God bless Fern," he said fervently.

Maggie pressed her back against him. "Aye. She's a guid friend." A sudden chill brought a shiver.

"Let's go inside and sit by the fire. Your dressing gown and baffies aren't enough. The sun may be oot, but it's still cold."

She turned sideways and slipped her arms around him. "Mmm, I'm wondering if a certain man with verra talented hands could give his wife a back rub."

"Your back's aching, then?"

She smiled at the alarm in his voice and rested her cheek against his chest. "Don't fash yourself, 'tis no more than usual."

Rob led her into the bedroom. Her back ached? He shivered, and it wasn't from the cold.

Maggie removed her robe, kicked off her baffies, and lay down on her side. "'Tis too cold to take off my nightgown. Can you just pull it up a bit?"

He rummaged in the bedside table drawer and held up the

bottle of lotion. "Here 'tis." He pulled up her nightgown and poured some lotion into his palm to warm it, then massaged her back, kneading the tight muscles carefully so he wouldn't hurt her. "Feel guid?"

"Wonderful. This is one of those times I'm grateful your hands are so large and your fingers so long." She lay with eyes closed, a dreamy look on her face.

Was there ever a bonnier lass? He pulled her nightgown down, climbed onto the bed, and took her into his arms. "Just relax. It's what you've been needing."

She caressed his face with her fingers, her eyes filled with so much love, it was almost more than he could bear. He struggled to put what he felt for her into words but the flowery phrases attempting to escape from his brain to his lips died in his throat, strangled by a lifetime of feigning indifference. *If they don't know you care, they can't hurt you* had been his guiding principle. But all of that was behind him. Maggie would never take advantage of his feelings. He caught her hand and brought it to his lips. "Och, Maggie, I luve you so much and I never have the words to express it."

"I know what you mean. I still can't believe you chose me."

"There could be no other. God had it all planned, and His plan is always perfect."

She wriggled closer and brushed her lips against his. "Kiss me," she whispered. "Really kiss me."

His heart swelled as he tasted her sweetness, the depth of her love.

She gasped and drew back, eyes wide as she grabbed his shoulders. "Och, my water just broke."

He bolted upright. "No' again, Maggie. You can't do this to me again." He scrambled off the bed. "What can I do? I can't get to kirk and back quick enough."

She grabbed his hand. "Don't you dare leave me!"

Chapter Eighteen

Rob's mind raced. He had been alone with her when she birthed Robbie. He could do this—but, och, he didn't want to. "First things first," he mumbled to himself. He got the rubber sheet, pressed it beneath her, and rolled her over onto her back. "The water. I'll set the kettle on." He ran into the kitchen and shook the teakettle— enough water to sterilize the scissors. He set it on the hottest part of the stove, then tore back into the bedroom.

Maggie was already straining, back arched, breath coming in gasps.

He took her hands and held them tightly. His heart thumped so loudly he was sure she could hear it, but he forced himself to act calm. "Tell me what you need me to do."

She nodded as the contraction eased. "Put towels 'neath me." Another spasm racked her body.

When it eased, he pulled her nightgown up over her knees, got the towels, and pushed them under her.

She strained, grunting and panting, beads of perspiration running down her temples. For another fifteen minutes, she laboured hard.

The top of a tiny head appeared.

"It's coming!" He knelt at the foot of the bed and leaned over, arms extended.

Another contraction.

Maggie cried out as the head emerged.

He eased out one tiny white shoulder, then the other. When the next contraction hit, he gently guided the emerging baby into his waiting hands. "It's a lass!" he cried. "Och, Maggie, she's so wee." He lifted the bairnie and placed her carefully into her mother's waiting hands.

The tiny lass gasped and cried, the noise so thin and weak, it sounded like the mewling of a newborn kitten.

Tears blurred Rob's vision. "She's too wee. Is she all right?"

Maggie examined the tiny body. "She's fine, just no' a braw lad. You have a bonnie lass, Rob."

"You're certain?"

"Biddy certain."

His shoulders shook. "Our bonnie, bonnie lass."

Smile tremulous, voice weak, she said, "She has your brown hair."

"But she's wee like you." He swiped a sleeve across his face.

"Get the scissors and string, luve. You know what to do."

His hands shook as he tied off the umbilical cord, again twa knots just to be sure. This time he didn't hesitate with the scissors. Though his hands shook, he knew just where to cut. He cleaned Maggie up a bit before starting to take the soiled towels into the bathing room.

She grabbed his sleeve. "Come right back. 'Tis our lass's bath time."

He reared back, heart galloping. "I can't do it. She's too wee and my hands too big. I'll hurt her."

"Don't be daft. Get the basin. Remember, no' too hot nor too cold, and a face flannel and towel. And while you're up, fetch a hippen, gown, and blanket. You know where they are."

When everything was ready, he was so frightened his entire body shook. *Help me, Lord, please help me. I don't want to hurt her.* He picked up the lass and cradled her in one large hand. When he dipped her into the water, the bairnie wailed again, her voice so thin and reedy, he prayed nowt was wrong with her. He gently bathed her face, head, and neck, then her tiny body. He counted her fingers and toes and gazed in wonder at their daughter.

She had a mass of light brown curls and features so delicate she looked like a wee wildflower, newly opened. She screwed up her face and cried again, tiny chin quivering.

He lifted her out of the water and wrapped her in the towel, blotting her dry. "You're my wee lass," he whispered. "My Wee

Annie." He handed her to Maggie and removed the basin. "Hurry," he said as he spread out the blanket. "She's so cold she's sheevering."

"She doesn't like being in the scud. It frightens her." Maggie fastened the hippen and dressed the lass in the gown before swaddling her securely in the blanket.

Rob leaned over them, heart almost bursting with gratitude. "She's perfect."

Maggie fingered the light brown curls alight with blonde and red highlights in the sun streaming in through the window. "Her hair looks just like yours in the sun." She pointed out the muzzy, blue-grey eyes staring up at her. "And she looks like she's going to have your hazel-brown eyes, too."

"But she's got your bonnie eyebrows and mouth, luve, and she's going to be wee, just like her mither."

Maggie smiled as she placed the bairnie beside her on the bed, cuddling their new lass close. "Nothing lots of nursing won't fix."

"Will it be harder, then?"

"It will just take her a little longer to learn how, is all, but she soon will. Right now all she wants to do is sleep. She's fair exhausted."

"I'll bring you some tea. You need the liquid."

"Listen to you. You're getting to be an auld hand at this."

"No' by choice. I was determined no' to go through it again."

"But you did. And nobody could have done better."

When Fern and the bairns returned from kirk, they were astounded to hear that the bairnie had been born. Fern rushed into the bedroom where Maggie lay on her side, cuddling the tiny bairnie in the crook of her arm. Fern smiled down at her. "So you just couldn't wait. Poor Rob, you did it to him again."

Maggie's smile was radiant. "You should have seen him, Fern. A doctor couldn't have done better."

Fern eyed the bedclothes. "It looks like you didn't make it 'neath the bed covers."

"Och, my water broke just after Rob gave me a backrub. He

took care of the worst of it, but I do need a bit more cleaning up."

Fern pulled the blanket down from the sleeping infant's head. "She's a verra wee one. I'm sure Robbie was much larger. And she has Rob's brown hair, but lighter. What a bonnie wee lassie."

"Aye, isn't she?"

"Shall we clean you up properly and get you into fresh linens?"

"Bring Robbie in first. 'Tis time he met his sister."

"Rob called her Annie?"

"Anne Margaret Savage. She's so sma', he was worried sick there was something wrong with her."

"I'll go fetch Robbie."

"Bring Katie, also. It wouldn't be fair to exclude her."

Robbie quickly tired of the bairnie and tried to climb into bed with his mother, so Rob picked him up and took him outside with Shep.

Maggie pulled the blanket aside so Katie could see the bairnie's tiny hands and feet.

"Och, she's so bonnie," Katie said. "Can I hold her?"

"When she's aulder," Maggie said, smiling fondly. "I'm going to need your help with this wee one."

Katie planted a gentle kiss on the bairnie's head. "Guid-bye, Wee Annie." She tiptoed out of the room.

Fern helped Maggie bathe, then changed her bedding.

"And I thought the rubber sheet would help," Maggie said. "I didn't think about my water breaking while I was lying on top of the covers."

"There's just no way to plan ahead for everything."

"Do you suppose I could bother you for another cup of tea? I'm going to have to wake this wee one and see if I can get her interested in suckling."

"Of course. I'll feed the others some dinner, too. How about you? Does owt sound guid?"

"Just a long nap. I'm no' hungry now. But don't bother with supper. As soon as the kirk bell is rung, almost every woman on the island will be at our door with a dish of something from her kitchen. 'Tis a custom on Innisbraw."

After he fed Robbie a jelly buttery, Rob ran down to the manse.

Hugh hugged him and pounded his back with the news of another safe delivery. "You amaze me," he said. "You don't even look tired."

"Och, Hugh, I didn't do any of the work. Maggie did all of that." Tears stung Rob's eyes. "Birth is such a miracle. In just a few minutes, you're holding a perfectly formed, wee human being in your hands. There's nowt on earth can compare with the feeling that brings."

"Then you should be the one to ring the bell."

"May I? It would be a joy."

"Of course. Remember the number for lasses?"

"Aye. Five for a lass."

Rob stopped at Elspeth's cottage on his way home.

She embraced him at the news. "Anne Margaret. 'Tis a bonnie name."

"Would you like to go see her? I can get Angus's cairt."

"Och, I wouldn't want to bother you after all you've been through."

Rob kissed her cheek. "'Tis no bother. I'll be back in a tick."

Elspeth shook her head as he raced off. So eager to show off his new lassie.

There was a sharp bite to the air.

She found her heavy winter coat and put it on. She waited on the front flags, head bowed in a prayer of thanksgiving that the wee lass had been delivered safely.

She had held Maggie only an hour after her birth. The warm feeling the memory invoked brought a smile. How she treasured that lass—and her Rob. Once again he had proven the kind of man he was.

Tears pooled in her eyes. "Keep him strong, Faither. 'Tis a perilous path through life You've chosen for him and it won't be all good that comes his way. Keep that precious lad strong."

Chapter Nineteen

"Och, Robbie, quit your whinging! I can't hold you in my lap and suckle your sister at the same time." Maggie pushed the lad away, trying to close her heart to his shrieks. After hours of frustrating coaching, Annie had finally latched onto the nipple and was sooking properly. Now this—sibling jealousy rearing its ugly head.

Fern set a cup of tea at Maggie's elbow and captured the struggling lad, pinning his flailing arms. "Hush, you wee skellum. Go find your ball. Katie's waiting on the front entry for a game of keep-away."

In an instant, Robbie relaxed his stiff body and slid to his feet, smile replacing a scowl. He ran into his room and returned with a large red ball. Grabbing Shep's ruff, he tore out the door, the dog at his side.

"Thank ye for that, friend," Maggie said with a grateful smile. "I was happy to see the back of Rob when he returned to the shed. His hovering over me drove me near daft. But I didn't realize how much time he must have been spending with our laddie."

Fern returned with her own tea, taking a sip as she sat. "'Tis just like my neighbor's experiences on Harris. When she had her second lad, the first—about Robbie's age—pestered her constantly, wanting to be the center of attention."

Maggie put Annie over her shoulder and patted her back. "What happened? Or more important, how long did it last?"

"Och, after a few weeks, he returned to his sunny self and even tried to entertain his new brither." Fern laughed. "Of course, he got a bit rough at times but at least the tantrums stopped."

"A few weeks? I don't know if I can last that long. No' only do I feel guilty about being happy no' having to answer Rob's constant questions about how I feel, I'm going to have to confess to the Lord that I snapped at my lad. And I say I want eight bairns?"

Fern squeezed her arm. "This is the hard part. Give it time and you'll be eager for another." She got up and stretched. "Speaking of Rob, 'twill be suppertime soon. I'd best check on Katie and Robbie and take myself oot to John's cooling shed for some of that food the womenfolk have been dropping off. That's a custom I wish I could have enjoyed."

When Fern quit the house, Maggie closed her eyes and laid her head back. *Och, Faither, I've been judgmental and unkind. Rob's questions were perfectly natural—like mine when I nursed him through his terrible injuries. And Robbie's accustomed to my undivided attention. Please give me patience, and calm these raging hormones that are causing such havoc in my mind and body. Thank Ye for bringing Fern into my life. She's such a guid friend.*

She smiled down at Annie, who'd fallen asleep. Such a perfect, wee lassie. The Lord had blessed Maggie with so many girlfriends. Susan and Siobhan when she was young, with their girlish giggles, sharing secrets behind raised hands, racing across the girse while plucking wildflowers and laughing with abandon at the simple joy of being alive.

Mary, Janet, and Lizzie at the academy on Harris, reading letters aloud from their families, mooning over the lads who had caught their fancy, or huddling close, tears flying, when the yearning for home swept over them.

And not just girls.

Will, the English orderly at her last RAF hospital posting—gap-toothed, ruddy-cheeked, always ready with a cheerful smile and humorous turn of words—or a warm shoulder to cry on when a patient died and her weary heart shattered from the hopeless futility of a war that ground on and on, slaughtering the young, the future.

Faithful, patient, luving Elspeth.

Hugh, never too busy to offer a prayer or guidance in the Word.

Morag and Alec. Flora and Angus. Katag and Gordon.

Graham, Fern, of course—och, the list was endless.

145

But dearest of all, her Rob. She brushed tears from her cheeks. Rob, luving her beyond reason, and when she was weary, nearly suffocating her with the depth of his need to show that luve. Tender, stubborn, impatient, unable to see his own worth, with an eager thirst for God's Word that often shamed her.

Her soul mate, now and forever.

Rob trudged up the path past Elspeth's cottage. How had he ever had the energy to run up the hill? His Maggie would be upset that he had missed another supper with the family. And Robbie would already be abed, lost in a wee lad's dreams, beyond caring how much his faither treasured him.

The soft lamplight from Elspeth's window cast a warm glow across the path. She was most likely still on her knees, petitioning the Lord in behalf of the island's folk. Hopefully she remembered his family.

His family. Och, what had happened to the peaceful, happy eens when he went home with a light heart, eager to be greeted by a smiling Maggie? Mebbe he wasn't cut out to be a faither of eight bairns after all.

Guilt slowed his steps. Aye, Robbie was always whinging about all the attention his new sister received, but that was only natural, wasn't it? And Maggie, impatient and sober, had been through childbirth only a week ago. Lack of sleep and trying to get the less-than-eager lass to suckle was a hard burden for any woman to bear.

He stopped at the gate to his home and turned to look out over the harbour. Fleeting moonlight kissed the tops of the waves as clouds pushed their way across the sky, dropping a thick veil of inky blackness. *Give me strength, Lord—and Your patience. Break through my Maggie's exhaustion and help her see how much I luve her.*

The bad dreams that plagued Rob months earlier returned, thrusting him from sleep into a welter of sweat-soaked bedding, heart pounding, the vision of the boat sinking when she was launched playing over and over in his mind.

146

Though Maggie offered soft words of encouragement as she changed the sheets, he lay awake the rest of the night, fearing sleep and another heartbreaking dream. He prayed for confidence, that the plans he had drawn were correct, and claimed the promises of God, but every day his doubts returned, cramping his stomach and bringing beads of sweat to his forehead. After all, when he began the design, he had absolutely no knowledge about boats. Had he been a fool thinking he could learn from books and the hours spent questioning the Innisbraw fishermen?

Ⓐ

As spring approached, Maggie established a relaxed suckling schedule for Annie. Fern read all of Katie's picture books to Robbie and even taught him how to brush his teeth and fold his nightclothes to put beneath his pillow.

With the advent of April, the constant heavy rain turned to occasional showers and Robbie was allowed to play outside again. Life returned to a semblance of normality. Rob curbed his impatience to have the boat built ahead of schedule and cut his hours at the shed. He and Maggie spent long evening hours in front of the fire, talking and making plans for the spring and summer, reveling in their renewed closeness. Rob's shorter hours did much more than lessen his exhaustion and warm his heart. The bad dreams occurred less often.

May was not as kind.

Rob had just finished meeting with Graham and outlining what the crew had to tackle the next day when Angus burst into his office, red hair beaded with rain, cutty pipe clenched in his fist. "Rob! Come outside and have a keek. There's a big boat at the dock loaded with poles and crawling with men. Some sort of official strutted down the gangplank and said they've come to electrocute the whole island!"

Not knowing whether to curse at the interruption or to laugh at the picture Angus's wild words painted, Rob pushed himself from his desk, shrugged into his A-2 jacket, and accompanied the panting crofter down the main pier and out to the dock.

Sure enough, there was a large boat with a crane unloading

long, smooth poles onto the dock. Could they really be bringing electric power to the entire island? Men clad in waxed jackets and heavy boots strong-armed a crowd of curious islanders out of the way.

This was no longer funny.

He told Angus to stand fast and pushed aside several burly men as his eyes swept the dock for the official the crofter had mentioned.

That must be him, the one in the long woolen greatcoat standing at the side of the dock, conferring with a man attempting to shelter a clipboard from the rain.

Using all the intimidation his height could bring, Rob stepped close and squared his shoulders. "What's going on?"

No sign of reply, or even recognition.

He put his hand on the official's shoulder, sinking his fingers into soft flesh. "I asked what's going on?"

The man with the clipboard raised his head. "Mr. Maxwell, you'd best answer him."

"Aye, Mr. Maxwell, you'd best answer me." A deep-voiced, soft-spoken threat.

Maxwell stopped pointing at the clipboard and looked up—and up. He stepped back, his face a blur of white. "Who ... who are you?"

"Rob Savage. I own the boatworks and I want an answer. Right now."

"Is this the thanks we get for bringing you folks into the twentieth century?"

Stepping closer, Rob said, "Not good enough. For the last time, what's going on?"

"Why, we've come to erect the poles needed for your electricity, man." Maxwell waved his hand, flashing a ring with a large ruby-red stone. "Surely you've been informed about our need for housing and meals for the men we've brought to erect the poles."

"Informed how? We've no telephones on Innisbraw. Who did you write with this information? The Island Council?"

Maxwell backed into a mooring post. "That's not my department. You'll have to contact our office."

Electricity for the entire island! Rob swallowed a grin. "Then I hope your men have some silver to pay for their meals at the howff—that's a pub to you—and I suggest you rethink the need of housing. Most of these folk have no room in their wee cottages. Of course, you could ask our minister, Hugh MacEwan, if your men can stay at the manse, though beds could be a problem. Your only other choice is a sheep fauld."

"But we were assured your people would welcome us with open arms. Surely this island has someplace my men can rest their weary bones after labouring all day. After all, this will benefit each of you."

Rob ignored Maxwell's simpering smile. "Enough of the violins. And tell your men to stop shoving the folk aside like they're wild creatures." He grinned. "After all, you're here to benefit each of us." He turned on his heel and strode back to Angus.

⚓

Hugh opened the manse to the crew, saw that they at least had blankets against the cold, and kept pots of coffee going far into the een.

Paddy was delighted with the hearty meals the men ate after digging holes and erecting poles along each path leading to a cottage. A nice bit of silver for his pocket. The cannie Irisher's glee erupted into laughter when another boatload, this of electricians, landed on Innisbraw.

The workers strung wires from pole to pole before connecting auxiliary lines to each cottage, then worked feverishly, drilling holes in stone walls to pass wires into rooms and install accessible plugs.

Not all of the islanders were pleased.

The Island Council called a meeting to hear the complaints racing around the island.

Fergus was the first to his feet. "We've no use for such modern whigmaleerie! And we have no silver to pay for it." He turned blazing eyes to the crowd. "Betterments? Better for who? Why just yesterday, Gordon had one of his ewes fried to a cinder when it wandered too close to one of those wires. Now, I—"

Gordon MacLeod leaped up. "May the Lord strike him dead for

a liar," he roared. "I've lost no sheep—ewe, ram, or lamb." He cast an apologetic smile at Elspeth and lowered his voice. "And I for one am happy we can stop wasting our silver on paraffin for our lamps. It's better spent bringing real progress to Innisbraw."

Maggie, with Annie cradled in her arms, and Morag and Flora spent the better part of twa weeks hurrying from cottage to cottage with an Anglepoise lamp from Rob's home office, plugging it in, and demonstrating how much more light it cast than a paraffin lamp.

Most of the women welcomed the trio and offered tea and whatever sweets they could scrounge from their near-bare armoires. But a few, mainly the old widows, could see no benefit when they had no silver for new lamps.

"We're facing a problem," Morag said as the three women turned weary steps toward the next cottage. "Fergus is right. The folk now have electricity but no silver to buy new lamps or any of the other betterments it could bring into their lives. If they bought a pump to bring water inside their cottages, they wouldn't have to haul it from the nearest burn in buckets. Or they could buy a boiler to heat the water. And what about a digester for the waste water from their jawboxes or an indoor watterie or bathing tub?"

Maggie pulled Annie's blanket over the sleeping bairnie's head. "I'm thinking the Women's Aid Society must make this a priority. We should contact our sister associations on all the Western Islands and ask their help in providing at least one working lamp for each cottage."

Flora humphed. "But what about the cost of the electricity itself? We often leave off lights we could be using because we can't afford to burn them—and we're better off than most folk as we take in enough silver from the sale of our wool, mutton, and herding dogs to get by."

"I'll have Rob send off a letter to the government," Maggie said. "They surely have funds to help those too poor to afford anything more than the barest necessities, especially since none of our folk are on the dole."

Rob, impatient as always, did not bother with only one letter.

He, John, and Hugh began a letter-writing campaign asking for a stipend for those too poor to afford pumps, boilers, or digesters, targeting those officials governing the county of Inverness who made the decisions affecting the Western Islands. A week later they received their answer—a terse, stiffly worded refusal.

Chapter Twenty

"They say there's no rest for the wicked, so we must be flirting with the de'il." Rob's gaze pinned Alec. "When's all this to take place?"

"Starting later the day." The crofter shuffled his feet. "I thought you'd be dancing a jig, Rob. You're the one who's always nattering about no phones on Innisbraw. Now they've laid the cables, they're ready."

Rob sat back in his office chair, blowing a sigh. "Och, 'tis past time. But I'm no' sure the folk will take kindly to another one of those betterments they've been on about. We could have used a bit more time."

Alec ran callused fingers through his greying hair. "You've no reason to be involved. They're going to partition off a corner of the post office for what they call a 'switcher board,' or some such nonsense. Morag's visiting some of the cottages, asking the women to pass on the news so we can have lasses ready to be trained." He ducked his shoulders. "You're angry?"

"Och no!" Rob leaped up and threw his arm around Alec's shoulder. "'Tis just that things have been stacking up till my mind feels like brose with the water boiled off. And we'll have to keep pressuring Inverness for that stipend for the electrical bills. Thank ye for bringing the news, friend."

❧

Within twa weeks, lines were strung from the electric poles and into the cottages and a switchboard set up. Young local lasses, already fluent in Scots and the Gaelic, who promised to enroll in an English language class to be taught by Elspeth, were trained to handle answering and transferring calls, twa to each of three shifts.

For the very first time ever, the folk of Innisbraw could

communicate by telephone with someone on Harris and Lewis Islands or Scotland, as well as almost anyone worldwide.

But many on the island, who had no silver for electricity or telephones, opted to remain in contact by radio or word of mouth, and a few of those who could afford it had a difficult time learning to use the new device.

Hugh opened the kirk hall for a demonstration by telephone personnel.

"I don't understand how anyone could find it hard when all they have to do is pick up the receiver, jiggle it, and wait for the operator to answer," Graham complained to Rob the morning after the demonstration.

"Och, I don't think that's what has them in a fash. 'Tis having to wait if she's busy with another caller, or remembering how many rings they've been assigned." He chuckled. "Since there are three cottages on each line, I'm thinking the lang-nebbits and gossips will soon learn to answer any ring, just so they can hear what their neighbors are saying."

"That means none of us can have any privacy," Graham said, fuming. "What happens when we're finished with the rescue boat and open for business? We don't want just anybody listening in."

"Don't get in a fash over that. I've had three phones installed in the shed—one for my office with one ring, another in your office with twa, and the last in the rescue controller's cubby with three. He mainly has to be able to call oot since he'll be using the maritime radio to take distress calls." He raised his eyebrow and grinned at Graham. "Unless you're going to be whispering sweet words to your Rinait over your office phone, you're safe." He held up his right hand. "I promise I won't tell anybody your secrets."

Graham's face turned red. "If I hear any heavy breathing while we're talking, I'll bloody some nobs."

"Just make sure it isn't Rinait doing the breathing," Rob said and ducked the pencil Graham threw. When he was alone again, Rob plonked down at his desk. 'Twas a guid thing Graham was not like Den. His old West Point buddy would have delighted in listening in on Rob's calls home to Maggie, and then outrageously embellished them in front of the crew.

Rob had a telephone installed in his home office. He also insisted that Elspeth's cottage be wired, paying the installation fee and having her monthly charge added to his personal bill. She initially turned down his offer, but he was adamant. "I need to be able to contact you without having to run down to your cottage, so you'll be doing me a favour. Besides, now our folk can reach you with prayer requests without having to brave bad weather."

She finally acquiesced, but only after Hugh intervened.

"Let the lad do this if he wants," Hugh said. "If it sets his mind at ease, it's worth it. He's already run ragged with all he's trying to accomplish."

At first, Maggie had a hard time understanding that a call to a neighbor did not cost extra. Rob finally convinced her by showing her their telephone contract. "See? All local calls are included in the monthly fee. You can call anyone on the island and it won't cost owt extra."

"But—"

"No buts from you, bonnie lassie."

The shore glistened beneath a midday sun. A gust of wind kicked the sand and gritted his eyes, blurring the rescue boat on her skids. A bloom of panic blossomed in Rob's chest, driving the air from his lungs. He knuckled his eyes.

He couldn't bear watching the boat slide into the water and sink into an early grave. A fitting end to a fool's hopes and dreams.

The glare splintered his eyes. His lids wouldn't close.

Och, Faither, don't let her sink. Lift her up on wings of Your angels. Please, please!

The sand beneath his feet, the glistening harbour waters, suddenly blurred and receded as he felt himself rising like a silken milkweed pod caught in a blowsterin wind.

Up, up, up.

Not the boat.

Him.

154

A sob burst from his throat. Then another.

He woke with a start, heart pounding.

Maggie's soft fingers caressed his cheek. "Och, luve. Another bad dream, was it?"

He pulled her close, needing her touch to anchor him to the present. "Sorry to wake you."

She pulled over a corner of the sheet and wiped his forehead. "I haven't gone to sleep yet. You only turned off the light a few minutes ago."

"I ... I don't know why, but instead of keeping the boat from sinking, the Lord raised *me* up."

"So it wasn't like your other dreams?"

He traced a quivering finger over her cheek. "I didn't have to watch the boat sink to the bottom of the harbour, like usual."

She sat up. "Our Lord was showing you His power over the de'il and his lies." Her lips trembled. "'Tis like Him throwing the stars into the skies when He created the earth. Satan may rule the earth and deceive hardened hearts, but his power is limited to those who turn away from the truth of the Word." She lay down again and rested her cheek on his chest. "I'm thinking we both have praises to offer a verra loving Lord."

He fisted his hand in her hair. "Aye, we do that."

Chapter Twenty-one

One week after the phone was installed, Rob received a call from a shipping clerk in Oban. "We have two large crates here at our facility. They're addressed to you and are to be shipped on to Innisbraw. If you lived on Barra we could send them on the mail steamer, but it doesn't stop at Innisbraw. How do you want them delivered?"

Rob tapped his fingers on the desk. "Can you get them to the commercial fishing dock?"

"Our truck can take them to any facility you choose as long as it's in Oban."

"Then take them to Pier One. Skipper Malcolm MacNeill of the *Sea Rouk* will be expecting them. Can you load them for him?"

"Of course. It's all part of our service."

"Verra well, I'll tell him to expect them at the dock on the morra's mornin. He sails at around 0600."

"I'm not sure we can have them there that early, sir. There is a charge for early deliveries."

"So be it. I'll pay the charge—just have them at Pier One before 0600 on the morra's mornin."

Rob put in a call to the harbour master in Oban, requesting him to advise Skipper MacNeill that he would have twa large crates delivered the next morning before he sailed. Maggie had been looking forward to her new washing machine and refrigerator since he had ordered them shortly after the war ended, but he would keep them a surprise until they arrived.

He forced his thoughts back to his concerns at the shed. The deck planking on the rescue boat was being installed today. The boat was taking shape. It wouldn't be long until the final fittings were installed, then came the rescue equipment. Thanks to the new telephone service, he had been able to track down the latest in radar equipment, an FFR system just available on the market. He had also ordered the newest model radio he could find. With a government waiver on engines for a boat involved in rescues, the twa 460 hp diesel engines had been installed the week before. It wouldn't be long before the *Maggie* was ready for painting and the first of many sea trials.

But first, she had to be launched and float. He prayed silently as he made his way to the door of the office. *Och, Faither, forgive me for no' trusting You to take care of my mistakes. Please help me have faith in the design. I know You were guiding every line I drew, just give me the courage to see this through.* He walked into the center of the shed where the boat was being constructed.

Graham cut the outer deck planks to fit, working one step ahead of the crew who installed them.

"How's it going?" Rob shouted.

Graham turned off the power saw. "Verra well. These boards are in prime shape, just like those we put down in the cabin. Your mill in the States really came through."

Rob grinned. "Sounds guid. Think you can carry on here without me? I've got some plumbing work to do at home."

"I don't envy you. From what I've heard, there's nothing worse than a leak or a clog."

"'Tisn't that. Maggie's washing machine should be here the morra's een. I need to put the drain pipes in."

Graham whistled. "Washing machine, is it? First the telephone, and now this. Soon you'll tell me you're getting one of those new refrigerators Rinait's been talking about."

"That'll be here on the morra also."

Graham's mouth opened and closed like a beached fish. "You're playing me for a daftie, right?"

"No' at all. I ordered them both months ago."

"You know what you're doing, don't you? You're upping the price of our new house every time you get one of those new machines. Now, Rinait will want them, too."

157

"Then order them."

"With what? I'm living on my savings so silver's in short supply right now, what with saving every pence to build the new house."

"You need an advance?"

Graham recoiled. "No! I'll just have to remind her how long Maggie's done without a washing machine. It isn't like we'll be having a lot of wash at first, but the refrigerator? That's going to take some mighty fast talking to convince her we can wait. Do you suppose it's time for the captain's cap?"

Rob raised his hands. "Don't look to me for advice. The last time I planned to try mine, it didn't work so well."

"I'd like to have seen that."

"No, you wouldn't have. It was ugly." Rob put on his jacket and picked up his thermos. "See you on the mornin." He selected some pipe, elbows, other fittings, and a few tools he would need and headed up the path. Maggie was at a Women's Aid Society meeting. He might be able to finish the plumbing before she returned home.

It was oddly disquieting coming home to an empty house. He grabbed a couple of butteries, filled them with bramble jelly, and ate them while planning what he needed to do. First, he had to change into his denims and his oldest shirt. It would be dirty and probably wet under the house.

Twa hours later he had his trench dug and the pipe installed. He should have done the work when the house was being built, but his legs had not been strong enough to do all of the squatting then. He climbed out from under the house and screwed the crawl-hole cover back into place. Now all he had to do was connect the water pipe to the hot water boiler, the outlet drain to the digester line in the washroom, and fasten the hot and cold pipes to the wall. He laid his pipe wrench on the back entry and looked down at his mud-covered body.

Good thing Maggie was going to have a washing machine. With him around, she needed one.

He went into the washroom and took off his muddy shoes and clothing. He'd have to take a shower before he could do any more work, and that meant almost a fifteen minute wait for the water to heat. Leaving his muddy clothes in a pile, he raced through the kitchen and living room to the bathing room, wearing only a pair of boxers—a better place to wait in case Maggie and Fern returned before his shower was ready.

He barely made it when he heard the telephone ring their three rings. This had better be important. He knotted a towel around his waist and tore into his office, grabbed the receiver, and said a hasty, "Hoy."

"Rob, is that you home so early? You aren't feeling poorly are you?"

Elspeth. "No, just doing some work on the house." His heart pounded. If Elspeth was already home, Flora would soon be dropping off Maggie and Fern. He was trapped.

"Well, that's a nevermind, then. You should know I received a letter from the Inverness County Council. Hugh thought you should be advised, but he feels 'tis the best offer we can expect."

"An offer? They didn't turn us down this time?"

Her laugh sounded even throatier on the telephone. "I'm thinking your weekly letters wore them down. They've promised a stipend for each household on Innisbraw with a need. They did refuse to consider providing silver for a digester, insisting the cost would be too high and rationing made them impossible to find."

"But a water pump and boiler?"

"Aye, if the boilers can be found."

Laughter outside.

"Look, Elspeth, I'm all muddy and I need a shower. Can we blether another time?"

"Of course. Guid-bye, lad."

Rob flung down the receiver and, hunkering down, dashed back to the bathing room.

The front door opened and closed.

"It's late and I haven't even thought about supper," Maggie said from around the corner. "Rob will be starving to death when he comes home."

Och, he had some explaining to do. He opened the door a crack. "I'm already home, lass. I'm going to take a shower."

Maggie pushed open the door. "What have you been doing?" she asked, eyeing his muddy arms, hands, and face.

"Just running some pipes under the house."

She reached up and gave him a cautious peck on the chin. "I've never seen you so dirty. Pipes for what?"

He'd have to tell her now and just hope there was no hitch in the delivery plans. "Your new washing machine."

Her mouth flew open in surprise. "You mean it's finally come? Och, Rob, why didn't you tell me?" She started to dart out the door, but he caught her hand and pulled her back.

"Because it isn't here yet. It should come in on Malcolm's boat the morra's een."

"Well, from the looks of all the mud on you, it's a guid thing. I can just imagine what your clothes look like."

"No, you can't."

"That midden then?"

"Worse."

"Where are they? You didn't put them to soak in the bathing tub."

"They're in the washroom where they're going to stay until your machine gets here."

"My machine. Och, Rob, I can't believe it." She threw her arms around him. "Thank ye, luve."

His eyebrow arched. "You just got mud on your dress."

"Who cares? I'm going to have a washing machine!"

"You really don't care, then?"

"No' a dottle."

"Well, in that case." Rob grabbed her and lifted her up so he could kiss her soundly.

She threw her arms around his neck and returned his kiss.

When they parted, he grinned and shook his head.

"What?" she demanded. "What are you laughing at?"

"You. You're almost as muddy as I am."

She pulled away and looked into the mirror above the sink. "Och, blethers. I look a midden."

"You could join me in the shower. You still haven't tried it."

She wiped at the mud on her cheek. "I can't. I've supper to

make."

"So it will be a wee bit late." He dabbed more mud on her chin.

"Rob Savage, you did that a'purpose."

"I did. What are you going to do about it?"

She swatted at him. "Take a shower, what else?"

His grin widened. "Are you now? And what are you going to put on after your shower?"

"You surely don't expect me to go to the bedroom for clean clothes looking like this. Fern's oot there."

"Better you than me. I'm almost in the scud."

She swatted at him again. "I'll do it, but I'll get even, you can count on that."

His eyebrow rose to new heights. "I *am* counting on it, lass."

She laughed and hugged him. "You'll be sorry." She opened the door and darted out, closing it quickly. He heard a startled exclamation, and, a moment later, gales of laughter, including Katie's giggle.

Maggie returned with their clean clothes, a smug cat-that-ate-the-mouse look on her face.

"Why are you smiling like that?" Rob asked. "What happened?"

She started to disrobe. "Nowt. Fern just wondered why I was all muddy, is all. And of course, Katie was dying to know."

"What did you tell them?"

"The truth—sort of."

"That I was laying pipes?"

"Well, no' exactly."

"What, then?"

She launched herself into his arms and nestled close, a vibrating sigh tickling his chest hairs. Definitely a purring cat.

"Maggie?"

She pulled away and looked up at him, blue eyes sparkling as she stripped off her undergarments.

"Maggie, answer me. What did you tell them?"

"That you were plowtering about in the mud."

"Plowtering in the ... Och, I've no' plowtered in the mud since

161

I was a lad."

"Then 'tis past time." She wiped a glob of mud from his arm and smeared it on his chest.

He stared at her in amazement, before running his arms down her sides, leaving muddy streaks.

"That's better." She wrinkled her nose. "Now we can take that shower. I've been wondering if it's as guid as the bathing tub."

Supper was very late that night, as Rob had to complete the inside plumbing, but the mood around the table was cheerful. Katie kept eyeing him, eyes sparkling with laughter.

"What's so funny, lass?" he finally asked.

The dimples danced in her rosy cheeks. "I didn't know big lads plowtered in the mud."

He cast Maggie a warning glance. "They don't. I wasn't plowtering, I was working."

"But Aunt Maggie said—"

"She was having you on."

Her smile faded. "Then you weren't plowtering after all?"

"Well, it was work, but I guess I was plowtering a wee bit, too."

Her smile returned. "Was it all gushy and squishy?"

He grinned. "Verra gushy and squishy."

"Gushy kwishy," Robbie said.

They all stared at him in amazement.

"Did he say what I think he said?" Rob asked.

"Gushy kwishy," Robbie said again with a crooked grin. He took a drink of milk and some dribbled down his chin. "Gushy kwishy," he repeated, giggling.

Rob wiped the lad's chin with his napkin. "I'm thinking we're going to have to watch what we say from now on or we're going to be in trouble."

Maggie put Annie over her shoulder and patted her back. "He's saying all sorts of words now, even in the Gaelic. He called Shep by name this morning. That poor dog looked so surprised, I couldn't help but laugh."

"He blethers all the time," Fern said. "But every once in a

while, an entire sentence creeps in."

"He waved bye-bye to Hugh today," Katie said, "and he kissed Elspeth's cheek."

"Did he now? Well, perhaps he's finally learning some manners."

Katie gave a deep sigh. "I'm no' certain. He kept pulling Kaitlin's braid at the meeting."

Maggie put Annie in her cradle and sat down to her own supper. "We had a guid meeting. The women took a vote and decided to put the funds we collected from our Yule Bazaar toward buying medical supplies for the rescue boat instead of buying lamps for the folk without silver."

"But what about the lamps? They'd make a big improvement in every cottage."

"Malcolm brought over twenty large boxes filled with lamps collected from the Women's Aid Societies on Lewis, Harris, North and South Uist, Mull, Skye, and even some from Oban. They're all used and some need a bit of repair but Dougal has those at his cottage, being worked on."

"Shouldn't that money be spent on women's needs?" Rob swigged his coffee.

"As far as they're concerned, it will be. Taking guid care of the men on the island meets a verra big need."

"You know, most of the time we'll be shouted out to help a boat that isn't from Innisbraw," Rob said. "We'll answer any distress signal that comes from our waters."

"The women know that." She leaned forward, her eyes sparkling. "Och, you can't begin to realize what this rescue boat means to our folk. Women, men, it matters nowt. They've lived close to death for so long, 'tis a miracle to think of help only a short time away."

"That's why she's being built. I can remember what it was like to have my radioman contact Coastal Rescue when I had to order a bailout over the Channel. Knowing the boats were close gave me confidence I was making the right decision."

"Did you have to do it often then?" Fern asked.

"Only twice, but no' a member of my crew was lost at sea."

The phone in Rob's office rang their three rings.

He raced to answer it.

※

When Rob finally came back to the table, his grin was broad enough to choke on. "You'll never guess who that was."

"Who?"

"Den Anderson."

"Den?"

"Aye. He got our number from John. He contacted John several months ago, but you know Den. There's no way he was going to track down a radio to get in touch with us. He told John to call him if civilization ever got this far east. Your father must have done so, now that he's back at work to finish up."

Maggie giggled. "That sounds like Den. How is he?"

"In a wee bit less than twa months, you can find out firsthand. He'll be here at the end of July."

"Never! Den's coming here?"

"He's hiring a floatplane in Oban and flying in." Rob sat down at the table and turned to Fern. "Den's an auld friend. He was my second-in-command at the 396th."

"Is he still in the Air Forces?"

"No, and I can't believe it. He's teaching flying at some airstrip in California—San Diego, I think he said."

Maggie's brow creased. "I thought he was a career man."

"He was. But when the war ended, they wanted to put him behind a desk at the Pentagon. You know Den. He's like me. The last thing he ever wanted to do was fly a desk."

Katie's eyes widened. "Desks can fly?"

Rob laughed. "That's just an expression pilots use. It means you no longer pilot an airieplane, but you have to sit at a desk to do your work."

"I can't believe he'd come all the way here," Maggie said.

"You know Den—owt for a bit of excitement. When I told him there were no cars on Innisbraw, he almost backed oot."

"What changed his mind?"

"I told him the local lasses are verra bonnie."

164

Maggie choked on her tea. When she stopped coughing, she eyed her husband incredulously. "You didn't. That was mean."

"Why? Our lasses are bonnie."

"And about as likely to fall for someone like Den as they would a Sassenach."

"You've forgotten about Anna's Elam—he's from England and the folk like him. As far as Den is concerned, I don't know if they'll take to him but let him find out the hard way. He was the one who convinced my classmates at the Point I snored."

Fern waved her fork at Rob. "What did you mean when you said, 'someone like Den'? What's wrong with him?"

"Nowt. He's just a real tease, a confirmed bachelor. But he has a line he uses on the lasses that he swears has them swooning."

She sat back with a frown. "He sounds conceited."

"Den? No, he just likes to have fun. You'll like him."

Chapter Twenty-two

San Diego, California, USA

Den Anderson pulled a comb through his short, thick red hair. When should he stop asking his barber for a military haircut? The war had been over for almost a year and he'd resigned his commission in the American Army Air Forces over six months ago, but how could he wear sideburns and a forelock swooped high with Brylcreem like all his buddies sported?

He studied his bloodshot blue eyes in the bathroom mirror. He'd have to wear his aviator's shades today so no one could see how little sleep he'd had after spending eight straight hours dancing with a hot new date. "But what a night!" He slapped Old Spice aftershave over his smooth jaw and reached for his shirt hanging on the doorknob.

He glanced at his watch, blinked, and took a good look. What was he doing up and ready for work at 0700? His first student wasn't scheduled for another two hours. Idiot that he was, he'd been too pooped to even think of resetting the alarm clock.

Sighing deeply, he threw himself onto his old couch and pawed through the litter on his coffee table. Where was that envelope? There it was, under a copy of the latest Life magazine, which had a picture of a pair of ice-skaters on the cover.

Not a bad investment for a dime. The girl's legs were as shapely as Betty Grable's on the poster that decorated the walls of countless barracks during the war.

He pulled the envelope out and opened it. He hadn't had a real vacation since he was fifteen and he and his family piled into their Packard Touring Car for a trip from their home in Seattle to

Vancouver, B.C. His hands trembled as he took out his plane tickets.

From Los Angeles to New York, connecting to Heathrow in London, and again to Prestwick Airport in Glasgow, Scotland.

He scanned the automobile rental agreement. Could he still remember how to drive on the wrong side of the road? Maybe he should have opted for the train from Glasgow to Oban on the western coast, but a train was too slow for a man who valued speed—any kind of speed, but especially in an airplane—above safety.

A wide grin split his face when he removed the last set of papers. What a hoot it would be to fly a spiffy little floatplane to that chunk of rock in the Atlantic Rob called home. His grin faded.

Rob. He hadn't seen the man he loved like a brother for almost three years and now he would get to visit Rob and his family on Innisbraw, that tiny three-by-four mile island at the southernmost tip of Scotland's Outer Hebrides Islands.

His eyes were instantly drawn to the only photo he'd hung on the wall. The ten-man crew of the *Bonnie Maggie* all grinned like idiots. Rob, standing at least a head taller than anyone, had his arm thrown around Den's shoulders. What he wouldn't give to step back into that picture and relive those few moments of intense brotherhood.

He pushed everything into the envelope and lay back, putting his arm over his eyes. Life must have been tough for Rob after the medical discharge, but he'd sounded fine on the phone, same soft, deep voice that commanded attention from even three-star generals. And his pal *did* have a pretty strong accent after living in Scotland for several years.

When he'd first heard Rob had married Maggie, that drop-dead gorgeous Scots nurse, he'd gaped. Rob Savage? He was the guy who clammed up and beat a hasty retreat from any encounter with the fairer sex. Yet now he was married with two kids.

Even when they met as seventeen-year-old plebes and roomies at West Point, his old pal was scared to death of anyone wearing skirts. But that was the only thing he was afraid of. There wasn't a better pilot, a more strategically adept commander in the entire Eighth Army Air Forces, than Colonel Rob Savage.

And Den planned to present the medals to prove it.

But there was a lot of water under the bridge after all this time. Would that old spark still be there? Or would three years of not seeing each other kill their fourteen-year-old friendship?

He got up and padded into the cramped kitchen in his stocking feet. Too late to worry about it now. In a little less than two months he'd be on his way. And Rob better not have lied when he'd claimed there were some really "bonnie lasses" on that piece of rock.

He hated instant coffee but he was out of the real stuff, so he spooned a heaping tablespoon of granules into a cup and poured boiling water over it and stirred briskly. One sip elicited his usual grimace, followed by a shiver of distaste.

What if the Scots drank tea like the English? What if they didn't have any coffee on that island?

He stifled an oath. Too little sleep had scrambled his brains. Knowing how Rob loved his coffee, he'd have found some even if he had to import it.

Den stood at the cluttered kitchen counter and gazed out the window at the rising sun. A soft breeze rustled the fronds of the tall palms lining the street and the Jacaranda tree in the front yard was covered with purple blossoms. They'd make a slippery mess when they fell.

A milkman stopped his white truck at the front curb, rummaged around in back, and pulled out a wire basket jammed tightly with four glass quarts of milk, probably for the family that lived in the apartment below. They were good neighbors, but a little noisy when their kids started screaming. It was the couple on the floor above that gave him a headache. What did they wear on their feet—tap shoes or lumberjack boots?

Yeah, San Diego was a beautiful place to live—lots of sunshine and warm weather, unlike Seattle—but he'd have to look for another place to live. Maybe one of those small Spanish-looking bungalows somewhere closer to the airstrip, though knocking around in a place much larger than this apartment would be a nightmare. Too much room for a single man who was seldom home and never cooked.

Single man. But that was the way he liked it. No little woman nagging him about dropping dirty clothes on the floor or complaining that he needed to stay home more. Or, even worse, dragging him off to church every Sunday. That God stuff was for others—even Rob—not love-'em-and-leave-'em Den Anderson. The last thing he needed was a set of hard and fast Bible-thumping rules to put a crimp in his lifestyle.

Whistling, he finished dressing and left the apartment. His first student for the morning was a real looker. She'd served as a Women Airforce Service Pilot during the war, ferrying aircraft from factories and airfields to military bases across the nation. A month ago, her boyfriend had bought an old Piper J-3 Cub and all she wanted was the hours it took to become proficient enough to get her civilian pilot's license.

He raced down the stairs and did a little shuffle as he made his way out to the curb. Maybe she'd be early and they could go out for a coffee or two, but he'd have to watch his language. She'd made it clear during her first lesson that she didn't like him swearing or using colorful vulgarities, and he had a tendency to lace his language with both.

He spit on his finger and smoothed his eyebrows as he jumped into his 1941 Hudson Coupe. So what if she already had a steady boyfriend? He thrived on competition. Give him a few more days to work his magic and she was as good as his.

Chapter Twenty-three

The moment Rob spotted the *Sea Rouk* entering the harbour, he wheeled one of the heavy dollies from the shed to the dock.

His building crew followed. Angus's cairt waited on the path, Feona in the traces. This would be too heavy a load for old Jack to pull.

Once the *Sea Rouk* docked, the crew lifted the twa crates down the gangplank. It was hard work manoeuvring the loaded dolly over the gaps in the rough boards, but with so many helping hands they soon had the twa crates loaded.

Feona balked and reared, the whites of her eyes flashing.

Rob climbed onto the bench, released the break, and took the reins. "Up you come, lads. I've dealt with this stubborn cuddy too many times to count." He flicked the reins.

She snorted and stood fast.

Rob slapped the reins harder.

Dust rose from her shaggy coat. Though her ears remained flat against her neck, she put her shoulders into it and they were on their way.

Maggie and Robbie waited on the flagstone path, the gate opened wide. "They're here!" she cried. "Och, they're finally here."

She looked so bonnie, he wanted to leap off the cairt and shower her with kisses, but she was eager to see her refrigerator and washer. He guided Feona through the gate, around Maggie's newly planted garden, and over to the side of the house.

The lads made short shrift of the unloading and Rob opened the largest crate with a crowbar from the cairt.

Utter silence settled as everyone looked at the gleaming white refrigerator.

"Och, what a beauty," Colin MacCrae breathed.

Alan MacKinnon caressed the door with a touch of reverence. "It's a lot larger than the one where I boarded on Lewis Isle."

Shooting a glance at Maggie's expectant smile, Rob grinned. "Let's get it into the kitchen, lads. I left a place at the end of the presses. Come away in, I'll show you."

Colin uncoiled the cord. "I thought America used different connectors. This looks like it will fit ours."

Rob quelled his impatience. No' a time to bark at one of his lads for being curious. "I made sure the refrigerator and washing machine were both wired for use here. Had to pay extra and it delayed the shipment, but with rationing, I couldn't have bought them anywhere in the UK."

In a few moments, the refrigerator was in place and the lads went back outside.

Rob clipped the wire racks into place and pulled down a door at the top. "This is called the fast-freeze compartment. 'Twill make ice cubes in yon metal trays and hold several packages of meat."

Maggie washed and dried the inside, then hugged him, body trembling with excitement. "Listen to it hum."

"It'll take a while to cool off inside, then I'll fetch the food from the cooling shed and you can fill it." Who could resist returning her radiant smile? "Now for the washing machine."

Maggie followed them outside, holding Robbie's hand so he wouldn't get in the way.

The lad's eyes shone with wonder, his usual jabber absent.

"Where's Fern?" Rob asked as he began removing the crate.

"She's over at the infirmary. Katie skinned her knee and she wanted to put tincture of Merthiolate on it so the lass wouldn't get impetigo. With all of Robbie's and your wee scrapes, ours was gone."

"Was it bad, then?"

"Just a small abrasion. She was verra brave."

"That's my lass." Rob pulled away the last side of the crate. He grabbed Maggie's hand. "Well, what do you think?"

"I can't believe it. See how big it is?" Her fingers tightened on his. "I can wash all the hippens at once. And look at that wringer."

Rob caught a flash of movement.

Robbie dashed from behind Maggie and launched himself at the washer.

Rob caught up his son and held him high. "No' yet, lad. Stand oot of the way with Mither while we move it inside. Then you can touch it."

No protest, but his son's hands opened and closed as fast as Shep's jaws nipping at a cloud of midges.

"On you come, lads. This goes just inside the door and on the far wall under the hot and cold spigots." Once it was inside, Rob connected the hoses and plugged it in, then pulled Robbie to his side. "You can touch it now, but when Mither's using it, stand back and watch."

Maggie stared at the washer, tears filling her eyes.

He kissed her forehead. "Well, what do you want to wash first?"

She turned to his clothes lying in the corner, the mud dried and cracked. "Will it really get those clean?"

"You may have to put them through twice to get all the dried mud oot, but why don't you try it and see? Here's the instruction booklet." He grasped her shoulder and turned her so he could look in her eyes. "Just be verra, verra careful using the wringer. Don't get your fingers too close to it or let the bairns near when you're using it—and always pin your hair high atop your head or you could get it caught. I've got to take the cairt and cuddy back to Angus. He needs them this een."

"I'll do it," Danny called from the entry. "And we'll stack the crates next to the side of the house. There's some guid wood there."

Rob thanked the lads, paid them, and closed the door.

Maggie scanned the instruction booklet, but the tears in her eyes surely blurred the words.

He took the booklet from her and pulled her into his arms. "Don't cry, lass." He ran his lips over her forehead.

"I'm just so happy," she said, smile tremulous. "Do you have any idea of the hours this will save me?" She hugged him, resting her cheek against his chest. "Thank ye, luve, from the bottom of my heart."

Robbie pulled on his faither's pant leg. "Oop, Faither, oop."

Rob picked up his lad and brushed the curls from his forehead. "What's for supper? I'm gleg as a gled."

"Greg a greg," Robbie parroted.

＊＊＊

As soon as she and Fern finished the supper dishes, Maggie sent Rob after a box of food from John's cooling shed.

He handed Maggie a large earthenware jug of milk.

She wiped it dry, set it in the refrigerator, and stood back, beaming. "In the winter, when the rain's plomping down, it will be wonderful no' having to run to Faither's cooling shed before I can start a meal."

"Aye, and the butter and cheese won't taste rancid in summer." He unpacked the box, lining the bunker with all the perishables. "I'm glad the handle's too high for a certain lad to reach or we'd be in a muddle."

"There's the truth."

They soon had the box empty and the refrigerator shelves almost full.

Rob stretched. "Och, I'm tired."

"So am I. I'm thinking I'll leave the washing for the morra. Why don't we go sit by the fire? Robbie's fast asleep and 'tis time for Annie's feeding."

"Where are Fern and Katie?"

"Already abed. She's reading the lass a story."

"You mean we're all alone?"

"Aye, except for our Annie."

He pulled their rockers closer together. "I can't believe it, but our wee lass is finally growing."

Maggie settled Annie at her breast. "Aye, and she's so guid-natured."

He touched Annie's elbow. "Look, she's got a dimple. She's trying to smile and suckle at the same time." He fingered Annie's fine hair. "It's wavy like yours."

She smiled at her husband, love softening the violet flecks in her blue eyes. "And see how the firelight brings out the blonde and the red? This is one lass who truly belongs to her faither."

"She's such a quiet, wee one. Remember what a lusty cry Robbie had at her age? There's none of that from her."

"She does make her wishes known. She just goes about it like a lass, no' a lad."

"When she smiles at me, she melts my heart." Rob leaned over and tenderly kissed Annie's nape. "There's nowt I wouldn't do for you, my Wee Annie." He settled back in his rocker, fingertips tapping on his thighs.

"What are you thinking?"

He uttered a sound between a snort and a humph. "Just an idea I've come up with. Mind if I run it by you?"

She put Annie over her shoulder and patted her back. "Of course no'. What is it?"

"I've been racking my brains trying to come up with a way to signal the crew of the rescue ship when a shout comes in. Remember, they'll be volunteers with full-time turns so they'll be scattered all over the island. Even if they have telephones, I can't expect them to be at home to hear the ring."

"So what have you decided?" She put Annie to her other breast.

"I'm thinking a siren of some sort. At first I thought we could use a bell, but that would be hard to hear inside, and would conflict with the kirk bell."

"A siren? Where would you put it?"

"Right up here on Innis Fell. 'Tis a high enough point for the sound to carry into every cottage on the island. I'm biddy certain I can find one in Oban that they used for air raids. Do you think the Island Council would approve?"

"I can't think why no'. You do need a way to call the crew."

"Then I'll take the idea to Elspeth first. As Council Elder, she has the most say." He got up, added peats to the fire, and stared into the flames.

"There's more. What else are you thinking?"

"You know me too well, Maggie, lass. Who am I going to get to crew the boat? Sea trials are just weeks off and the crew will need a lot of training aboard the boat, and medical training, too."

"How many lads do you think you'll need?"

"At least nine. It will only take six for each rescue, but we should have three in reserve so I can rotate them if we have shouts in succession, or even use all nine if we must."

"Why don't you have Hugh make an announcement at kirk on the Sabbath? He could ask for anyone who's interested to contact you."

"I thought about that, but I hate to turn anyone down. It will require a lot of strength. Every lad will have to be a guid swimmer already, for there's no time to teach such basics now. They'll have to be trained in diving and searching for victims who might have slipped underwater, but I can do that later."

Maggie's heart skipped a beat. *Diving for victims?* She'd been doing so well that she could not allow her fears to take over now. "Then give a list of requirements to Hugh to read off. That way, only qualified lads will answer the call."

"Leave it to you to have the solution."

"You have too much on your mind, luve. You can't expect to think of everything."

"You wouldn't believe the lists on my desk down at the shed. Every day I add things." A sigh escaped his lips. "And I thought commanding an air group was complicated."

"Will Graham be your second-in-command like Den was at Edenoaks?"

"They're called second coxswains, but Graham made it clear he's no' a guid sailor. He gets verra seasick. That was the main thing wrong with him when we took him off the *Sea Rouk* when he came home injured."

"That could be a tickler."

"Aye, a big one. I'll just have to see who's interested in being more than just a member of the deck crew. There may be one who stands oot above the rest."

Maggie lifted Annie to her shoulder. "Can you take the cradle into the bedroom? 'Tis getting late." Once the cradle was beside their bed, Maggie settled Annie and covered her, tucking in the blankets.

Rob looked down at their little girl. "We're so blessed," he whispered. "A braw lad and a bonnie lass." He pulled Maggie into his arms. "And a luve between us that will never end."

"Never." She raised her face for his kiss.

Rob stood alone on the shore, the sun glinting off the white sand almost blinding him. Another metre and the rescue boat's stern would reach the harbour waters. Not a wave or riffle marred the glassy surface—still as a loch on a rare windless day. Too spellbound by the sight of that red and black boat being launched, he didn't stop to wonder how the boat glided effortlessly over the sand without any skids to guide it, or why the waters parted without a splash when her broad stern breached them.

She slid slowly into deeper water, her black keel disappearing, railing and decks vanishing without a ripple, until only the top of her red cabin remained as a bitter reminder of his folly.

The sand gripped his feet, then his knees, his hips. The harder he struggled, the faster the sand rose. When it reached his armpits, he stopped fighting and waited for the inevitable. A fitting end for a fool.

Chapter Twenty-four

Maggie switched on the lamp and sat up.

Rob lay still, eyes closed. Sweat ran down his face and body, wetting the sheet tangled beneath him.

Och, he'd had another bad dream. But usually his thrashing legs and arms woke her. Why wasn't he struggling? She shook his arm and whispered his name.

No response.

She grasped his slippery shoulders and shook him again. "Rob, wake up. Wake up, luve."

Still no response.

Trembling fingers sought his carotid. *Fluttering, weak pulse.* She had to wake him! She straddled him and lifted his head from the pillow. "Wake up right now, Rob Savage!"

He sat up so suddenly, she tumbled to the side of the bed.

He drew in one huge breath, then another, hands brushing at his face, eyes wild.

She scrambled to his side, grabbing his hands. "A dream, Rob, only a bad dream."

Fingers clutched hers. He panted, chest heaving. "Maggie?"

"Aye. Lie down, luve, so I can pull up the bed covers. You're sheevering."

Annie, snug in her cradle at the side of the bed, whimpered.

Maggie pushed on the rocker with her bare foot and set the cradle into motion.

⚓

A shudder shook Rob's body. He brushed his face again. *Sand. In his mouth, in his nose, covering his eyes. Just a dream?* He couldn't lie down. It might come back. "No' cold." His whisper rasped harsh in his ears. "Hold me, Maggie, please hold me."

Her warm, soft arms encircled his chest. The rapid beat of her heart echoed the blood pounding through his body. Only a dream. *Och, help me, Faither. I gave up. I didn't even fight it. I can't tell my Maggie.*

"Was it about the rescue boat sinking again?"

He rested his cheek against her hair. "The boat, aye. But this dream wasn't like the others. 'Twas like I was living inside a dream with no sound, no' even a breeze, and nobody there. Just me— alone."

"You'll never be alone again, Rob. You have me, and Robbie and Annie, and an island filled with folk who luve you."

"I've failed God, Maggie. He tested me and I failed."

She jerked away, taking her softness, her warmth, her heart beating as one with his. "Our Lord would never test you with a bad dream. But the de'il would. He seeks out the things that frighten you, plants seeds of doubt in your mind, takes advantage of your lonely past. You can't let him win, Rob. Remember our Lord's promise? 'I can do all things in Him that strengthen me.' No' some things, luve, but *all things*, especially fulfilling a promise you've made." She pulled his face down and kissed his cheeks and forehead.

Each touch of her lips calmed him, lessened the shame of failure. *She's right, Faither. I can't let the de'il win. Give me Your faith when I falter.* A warm flush bathed his head and covered his face, his shoulders, his body. *You anoint my head with oil. Thank Ye, Lord, thank Ye!*

On the last day of May, the cut stones for Fern's house were delivered to the site. Rob had drawn detailed plans after talking with her for many weeks to determine not only what she needed, but what she wanted. A vast difference, that.

His plan of the exterior walls was especially detailed since he could not be present when they were being erected. Because her house would be very similar to his and Maggie's home, just smaller, he was certain there would be no problem in erecting the walls, but he met early in the morning with the twenty-five men who would be doing the construction.

"Just watch the fit of the wooden window frames," he told Alec, who would be doing the woodwork. "Make sure your miter's true or we won't get a guid fit when we install the glass."

"I'll do it right. You just see to building the boat. No need to fash yourself over this too."

Rob grinned and clapped him on the back. "I know you will. I've just got so much on my mind right now I don't know whether I'm coming, going, or spinning my wheels in one place."

"You're worn out, Rob. You can't keep working such long hours. You need to cut back even more."

"Just another week or twa and the boat'll be ready for launching. Once she's in the water I can take a breather."

Alec's gaze still looked anxious. "You'd better. A man can go daft trying to juggle so many projects at once."

Rob grabbed his thermos off the croft wall. "Thank ye for all the help, Alec. I couldn't have done any of this without all the support you folk have given me."

A smile teased the corners of Alec's lips and he ducked his head. "'Tis our pleasure."

Late to the shed, Rob took off down the path at a run. Though he had been spending so many hours a day on the boat, he should be doing more. Such as going over the final specifications one more time before the boat was painted.

He ticked off items in his mind. Much of the equipment needed for a shout had already been delivered. Stacks of rope, life jackets, and stretchers were ready to be put aboard. A transfer sling was due to arrive any day, and the wetsuits and swimming fins for the crew would be ordered as soon as the final crew selection was made and measurements taken.

From what he had read about the Royal National Lifeboat Institution, his boat and manner of executing rescues would differ greatly from the norm. They seldom did in-water rescues. Instead, they attempted to save the crews of disabled boats by manoeuvring close enough to have the men jump to the deck of their lifeboat. But there were too many rocks jutting out of the Atlantic south of

Innisbraw. And those same skerries made it impossible to get close enough to transfer survivors from boat to boat.

That's why he always referred to his boat as a rescue boat, not a lifeboat. Hopefully the RNLI would license and certify it despite the differences. If not, he was determined to go it alone, though that could prove a legal nightmare if there were any fatalities.

Hugh's announcement at Sabbath service had brought a gratifying response. Eight of the lads who had returned from military duty volunteered right after the kirk service ended. They were highly qualified and all were experienced swimmers. One lad in particular, Matthew Campbell, was a trained medic with three years battlefield experience. All Rob needed was one more qualified lad and he would have his crew, if they all passed the swimming test—another instance where he differed with the RNLI. Some of their lifeboat crew members didn't even know how to swim.

The only thing giving him pause was the mental condition of the ex-military lads. He'd seen them at kirk and recognized the dark shadows lurking behind their somber gazes. Had they been given enough time to overcome all they had seen and done? If not, they would be in no condition to face rescuing someone from a wild, turbulent sea.

He arrived at the shed to find the crew hard at work installing the final fittings. He eyed the large, forward-positioned cabin. It might be unconventional, but its wide windows would afford a one-hundred-eighty-degree view of the surrounding sea.

Graham appeared on the deck. "Guid mornin. The stretcher fittings are all up, as well as the shelves for medical equipment." He climbed down the rope ladder and followed Rob into the office.

Rob poured them both a mug of coffee. "That's grand. Sorry I'm late. They're starting Fern's house the day and I had to talk a few things over with your faither." He pulled a napkin from his pocket and handed Graham a scone.

"Can they build your design without you being there to oversee?" Graham sipped his coffee.

"They know what to do when it comes to working with stones better than I."

They finished the scones in several bites and drained their

180

mugs.

"When are you going to install the radar and radio?" Graham asked.

"I've an electronics expert coming over from Glasgow at the end of the week, and I'm hoping to have one more lad for the crew lined up before then. I'd like to have all nine trained to use the equipment."

Paddy appeared at the door, bunnet in hand, a huge grin lighting his braw, ruddy face. "Mornin to you."

A twinge of impatience made Rob blink twice. He didn't need one more curious islander poking about the day. "Guid mornin," he said, words clipped.

Paddy gestured out the door at the boat. "She's a sight to behold," he said, his Irish brogue singing. "I'm here to add me name to the list."

"List?" Rob asked.

"Aye. The rescue boat crew. I'm here to volunteer."

Graham closed his open mouth with a snap. "But what about the howff? You'll have to spend a lot of time training if you're chosen, and if you're called out on a shout, you have to go right then."

Though it didn't seem possible, Paddy's smile broadened. "There's no problem. Jack Ferguson, me bartender, can fill in for me. He practically runs the place, anyhow, what with me playin' gigs."

Rob brushed aside his surprise. "Are you a strong swimmer? That's a must."

"Am I a strong swimmer, you ask?" Paddy rolled his eyes "Why, I was raised on the shores of the Irish Sea. Swam before I walked, they tell me."

"You'll have to pass the test."

"Bring it on. I'll outswim all comers."

Rob eyed Paddy's broad-shouldered build. The lad was strong, which would be a plus, and his good nature would help build camaraderie among the crew. The main thing in his favour was the fact he had never been to war. But one last question remained. "Do you get seasick?"

The Irishman roared with laughter. "Seasick?" he sputtered. "Are you puttin' me on then? Me da was a fisherman. Why, I've spent more time on water than on dry land, and that's the truth."

Rob grinned. "Then I'll be glad to put your name on the list." He extended his hand.

Paddy shook Rob's hand, then Graham's. "Let me know when that swimmin' contest's to be held. And warn all the others Paddy McDonald's never been bested."

Rob watched him walk across the path to the howff. "If that doesn't beat all. It never occurred to me Paddy would be interested."

"Me either. But I always hoped there was a serious side beneath all that glad-handing."

"That makes nine volunteers. I'd say 'tis time to order wetsuits for each crew member from that supplier in the States. At least three each, in case some get damaged. And then set up that swimming test."

"I'll take care of it. I'll get the lads over here for measurements and place the order."

"Be sure to tell them all to be here on Saturday mornin for some radar and radio training."

"Consider it done."

Later that evening, Rob walked around the partially-erected walls of Fern's house, tape measure in hand.

"How does it look?" Fern sounded anxious.

"Grand. They should finish the exterior walls by Friday een."

"Then what?"

"If this clear weather holds, they'll frame the roof and put the slates on as quickly as possible. 'Tisn't summer yet. We're still in for some rain."

Katie skipped up to them. "I found my bedroom window." She hopped from one foot to the other, grabbing Fern's hand. "Come look, Mither."

Rob smiled at the lass's fluent Scots. "On you go—do some exploring. I need a cat's lick before supper."

Fern laid a hand on his arm. "You look so tired. I hope you're through for the een."

"I am. This night belongs to my family."

Katie pulled on her mother's hand. "On you come. I want to show you my window."

Rob smiled at the kittled-up lass. "Don't be late for your supper."

"I already set the table," Katie called as they rounded the corner and disappeared.

He stretched, flexing his shoulders and neck muscles. Fern was right, he was tired, but he was also excited. Things were coming together. In another week, twa at the most, they would be ready to launch the rescue boat. Just the thought brought a stabbing pain in the pit of his stomach. He still suffered bad dreams about the launching, but none had been as horrible as the one in which sand swallowed him. *Please help me, Lord. I know this is Your plan, for You planted the need in my heart and guided each line I drew. Please give me the faith she'll float.*

Chapter Twenty-five

Mouth-watering aromas filled the house. Maggie stood at the stove, moving a bowl of beans to the warming shelf. The warmth of the kitchen, the soft light pooling from lamps onto polished floors, and the sweet reek of burning peats brought a swell of contentment—of *belonging*—to Rob's heart. Home. Such a simple word, that, but one filled with so many meanings, it amazed him. He hugged Maggie from behind, burying his face in her hair. "Mmm, you smell so guid, even better than whatever you're cooking."

She leaned against him. "And you feel guid. I'm surprised you're still on your feet after such a long day." She turned and rested her cheek against his chest. "Can you stay oot of your office for just this een, luve?"

"The night belongs only to you." He kissed her. "Let me help you get supper on the table. I'm gleg as a gled."

She pushed him away with a laugh. "Supper's almost ready. We're having a beef joint."

"Beef joint? What's the occasion?"

"I was hoping to lure you away from the office the night."

"Och, you were?" His right eyebrow rose as he patted her bottom. "You're a designing little wife, aren't you?"

She smiled wickedly and returned to the stove.

Rob ate three large helpings of supper plus a handful of Maggie's melt-on-a-tongue shortbread. The food gave him a surge of energy and he played ball with Robbie and Katie on the entry for an hour while Fern and Maggie did the dishes and set the following twa days' bread to proof.

After Fern, Katie, and Robbie disappeared upstairs for their story time, Rob brought in some peats and relaxed in his rocker while Maggie put the bread in the oven and sat beside him to suckle Annie. He laid his head back with a deep sigh. "This is the way every een should be. When the boat's finally launched, I'm planning on making this permanent."

"I've been wondering, how will you keep your boat-building crew busy until you get an order for another boat?"

"I've had some interesting calls the past month. Both Harris and Barra Island's Lifeboat Services want to see our sea trials, so I'm thinking the word must have gotten out. I'm hoping they'll want a larger boat that will right herself if she capsizes."

She patted Annie's back. "That could take time."

"Aye, but I'm planning on keeping the crew busy doing the interior of Fern's house. After seeing the work they did on the boat, I've no doubt they'll do a fine job."

She reached for his hand. "I don't see how you keep everything straight in your mind."

He brought her hand to his lips. "This is one of those times I'm grateful for the organizational skills I used at Edenoaks. I'm no' sure I could have done this without having to wear so many hats there. The turn may be different, but I go about it the same way."

John MacGregor, the electronics expert, helped Rob and Graham install the radio and radar and make sure the antennae were positioned correctly. Next, he talked Rob through the steps he needed to know before using either device. They broke for a quick dinner at the howff before meeting with the crew.

All of the lads on the island were familiar with radio frequencies and protocol but the navigation equipment was another story. Rob was the only one of the ten men who had any understanding of how radar worked. But the lads were intelligent and eager to master the new device. By early evening, his crew had a rudimentary knowledge.

MacGregor cleared his throat. "I'll be back when you're ready for the sea trials. Then you can see the FFR in action on the seas where it belongs. You'll be amazed how much easier it makes navigating in high seas, or with a gale blowing the rain so hard it's like the sea's swallowed you up."

Because Rob and Maggie's extra rooms were in use, MacGregor had arranged to stay at the manse for the night. Rob walked him over to the kirk and saw him settled in before turning his steps toward home. He had a headache—a sign of trying to cram too much information into his brain in too short a time. He massaged his stiff neck muscles as he walked up the hill.

The glowing lamp in Elspeth's cottage brought a flush of guilt. It had been almost a week since he'd seen Elspeth, and at least three days since he had called her. He reminded himself to call her when he got home, determined to add her name to his list of things to do so this would never happen again. There were just too many things to remember.

He opened his front door and walked in.

Maggie held a crying Robbie in her rocker, a bulky face flannel pressed to the lad's mouth.

Robbie took one look at his faither and bawled harder.

Rob picked him up and lifted a corner of the flannel.

A bruised cut on Robbie's upper lip.

Rob rocked him, telling him a story about a silly rooster to detract his attention from the makeshift ice bag. When the lad quieted, he asked Maggie, "What happened?"

"He was over at Fern's new house and pulled away from Katie. He tripped over a stone and fell against our dyke. The split's no' deep, so there's no need for stitches. 'Tis more an abrasion than owt, so I have ice on it to keep the swelling down."

Rob cradled his son, heart aching. This was the first time the lad had suffered anything worse than a minor bruise or scrape.

Maggie held out her arms. "Give him to me while you eat your supper. 'Tis on the warming shelf."

"I'll wait. I'm no' hungry now."

She knelt by his chair. "What's the matter? Are you hurting or fashed about something?"

"Just a wee headache is all. I'm no longer accustomed to cramming so much information into my head in one day.

She fetched him twa APCs and a glass of water. "Do you want a cold flannel?"

"The aspirin will do the trick." He looked down at Robbie, who was nestled in his lap. "Is he asleep?"

"Aye, poor laddie."

"I'll carry him away to bed." He took Robbie into his bedroom, carefully undressed him, and put his hippen and nightclothes on. After he tucked the lad in, he stood for a long time looking down at him.

The chubby, wee lad was slimming down and growing tall. It wouldn't be long before accidents became commonplace. Robbie was all boy. He never walked, but ran. He climbed everything he could, and many things he should not, fearless and more than a little impetuous.

Like Rob in his own boyhood. A fall from a Sycamore tree when he'd been pretending to fly a bi-plane had resulted in the only broken bone he'd ever suffered as a lad, but he still had many small scars from cuts suffered when he was growing up. *What goes around comes around.* He pulled the bed-plaid up a wee bit higher on his son's shoulders and quit the room.

Maggie was settled in her rocker, nursing Annie.

"Where's Fern and Katie?"

"They went upstairs early so I could try to settle our lad down. Every time Katie looked at him, he began crying again."

Rob caressed her shoulders. "He's fast asleep. Are you all right?"

"I'm fine. I have to admit, when I first saw all the blood I could hardly think, but I'm grateful for my nurse's training. A quick look eased my fears, and then it was only my heart hurting."

He sat in his rocker and leaned back, closing his eyes. "I don't like to see our lad hurt."

"I don't like to see my man hurt, either," she said, voice soft as a morning mist.

"The headache's almost gone. Have you had your own supper?"

"Aye. We had just finished the dishes when Robbie fell. Can you eat now?"

"In a minute. I'm just sitting here angry at myself for no'

calling Elspeth again the day. She's going to think I've disremembered her and all she's done for me."

"Stop being so hard on yourself. I've called her every day the week and she's grand. She knows how busy you are."

"Too busy for dear auld friends? That's no' right."

She squeezed his arm. "Just for a few days, is all. She understands. After all, what you're accomplishing is bringing a dream of hers to fruition, too."

He sighed and covered her hand with his. "Just a few more days. Can you hold out that long, lass?"

"As long as you don't make yourself sick with work and worry."

The following day brought a much-needed day of rest for Rob. He planned to run that morning before kirk, but slept later than usual, so he bundled Robbie up and they went outside to throw a stick for Shep.

The lad's upper lip was swollen and bruised, but he didn't seem to notice. He jabbered and laughed as he and the dog cavorted about in the crisp, clear air.

The family walked to kirk, Rob pulling Robbie and Katie in the cairt. The service soothed Rob's soul. He had been too distracted by decisions to pray as much as usual. No wonder he had been so tired—he had distanced himself from the Power that kept him going.

They spent time talking with Elspeth and Hugh after the service. If Elspeth was upset by him being too busy to call, she gave no indication. She was her usual warm, loving self. For someone who would soon be turning a hundred twa, she was amazingly spry.

"I have some lily tubers I divided to give you," she said to Maggie. "They bloom all summer and have the most delightful fragrance. Drop by sometime next week, for 'tis almost past time to get them in the ground." After Maggie promised she would, Elspeth turned her attention to Rob. "I understand your boat's almost ready to launch. This is one more thing that makes me grateful for where I live. I can watch it all from my front entry."

"I'll drop by on my way to the shed the mornin we're putting

188

her into the water. 'Tis still too cold out on your entry unless there's something to watch."

"Och, blethers. I have the common sense to dress warmly." Her keen gaze swept his face. "You look tired, lad. Don't push yourself too hard. A day or twa one way or the other won't make any difference in the outcome."

His eyebrow rose. "I'm thinking you and Maggie've been talking about me. She said the verra same thing this mornin."

"Then listen to us. You're pushing yourself as hard as you can to see this boat put to use, but it will do no guid if the boat's commander is too tired or sick to take the helm."

His crisp salute was automatic. "Aye, Commander."

She laughed. "Maggie, I don't see how you put up with this lad. He always comes up with a smart answer."

"Are you going to have a christening service?" Hugh asked. "Several of the folk have suggested it."

"Aye, but it'll have to be after she's launched. I know that flies in the face of tradition, but 'tis too dangerous to have a lot of folk around while she's on the skids. And I really don't need the superstition, just want a blessing." He eyed Hugh. "Do you suppose you could offer a prayer when she's christened? That boat and her crew are going to need all the divine help our Lord will provide."

"Of course I will. What better time to invoke the Almighty's blessing than on an endeavour meant to save lives?"

"Guid. We begin painting her on the morra. Depending on the weather, we may be able to launch her in about a week."

"Did you find enough lads to crew her?"

"Exactly nine. I just hope they all pass the swimming test. But I'm worried about most of them being ex-military. I ken how hard it can be to leave the war behind."

Hugh appeared to ponder his words. "Och, I've counseled all those lads who're home from the war since they returned. Some were in worse condition than others when they came home, but I'm thinking they've all put the worst behind them."

"I hope so. They can't falter when they're in the water saving some poor soul."

No elfin smile now. "So rescues will call for you going into the water?"

"Some will. I'm putting an inflatable on the cabin roof to use in shallow water or when there are too many victims for the lads to handle. But if a boat gets into trouble around the skerries, 'twill be too dangerous to use the inflatable. We'll have to rely on the transfer sling. Or, if the boat's already broken up, on one-on-one rescue techniques."

"Och, it sounds dangerous."

"It can be. We'll have to lay off far enough to keep the *Maggie* oot of trouble, but close enough to be of help. Every shout will be different. I'm convinced the lads who've volunteered will make the difference between certain death and survival."

Hugh took Rob's hand. "Your dream has brought hope to our folk. Thank ye for that, lad."

"It was my pleasure," Rob said, grin wide.

Chapter Twenty-six

That afternoon, Rob took Robbie out into the yard to play while Maggie watched and Annie napped. The lad ran and climbed as fast as he could, giggling with glee when he caught his mither watching him. Katie pulled him in the cairt until she tired and Rob took over. Shep still barked whenever his small charge was seated in that contraption in the yard as if sensing how impossible it would be to herd something on wheels.

When Robbie fussed and rubbed his eyes, Maggie took him inside for his nap. Katie pestered Fern into resuming her knitting lessons, so Maggie hurried out to the entry and pulled her rocker close to Rob's, looking out at the Minch.

Though there were high clouds, for the first time in months only a light breeze tickled her cheeks. "'Tis hard to imagine the need for a rescue when the sea's so calm," she said. "It's almost as smooth as a loch at dawn, before a wind rises with the sun." But it could be so wild during a storm—wild and dangerous.

"Aye, but boats can get into trouble even when 'tis calm like the day. They can lose power or steering and drift, for instance. That's one of the reasons I installed twa powerful diesel engines. I'm biddy certain we'll be called to do some towing once in a while."

She reached for his hand. "Rob?"

"Aye?"

"Are you going to join the crew in the ... water ... when they take the swimming test?" Och, why had she hesitated? And her fingers trembled. Now he knew she was fretful.

He didn't answer immediately and when he did, his voice was a low, soft rumble. "I am that. As commander, I can't expect my men to do something I'm no' willing to do. Remember, that's the way I command. As Elspeth always says, "Tis only fitting.'"

She knew well the way he commanded—flying lead plane on the most dangerous missions during the war. Why had she asked such a pointless question? But she had and he was waiting for a response "I ken that. But I've never seen you in the water."

"I'm a guid swimmer. I learned in a pond at the orphanage when I was four or five and I did some competition swimming at the Point. I've always felt at home in the water."

She couldn't stop now. "But you haven't done it for a long time."

A small smile played across his face. "It isn't something you forget how to do, lass. Besides, I'm in better shape now than I was as a young lad, especially my upper body. I hope I don't place dead last in the test, but even if I do, I have to show the lads I'm willing to go into the water with them."

This was serious, no' something to smile about. "But who'll run the boat if you're in the water?"

"There isn't a lad who volunteered who can't operate that boat, some better than others, but that's another part of their training— and mine. Don't disremember, I'm the novice sailor around here. Malcolm's going along the first few times I take the *Maggie* oot, and I'm praying I'll be a quick learner. I might ken how to design a boat now, but I need experience operating one."

Rob, struggling through the waves, sinking 'neath the water. She couldn't speak.

He got to his feet and pulled her into his arms, resting his cheek on the top of her head. "Don't fash yourself, lass. It'll all work out, you'll see."

She'd already seen—the same picture she saw every time she thought of him going out on a shout.

⚓

The crew began painting the rescue boat the following morning. Thin primer coats were applied to the inside, outside, and bottom. Because a light drizzle had set in and the humidity was high, this had to dry for twa days.

While the primer coat dried, Rob took his crew up to Fern's

192

house and laid out the plans for the interior. None of them were experienced plumbers, so he showed what was required before the floors could be installed. He worked with them, relieved with how quickly they learned and how much they accomplished in twa days.

The following day, work resumed on the rescue boat. The inside and outside were each given one finish coat, but the final coat on the keel was postponed until the day before the launch.

Rob was anxious to apply the final finish to the interior and exterior but the drizzle turned to a steady downpour. Once again his crew returned to Fern's house, and finished the plumbing work that evening.

The rest of the week the crew alternated between the boat and the house. After the final coat of paint was applied to the boat, the crew laid the floor in the house. Rob instructed them in the construction of the interior walls, choosing one short wall and showing them the plans and technique before leaving them hard at work. He had a quick dinner at home, then trotted down to the shed. It was time to paint the numbers the Royal National Lifeboat Institution had assigned him on each side of the cabin in bold black paint. *Please don't let them ask me to remove them once the boat is launched and inspected.*

Above the numbers, in smaller white letters, would be *Innisbraw Rescue.* The white and black would show well against the brilliant red he had chosen for the large cabin. Also, the name *Maggie* would be painted in white letters on both sides of the black prow.

Graham, still at the shed, had the stencils, paint, and brushes ready. They each took a side.

Though rain plomped down the next day, they worked on the skids. By late afternoon the final piece was laid and they were ready for the launch. The skies filled with black, heavy clouds as they gave a final coat of paint to the boat's keel.

At kirk, Hugh offered a prayer for a successful launch.

Though Rob prayed diligently for peace of soul, his heart still beat faster than normal and he had a hard time concentrating on the lesson Hugh taught that morning.

Maggie must have sensed Rob's unease. She clasped his hand and held on tightly throughout the service.

Or did she have her own fears?

Rob was thronged by well-wishers once they were outside.

"It looks like the weather's clearing," Alec MacDonald said.

Angus grasped his arm. "We're planning on watching from Innis Fell. I know you don't need a crowd around you on the shore."

"Thank ye, Angus. 'Tis going to be too dangerous for anyone to be too close."

"I'll pass the word, then. There's plenty of room up on the fell for those who want to watch."

Rob sought out Elspeth. "If it's no' blowing a gale, we'll launch the *Maggie* on the morra, but you may no' want to watch the whole thing. It'll take a lot of time to get her from the shed to the water."

"If I see any activity down there, I'll no' miss a minute of it, even if the rain is plomping down." Her faded blue eyes glowed with an inner spark. "I know 'twill be hard for you to sleep the night, lad, but don't fash yourself. By the morra's een, the *Maggie* will be tied up at her berth where she belongs."

"I pray you're right. I hope this whole thing hasn't been a wild plan dreamed up by an eejit."

Her mouth fell open. "Don't even think such a thing, Rob Savage. Our Lord's hand has been on this from the beginning."

"So much depends on a successful launch."

"And successful it shall be." She stood back and eyed him critically. "You've lost weight again, lad. Are you no' eating?"

"As much as usual—too much."

"And working twice as hard, I'll warrant." Her gnarled finger poked his chest. "Stop by my cottage on your way to the shed on the morra's morn. Malcolm finally found me a few almonds and I've baked some of those almond scones Maggie says you like so much."

"Och, Elspeth, you know the way to a man's heart, and that's the truth."

The family ate dinner before walking over to Fern's house.

"I can't believe how quickly it's all come together," Fern said, tears blurring the blue of her eyes. "I can't thank you enough, Rob."

"You're more than welcome, lass. The crew should be able to put in twa or three days next week. After the *Maggie's* launched, they'll have to outfit her with all the rescue supplies. When that's done, they'll be working here full time. Your house should be ready sometime around the mids of July at the latest."

"I don't want to take you away from the rescue boat. I know how much it means to have it ready as soon as possible."

"You won't. Come autumn she should be certified seaworthy and ready for shouts."

She laid a hand on his arm. "Just don't fash yourself about the morra. Everything will go as you planned."

He tried to hide his surprise. She seemed as perceptive as his Maggie. "'Tis that obvious, then? I thought I was doing a guid job hiding my fears."

"I just know how I'd feel, is all. And remember, I'm planning to help Maggie train your crew in medical procedures."

"I'm grateful for your help."

"Have you heard from John? I thought he might be home by now."

"He's working on it. He's given his notice, but he still has to finish his work at the university."

"Of course. I forgot how long that can take."

Maggie came inside, holding Robbie's hand. "I found this skellum on top of the dyke, teetering for a fall. Those capstones are sharp."

Rob picked up his son. "Where was Shep?"

"That's what alerted me. He was barking and gathering himself to jump when I got there. Katie was trying to help, but she's no' strong enough to lift the lad down."

"What are we going to do with you?" Rob hugged the lad. "The dyke is no' for climbing, understand?"

Robbie grinned and clung to his faither's neck, shaking his head. "No' for climbing."

"It's my fault," Rob said. "I wouldn't let him in here because of all the tools lying around. I'll know better next time."

Maggie swatted at him. "It'll be something entirely different next time. Your lad wants to explore everything."

"Then he is my lad, aren't you?" Rob squeezed his son. "But you have to learn what's right and what's wrong. I just hope you don't have to learn it the hard way."

"Hard way," Robbie echoed, shaking his head with such enthusiasm his curls bounced.

Later that evening, Rob took the family to see the *Maggie*. When they reached the shed, he picked up Robbie. "You're no' going to explore now, lad. This place really is dangerous." He cautioned Katie to hold Fern's hand tightly, opened the shed door, and turned on the lights.

Maggie gasped as she walked toward the boat. "Och, Rob, she's so bonnie. I can't believe it."

The boat looked enormous in the shed, the red and black paint shining in the glare from bright arc lights Rob had installed so they could work day or night.

Tears filled her eyes as she hugged him. "You've done it. The dream that started almost four years ago has finally come true."

Rob ducked his head. *If she floats.*

"Can we go up there?" Katie pointed to the deck far above her head.

"No' this een. The paint's still tacky so there's no ladder in place. But as soon as she's in her berth, I'll give you the grand tour."

Maggie walked around the boat. "She doesn't look a thing like the Barra lifeboat. How could you take those plans on paper and turn them into such a wonder?"

"A lot of hard work. And there's no way I could have completed it in time myself. It would have taken me at least twa years without my building crew. She's over sixteen and a half metres long."

Fern wiped her eyes. "It makes me proud my failure played a part in your success."

Och, all she had done when running her own boatyard, and how long she had held on when most experienced men would have given up ...

He could never have done all she accomplished while having to spend his early mornings and evenings parenting a young lass. "Don't ever call it a failure, Fern. You gave it your best. You can never expect more from yourself."

Chapter Twenty-seven

After trying for hours to fall asleep, Rob crawled out of bed and sat in front of the fire so he wouldn't awaken Maggie. "Please, Lord," he whispered, staring into the glowing embers. "Please make this work. Like Fern, I've done my verra best and so much depends on it." He closed his eyes and leaned his head back.

Faces of the fishermen who had perished at sea since he had come to Innisbraw paraded before his closed lids. All that grief, lives changed forever. Faithers and mithers burying their lads or attending a memorial service, widows trying to scratch out a living, and bairns growing up without a faither's luve and example.

If the *Maggie* performed as well as he hoped, a successful boat-building business on Innisbraw would follow. With work coming in, he could hire more lads, reunite families, and the island could grow and prosper. Maggie's Cottage Weaving Industry was off to a good start. Soon the lasses would return to the island of their birth. In time, lads and lasses would fall in luve, new families would be formed, and bairnies born out of those unions.

His breath caught in his throat.

The *Maggie* had to float. She had to.

Clutching her pillow, Maggie battled her fears again. Over and over she imagined the Lord throwing the stars into the heavens. But an image of Rob sinking beneath the waves always followed. She recited Bible verses she had memorized, repeating 2 Timothy 1:7 over and over. "For God gave us not a spirit of fearfulness; but of power and love and discipline."

Brand those words on my soul, Faither. Rob's worked so long and hard to bring Innisbraw its own rescue boat. Give me the faith to get through the morra.

⁂

Rob woke with a start.

Maggie leaned over him, eyes soft with love. "I'm sorry to wake you, but you were blethering in your sleep."

He looked around, bewildered, until he realized he was in his rocker. "I'm sorry, lass. I'm the one who woke you."

She sat on his lap and cuddled close. "You're cold. The fire's almost oot."

He yawned and flexed his neck. "What time is it?"

"Almost 0500. Annie's stirring, so I'll have to suckle her soon. You've been oot here a long time."

"I couldn't sleep, and didn't want to wake you with my tossing and turning." He nuzzled her neck. "You're warm."

"That's because I stayed abed." She ran her fingers through his hair. Probably checking for sweat. "Bad dreams?"

"Don't think so. I can't remember what I was dreaming."

"Why don't you come back to bed? I'll turn the boiler on for your shower."

His smile was fleeting, but it was the best he could do. "Mmm, sounds guid, but 'tis getting late. I'm meeting Graham and the crew at the shed at 0530."

"So early?"

"We have to start moving the boat so we'll be ready to put her into the water at high tide."

Her fingers brushed his cheeks. "'Twill take that long to move her?"

"It may. We'll have to winch her by hand and I don't know how long that will take. It won't be easy."

"So you're going soon?" More than regret in her voice. A hint of fear, maybe?

His own regret turned to guilt. "A lot to be getting on with."

"Then let me start your coffee." She gave him a quick kiss and got up, belting her dressing gown against the chill as she went into the kitchen.

He got out of his rocker and stretched—stiff all over. He added peats to the fireplace and went into the bathing room to shave. When he turned off the water, Annie's fussing carried from the living room.

Maggie had the bairnie in her lap, changing her hippen. "Have you taken a keek ootside? The sky is clear. Looks like you'll have a bonnie day for the launch."

He kissed Annie's plump cheek. "Sounds guid." He waited until Maggie had their lass settled to breast, then kissed his wife tenderly. Her lips were soft with promise. More guilt about leaving so early.

When their lips parted, she took his hand. "I'll be praying. All the day."

"Thank ye, luve." He squeezed her fingers. "So will I." He dressed, hands trembling like an auld man's. He put on faded, patched denims and one of his oldest shirts with his gansey sweater to ward off the early morning chill. Though his stomach didn't feel ready to eat, he picked up the bacon buttery Maggie had left on the bunker near his thermos. Somebody in the crew would eat it if he couldn't. The coffee looked as if it had perked long enough, so he moved it to the back of the stove.

Maggie finished burping Annie and returned her to her cradle, then came into the kitchen and filled Rob's thermos. "Is that bacon piece going to be enough?"

"Aye. Thank ye, lass."

"I don't suppose you'll be home for dinner."

"There's no way I can. Once we start winching, we can't stop till she's at the water's edge."

She gripped his arm. "Please eat the piece, Rob, even if you have to choke it down. You'll need it for energy."

"I promise I'll try. Elspeth has some scones for me to pick up, too. I'll do the best I can."

"That's no' good enough."

The words popped out of his mouth. "What if she doesn't float?"

She gazed up at him, heart aching at the pain in his voice. This put him one giant step closer to the time he would be risking his life in the sea. But he had laboured too long and too hard to allow her fears to keep her from saying what he needed to hear. "Look at me," she said.

He averted his eyes.

"No' over my head. Look at *me*, Rob." She waited until his gaze met hers. "You once told me we had to have faith, that without it we had nowt. Remember?"

He nodded.

"All those missions you flew, I was afraid you would die but I clung to your words, claiming our Faither's faith when mine faltered and listening to His still, quiet voice that you would come back to me alive. And even that last terrible time ... you did come back to me alive, something nobody could believe when they saw your airieplane after the crash." She framed his face between her palms. "'Tis all right to be fearful, luve, 'tis only human. But you have to have faith in what our Lord has mandated. The *Maggie* will float. Hang on to that thought. She will float."

He picked her up and cradled her close, face buried in her hair.

She hugged his neck, trying to impart her faith through her embrace. She had no doubt the boat would float. Though the very thought of what might happen when it did terrified her, she had to make him believe, too.

"I'll have someone call you when we reach the water," he said. "Come stand with me so we can watch her float together."

"I'll be there." She watched from the kitchen window as he vaulted the dyke and raced down the path. Could she have said more to encourage him or had her own fears for his ultimate safety held her back?

Och, Faither, please be with Rob the day. Give him Your assurance and guard his heart against his fears.

She shook her head as she set a pot of brose to boil for Robbie's breakfast. Rob feared the *Maggie* wouldn't float ... and she feared what would happen to him when it did. What a fankle.

It took a long time to grease the skids with a thick layer of axle grease, dismantle the cradle, and pull the boat into position on the skids. The winching itself was a slow, tedious, back-breaking job. When the boat finally left the shed by the large door, shouts rang out from the fell. It looked like everybody on the island had gathered there.

Rob took off his gansey and wiped the sweat from his face with his shirt sleeve before bending to the task again.

The job became easier as the shore started its downward slope. By noon, they had the boat at the water's edge.

Rob called Alan MacKinnon over. "Would you go telephone Maggie for me? We have a few minutes before high tide, but I don't want to leave."

"Aye. Be back in a tick."

Rob stood back, looking at the boat. Tears filled his eyes.

She loomed over him, tall and proud, the sunlight glinting off her new paint. It was as though the vessel was talking to him. *Don't doubt. I was born to sail, and sail I will.*

Maggie appeared at his side, panting. "I was watching from our entry." She grasped his hand. "I came as soon as I saw her about to reach the water."

So soft and warm, that hand. "We're almost ready to cut the ropes. Will you ... will you come aboard with me?" He repressed the fear he could be putting his Maggie in danger. He would be close enough to grab her and swim ashore if the boat sank.

Her smile shone bright as the sun overhead. "I'd luve to."

He lifted her over the top of the skid, helped her climb the rope ladder, and followed her up. "Go stand in front of the cabin on the port side. I'll catch you right up." When he reached her side, he bowed his head and silently prayed the three words that Hugh called a believer's most potent prayer. *Your perfect will.* He took a deep breath and raised a trembling hand to Graham, who nodded.

Axes raised.

Rob dropped his arm.

The axes descended, severing the ropes holding the boat back.

The *Maggie* moved.

Chapter Twenty-eight

Rob grabbed Maggie's hand as the boat gained momentum. Bile filled his mouth as her stern slid into the water with a huge splash. He held his breath as her bow dipped into the water.

Whistles and shouts filled the air as she moved backward into deeper water. A huge roar resounded from the fell. The *Maggie* was afloat!

Maggie sobbed.

Rob's heart almost burst. He dashed inside and took the helm, swiping his sleeve across his face. *Thank Ye, Lord, thank Ye, Lord, thank Ye.* He put the diesel engines on idle and pushed the start button. As they chugged to life, he eased them into reverse and turned the helm.

The boat moved slowly backward into deeper and deeper water.

When she was well clear of the dock, he put the engines into low-forward and manoeuvred the boat toward her designated berth at the shed dock. Anxiety tightened his chest. Though he had memorized the steps Malcolm had told him and gone over them time and time again in his mind, the reality was terrifying. If he came in too fast, he could damage the dock as well as the boat. But really this was no different than jockeying his B-17 into her space on the hardstands after a flight. The tight band constricting his ribs relaxed. He eased the starboard side of the boat into position and cut the engines.

Maggie had anticipated his move and was already throwing the stem line to Graham who stood ready on the dock.

Rob sprinted aft and tossed the stern line to Danny MacIntosh.

When they had the boat safely moored, the kirk bell rang and crowds of folk streamed down the path from the top of the fell. Graham and the lads who had helped build the boat swarmed over the railing and leaped on board. They surrounded Rob, pummeling his back and shouting their congratulations.

He grinned so broadly, it felt as if his face would split. He shook hands and slapped backs as he made his way through the crowd of lads to where Maggie stood, tears spilling down her face. He scooped her up into his arms. "We did it, Maggie," he said into her ear. "The Lord and you and me—we did it."

She was sobbing so hard she could only nod.

He kissed her fervently.

She buried her face against his neck. "You did it, luve," she said brokenly. "You've brought life back to Innisbraw."

Graham pushed his way through the lads and pumped Rob's hand. "What a sight. What a bonnie, bonnie sight."

Rob kissed Maggie's cheek and set her on her feet. "There's someone on shore who deserves a salute, lass. Want to help me?"

She wiped her cheeks with the backs of her hands and nodded.

"Stand back, lads," he shouted. "'Tis time you heard this boat's voice."

He pulled Maggie into the cabin and showed her a short rope hanging above her head. "Pull it slowly three times."

Three loud wails split the air.

Rob guided Maggie over to the port railing. "See Elspeth up there? She's standing on her entry."

"I do."

"Come on lads, stand at attention like you're on parade. Now, on the count of three, snap a salute to the grand auld lady up there watching us. This boat was her dream too." He counted and when he reached three, Rob, Graham, and all the lads snapped brisk salutes in the direction of Elspeth's cottage.

By then, the shore and pier were covered with the folk who had been on the fell or watching from the safety of the path. Paddy McDonald and his musicians pushed their way up the pier, playing a rollicking reel. Fern carried Annie towards them as Katie clung to the back of her sweater to keep from being swept away in the crowd. Rinait, next to Fern, pulled Robbie in his cairt.

Rob grabbed Graham's arm and pointed. "On you go—rescue them. I'll have the lads put the gangplank in place before you get back."

When Fern, Rinait, and the bairns were safely on board, Rob scooped up Robbie. "Well, what do you think, lad? You're finally on Faither's boat."

Robbie giggled and hugged Rob's neck shouting, "Boat! Faither's boat!"

Maggie took Annie so Fern could have a look around. Graham and Rinait had already disappeared into the cabin.

Eyes wide, Katie stared around her as she tugged at Rob's sleeve. "Uncle Rob, why is the floor so rough?"

"Smart lass to notice," he said, hugging her. "We put sand in the paint when we did the deck. 'Tis so you won't slip and fall when it's wet."

"It's all so pretty and shiny. No' like that reeky auld boat we sailed on before."

Rob touched Maggie's shoulder. "Take Fern and Katie with you and explore the cabin. Just make sure the lass doesn't go near any of the equipment."

"Shouldn't we wait? 'Tis getting wild out there." She indicated the crowd on the shore. Many of the younger folk had removed their shoes and danced to the music, bare feet sending spurts of sand into the air while others milled about, shouting and gesturing.

"Better take advantage while you're aboard now. On the morra we start getting her ready for service. On you go. You helped build this boat too. You deserve to see what you sacrificed so much for."

She shook her head, probably at his choice of words, but her innate curiosity won out. She, Fern, and Katie entered the cabin just after Rinait and Graham slipped out the door.

Rob smiled at the freckle-faced redhead's tight grasp on Graham's arm. "Well, what do you think, Rinait? Was it worth all those lonely eens?"

She blushed. "'Tis bonnie. I'm so proud of Graham."

"And rightly so. I never could have built this boat without him."

Graham threw back his head and laughed. "Och, you'd have built her. If you think I'm stubborn, Rinait, I don't hold a candle to Rob here."

Rob squirmed. "I'm thinking our schedule's going to have to slip a day. So many people had a hand in helping build this boat and they all deserve to have a keek. What say we put off bringing that equipment aboard and escort groups of folk all day the morra for a quick tour?"

"I like that. But mind you, there aren't really that many people who had an active hand."

"There isn't a person on this island who hasn't spent time in prayer, and prayer's what made it happen, lad."

"That's me sorted, then." Graham studied the deck planks. "Why don't we bring them aboard in groups of ten?"

"Sounds guid."

⁓⁂⁓

That night, Rob added peats to the fire, then sat back in his rocker next to Maggie's and held her hand. "I wish I could have watched her enter the water from the fell. That must have been quite a sight."

"I was thinking the same thing."

He squeezed her hand. "We do that a lot, don't we? Have the same thought at the same time?"

Maggie smiled. "Of course we do." She held up her right hand, displaying the inscribed ring he had given her. "That's what happens when you're connected mind, heart, body, and soul."

He ran his lips across her knuckles. "Did you ever think it possible to be so closely connected with another human being?"

"I suppose 'tis what happens when the Lord brings twa people together He had destined for one another."

He dove into the depths of her violet-blue eyes. "There's no way I could ever luve you more than I do at this very moment, yet every day my luve for you grows deeper."

She blinked back tears. "You're my life. Without you, I might continue to live physically, but I'd be nowt but an empty shell."

He got up, pulled her into his arms, and sat again, cradling her in his lap. "I meant what I said the day." He tangled his fingers in her hair. "I never could have designed or built that boat without you."

⚓

She hushed him with a kiss. She was so proud of him a warmth infused her body. He was such a good man, such a dedicated man, she still couldn't believe God had chosen him for her. *Och, Lord, take care of this precious gift of a husband.* She pulled back and looked at him. "How are you going to test the boat's stability when we're entering the season of calm seas?"

He turned his gaze to the burning peat. "There are ways." Only a whisper.

She cupped his chin in her palm and turned his face. "What ways?"

"I'm no' sure you really want to ken."

"But I do. How else can I pray if I don't ken what to pray for?"

He pulled her close and pressed her head against his chest. "You'll no' like it."

"I'm no' a bairn. I'm your wife. I have the right to hear your plans."

He was silent for a moment, then sighed deeply. "All right, I'll tell you, but you must know there's no other way. The boat has to be tested before the stormy months."

She forced herself to calm and nodded.

"We'll use the surf around Heuch Fell."

Och, no' Heuch Fell. Those were the most dangerous waters around the Hebrides. The only reason fishermen never got into trouble there was that none were foolish enough to try to navigate the narrow strait that ran between the fell and the rocks. She stiffened, biting back a panic-fueled protest. "And how can you get close enough to the rocks without going aground? You know there isn't a boat around that ever ventures near those waters." As hard as she tried, she couldn't keep her voice from trembling.

"We'll go in at high tide. The Barra Lifeboat has already agreed to stand off a ways in case the *Maggie* doesn't right herself when she capsizes."

"And who will be aboard?" she whispered.

207

"Myself and five of my strongest swimmers." This time it was Rob who turned her tear-streaked face to his. "Faith, luve, that's what it comes down to, remember? I know the *Maggie* will right herself, but I have to prove it before I can build the same rescue boat for others. It never occurred to me I'd be building anything but fishing boats, but with all the interest, I'm sure we'll get orders for rescue boats, too." He traced the outline of her jaw. "Once the *Maggie* floated, I knew I'd designed and built her right. The waters around Heuch Fell are the roughest in the Hebrides, even rougher than those around Barra Head, so it's the ultimate test. And she'll pass the test, luve. I know she will."

"But can't someone else test her for you?"

"Of course no'. And I'll no' do it until I know how to operate that boat as well as I knew how to fly the *Bonnie Maggie*. I'm no' daft, lass. 'Twill be weeks, mebbe even months before I'm ready."

"But you spent years flying, no' weeks or months."

His smile brought a niggle of irritation. "Getting an airieplane into the air and keeping her there is a wee bit harder than steering a boat. Besides, I already have the advantage of knowing how to operate controls and do several tasks in order. The main thing I have to learn is this boat's particular idiosyncrasies. They all have them, just like no twa airieplanes behave exactly alike. That's what I have to learn before I tackle Heuch Fell."

She closed her eyes and nestled her face against his neck. "Thank ye for being honest," she said, voice a whisper again. "Now I ken how to pray."

Chapter Twenty-nine

Three Royal National Lifeboat Institution inspectors arrived early the next day, the morning sun glinting off the brass buttons on their navy-blue uniforms.

Rob was on board the *Maggie*, roping off the cabin doorway so the touring islanders could look in but not accidentally engage the engines or touch any of the sensitive equipment.

"Mister Savage," the leader of the group hailed from the dock.

Rob dropped the rope, stomach clenching. This was the visit he had been dreading. Though he had sent detailed plans of his rescue boat to the RNLI and kept them abreast of all of the progress, he hadn't expected them to arrive until he'd had time to train his crew and conduct some sea trials. And certainly not when he wore auld denims and a patched Jacobite shirt. He clambered down to the dock and shook all three hands as they were offered. "I didn't expect you so soon," he said to David Elliott, the Englishman who seemed to be in charge.

Elliott's grey eyes narrowed as his gaze swept over the *Maggie*. "We've been in Scotland for several weeks, doing some spot inspections in the Shetlands and Orkneys. I see you've had a successful launch."

"Just yestreen—yesterday—" Rob ground his teeth over lapsing into Scots. "Come aboard. We have the gangplank down so the island folk can have a look before we bring the rescue equipment aboard."

The men all boarded quickly, heads pivoting as though attempting to absorb all the differences this Yank had built into his boat. Surely they were all members of the board that had poured over his plans. But they still stared as though awestruck by the actual sight of the large cabin with its many windows and the size of the boat.

"I'm gobsmacked," the man called Graves muttered beneath his breath.

Might as well get it over with. "Is there any place you'd like to see first?"

"The engine room will do for a start." Elliott's gruff voice did nothing to alleviate Rob's concern.

Rob led them to a hatch behind the cabin. "I'll go down first and turn on the light, then leave you to it. There isn't room for four down there at one time."

Though he could hear the murmur of voices coming from the engine room, none of the men offered a word when they finally turned off the light, climbed the ladder, and gestured for him to close the hatch.

Elliott entered the large cabin next, the other twa men almost tripping over his heels in their eagerness to join him. They spent a long time inspecting the dual controls, one for the coxswain—who Rob had decided to call the commander—and a duplicate for the second coxswain.

Elliott nodded at the FFR. "I see you've installed a radar unit. Are you familiar with how it works?"

An easy question to answer, that. "I am, and my crew will be trained in its use before we apply for certification."

Some raised eyebrows.

"From your correspondence, we were surprised to learn that you expect each of your crew to also have medical training," Graves said. "Aren't you asking a great deal from men who will receive no wages for their efforts?"

"How do you put a price on a soul you've saved from hypothermia, drowning, or life-threatening injuries? My crew are all local lads, ex-military with the exception of one. They're looking forward to the opportunity to save as many as possible and they have guid-paying jobs already."

A curt nod from Graves.

Rob explained the cupboards would house medicaments and demonstrated the use of the stretcher racks. "The center of the cabin will be used for artificial respiration when needed." His heart sank at their skeptical looks. "We've learned from experience that if AR is given early enough, many can be saved. Even if the victim has stopped breathing."

Once the three men had examined every inch of the *Maggie*, their dour expressions remained.

They must have already decided not to license her. *Please open their minds to something different. I don't want to be operating a rescue boat without their license on my wall.*

Elliott pivoted on his heel. "Is there somewhere we can go to talk in comfort?"

"My office. It's in the boatshed." Rob waited until the men were on the dock, then pulled in the gangplank and secured it before climbing over the railing. "You'll find it quiet the day," he said as he led them down the pier. "I've given my building crew the day off before they start cleaning up."

Though there was some clutter in the center of the shed and piles of sawdust beneath several of the saws, the men appeared surprised by how organized the crew had left the hand tools and equipment bins.

Rob grabbed a chair from Graham's office and pulled it into his.

Instead of sitting immediately, the three men wandered around, studying the pictures of Rob's planes and crews on the walls and peeking into the small room off to one side.

"That's where Control will sit," Rob said before they could ask. "He will have the latest radio I could find for receiving Mayday calls from boats or Maritime Rescue and communicating with the *Maggie*. And he'll also throw that switch to activate the siren we're installing on the top of our highest fell so it can be heard no matter where the crew is working. That phone is for him to contact the infirmary to prepare them for any injured they might expect."

Elliott's stiff stance relaxed. "I'd forgotten you have an infirmary on Innisbraw. Very handy, I must say."

"With Doctor John McGrath in charge and two of the finest nurses on staff, any victims we bring here will have a good chance of surviving."

The man called Graves whirled around. "John McGrath is here? I didn't realize he'd left the Royal Infirmary."

"You've heard of him then?"

Graves grinned. "Heard of him? Goodness, man, he saved my son's leg when it was almost severed by a German machine gun. There isn't a finer orthopaedic surgeon in the United Kingdom—perhaps in the world."

"He's not here for good yet, but he will be soon."

Elliott cleared his throat. "Well, I'd say we have a decision to make."

The other men nodded in solemn agreement.

Elliott sat back. "You realize your boat is unlike any other in our service. She's much larger, for one thing. And if you are correct in your assumption that the air baffles will right her if she capsizes, you have eliminated the need for an air bladder on your aft-deck—and there is the large cabin, of course."

Rob nodded. No need to waste words on the obvious.

"Your design has caused our board to miss many an evening tea while we discussed what to do with this boat of yours." Elliott paused and puffed frantically for a moment until the pipe was glowing again. "Added to our dilemma were several requests from other Outer Hebridean services to consider allowing them a boat just like yours."

Rob's breath froze. He hadn't realized how far word had traveled about his rescue boat. Would he be asked to build them?

Elliott reached into his breast pocket and pulled out a piece of paper, handing it to Rob. "This is only temporary, of course, until your boat passes its sea and capsizing trials. If it does—and I personally will be aboard during your capsizing trial—the RNLI has decided to add a second category to those lifeboats we license and oversee. That of 'Rescue Boat.'" He extended his hand to Rob. "Congratulations, Commander Savage. I trust your trials will not disappoint us."

Graham arrived a few minutes after the men quit Rob's office.

Rob still sat on the corner of his desk, holding the paper, eyes filled with tears. He held it out for Graham to read.

All the long hours and hard labour had paid off. Once the *Maggie* passed her trials, Innisbraw would have its own officially licensed Coastal Rescue Boat.

⚓

Rob left Graham to organize the tours for the islanders and ran up the hill to home. Something this important couldn't be told on the telephone or wait all day. He found Maggie singing a ballad in the Gaelic as she hung washing in the side yard.

Robbie wrestled with Shep.

Annie lay on a nearby blanket, struggling to put her bare toes into her mouth.

"Rob!" Maggie dropped a sheet into the basket. "What's happened? If you were smiling any harder your face would crack."

He grabbed her up, whirled her around, and thrust a paper into her hand. "Read this and you'll understand."

Robbie dove for Rob, trying to climb his leg.

"Show me how far you can throw a stick for Shep," Rob said.

Robbie raced to find a stray twig.

She read the paper quickly, then looked up at him, face beaming. "Och, it's happened, luve. I know how you've worried about the RNLI certifying the boat and they've done it."

"No' yet, lass, but they will." He took her into his arms. "Our Lord had it all planned, Maggie, from the first idea He planted into my stubborn head to this. He guided your faither to the books I needed to design the boat, then made certain I no' only survived that crash in '43 but came out of it able to do the work ahead of me. And every lad He provided knew his turn well and everything I needed was available. Mebbe no' as soon as I wanted, but in His perfect time. How could I ever have doubted Him? The Holy Spirit must have been working doubles to pull this off."

Maggie threw her arms around Rob's neck. "His perfect will, luve," she whispered, as he picked her up.

"For ever and ever and ever," he said softly before his lips claimed hers.

Chapter Thirty

Malcolm delivered the wetsuits for the crew that evening. Rob and Graham laid out a course on paper for the swimming test, keeping in mind that none of the lads who had volunteered to crew the rescue boat had been in the water for some time. At gloaming, Rob and Tormad used the fisherman's coble, a small rowboat, to run a line of buoys from the shore to the entrance of the harbour.

Early the next morning, Rob and Graham gathered the nine volunteer crewmen in the *Maggie*'s cabin and issued each his red wetsuits, showing them how to work the tight rubber suits over their bare legs, bodies, and arms.

Groans and a few laughs filled the cabin when everyone—including Rob—struggled learning to walk wearing the fins on their feet. When they were all suited up and could manage to walk without tripping, Graham clasped Rob's arm. "Don't kill yourself trying to be the first ashore. Those lads are a lot younger than you."

"Thirty-one isn't ancient, but I have to admit, I've never been for a long swim in cold sea water."

"Godspeed." Graham leaped to the dock and raised a hand in greeting as Malcolm approached the boat.

A broad grin creased the skipper's weathered face as he clapped Rob's shoulder. "Ready, Commander?"

"We're ready."

Graham untied the mooring ropes and tossed them aboard as Malcolm entered the cabin and took the helm. A moment later the twin diesels chugged to life and the *Maggie* eased away from the dock.

Rob studied the lads' faces. They looked anxious, but all their eyes were clear and sparkling with excitement. Hugh must be right—they had managed to put the war behind them. Paddy McDonald stood on deck, swinging his arms vigorously. Several of the other lads copied him.

Rob flexed his neck and shoulders. He wasn't afraid he couldn't make shore—but it would be nicer not to be too badly beaten by the lads he would be commanding. When they reached the outer buoy, Rob lined the lads up along the top deck railing. "During a shout, you'll be jumping from the taffrail, but there isn't enough room for all of you to go at the same time down there so it's a bit more of a drop from here. There'll be no diving," he instructed, voice firm. "Just like you'll never dive in a rescue attempt. You'll jump into the water feet first. Is that understood?"

They all nodded, but Paddy did not look pleased with this turn of events. The lad had undoubtedly planned to make a long dive, giving him a head start.

Rob pointed. "Follow the buoys. You can see Tormad at the second buoy and he'll keep the coble even with you all the way in. Don't try to be heroes. If you tire before you reach shore, he'll throw you a life ring to put over your head. Use it. That's an order."

They nodded again.

Rob scrambled up on the railing. "Don't try to stand. Just crouch here and when I say 'three,' jump. Godspeed."

When they were all on the railing, Paddy leaned forward.

"Mind you, jump, don't dive." Rob held up his hand. "One, twa, three." He jumped. The shock of the icy water stunned Rob for a second. He pulled himself to the surface and took a deep breath, then began stroking, counting to himself. *One, twa, three, breathe. One, twa, three, breathe.* Quickly he established a rhythm. He had never felt so strong in the water and his left arm moved as effortlessly as his right. He kept himself within the buoys, but paid no attention to the swimmers around him. As always, he competed with himself, not others. But he also didn't want to embarrass himself and lose their respect. At a little over six-foot-five, his long arms and legs gave him an advantage over the shorter lads, but he was several years older, so he paced himself carefully.

As the wetsuit warmed the water trapped against his body, the

215

chill of the icy sea faded.

He stroked and pulled, stroked and pulled, fluttering his feet, adding speed with the swimming fins.

Another swimmer neared his scissoring fins.

Rob didn't break his rhythm to see who it was. By counting the buoys, he figured he was over three-quarters of the way to the shore. He thought he heard shouts and whistles, but the tight hood covering his ears made him unsure.

Soon, fatigue factored in. His strokes weren't quite as long or as powerful. He kicked it up a notch and forced himself to reach farther, pull harder. His left shoulder burned, but he ignored the discomfort. Almost there, no quitting now. His right hand suddenly dug into the sand as he pulled it toward his body. He looked up. Already in shallow water? He scrambled to his feet and waded awkwardly ashore, chest heaving. He'd made it! He pulled down the hood, unzipped the front of his wetsuit to his waist, and tugged off his flippers as Graham came trotting across the sand, smile broad.

"You didn't tell me you were part seal." He laughed. "You just beat Paddy by at least five strokes."

Rob looked back, panting heavily.

Paddy knelt on the sand behind him, a look of disbelief on his ruddy face. Ewan MacGregor and Matthew Campbell battled it out just at the shoreline. Brothers Artair and Duncan Frazer were only a few strokes back, followed closely by James MacIver, Stephen Ross, Danny MacIntosh, and Neil MacLean, all almost neck and neck.

They had all made it, and he in the front! He clapped Graham on the back. "We've got a crew!" he exclaimed, "and, what a crew!"

There was a great deal of hilarity while the lads changed at the boatshed. The brothers each claimed to have beaten the other by a stroke, while the others teased Stephen Ross, claiming he was the last ashore. Only Paddy McDonald was quiet, his usual good-natured grin absent, most likely because he had boasted that no one could outswim someone who had learned to swim in the Irish Sea.

Rob toweled dry and dressed, enjoying himself enormously. This was so much like the camaraderie he and his B-17 crews had enjoyed after a successful strike. He passed among the lads, offering congratulations on a job well done. When they were all dressed, he stood by the door and raised his hand for silence. "I want to welcome every one of you as crewmembers of the Innisbraw Coastal Rescue Boat *Maggie*." He gave them a thumbs-up. "Well done, you. I couldn't be any prouder."

Paddy came forward, extending his hand. "We'll be proud to serve with you in command." He shook Rob's hand vigorously. The rest of the lads shook his hand and saluted smartly before they filed out the door.

Blood roared in Rob's ears. There was no longer any doubt about the outcome of the boat-building enterprise. With a crew like this aboard the prototype, success was a given.

Chapter Thirty-one

Maggie's Cottage Weaving Industry continued to grow as young lasses returned to Innisbraw where there was finally an opportunity to earn a living. Every week, Malcolm brought at least one on his regular post run. Family reunions became commonplace as parents and siblings welcomed the lasses some had not seen since they went off to help in war efforts.

Several of the men built a large addition onto Mary MacCrae's weaving shop. Looms were set up, ready to accommodate the returning lasses. The older women had already completed hundreds of metres of woven material and were very adept at instructing their daughters in Rinait's pattern.

⚓

Maggie welcomed Elizabeth MacGruder, the marketing consultant from Edinburgh, to the island the last week of June.

"I'm surprised by how much you've already woven," she said in her broad, burred Edinburgh English. "I like your choice of colours. What did you use for dyes?"

"Local plants and herbs," Maggie said. "They've been used for generations by the local islanders."

"They'll not bleed or fade?"

"Och, no. See the skirt I have on?" Maggie fingered the pleats. "'Tis over eight years auld and the colours are as true today as when it was woven."

"Excellent." Elizabeth handed Maggie a slip of paper. "Here's your first order, and you already have enough material woven to fill it. I'll take the goods back with me and you should expect a check as well as another order in a few days. Keep on weaving."

A sigh of relief escaped Maggie's lips. "I was afraid we were

218

too late for the autumn market."

"Normally you would be, but there's such a need for woolens since the war ended, the garment industry's been turned on its head. Just keep producing as much as you can. I guarantee I can sell every yard."

Rob's lads showed a remarkable affinity for rescue work. They had laboured a week learning how to work the transfer sling, using Malcolm's *Sea Rouk* when she was in port or one of the other fishing vessels when available. Not only was the rescue crew being trained, but the crews of the trawlers and creelers obtained invaluable knowledge should an emergency arise involving their own vessels.

Rob also spent a great deal of time with his crew, taking them into the sea, where he showed them the correct way to use their swimming fins to propel them deeper under water. "Pay close attention to what I'm teaching, lads," he said. "There may come a time when you have a victim slip from your grasp and sink beneath the waves if he's no' wearing a life jacket. If you don't know how to safely search for him, you'll lose him for biddy certain, and mebbe your own life." They also swam long distances in the harbour for hours every day, building up their endurance.

Maggie often stood on their stone-flagged entry, looking at the buoys Rob had set around the various points of the harbour where the water was the correct depth for what he was teaching. She even borrowed Rob's binoculars and watched the men diving, holding her own breath until they resurfaced.

One time, she was amazed to see each of them struggle to the surface holding a heavy building stone. She supposed that was to train them in what it would feel like to pull a rescue victim's weight up from the sea. A sharp stab of fear pierced her chest. Sometime in the future, Rob could very well be diving and searching for a victim. She dropped to her knees, praying again for faith that the Lord would see that Rob always returned to her.

Fern accompanied Rob as he inspected every detail of the construction of her new home. She walked slightly behind him to hide the tears of gratitude pooling in her eyes. This had been a year of so many changes, but she didn't regret seeing the last of Harris Island, and working with John in his infirmary would be so rewarding. Only two days before, she had received a check for the sale of the boatyard. She glanced up at Rob, who was using a spirit level to check the front door frame.

The sun glinted off the red streaks of his brown hair. His hazel eyes narrowed as he made sure the frame was straight so the door would open and close properly. What a fine man he was—caring and loving and always putting everyone's needs ahead of his own. Yes, he was impatient with his own goals, always wanting everything to be done yesterday, but he had put up with her and Katie's presence with warmth and understanding. He looked tired, but it was amazing he could work at all after being injured so badly. Maggie was so fortunate. Though Fern knew Rob's body was covered with scars, at least he was alive. If only her Edward ...

Rob glanced at Fern. Tears? "There's nowt to worry about, everything's shaping up." He slipped the level into his back pocket. "The interior walls are in, the electrical work finished, the walls limed, and the woodwork is coming along well." He joined her and turned his steps toward home. "They'll hang all your doors on the mornin. Looks like it'll be ready for you to move into by the second week of July. By then your presses and all the woodwork should be finished."

Fern dabbed at her eyes and cleared her throat. "What about Angus and Flora's windows? You promised you'd do them when their lass Rinait won the contest for the best weaving pattern. Shouldn't they be refurbished first?"

"They will be. I'll take the crew over to the MacPhees on Monday mornin to teach them what to do. It shouldn't take them more than a day or so to finish and then they'll start yours." He left Fern to herself. The minute Rob walked in the door to his house, he washed his hands and plucked Annie from her cradle, pacing the living room, kissing her cheeks and that sweet spot at the back of her neck.

She smiled up at him, delighted by the attention.

"Is that a wee tooth I see?" Rob asked.

"Aye," Maggie said. "It broke through just this mornin."

Fern slipped in the door.

"Och, my Wee Annie is growing up." Rob sat in his rocker and put the bairnie over his shoulder. "Look at how her hair has grown. 'Tis much longer than Robbie's."

"Her hair might be the same light brown as yours when you were a lad, but it's growing like mine does. Faither says my hair was down to my shoulders by my first birthday."

"Was my hair that long?" Katie asked her mother.

"Almost. Speaking of which, 'tis time to trim the ends." Fern made as if to snip the hair with finger scissors.

The lass tossed her long, copper-coloured curls. "But I want my hair as long as Aunt Maggie's."

"It will do, but no' unless you keep the ends trimmed."

Katie sidled up to Rob. "You like long hair, don't you, Uncle Rob?"

"I do that. Nothing's bonnier than a lass with her hair spilling down her back."

The phone rang and Maggie hurried into Rob's office to answer it. When she came back a short time later, she was both smiling and crying.

"What is it, luve?" Rob asked, rising.

She pushed him down. "It was Faither. He's finally officially retired and is coming home to open his infirmary permanently."

He handed Annie to Fern and took Maggie into his arms. "I can't believe he's really retired after all the years he's promised you he would." He held her out at arm's length. "Now, no' only will your faither be home with his family where he belongs, but Innisbraw will have a full-time doctor, one of the best in the world. Luve, guid things are happening here and I couldn't be happier."

Rob took the following Monday off from sailing the boat,

instead helping his building crew rebuild the MacPhee's windows so they could open and close. By noon the following day, they were finished.

Flora opened and closed the windows several times, then left them all open. "'Tis a marvel. I've always wanted to smell the sea and the heather inside and now I can."

Maggie sat down to fold laundry just as Rob burst through the door. She looked up in surprise. "Why are you so early? I haven't even started dinner."

"With Fern and Katie at the infirmary, I thought we'd take the bairns someplace for a basket dinner—just our family."

Maggie hugged him, unable to control a giggle of delight.

While he changed both bairn's hippens and had a cat's lick, she packed a hearty dinner of Scotch eggs, cheese and pickle sandwiches, and shortbread.

Rob loaded the food into Robbie's wooden cairt and took off down the path toward their favourite cove on the eastern shore.

Robbie was so excited by this new adventure he didn't even mind sharing his cairt with the food and blankets. He talked nonstop, pointing excitedly at every new sight.

Shep, plumed tail held high, kept the family together, his herding instincts sharp as ever.

The early summer air was redolent with the warm scents of marsh and sea. Marram grasses waved in the light breeze, covering the upper shore with ever-changing shades of green. Further inland, the low-lying sandy grassland just above the high-water mark was a riot of colour as purple wild pansies, yellow bird's foot, and purple knapweed flowers bloomed amid thyme and silverweed. Oystercatchers piped at the edge of the tide, and red-breasted mergansers rode the surf, diving occasionally with incredible speed. Sea pinks and yellow marshmallow carpeted the ground between the rocks, adding bright patches of colour.

Rob leaned over and kissed Maggie's cheek. "It's been too long, lass. We haven't been here since the week before Robbie was birthed."

"Aye. It seems we're always too busy."

"You mean *I'm* always too busy." He hugged her shoulder.

Which smelled better—the briny sea air or his unique, manly scent?

"Well, that's going to change." He kissed her cheek. "Let's make a date for the first Sabbath afternoon we have free and spend it right here."

Her stomach flitted with butterflies. "Och, could we? It would be so wonderful to look forward to."

"Consider it done."

A thought transformed butterflies to stones. "But Faither will be home and it doesn't seem right to exclude Fern and Katie."

"Maggie, we need time for just our own family. I know the others will understand. Memories of times like this will stay with our bairns for all of their lives. Even when they've grown up and moved on."

The knots in his stomach relaxed when her smile returned. "The first free Sabbath afternoon it is, then." Maggie laid Annie on her blanket and spread a cloth for the food.

While she set out their dinner, Rob, Robbie, and Shep explored the shore. Rob led the lad down to the water and delighted him by skipping pebbles across the shining surface just past the breaking wavelets.

Robbie grabbed up a rock and tossed it half a metre in front of him.

Rob swallowed a laugh at the splash, picked up his son, and hugged him. "Someday you'll be skiffing them farther than I can and we'll have a grand game of Ducks and Drakes—'tis a promise."

They made their way behind the large rock which sheltered their blanket from the wind and sat. Soon they had eaten everything Maggie had packed. Rob poured coffee and tea from the thermoses, and he and Maggie sat with their backs propped against the rock while Annie slept and Robbie played fetch with Shep.

"There's something comforting about the smell of the sea." Rob closed his eyes.

She put her arm around him and rested her cheek against his

chest. "Thank ye, luve, for this afternoon. It's brought back so many glorious memories."

"Aye, it has." He put his palm beneath her chin and raised her face to his. Their kiss was filled with those memories, and also with the promise of many more to come.

"I luve you, Rob Savage."

Maggie's whisper clogged his throat with tears. "And I luve you, Maggie Savage."

Chapter Thirty-two

Through occasional rain showers, high cloud cover, and brilliant, sunny days, Rob spent hours at the helm of the *Maggie*. He always took at least one of the lads with him and together they manoeuvred the boat through the waters beyond the harbour, getting to know how she responded to changes to the screws and helm. She displaced over thirty-seven tons of water and was over sixteen and a half metres long, yet with her twa powerful diesel engines, she could still do eighteen knots. They practiced bringing her into the harbour at full speed, as they would when they had a medical emergency. He used his siren to signal other craft that he was approaching, and often, when they came in from a long practice run, they would see a crowd of folk watching them from the top of the fell.

John McGrath arrived home on the *Sea Rouk* Friday evening. The emotional reunion, filled with hugs and tears, was the event Maggie had been dreaming about for well over ten years. Her faither was home to stay! Never again would he miss his grandbairn's first tooth or steps. And perhaps even more important, she wouldn't have to rely upon a radio or telephone to hear his voice. Or wait until he made the long journey from Edinburgh when she felt a need to hug him close and feel the familiar, rough texture of his tweed jacket.

The first thing John requested was a tour of the *Maggie*. "I can eat supper anytime," he told her, running his fingers through his short, windblown, salt-and-pepper beard. "I've been waiting over three years for this opportunity and I'll no' wait longer."

Anticipating this, Maggie had left the bairns at home with Fern. She and Rob escorted John to the rescue boat's berth.

Her faither's dark brown eyes widened behind his wire-rimmed eyeglasses. "I can't believe it, Rob. She looks even larger than she did in the shed."

They took him aboard where he spent over an hour exploring every nook and cranny, inspecting the equipment, the small inflatable boat clamped to the cabin roof, the engine room, and even looking into all of the many cupboards inside the large cabin. "It looks like a small infirmary in here," he told Rob, "and it's all top of the line. You've done your homework."

"Maggie was a big help when it came to the medical equipment. I'm hoping, now you're here, you can make sure we have everything we'll need."

"Other than the supplies you won't put aboard till she's certified, like saline, I'd say you've got it all."

When they arrived home, they found the table set with Maggie's best china. Delicious aromas tickled their noses.

Robbie threw himself into John's arms, exclaiming in his usual mixture of languages.

John picked up his grandson and hugged him tightly. "I'm excited to see you, too, Robbie," he replied in the Gaelic, showering the lad's face with kisses.

Robbie held out his stuffed rabbit. "And my bunny?" he said in Scots, holding the frayed face close to John's mouth.

John roared with laughter before planting a kiss on the rabbit and lowering the lad to his feet. "Och, I can't believe how well he's talking, in both Scots and the Gaelic." He wiped his eyes on his handkerchief. "And other than his black hair and blue eyes, he's looking more and more like you, Rob."

"'Tis only because he's so tall."

Maggie appeared at John's elbow, holding Annie out. "You've another grandbairn to greet."

Her joyous smile shattered his heart. Why had he waited so long to retire?

It was a good thing he hadn't returned his kerchief to his pocket, for one look at the bonnie, dimpled lassie in Maggie's arms flooded his eyes with tears. He held out his arms and gathered the lass to his chest, cradling her close, nuzzling her light brown curls. "My lassie, you're so bonnie you take my breath away. And you smell so guid, like milk and heather." He turned to Maggie. "You're looking at an auld eejit who's missed so much."

"But never again." She took Annie and gestured. "And there's another lass who has been waiting on heckle-pins all day to greet you."

Katie peeked out from behind Fern. "I set the table and I was verra careful no' to break owt."

John wiped his cheeks again and hugged and kissed the lass and complimented her on her Scots before pulling Fern into his arms. He kissed her cheek and held her at arm's length so he could study her face. "You look even bonnier than the last time I saw you. Living on Innisbraw must agree with you."

Fern laughed. "Och, more than you'll ever ken. And you'll find the infirmary clean, stocked, and ready to open the minute you say the word. Rob even printed a sign to Sellotape to the front door. 'Open from tomorrow till Nevermass.'"

John chuckled. "A bit optimistic, aren't you, lad?" he asked Rob. "Expect me to live forever, do you?"

"Aye, whether here or in heaven, I do that."

John looked fondly at the lad he had grown to love so much, then allowed his gaze to take in the group gathered around him. He *was* an auld eejit. This was where he belonged, with his family, with those he loved. "I'd say 'tis time to eat," he said, his voice hoarse with more unshed tears. "If what you put on the table tastes as guid as it smells, I've already died and gone to heaven."

Fern's house was finished on Friday, the sixth of July. Though rationing was still in effect throughout the United Kingdom, she had been buying used furniture. Between those finds and a few household things Malcolm was able to secure in Oban, she was ready to move in. Rob's work crew brought her boxes and two beds from the storage room in the infirmary, and Maggie and Flora helped her put everything away.

"I'd appreciate it if you could provide the embers for my

fireplace and stove," she told Rob and Maggie when the last of the furniture was in place. "If my house becomes even half as warm and welcoming as yours, I'll be more than satisfied."

≈✠≈

Maggie stopped at the entry to the washing room. "How grand to continue the island's tradition. Remember when Elspeth provided the embers for our new home?"

"I do that." Rob opened the door and picked up a bucket. "You'll have to tell me if there's a special way they're gathered. I only remember her placing them in our stove and fireplace."

Maggie picked up the glowing embers with tongs while Rob held the bucket. "A prayer goes with each burning peat," she told him. "It doesn't matter what you pray as long as it involves Fern's home and the family that will live in it."

Rob and Maggie bowed their heads and offered a brief prayer as each ember was placed in the bucket.

Robbie clasped his chubby hands together in front of his chin and after his parents said "amen," he launched into a jumbled version of the now-I-lay-me-down-to-sleep prayer, ending with a shouted "amen!" His blue eyes glistened with delight when Rob grinned at him and gave him a thumbs-up.

Once the bucket was full, Rob carried it over to Fern's house, Maggie at his side carrying Annie, and Robbie and Shep running ahead.

"Welcome to our home," Fern said, opening the door.

Katie stood next to her, dimples deep in both cheeks, red hair bouncing wildly as she hopped with excitement.

"Stay ootside, lad," Rob ordered Shep as they crossed the flagstones and stepped inside. They placed some embers in her used kitchen stove and, after the peat Fern had already placed inside caught fire, deposited some in the fireplace. "I've stacked you a small pile of peats for now, and I'll see that some of the lads stack a guid one to add to what I've begun," Rob said as the fireplace began to burn. "I cast extra this spring, so anytime you need more, just let me know."

Fern embraced him and Maggie. "I've never had such close friends. You've always been there for me. Know I'll always be here for you."

Katie took Robbie's hand and pulled him into her bedroom as Rob eyed the large and small rockers before the fireplace. Though she would have to add more new furniture once rationing was lifted, Fern's possessions fit the home well. Like Maggie, she had accumulated a large number of handmade bed-quilts and haps which were stacked on a small table, a kaleidoscope of vibrant colour. He walked over to a picture Fern had hung on the wall.

A smiling, young soldier, hair slicked back beneath his military cap, deep dimples in his cheeks.

Katie looked so much like her faither, Rob's eyes burned with tears.

"'Tis Edward," Fern said. "I may take it down some day, but for today it seems fitting."

"Of course 'tis fitting," Maggie said. "Now, I'm going to take this strong man home with me so he can help carry over the supper I cooked. If you'll set the table while we're gone, we can eat before he starves to death."

John joined them for supper. After they ate, Fern and Katie took him on a tour of the house. Though the layout was similar to Rob and Maggie's home, Fern's decorating style was more eclectic and she mixed colours and textures with a more relaxed hand.

There were three bedrooms downstairs—one devoid of furniture—and a loft bedroom with a large storage closet upstairs. The single bathing room downstairs had a bathing tub and a shower.

"I don't take showers." Fern laughed. "But you never know what the future holds."

John nodded. "Guid thinking. You're young and bonnie, Fern. I'm thinking you'll no' be alone with Katie for long."

Her cheeks flushed. "I'm no' certain about that, John. I luved Edward so much it will be hard to ever feel that way again. Besides, after seeing how Rob and Maggie feel about each other, I'll no' settle for less than what they have."

As they walked home, Maggie cradled Annie and listed all the

229

names of eligible men. "There's no' a man on this island suitable for her. They're all either too young or auld or already merrit."

"That's true. We'll just have to pray the Lord provides someone special."

"Like He did for us."

"Aye, like He did for us."

Chapter Thirty-three

"It's time for the test."

Maggie stared at Rob, her eyes dark blue. "When?" A ragged whisper. "Surely no' so soon."

He reached for her.

She pulled away, shaking her head. "You said weeks, or even months. You can't be ready this soon."

"It has been weeks, Maggie. 'Tis almost the mids of July, and I am ready or I wouldn't have scheduled it. Remember, the Barra lifeboat will be standing by."

She whirled around and strode to the window, back stiff.

He followed and grasped her arm.

She wrenched away.

Her reaction pierced his heart. "Don't turn from me, Maggie. With all we've been through to reach this day, you've never turned your back on me before."

Her shoulders shook. "You'll die!" A terrified cry.

He backed up to the bed and sat down, head in his hands. He felt hollow, as if the blood had been drained from his body. Though months before she had voiced fears of him drowning, he had no idea the capsizing trial below Heuch Fell terrified her so. What could he do or say? If Maggie was not in this with him, it would fail.

But he'd invested almost three years of his life in the rescue boat. The back-breaking work, the hours spent making lists and worrying about shipments and schedules, plus the grand plans for a prosperous Innisbraw. And what about his mandate from the Lord? How could Maggie expect him to quit now when he only needed to prove the boat would right herself if she capsized?

She still stood by the window, her back to him.

"So what do you expect me to do? Forget about getting the boat certified after all we've been through to get this far?" His voice faltered. "Elliott from the RNLI will be aboard. He's made it clear he won't certify her if she doesn't right herself."

No reply.

He staggered from the bedroom, and lurched to the front door, tripping over Shep who waited to go out. He couldn't bear it. He had lost Maggie's support. After all that had happened, all they had been through, he had finally asked too much of her.

"Rob!"

He didn't stop. He opened the door and stepped out onto the entry, the brilliant morning sun almost blinding him.

She grabbed him from behind and tried to pull him back into the house. "Where are you going?"

He pulled away. "For a run."

"Don't go. I was wrong. Don't leave me like this."

He stumbled to the railing and gripped it so tightly, his palms stung. *Och, Lord, don't make me choose between my Maggie and the boat. Haven't I paid a high enough price, giving up flying? What more do You want from me?*

Her arms encircled his waist. "I can't bear the thought of losing you. Can't you understand that? But I know you have to test the boat. I'm just so afraid."

He sat on the railing, face buried in her hair as he struggled to talk. "I'm sorry you're so afraid, Maggie. I don't ken what to do. All this time ... I thought you and I shared the same dream. I thought you were in this with me all the way, no matter what."

She squeezed his hand between her palms. "I am. I didn't expect the trial to be so soon. I just need to know you'll come back to me, that you're really ready for this."

He raised his head and looked at her face. Streaked with tears, it was, and pale as the petals of her favourite white rose. "I've been oot to the skerries and sailed her close to Barra Head. I've put her into the roughest water I could find short of Heuch Fell." He grasped her shoulders. "I know how the boat reacts, how she responds to the helm and screws. I can't be any more ready."

The pain in her dark blue eyes was agonizing to see. This was his precious Maggie, the love of his life, and he was putting her through anguish again. She had stood by him when he was hurting so badly from the crash injuries. Her voice, her smile, her faith and prayers were the only reasons he was alive now.

He had a sudden picture of life without Maggie: no warmth, no joy, no reason to live. And it would mean giving up his bairns. He would lose the only family he'd ever had—the family that meant more to him than his own life.

The black whisper of a bleak future.

It was too much to ask of him. He was no Job, so filled with fire and commitment he would do anything for the Lord, even if it meant losing everyone he loved.

He could not do it to her again, dream or no dream, mandate or no mandate. Surely the Lord he worshipped wouldn't expect him to throw away his family. There had to be another way. *Please, Lord, please help me. I feel like I'm being torn in twa.*

Chapter Thirty-four

Tremors rippled through Rob's body.

His heaving chest and ragged breathing shredded Maggie's resolve. Shame struck like an unexpected spring gale, threatening to carry her away on a raging wind of guilt. What had she done? How could she do this to the man who was the center of her universe? Her faither had told her how, when she had returned to duty, Rob laboured over the plans for the rescue boat night after night, surviving on short naps during the day and spending the rest of the daylight struggling to walk.

But the second crash robbed him of the one thing he prized so dearly—flying.

And after the war ended and he could get the supplies he needed, all the hours of hard physical labour it took to build the boat, the broken blisters and calluses on his hands, the leg cramps, the nightmares, the fatigue stamped on his face every een.

She had almost driven him away before with her fears he would be killed. She could not do it again. *Faither in heaven, please show me the way. Give me the faith, please, give me what I need to undo what I've done.*

The words of a scripture from Isaiah came to her so suddenly, her knees felt weak. *But they that wait upon the LORD shall renew their strength; they shall mount up with wings as eagles; they shall run, and not be weary; they shall walk, and not faint.*

⚜

Rob framed her face between his palms. "I once swore I'd never hurt you and I've broken that vow." He strained to talk around the grief threatening to close his throat. "And when we were merrit, I promised to luve you as Christ luves the Church. I didn't know

234

you were so afraid, but that's no excuse. I can't put you through this again. When I was in the Air Forces, I was following orders. Now I'm the one in charge of my actions. I'll try to find another commander to take my place." The words he never expected to say scrambled his thoughts. He fought to stay focused. "It'll take time for whomever I find to get familiar with her, but we still may be ready before the stormy winter months."

Maggie clutched at him. "Will you listen to me, please? I mean really listen, with your heart as well as your ears?"

What now? His muscles tensed, but he nodded.

She gazed up at him, luve shining in her eyes. "It isn't you who broke a vow, Rob, 'tis I. When we were merrit, I promised to luve you as the Church luves Christ and I faltered. The Church puts its trust in our Lord, for He never asks us to give up on our dreams for fear we may be injured or even ... even die. And His love is always there, through the guid times and the bad. I lost my faith for a while, but not my faith in you. You've told me you're ready, and I believe that now. I just failed once again in trusting our Lord to protect you."

Brave-sounding words, but would they stand the test of time? "I can't put you through this again, Maggie. 'Tis just the beginning. There will be rescues around the skerries and most at the height of winter. It's too much to ask of anyone, especially one I luve more than life itself."

"But you must. Don't you see? If you give it all up now, because of my lack of faith, I'll never have an opportunity to make that faith grow. How will I ever get through raising the eight bairns we want without the faith our Lord is watching over them?"

Her pleading gaze took his breath. "That's different," he whispered.

"No, it's no', for faith is faith. As much as I luve you, our Lord luves you more. He has a plan for your life, like He has for mine. I can't be the one to tell you your plan is wrong, only He can—and He hasn't. He's blessed the rescue boat from the beginning. He's seen that everything you worked so hard for has come to pass." Trembling fingers smoothed the forelock back from his forehead.

"Give me another chance, luve. Please."

But what if something happened? He couldn't go through this again. "I can't concentrate on the trial if I know you're here at home, afraid out of your mind."

"But I won't be here, and I won't be afraid. I'll be on my knees at the kirk where I belong."

He looked deep into her eyes, beseeching her to be truthful. "Are you certain? Biddy certain?"

A radiant smile broke through her tears. "Biddy certain."

On Friday, the twelfth of July, the *Maggie* rendezvoused with the Barra lifeboat at 0700 just off Heuch Fell. The tide, at its apex, sprayed spume high onto the fell and over the rocks lining the narrow channel. The coxswain of the Barra lifeboat manoeuvred into position and radioed the *Maggie* that he was ready, with all personnel on alert.

Conscious of David Elliott's presence, Rob donned his wetsuit and shot his men a thumbs-up. Though a bit pale and serious, they'd come through for him. He placed his crew into position in the cabin, telling them and Elliott to hang on tightly when the boat capsized. "She should right herself almost immediately, but it'll be a ride you're no' likely to forget."

He braced himself at the helm and turned the *Maggie*'s prow into the seething water between twa large rocks.

The boat bucked violently and churned forward through the pounding, surging sea. She hesitated when her screws left the water as she was carried high onto a wave, then lurched forward again, only to be inundated by a giant wall of water. She tipped to port, caught in a trough between waves.

Rob fought the wheel to bring her prow around and goosed the engines.

They both died.

He hung onto the helm with his left hand while he tried to start the engines with his right, hitting the starter again and again.

No roar, no trembling deck beneath his feet.

Pain like a knife ripped through his stomach. It didn't get any worse than this. Without power, they were at the mercy of the sea.

The Promise of Dawn

The *Maggie* tipped further and went over, floundering onto her side.

"Hang on," he shouted. "Be ready to abandon ship!"

Chapter Thirty-five

Another wave hit, driving the starboard side deeper into the water. Even if the *Maggie* righted herself, without engines, she would capsize again.

He hit the starter button over and over.

Both engines backfired.

Chugged to life.

He gulped in a huge breath.

But the *Maggie* had not righted herself. The screws were out of the water and useless. What had gone wrong? Was his design faulty? Had his idea of using air baffles in the hull to bring her up failed? *Faither, don't let this happen now. Take her up, Lord. You can do it even if I can't. Please, please take her up.*

Though it had only been seconds, he couldn't wait much longer. He had a crew to think of. "Aband—"

The *Maggie* trembled, stopping the words in his mouth.

The port side inched up.

Another wave hit.

The *Maggie* continued to right herself. Within one long, gut-wrenching moment, she was upright.

Rob shook from exhaustion, but excitement surged through him. *Thank Ye, Lord, thank Ye, thank Ye.* He grasped the helm and turned the prow into the next wave.

Sea water rushed over the deck, but the *Maggie* did not flounder again. The roar of the surf drowned out the roar of the engines.

He glanced at Elliott in the second coxswain's seat, knuckles white from gripping the shelf above him. Rob concentrated on fighting the waves and eddying currents, eyes darting from side to side as he turned the boat to starboard and slowly guided her through the long, narrow strait between the sheer, rocky face of the fell and the rocks.

Waves covered the deck almost constantly.

He fought the helm for ten minutes before he turned the boat into a narrow channel between twa huge, flat rocks at the west side of the fell.

The *Maggie* bucked and rose high as she charged between them, then dropped with a thud as she breached another wave and entered calmer water.

He gulped in air. His left shoulder throbbed, but he ignored the pain. He reached up and pulled the rope to activate the siren.

A loud wail split the air, then another and another. The *Maggie* had proven herself ready for any sea.

An answering wail came from the Barra lifeboat.

He peered out the salt-encrusted window at the Barra's crew waving from the deck. "Everyone all right?" he shouted to his own lads.

"All accounted for, Commander," Paddy McDonald answered.

Rob's radio crackled to life.

"That was quite a show," the Barra's coxswain said. "I thought you were goners. Over."

Rob pressed his mike. "You aren't the only one. Thank ye for the assist. Over."

"Wouldn't have missed it for the world. If you ever get to Barra, the drinks are on me. Barra out."

Rob grinned and wiped sweat from his eyes. "I'll take you up on that. Innisbraw out." He caught a movement from the corner of his eye.

The RNLI inspector.

Would the dying engines ruin his chances for having his boat certified? "You all right, Mr. Elliott?"

Elliott nodded, rubbing his hands together briskly. "Of course," he said, voice gruff. "I've been through much worse when I was a coxswain." Though strained, his smile appeared sincere. "Congratulations, Commander Savage. Once you get those engines signed off as sound, I'll personally sign your certification as the RNLI's first rescue boat."

The crew crowded around Rob. Other than Artair Frazer's bloody nose, they were all in fine condition and high spirits.

"Matthew, take care of Artair," Rob ordered the ex-Army medic. "The rest of you, run a quick check for any damage. We're going to have to investigate why those engines quit, but that can wait till we get back to dock." Rob checked his watch.

Only a few seconds gone 0715.

Strange. It seemed like hours since he turned the *Maggie* into that channel. He flexed his shoulder. Winced. Must have pulled a muscle—a small price to pay for what he knew now. In a few weeks, the island's fishermen could go to sea with confidence that help was near at hand. Innisbraw had a rescue ship that could answer any call in any weather.

Graham stood on the dock as they pulled in. He secured the mooring lines and leaped aboard. "You did it!" he shouted. "I heard the siren!" He pounded Rob on the back. "You did it!"

Rob grinned so hard his jaw hurt. "The Lord did it. And it was one wild ride, Graham. The carnivals would make a fortune if they could come up with one like it."

"How did it go? How long did it take her to right herself?"

Rob eyed Inspector Elliott who scaled the railing and walked toward the twa other inspectors who waited on the dock. "We had a problem with the engines. They both suddenly quit just before she keeled over. She took longer to right herself than I think she should, but those engines dying so early may have had something to do with it."

Graham crossed his arms. "Och, we need a mechanic. None of us is qualified to keep those engines in top form. We may no' have installed them right."

"I agree. Get on the phone and find the best available lad you can. Tell him it'll be a full-time, paid job and I'll expect him to act as second coxswain on our shouts."

Graham clapped his shoulder. "Consider it done. What did the inspector think?"

The inspectors huddled together, deep in conversation.

"He's so closemouthed, we'll never know. But he said we just have to get those engines checked and signed off as sound and we'll have our certificate."

"And the lads on the Barra lifeboat?"

"I'm thinking we knocked their socks off."

"Their socks?"

"Och, sorry, Graham, just an American idiom. They were verra, verra impressed."

"It won't take long for the word to get out. What will you do if you get orders to build twa boats at the same time?"

Rob laughed. "Bargain like a tinker with a cairt full o' trash. Then start hiring and ordering material. I've enough lumber for twa boats on order with the mill in New Hampshire that should be delivered by the end of the week. Any boatyard can turn out one boat at a time, but twa? We need that capacity if we're to succeed, Graham."

"No' a boat like this. You've set a high standard. Just you wait—the calls are going to start pouring in."

Rob looked at his watch. "That can wait. I have a date with a certain lass who's over at the kirk."

"Is that where Maggie is, then? I tried phoning her when I heard your siren, but she didn't answer."

"She was on her knees praying for a safe trial." He waved a hand at the *Maggie.* "I'm going to change, so could you take over for me? Have the lads hose the salt water off, then get busy finding that mechanic. I don't want to take her oot into rough water again until we find what went wrong."

Before Rob could depart, all three of the RNLI inspectors congratulated him on his design.

Even Inspector Reynolds, who had never uttered a word in Rob's presence, screwed up his usually dour face in a caricature of a smile and said, "We're astounded you could do that without a bladder on the deck to right her."

As soon as he could extricate himself, Rob trotted down the path toward the kirk, heart racing. He couldn't wait to share the good news with Maggie.

Perhaps it would help strengthen her faith for when that first difficult, dangerous shout took place.

He stopped at the kirk doors and brushed his hair back, then stood for a moment, composing himself. He opened the right-hand door and stepped inside the narthex, breathing deeply before peering in the doorway to the sanctuary.

Bright sunlight illuminated the stained-glass windows and cast a brilliant rainbow of colours across the interior.

His eyes were drawn to where Maggie knelt in their family pew, head raised to the stained-glass rendition of the Risen Christ soaring high behind the altar. He tiptoed down the center aisle.

Just before he reached their pew, she turned to face him with a radiant smile. She quickly stood and exited the pew, throwing herself into his arms.

He picked her up and held her close. "The Lord did it, Maggie. She righted herself."

"I knew she would." She buried her face against his throat. "The moment I went to my knees in here, I knew she would."

He sidled into a pew and sat, Maggie at his side. With the Lord's help, they had truly done it.

Chapter Thirty-six

Fern, Katie, Elspeth, and John joined Rob and Maggie for a late but high-spirited supper that evening. After they ate, Fern helped Maggie bathe the bairns and tuck them into bed, putting Katie in her old bed upstairs. The lass was so upset about missing the talk around the table that Rob had to promise her a new Selkie story at the first opportunity.

Once the bairns were settled and their prayers said, Rob gave the adults a detailed description of the capsizing trial. He expected Maggie to cloud up when he revealed how close he had come to ordering his crew to abandon ship.

Instead, she smiled and rested her head against his shoulder. "It must have been the stalled engines. Next time, she'll pop right back up where she belongs."

"I chose the sea at the base of Heuch Fell because the waves would approach us ahull—och, sideways—causing us to broach and capsize. From now on, I'll keep the bow into the waves." Rob ruffled her hair with his cheek. "She may never capsize again."

John sat back, steepling his hands beneath his chin. "It sounds like you're almost ready to go into service. When do you want to start the crew's medical training?"

"The sooner the better." Rob swigged his coffee. "The electronics expert is due back in three weeks to show the crew how the radar works at sea. Think we can get started before then?"

"Fern, Maggie, and I have been waiting for the word. Just tell us what you'll need."

Rob didn't hesitate. "The most important thing is how to revive and treat a near-drowning victim. And of course, the best treatment for hypothermia. Then there'll be the usual first aid for cuts, sprains, and broken bones. One member of our crew, Matthew Campbell, has three years' experience as an Army medic. His training should prove invaluable when trauma is an issue. Beyond that, I'll leave it to your discretion."

"What about triage, Faither?" Maggie asked. "They're likely to have multiple patients at one time."

John shot her a proud smile. "Excellent point. Knowing the order in which to treat your victims can mean the difference between life and death."

Fern set down her teacup. "Maggie's the one with the most experience in that department since she headed up the triage unit at one of the RAF bases."

"Will every man be expected to learn everything?" asked Maggie.

"I've given that a lot of thought and the answer is aye—absolutely aye. They all have to be able to handle whatever comes along, just like they'll all be expected to go into the water as needed. I'll be rotating crews, especially if we have a lot of shouts in succession. I can't be remembering who has what training."

Elspeth pinned Rob with a stern gaze. "But what about when you get back to Innisbraw after a rescue? How will you get your victims up to the infirmary if they need additional treatment?"

Rob studied her dear, lined face, heart swelling with love at all the prayers and support she had offered him over the years. "That's the one tickler I haven't worked out yet. All I can think of is to radio ahead from the *Maggie* to the infirmary with information on how many souls they can expect. And we have to come up with a way of getting cairts and cuddies to the pier before the *Maggie* reaches the harbour so they can be transported the minute we dock."

The old woman clucked her tongue. "What about using one of those telephones they just installed? Can't we ask those with cairts and cuddies to put their names on a list? Then someone at the infirmary can call as many as needed."

"Elspeth, you may be onto something."

John held up a hand. "Bide a bit. Only Fern, Maggie, and I will be available at the infirmary and we can't be tied to the telephone. We'll be busy getting ready for patients, or even waiting down at the dock."

Another cluck from Elspeth. "All anybody has to do is lift up the receiver and ask the operator to call someone who has the list of those who've volunteered their cairts and cuddies—someone like me or even Auntie Mairit. We're almost always home."

"I thought you hated to use that newfangled telephone." Rob smirked.

Elspeth's faded blue eyes sparked as she met his gaze. "Don't get smart with your elder, young man. I'm getting pretty good at using that device."

They all laughed when the telephone rang their three rings at that very moment.

Rob jumped up to answer it and almost laughed on his way back to the table.

"Who was it, luve?"

Grinning, he sat down. "That was the head of the Barra Lifeboat Foundation. They hold money-raising events to help pay their mechanic's salary and defray repair and equipment costs."

Maggie handed him a fresh mug of coffee. "What did he want? No' a donation, surely."

Rob didn't answer for a moment as his gaze wandered over everyone gathered at the table. "They want a boat like ours," he said at last, "and they want it as soon as we can build it."

There was a stunned silence before everyone began talking at once.

Maggie put her arms around Rob. "That's order number one," she whispered into his ear. "And you haven't even heard from the others yet."

Elspeth clanged her spoon against her teacup. "I'm thinking this calls for a celebration. I'll telephone Hugh with the news and ask him to reserve the kirk hall for the morra's een. If there was ever a reason for a ceilidh, this is it."

Rob rubbed the side of his nose. "Mebbe we'd best wait until I have a signed contract."

"Blethers." Elspeth tapped his arm. "This is the Hebrides, no' America. If the man says he wants you to build them a boat, he means just that."

Alone at last, Rob and Maggie sat in front of the fire, holding hands.

"I can't believe we have an order for a boat so soon," Rob said. "It's a guid thing I took a gamble and ordered that lumber several months ago. We're going to need the revenue. Our bank account's dwindling fast."

"Are we in trouble, then?"

"No' at all. But I would have a hard time making it through much more than another year."

"The folk of Innisbraw have guid reason to celebrate. We'll finally have a growing industry here."

"I suppose you agree with Elspeth that I should wear my kilt."

She got up from her rocker and sat in his lap. "You look verra, verra braw in your kilt, luve."

Was there a hint of a tease in her voice? "Och, you've disremembered something. Den's arriving here the morra's afternoon. The last thing I want is to give him a guid reason to crow about getting one over on me."

"If he does, it will be because he's jealous. All the men will be wearing their kilts. 'Tis a time to show pride in who we are."

"I'm no' a Scot, lass."

She wriggled closer. "No' by birth, mebbe, but I'm thinking in your heart you're more Scots than anyone I know."

His breath quickened. That tingle again. "And what does a Scotsman do when he's dying to show his luve for his lass?"

She unlaced his shirt, her forehead pressed against his. "What any other red-blooded man does, luve—only better."

Rob hung up the telephone. He looked for Maggie and found her making their bed. "I just got an order from Harris Island." He picked her up and twirled her around. "They want their boat as soon as we can build it." Maggie's exuberant kiss tasted sweeter than heather honey fresh from the comb, and her laugh bathed him in warmth.

"Can you do it? Build twa at once?"

He collapsed onto the bed, pulling her down with him. "We'll have to find more lads for the building crew—six at least." He chuckled. "I told him we already have an order from Barra, and the fellow cursed himself for waiting till this mornin to call. Then, to sweeten the pot, he said he was willing to let us have Neil MacLean, their second coxswain. Graham tried to hire the lad yesterday and he said they'd never let him out of his contract. He's one of the best navigators around—and a master mechanic."

"But where can you find that many lads with experience?"

"I'll put Graham on it right away. I don't care if he has to pull them in from as far away as Aberdeen or Perth, we'll find them." He rose up on one elbow and grinned down at her. "We're in business, Maggie. We're really and truly in business." His smile faded as a dark question intruded into his thoughts. "What about you, lass? Are you sure your fears won't return once the shouts begin?"

"I'll be too busy praying to be afraid. I have to believe our Lord's Word. You've been in the palm of His hand since the beginning and I know He'll no' abandon you ever."

"Do you realize what it's taken for the Lord to see us through this? I still can't believe He chose me, a bairnie Christian, to make all of this happen."

Soft fingertips caressed his face. "You grew up once you heard the Word taught by Hugh, a true teacher. I've seen your knowledge and faith grow every day. He knew what would happen and that's why He chose you. After all, His perfect plan needed the one man He knew would never give up, no matter how much pain and suffering he had to endure."

"Don't leave yourself out of that perfect plan, my Maggie." He rubbed his thumb along her jawline. "I could never have survived either plane crash without you, or designed and built the rescue boat. You're my anam-charaid, the one He created just for me to luve and cherish throughout eternity."

She melted against him. "Let's sneak oot to the entry before you have to leave."

"What about yon lass?" He nodded at Annie asleep in her cradle. "And Robbie?"

"She woke late for her last feeding and Fern has Robbie oot in the yard, tossing a stick for Shep. We should have time for a quick blether."

A few moments later, Rob fisted his hand in her hair, reveling in the warmth of her closeness as they rocked on the entry. "This was a grand idea."

Maggie smiled and tapped his chin. "You must be kittled up with Den coming on the morra."

"I've been so busy, I haven't had time to even think about his visit. And I don't ken what to do with him once the lumber comes and I'm working at the shed."

"Can't he watch while you work?"

Rob's chest shook with silent laughter. "Having Den stand around watching would be like putting a court jester in the mids of the British House of Lords. There's nowt he likes better than teasing, and he can be so humoursome nobody would get owt done."

"Then put him to work too."

"Doing what—answering the phone?"

"Why no'?"

"I can see it now." Rob placed his thumb in his ear and his pinkie beside his mouth. "Den picks up the receiver and in this fake burr says, 'You have rrreached the *Maggie*'s berrrthplace, that's berrrthplace with an e no' an i. This is MacDennis MacAnderrrson in charrrge of MacTelephone—sorrra, got carrried away—telephone verrrbal communications. To whom did you wish to speak? Orrr is it whom do you wish to speak to?—no, you canna end with a dangling parrrticiple.'"

Maggie buried her head against Rob's chest, her musical laugh muted. "Och, Rob, he surely wouldn't."

"I wouldn't put anything past him."

"Then he'll just have to stay here and follow me around while I do my turns."

"That might work, but won't he get in the way of your caring for the bairns? Speaking of which, I hear Annie."

"So do I." She got up and pulled him to his feet. "Don't disremember your thermos and scones."

Rob snapped his fingers. "I've got it. I'll put him to work fetching peats for Fern."

She pinched his arm. "Och, I'll no' have anybody named MacDennis MacAnderrrson anywherrre nearrr my best frrrieend."

Chapter Thirty-seven

A light onshore breeze, warmed by the sun overhead, riffled Rob's hair as he scanned the skies with his binoculars. Den was late and that was unlike him. But flights between the States and the UK were fairly new. He must have had a late connection.

Maggie sat on the bench by the pier, holding Annie. Robbie sprawled on the sand at Rob's feet, playing with a pile of empty cockle shells.

A low drone came over the horizon.

Rob raised the binoculars again.

There, coming from the east—a small floatplane. It grew closer and circled the harbour once before its final approach.

"He's here," he called to Maggie as he picked up their lad. "On you come, he's about to set down."

Annie in her arms, Maggie hurried to his side and they raced up the pier and out onto the dock.

Robbie pointed and bounced up and down with excitement as the plane taxied closer. "Airieplane! Airieplane!" he shouted.

The prop slowed and stopped. After a few minutes, the door opened. Den Anderson stepped out onto the pontoons and landing dock.

A wave of affection hit Rob.

Den tied the plane fast.

Rob reached for the redhead's bag and pulled him up the last step of the ladder.

They looked at one another for a moment before slapping each other's backs.

Blue eyes wide, Den's gaze swept from Rob's toes to the top of his head. "Why, you old reprobate. I thought that last crash about did you in. You don't have any right to look so fit. Don't tell me they have a gym on this godforsaken island. I swear you've grown another few inches, and look at those muscles."

Rob recoiled in mock horror. "I'm a reprobate? Look who just showed up with one of those California tans. And what's this about growing taller? At thirty-one, 'tis unlikely I'll grow more."

A snorted laugh. "Having a little trouble with the King's English are we? I detect a definite Scots burr."

"Ye hivna' heerd oniething yit, lad," Rob said. "I hivna' spaiken English fir months."

Den hooted and slapped his knee. "I'd give anything for the boys at the 396th to hear their commander now. You'd never live it down." Still chuckling, he stooped to pat Robbie's head. "So this is Rob Junior?"

"Aye, and you remember Maggie, of course. She's holding our lass, Wee Annie."

"Beautiful as ever, I see." Den kissed Maggie's cheek, fingered Annie's light brown curls, and grinned at Rob. "Well, this one is definitely yours, but I thought you said on the horn your oldest kid was almost two. Guess I heard wrong. Tall as he is, you must have said four."

Maggie tousled the lad's hair. "Robbie will be twa in September. Though he has my black hair and blue eyes, tall as he is, he's another bairn who's definitely Rob's."

"I can see that." Den picked up his bag. "Well, onward, troops. I want to see this house you built. I can't believe how domesticated you've become. It's enough to bring tears to my baby blues." He snapped his fingers and turned to Rob. "I forgot to ask. Is it okay to leave my transportation here? I mean I didn't lock the door or anything. All I did was tie her to the dock."

"'Tis safe. The worst thing you can expect is an occasional calling card from a pewlie gull."

"Ugh. Thanks a lot. So, we really have to walk? No taxis on this island?"

"No cars at all," Maggie said. "If you stay long enough, you'll be as fit as Rob."

Den recoiled. "Heaven help me, I've come to the very back corner of the planet."

They walked down the pier and onto a wide, sandy path heading up a hill. Several people, wearing quaint, old-fashioned, patched clothing exchanged smiles and "guid-days" with Rob and Maggie. Other than the large shed by the pier, there were only a few stone buildings to the right of the path, including a post office with the flag of Scotland flying from a tall pole. "This your downtown or is that on the other side of the island?"

"This is it," Rob said. "Doesn't look like much now, but give us a few years and you won't recognize the place."

Den looked out at the harbor one last time. It was fairly small, and the water was deep blue until it neared the shore, where it turned bright turquoise. A new-looking red and black boat with radio and radar antennas was moored at a dock connected to a pier leading to the large shed. A single, old, decrepit fishing boat rocked alongside the main dock. To the southwest, a tall, sheer cliff of rock rose out of the sea, waves curling at its base, sending plumes of spindrift high into the air. In the background to his right, purple bushes covered a tall hill. Wildflowers bloomed in each niche of every rock.

He sneaked a good look at Rob. A little thinner than before, but somehow, he looked bigger—thicker around the shoulders and chest, like he'd put on a lot of muscle. A memory of how he'd last seen Rob flashed in his mind, so graphic, so bloody and gut-wrenching. Den tripped over a stone.

"You're wobbly as a fisherman trying to find his land legs," Maggie said with a mischievous smile.

Den responded to her teasing tone with an exaggerated grimace. "Or a pilot who's just landed on water instead of tarmac." He concentrated on the here and now. "Seriously, guys, this is a very nice place. It sort of looks like one of those picture postcards you get from vacationing friends. Even smells different—sweet, somehow."

"That's the heather in bloom," Rob said. "The island's home, Den. I can't imagine living anywhere else."

252

"Here you are, living on a three-by-four mile piece of rock over seventy miles off the coast of Scotland, and you can still say that."

"You'll never find finer folk in all the world than those here on Innisbraw."

"Folk. Okay, folk it is." Den eyed Robbie, who was riding on Rob's shoulders. "Doesn't that big bruiser walk yet?"

Rob grinned. "Aye, he walks. He also runs and climbs and he's harder to catch than a runaway flight trainer with a dodo at the controls. If we want to get home before the gloaming, he stays on my shoulders."

An answering grin teased Den's lips. "I haven't heard the word 'dodo' since we left Randolph Field. I've often thought we must have led charmed lives to survive training all those cadets."

"At least a few of them. I've never had so many close calls in my life as I had with some of those dodos."

Maggie wrinkled her nose and squeezed Rob's hips. "What's a 'dodo'?"

"A flight cadet who hasn't soloed, lass. They could make some daft mistakes."

Den stole another glance at Rob as they climbed the gently sloping path. The only visible reminder of his best pal's last brush with death was a long, jagged scar over his right eyebrow but there had to be far more scars on his body. He remembered Rob's crash like it had happened yesterday: the long, careening drive over country lanes, horror at the sight of the damaged B-17, his spew of vomit when he saw a body dangling from a piece of metal.

"Go faster, Faither!"

Robbie's shout startled Den.

They passed a tiny stone cottage with a thatched roof and a yard filled with blooming flowers. "Now, that's what I call a quaint house. Whoever lives there must have a full-time gardener."

Maggie adjusted Annie on her hip. "She does—herself—and she's one hundred one years auld."

That stopped Den in his tracks. "You're putting me on. These primitive folk are unique, but a hundred and one?" He eyed the lush garden as they continued up the path.

"That's Elspeth NicAllister's cottage," Rob said. "She's our Island Elder. You'll never meet a finer woman or have a better friend."

"What's that big stone building up ahead? Not your house, surely."

"Och, of course no'. That's our infirmary. Maggie's faither, Doctor John McGrath, built it and runs it."

Den whistled. "Your own hospital." He flashed Rob a grin. "What do you do when you need an ambulance? Hook up the nearest nag to the old farm cart?"

Rob's grin mirrored Den's. "That's exactly what we do, and because Innisbraw's so small, a good cuddy—that's what the Scots call a cart-horse—can make it around most of the island's narrow paths faster than an ambulance could." Rob pointed. "That's our home straight ahead, next to John McGrath's cottage."

Wow, it was one big house. At least it didn't have one of those thatched roofs like the old lady's. Den transferred his bag to his other hand and wiped his sweaty forehead. "I haven't had to walk this far since I missed my ride and had to hike from the hardstands to Interrogation."

Rob unlatched the gate in the stone wall and when they were all in the yard, latched it again before pulling Robbie down from his shoulders.

The lad took off at a run, calling, "Shep! Shep!"

"I see what you mean. Does that kid have a low gear or is he stuck in high?"

"High, all the way."

A dog with funny-colored blue hair bounded around the corner of the house and came to a stop in front of Den.

"Whoa. Does he bite?"

"This is Shep. He's verra friendly unless you threaten one of the bairns."

"How can I know if I've threatened one if I don't know what the h—sorry, Maggie—you're talking about."

"One of the children."

"Oh, I'm okay with that." Den extended his hand.

The dog smelled it, lost interest, and trotted to the front stoop where Robbie climbed the railing.

Den studied the large stone structure. "This is some house. You really built it?"

"Everything but the stone walls. Lifting the stones was too hard on my busted shoulder. Between twenty and thirty of the men erected the exterior in five days."

"Your—" Den almost swore again before catching himself "— kidding me. In the States, that big a house would take months."

"They know their stone. That's all they use for building here."

Den scanned the house again. "Must have cost a bundle, bucko. Stone's expensive, especially with all those man hours."

"Didn't cost a pence. The stone comes from a quarry here on Innisbraw. It's the custom for the men to all get together and put up a house for whoever needs it."

Rob swallowed a laugh at the look of amazement on Den's face. This was one of the few times in their fourteen-year friendship he'd seen him without a quick, witty retort.

Maggie squeezed Rob's arm. "I'm going to have to get supper started. The ceilidh starts at 1800 and we all have to change."

Den's eyebrows arched. "What's a kaylee?"

"A party," Rob said. "You're in luck. Your first night here and you get to attend a genuine Scots ceilidh, complete with dancing, music, and storytelling."

"Oh, I thought we could hoist a few and catch up on what's been happening in our lives. Maybe we should take a rain check on this kaylee thing."

Maggie did not appear amused by Den's cavalier attitude. "This ceilidh is in Rob's honour, Den, to celebrate his success with his rescue boat and the twa contracts he has to build boats for both Barra and Harris Islands."

Den's mouth flew open. "You're building boats now? You mean you were serious at that pub in Edenoaks?"

A laugh rumbled in Rob's chest. "Let's go inside so Maggie can start supper. I'll tell you all about it over some coffee."

Chapter Thirty-eight

An hour and a half later, Den shook his head as he finished his third mug of coffee. "You talk about a one-eighty. I never imagined in a hundred years you'd be building boats and houses and furniture. I thought you were just having some kind of burnout that night at the pub. You know, too many missions, too many B-17s going down, no time to think about anything but how to replace those planes and crews—in other words, a nasty war that looked like it would never end."

Rob shrugged. "Things change. When I couldn't fly anymore, I had to come up with something to provide a living for my family."

Was there a hint of reluctance in Rob's voice? Maybe he should change the subject. But he really wanted to know. "Why can't you fly? You're in a lot better shape than I am."

"On the outside, maybe. I still have to run and lift weights to keep my joints from freezing up. I spent a long time thinking Wing made a bad call when they gave me that medical discharge after my last crash. Now, I'm no' so certain. But the war's over anyway. I'm no' like you. I don't have the patience to teach strangers to fly. I like my privacy too much."

"Geez, I didn't think you'd ever give it up. Don't you miss it, Rob?"

"Of course I miss it. There's nothing I'd like better than to be at the controls of a P-47 or a B-17 right now. But those days are over. I've had to move on with my life."

"When we were at the Point together, all you talked about was flying, flying, flying. I figured you for an Army Air Forces career man if there ever was one."

"You felt the same way and I don't see any wings on your

shirt."

"Once the Japs threw in the towel, I opted out. But at least I'm still in the air every day and the pay's pretty good. How could you give it up?"

"It hasn't been easy. But I'm finally getting to the point where I can look back at those years in a fighter or bomber and not get all torn up inside."

Not reluctance in Rob's voice. Something much deeper.

"Supper's on," Maggie called.

Den devoured a large bowl of something called partan bree, which tasted like creamy crab soup, and two pieces of what looked like English muffins. He sat back with a satisfied groan. "That was delicious, Maggie. After choking down the greasy fried pub food while at Edenoaks, I didn't know what kind of food you guys ate here, but if it's all this good, I'll be one satisfied puppy."

Maggie supervised while Robbie spooned mashed potatoes and carrots into his mouth. "Thank ye. Rob saved twa of the largest she-partans from the pot just for you."

"She-partans?"

"Female crabs. They're the meatiest."

He'd been right. It was crab. "That Robbie is really putting it away. Can you ever fill him up?"

That melodic laugh from the past. "Over time. He's like his faither. He takes eating verra seriously."

"Yeah, I noticed. Still packing it away, Rob. How in the—" Den ground his teeth in frustration. Cleaning up his language was tough. "Excuse me. How do you stay so thin?"

Rob coughed. "A lot of hard work, I guess. And luck. My problem is eating enough so I don't lose weight."

Lucky stiff. "What I wouldn't do to have that kind of problem."

Maggie gave Robbie the last of his milk and wiped his face before getting him out of his highchair. "We'll no' have sweets here the night. There'll be galore at the ceilidh."

Rob got up and began clearing the table. "I'll redd up the kitchen while you feed Annie," he told Maggie. "Then we're going to have to hurry and change or we'll be late."

"She's no' hungry yet, luve. I'll feed her later. You'd best shave and get your shower."

Den carried his bowl into the kitchen. "At least you've got a shower. I've had nightmares of trying to get clean in a bathtub."

"I'll turn the heater on, then," Rob said. "The shower water takes a while to get hot."

Another of Maggie's smiles. "I turned it on before supper."

Rob leaned over and kissed the top of Maggie's head. "Thank ye, luve."

Still the lovey-dovey couple. "Just how fancy is this kaylee, anyway? I didn't bring any really dressy clothes."

Rob squirmed. Here it came. He was about to make a complete fool of himself in front of the biggest tease he had ever known. "Just change into a clean shirt and breeks—pants. You're no' expected to wear a kilt like the rest of us men."

Den's mouth dropped open. "Kilt?" he sputtered. "You're wearing a kilt?"

"You know the old saying, 'when in Rome?' Well, special occasions on Innisbraw call for the dress kilt. I'm under orders to comply."

"Whose orders? The President himself couldn't make me wear a skirt."

"The head of the Island Council, for one, and it isn't so bad. All that shows is a bit of my knees, scarred as they are."

"A kilt! You take the first shower." Den backed away. "I'm going to need plenty of time to get over my laughing fit."

Maggie stiffened.

Oh, Den was in trouble now, especially with her finger wagging in his face.

"'Tis no laughing matter. 'Tis the custom of our country and we're proud of it."

Adam's apple bobbing, Den swallowed a grin. "Yes, ma'am." He offered her a crisp salute. "I stand corrected."

"Hurry, luve," she said to Rob. "We can't be late when you're the guest of honour."

Den grabbed Rob's arm. "I have just one question. I've heard about what they do—or should I say don't—wear under a kilt. What's the real skinny?"

Rob grinned. Payback time. He placed his hand over his heart. "'Tis sworn to saicrecy, I am," he said with his heaviest Scots burr. "I canna betray my countrymen." He chuckled all the way to the bathroom. This wasn't going to be so bad after all.

The look on Den's face when he stepped out of the bedroom clad in his McGrath tartan dress kilt and black jacket was even better.

A begrudging look of admiration quickly replaced astonishment. "Holy—I mean—oh, for heaven's sake. You look like a page out of one of Robbie Burns' poems. With that knife in your stocking and that scar on your forehead, I'd think a long time before taking you on."

"I thought the ruffles on the shirt would have you in stitches. You disappoint me."

"Is that knife sharp?"

"Razor sharp."

"In that case, I'll pass on the jokes. I know when to fold."

"Then get your shower. We're running late."

Den ambled down the stairs in a navy sports coat, light blue dress shirt open at the neck, and grey slacks.

Rob tapped his shoulder. "Maggie's almost got the bairns ready. Come next door with me to fetch our neighbors. Fern and Katie MacNeill will be walking to the kirk—church—hall with us."

"Fern and Katie?" Den's grin had a lecherous slant to it. "Two bonnie lasses, I hope."

Steady on. He asked for this. Rob tamped down a smile. "They are that. As bonnie as you'll ever lay eyes on."

"Lead the way."

As they walked, Den continued to question Rob. "These lasses, are they unattached?"

Rob swallowed another smile. "They are."

Den's grin widened. "And as beautiful as the ones you told me about on the phone?"

"Even bonnier. Fern's John McGrath's nurse. She's very talented as well as being bonnie."

"Then Rob, old pal, you're looking at a very happy man."

Den's grin evaporated when Katie answered the door and leaped into Rob's arms, her plaid, pleated skirt whirling.

"Uncle Rob!" she exclaimed, hugging his neck. "I'm gonna dance the Hieland Fling at the ceilidh."

"And you're all dressed up for it, too, Katie lass." Rob kissed her cheek and set her back down before turning to Den. "Katie, I'd like you to meet a good friend of mine, Den Anderson. He's from America."

Katie held out her hand. "I'm pleased to meet you," she said in perfect English as she shook Den's hand. "His hair's red like my faither's was," she whispered in Rob's direction.

"Aye, and like yours, too." Rob put Katie down when Fern appeared in the doorway.

She wore a soft blue, long-sleeved blouse, and long plaid skirt.

"You're looking very bonnie," Rob said. "There's someone here I want you to meet."

⚜

Den's funk vanished. This was more like it. Black hair, blue eyes. This was one beautiful woman—almost as good-looking as Maggie. He didn't wait for Rob. "I'm Den Anderson," he said, taking her hand.

Rob's eyebrows rose. "And this is Fern MacNeill, a very dear friend."

"Rob and Maggie have told me a great deal about you," Fern said, withdrawing her hand with a nervous laugh. "I'm pleased to finally meet you."

Den felt his smile broaden. "Same here."

There was an awkward silence until Rob took Katie's hand and Fern's elbow. "We'd best be away, then. 'Tis getting late."

"You look bonnie, Uncle Rob," Katie said. "Just like the Selkie's true luve in the story."

"Lads are handsome or braw, Katie," Fern corrected. "Only lasses are bonnie."

Katie looked up at Den. "He's handsome."

260

Den winked. "You're a very astute little girl. It's been a long time since anybody's called me handsome."

Katie peered up at him. "What's astute?"

"Wise beyond your years."

Her smile vanished. "Oh, I thought you meant bonnie."

"I just assumed you knew you were bonnie." He looked deeply into her eyes. "I never could resist a girl with blue eyes and dimples."

She blushed and hid her face against Rob's leg.

When they reached the Savage house, Maggie waited on the entry with Annie in her arms while Robbie sat in his wagon, pounding the wooden sides, shouting, "Go, Faither, go!"

"In a minute, lad." Rob stooped and kissed Maggie. "You're so bonnie, you make my heart hurt."

She caressed his cheek. "And you're verra, verra braw."

Den cringed at the sappiness, though Maggie had never looked more beautiful—or more Scottish. As well as the long plaid skirt and long-sleeved blue blouse, she wore a matching plaid sash over one shoulder, pinned at the center with an ornate silver brooch. He compared the two women. It was obvious they were sisters: same black hair and blue eyes—though Fern's were true blue with no violet flecks—and they had the same pale complexions and rosy cheeks.

Rob had said Fern was unattached. He pinched himself. This kaylee thing might not be such a drag after all.

Rob picked up the wagon tongue and took Annie from Maggie's arms. "She's getting too heavy for you to carry so far."

"No' even half as heavy as Robbie was at six months, thank the Lord."

"Aye, thank the Lord is right. I like my lasses wee."

They took off down the path, Shep herding the wagon the moment the gate closed behind them.

Though Den was itching to strike up a conversation with Fern, he grew uncharacteristically tongue-tied. He finally gave up and contented himself with walking at her side. A delicate, sweet scent surrounded her, very much like the fragrance in the air—heather,

Rob had called it.

He'd noticed the same perfume on Maggie. Must be something manufactured in Scotland for locals. Like the smell of warm honey poured over flapjacks.

When the path turned by the pier, they were joined by several other families. Rob called a greeting in a strange language to an older man and woman. They conversed rapidly for a while before the couple dropped back, unable to keep up with Rob's long stride.

Den sidled closer to Rob. "What was that language?" he whispered. "I know you speak several, but I've never heard that one before."

"It was the Gaelic. A lot of the older folk here on Innisbraw don't speak Scots or English."

"You mean you learned it since you came here?"

A flicker of amusement danced in Rob's eyes. "I had to if I wanted to talk to them."

"But Fern and Katie speak perfect English—with that Scottish burr, of course."

"They aren't from Innisbraw. They moved here from Harris Island a little over six months ago. They speak the Gaelic and English on Harris, no' Scots, though both of them have almost mastered it."

"You mean Fern speaks that language, too?"

"She does, and Katie. In fact everyone at the ceilidh tonight speaks it, even the younger bairns like Robbie. The stories will be told in the Gaelic, but don't worry, I'll translate for you."

Den hurried his steps to keep up with Rob's usual ground-eating pace. "You didn't tell me Maggie had a sister. That was sneaky, introducing her as a 'dear friend.' Not fair, keeping secrets like that from me."

"A sister? Fern?"

"You must be Katie's uncle by marriage."

"I'm sorry to disappoint you, but Maggie's only sibling is Calum, a six-foot-twa lad with broad shoulders. And her only other living relative is her faither. John will catch up with us later. A patient had a late appointment at the infirmary."

"But Katie calls you Uncle Rob."

"That's just a term meaning 'special friend.'"

What a bunch of rot. "But Fern and Maggie look like sisters. Same coloring, same small build, though Fern is a tad taller."

"Over half the women here share the same characteristics, and over half the men have the same black hair and blue eyes. Goes back to their early ancestors, I suppose."

Den digested this information for a moment. "What about Katie's father? You said Fern was unattached. Or was that some sort of a joke like how 'bonnie' they both were?"

Rob's eyebrow shot up. "So you don't think they're bonnie?"

"Stop playing games, bucko. You know what I mean."

Rob stopped for a moment and looked back at the others, several yards behind. "Take Annie for a minute, will you? Pulled a muscle in my shoulder yestreen—yesterday—and it's killing me."

Den placed Annie awkwardly over his shoulder. This was definitely not his idea of a good time. He shuddered when Annie smiled at him, a large stream of drool dripping from her lower lip. "Talk, Rob. What about Fern's husband? Are they divorced?"

Rob flexed his shoulder, pressing on the joint with his fingers. "Edward was in the British Army. He was killed helping the French Underground during the war, so Fern's a widow." He reached for Annie, wiped her chin with his fingers, and settled her against his chest after nuzzling her dimpled neck

Here I thought Rob was a confirmed bachelor like me. Boy, was I ever wrong. He takes to this father thing like a duck to water.

The others caught up with them.

So Fern was a widow and a good friend of Rob and Maggie. This was one conquest that would require some delicate diplomacy on his part—and he would definitely have to watch his language. Rob had never been one to use profanity, and though Maggie hadn't said anything, he'd seen her eyes darken. They had different beliefs and morals.

He had no use for Christianity or any other religion cluttering up his mind and giving him an instant out whenever something went wrong in his life.

He took another sideways glance at Fern. Even so, there was a

263

lass he could go for.

Chapter Thirty-nine

The Savage party arrived at the rapidly filling kirk hall. Men flocked around Rob on the porch, shaking his hand and slapping him on the back. No hope for introductions in all that confusion.

Once inside, Den stood back, grinning. The locals seemed to look up to Rob as some sort of hero. Time and time again he heard what sounded like "saved Innisbraw" from a couple of the younger men. Obviously, Rob had done something heroic and Den didn't have a clue as to what it was. Did it involve that sore shoulder?

Maggie was surrounded by a throng of equally exuberant women. What the h—rats, he'd done it again. If he was going to beat this habit, it would have to start with his thoughts, not his mouth. *What is going on?* he corrected in his mind.

Fern stood to the side, the only familiar face in a sea of strangers. And she spoke English.

He made his way to her.

She was deep in conversation with a tiny old woman dressed in a red and blue and green plaid skirt and shawl, sitting on a chair against the back wall.

The old woman tapped her cane as they talked.

When he got close enough to hear them, it was obvious they weren't speaking English, but this didn't sound like that Gaelic Rob had spoken earlier. This was as bad as being in a room full of chattering monkeys. After a few moments he could understand a word or two from every sentence. Again something Rob had done. He leaned closer.

They stopped talking and stared at him.

He turned to go, but Fern grabbed his sleeve.

"Elspeth," she said, "I'd like you to meet Den Anderson, a

friend of Rob's." At least she was speaking English.

The old woman fastened her gaze on his face.

His cheeks burned.

Her eyes were a faded blue, but there was no senility in that probing gaze.

"Den, this is Elspeth NicAllister, our Island Elder."

Elspeth extended her hand, grip as firm and warm as the smile lighting her wrinkled face. "I'm verra happy to meet you," she said in burred but understandable English. "Our Rob has spoken verra fondly of you."

Den relaxed a little. Ah, the centurion with the magnificent garden. There was something about her eyes and the warmth of her hand that put him at ease. He leaned forward and raised his voice. "And I'm pleased to meet you."

Her laugh was deep and infectious. "I'm no' deaf, lad. You don't have to speak so slowly or loudly, for I understand English. I'm just a wee bit out of practice speaking it."

"I apologize. Since I arrived this afternoon, I've been overwhelmed by so many different languages."

Elspeth nodded. "I imagine it would be confusing." She patted the chair next to hers. "Sit a moment so we can get acquainted. I don't handle such a crowd well on my feet anymore."

A sudden picture of that quaint cottage flashed through his mind. "But you manage to care for your flowers. I've never seen a nicer garden." He sat down beside her and Fern wandered away.

"Och, Rob was right. You may no' be an Irisher, but you do have a bit of the blarney about you."

"He said that?"

"No' in so many words, but he does consider you his best friend and has told me quite a few of what he called 'pranks' you twa pulled when you were at West Point."

What great memories. "And did he tell you most of them were his idea?" He squirmed. "Well, a few, anyway."

"Of course," she replied with a serene smile. "Rob is always quick to take the blame and slow to accept the credit."

"What do you mean?"

"Why, take this een—evening—for instance. Right now he's

telling that group of men over there that he never could have done what he's accomplished for Innisbraw without their help, that his role was small and that they should be thanking one another."

She'd lost him. "What are you talking about?"

"Why, the rescue boat, of course."

"You mean the boat he had built?"

She pinned him with her gaze. "Is that what he told you? That he had that boat built?"

"Something like that."

"Then that's what I'm talking about. Let me tell you the truth. As his best friend, 'tis only fitting you hear the true story."

"There's more to it than that?"

Her abrupt, throaty laugh startled him. "Och, far, far more, Den Anderson." The old woman told him all about Rob's painful rehabilitation, how he learned the languages. And while he was recovering, he learned to love the people and received a calling to build the rescue boat. "Rather than sitting around feeling sorry for himself, he got every book he could lay his hands on. By the time he could walk again and returned to duty, the boat was designed."

"When did he have it built? While he was back in command of the 396th?"

"Och, of course no'. Nobody here knows how to build a boat, especially one that can right herself if she capsizes."

"Right herself? Come on. I've done a lot of sailing around San Diego harbor, and I've never heard of a boat like that."

"That's just it. 'Tis unique. And we here on Innisbraw had to wait for Rob to return before we would have our own rescue boat."

"You must have had quite a wait." He forced the words from his lips, refusing to allow his own mind-numbing memories to stop the conversation. "From what I've heard, when he came back here again, he was more dead than alive."

Tears pooled in the old woman's eyes. "Aye. He was. For weeks he lay in a coma, his body shattered, but no' his spirit." She dabbed at her eyes with her handkerchief before tucking the cloth into the hem of her sleeve. "After his waking came the operations on his shoulder and legs, one after another, time and time again. But

Rob had no' let go of his dream for a rescue boat. And I shouldn't be leaving Maggie out of this account. That lass and her love is what pulled Rob through. That and prayer."

"Prayer?" Despite trying, he couldn't keep the scorn from his voice.

"Aye, prayer. Are you no' a believer, then, Den Anderson?"

"A believer?" He felt trapped. What was she talking about?

"A Christian, then."

"Oh, a Christian." His mind raced. She wouldn't find the truth acceptable. He would have to couch his words so he wasn't out-and-out lying. "My parents took us to church once in a while, like on Christmas or Easter. It wasn't like they were pagans, or something."

She smiled and patted his knee. "Well, niver heed. I'm almost finished with my story, so don't feel like you're going to listen to an auld woman all night." She held up a hand to stop his protest. "The moment the war ended and the lumber arrived, he began building that boat. He hired four local lads to help him, lads who had been forced to move elsewhere to find jobs. They laid the keel last September and you cannot imagine the hard work they di—"

"So he didn't build it by himself." Den winced when Elspeth thumped her cane. He'd better stop interrupting.

"I often saw Rob trudging up the hill for home long after dark," she said, eyes piercing, "his shoulders bent with fatigue. He got so thin everybody on Innisbraw was concerned about his health. But just yesterday Rob took that rescue boat through the roughest waters in all these islands, allowed her to capsize, and she righted herself." She held up a hand again to keep Den from interrupting. "And just last night he got his first order from the Barra Island Lifeboat Services for a boat just like his and this mornin, another order from Harris Island."

"So that's what this celebration's all about? His boat righting herself and two orders for boats?"

"Broadly speaking. But 'tis about far more than that. Because of Rob's dream for a rescue boat, our fishermen can now go out knowing they have a chance to survive if they get into trouble. And because of Rob's dream of bringing an industry to Innisbraw, many of our local lads can come home to work, rather than living away from their families. He's determined to save Innisbraw from wasting away till it's nothing but another abandoned island in the Hebrides."

He nodded. "I get your point. Rob always was a detail man. 'The devil's in the details,' he used to say. And if there was any way he could pull it off, he wasn't going to let his men go into unnecessary danger."

Elspeth's eyes sparkled as brightly as her smile. "You're a loyal friend, Den. I like you. A great deal."

Rob appeared at Den's side, shaking his head. "Whose idea was this anyway?" he asked Elspeth.

She tapped her cane. "Mine, lad, and 'tis about time you learned to accept the gratitude of others. 'Tis a lesson you obviously missed at West Point."

He kissed her cheek. "I see you twa have met. Well, what do you think? Will he pass muster?"

"More than that." She patted his arm. "You ought to think about keeping him on here. You could use another partner to take even more of a load off those broad shoulders."

Rob's elbow prodded Den's ribs. "You're in trouble now. When Elspeth gets an idea, it always has a strange way of coming true."

"Me? Live here? On an island that doesn't have a single automobile? Not even a proper downtown or night life? Get real. Not going to happen."

Rob threw back his head and laughed. "Those arguments sound mighty familiar. I made them myself just four years ago." He clasped Elspeth's hand. "The music's about to start. I'd better find Maggie or she'll never forgive me for missing the first dance."

"Have a guid time, Rob," she said, gaze and voice fond. "You've earned it."

"I enjoyed our talk." And strangely, Den meant it.

"So did I. But we'll meet again—often."

Den grabbed Rob's arm as they made their way through the crowd. "She's quite a charmer. I can't believe she's that old."

"It looks like she took to you. That's quite an honour."

269

"I know you've always had two left feet but old Den here is ready to boogie."

"We don't exactly 'boogie' here. This is Scotland, remember?"

"You mean I'm stuck on the sidelines while those little lasses go out on the floor and do their Scottish Fling, or whatever it's called?"

"It's the Highland Fling, and that's no' what I'm talking about. If you're willing to learn a few new steps, you can have a really good time tonight."

"Uh-oh, that sounds ominous."

"Just stick close to me and do what I do. They'll even play a few slow ones." Rob winked. "Watch the first dance or twa. You'll pick it up in no time."

Den stared at Rob's retreating back. What had he gotten himself into now? The only Scottish music he could recall was "Danny Boy" … or was that Irish? Either way, it was about as much fun to dance to as any other soppy ballad. He closed his eyes and heaved a deep sigh. This island was weird—the isolation, the clothes, the languages. Would this night never end?

Chapter Forty

The kirk hall swirled with colour and excited voices as Rob made his way through the crowd. There was Maggie, standing on her tiptoes, gaze sweeping the room. He pushed his way to her side.

"I didn't think I'd ever find you in this crowd," she said, hugging him. "Och, isn't this glorious?"

He put his arms around her and pulled her close. "It is. Where were you?"

"I had to feed Annie."

"I'm sorry, lass. I suppose you were stuck off in some back corner by yourself."

"No' by myself. Some of the younger lasses wanted a blether about the weaving."

Rob turned to Den, but he was gone. He searched over the heads of the crowd and spied him at the refreshment table, talking to Angus and Graham. Well, he was an adult, and at least Angus spoke some English and Graham was fluent. Besides, Den was one of the last people who needed to be babied like a bairn. "Where *are* the bairns?"

Maggie gestured toward the back wall. "Annie's fast asleep over in that corner and Robbie's off with Katie."

Paddy McDonald banged on his bodhrán, a one sided drum, for attention. "The first dance will be an Eightsome Reel," he announced. "If everybody who isn't dancing will gather around the walls, we ought to be able to have several going at once." He waited for the non-dancers to move off the floor and nodded to his lads.

As the music began, Rob took Maggie's hand and led her out to form part of the first eight dancers. Music and lively steps soon made him forget his fatigue. He led Maggie in and out of the

271

intricate pattern, paying little heed to what his feet were doing. His lass had never looked more bonnie. Lips rosy, smile winsome, and her glorious hair cascading down her back to below her waist in ebony waves. When it was Maggie's turn to stand in the center of the circle of dancers, he leaned over and broke rhythm to kiss those enticing lips, eliciting a few whistles from the younger lads.

Let them whistle. This was his Maggie and he'd kiss her anytime he pleased.

Den watched the dancers from his place at the refreshment table—not that lemon skoosh was his idea of a refreshment. But he had to admit, he was beginning to enjoy himself.

And Rob on the dance floor? This was the guy who was always so awkward he tripped over his own feet doing a simple two-step. Here he was, moving with assurance to what looked like a difficult dance for anyone.

He thought back to that night at the officer's club at Edenoaks when he had dared Rob to ask the tiny, beautiful Scottish Leftenant to dance. He had figured Rob would be such a klutz she would be relieved to be rescued by a really good dancer, someone who wouldn't step all over her feet or tower over her.

The fates had been smiling on Rob that night, not on Den. As unbelievable as it seemed, his once girl-shy buddy had found his true love. Now it was Den's turn—well, maybe not for true love—more like fun for a few evenings before he had to return to the real world.

Had to? Strange thought.

His toe tapped when the musicians played what looked like a free-style dance for couples. He could manage this.

Fern was talking to a redheaded girl and a young man with black hair.

He shouldered his way forward and tapped her on the shoulder. "Care to dance?"

She smiled. Beautiful smile. Beautiful woman. "All right."

He took her out on the floor and studied the couples around them. No two seemed to be dancing alike, so he improvised, a skill he knew well. Every time he tried to pull Fern close, she resisted.

That kind of "heathen" dancing must not be done at the edge of nowhere. He finally gave up and twirled her around the floor. She was an excellent dancer, anticipating his moves. Just when he realized what fun he was having, the music ended.

She blessed him with another of those beautiful smiles. "You're very good. You must dance a lot."

Don't out-and-out lie. Just hedge a little. "Not really. But I love it when I get the chance."

"You should have Rob show you some of the reels and jigs. You'll pick them up in no time."

The ultimate put-down. Have Rob show him? Good g— racious, what was he, chopped liver? He forced a smile. "Good idea. But he's probably too busy with his boat to teach dancing. Besides, I think women make better dance instructors."

She didn't take the bait. Instead, she thanked him for the dance and left him standing alone amidst a group of strangers.

He stared after her. Little tease. Well, two could play that game. He looked around, but there didn't seem to be any young, unattended females. Then he spotted the redhead he'd seen talking to Fern earlier. A little young, but pretty. She'd do.

Just before he reached her, that good-looking, black-haired young man appeared at her side, handed her a bottled drink, and kissed her cheek before they moved off, arm in arm.

The next song was a slow one. Rob led Maggie out onto the floor. They made a striking couple. The top of her head was below Rob's shoulder so she rested her cheek against his chest and they both closed their eyes as they swayed.

Den felt a sudden, uncharacteristic stab of jealousy. How would it feel to love and be loved like that? He shook himself. That was not for love-'em-and-leave-'em Den Anderson. He needed a short-term partner.

Fern, nearby, was alone again.

Oh, what the—nothing ventured, nothing gained. He walked over to her and tried his aw-shucks smile. "Care to try a slow one with me?"

"If we can cover the floor. I'm looking for Katie."

Not the answer he'd hoped for. He led her out to the dance floor, put his arm around her, and took her small hand in his.

They were a perfect fit. At six feet, Den didn't tower over Fern. He only had to look down a little to see her face while they danced. Again, she followed his lead perfectly. There was only one problem. She paid him scant attention. Instead, her head turned this way and that as she looked for her daughter.

What was with her, anyway? Was she playing hard to get, or didn't she realize how beautiful she was—how desirable? He stared at her full lips and wondered how it would feel to kiss her.

The song ended and she squeezed his hand. "Thank you, Den. Now, if you'll excuse me, I really must find Katie."

He watched her walk away from him for the second time in as many dances. Either he was losing his touch or these Scottish women were different.

Rob clasped his shoulder. "Having a good time?"

"Of course." Den felt his face burn. "Ever know me not to enjoy a party?"

"No' since I've known you."

Den caught Maggie's eye and winked.

She gave a slight nod.

Rob guided Maggie and Den toward the refreshment table. "I'm dying of thirst."

Maggie swatted his arm. "And probably starving, too."

"No' yet, but I'm working on it."

Maggie stopped so suddenly, Den bumped into her.

"Sorry," he said.

She didn't acknowledge his apology. Instead, she studied Rob's face. "Where do you hurt? And no lies. You've been favouring your left shoulder all the day. You only had one bowl of partan bree for supper and 'tis one of your favourites."

"'Twas a large bowl." Rob averted his eyes. "Is that coffee I smell?"

Maggie planted herself in front of him. "You're no' going one step farther until you tell me the truth. Did you hurt your shoulder yesterday?"

He sighed and gave a brief nod. "A little strain is all. I just need

274

to take it easy for a day or so."

The color rose in her cheeks. "And you pulled that cairt and carried Annie all the way here? Rob Savage, where are your brains? You know that shoulder is weaker than the other. Faither's told you that so many times."

A smart-looking man with a short, trim beard and silver-streaked hair walked up to the group. "Faither's told him what, lass? In trouble, Rob?"

Maggie grabbed the man's arm. "Och, you're finally here. Rob hurt himself yesterday. Mebbe just a pulled muscle, but it could be more."

Den was at a loss. Who was this guy, and what was Maggie doing, making such a fuss over a pulled muscle?

The stranger turned to Den. "You must be Rob's friend from America," he said in lightly burred English. "I'm sorry I didn't get to meet you earlier. I had patients to see all day." He extended his hand. "I'm John McGrath, this distraught lass's father."

Den shook his hand. At least one man looked normal, even if he was wearing a kilt like Rob. "Glad to meet you, Doc. Den Anderson."

"I understand you're an aviator. Did you have a good flight?"

"Any flight where I'm not in the cockpit is a drag, but once I got to Oban and could fly that snappy little float job, I was in heaven."

"Good, good," John said, his attention obviously on other things. He turned to Rob. "I'll expect to see you at the infirmary tomorrow before kirk. I want to take some X-rays of that shoulder."

Oh, Rob would put up a fight.

Instead, Rob said, "I'll be there, John."

Maggie smiled up at Rob. "Now would you like a mug of coffee? Morag just brought some oot."

Rob pinched her cheek. "'Tis just a pulled muscle, lass, that's all."

One more of those loaded, intimate interplays between those two and Den would explode. "Did I hear the word coffee? Lead me to it."

"Grab a mug and let's find a place along the wall," Rob said. "Katie's going to dance next."

Den scanned the crowd for Fern, but he couldn't find her. "What's with this Fern? Is she just a cold fish or doesn't she like redheaded men?"

"Why? Didn't she fall for you during the first dance?"

"Come on, bucko. I'm serious."

"She was married to a redhead, and she's certainly no cold fish. She's been through a lot during the past few years. Try being her friend first instead of using your usual line."

"Her friend? I'm only here for six weeks. The last thing I need is another friend."

"Then continue to come up a loser. 'Tis your choice."

A man with bagpipes strode to the platform at the front of the room and put his pipes at the ready.

A moment later, Katie appeared, cheeks flushed and dimples dancing as she struck a pose not far from the piper.

Rob stuck two fingers in his mouth and gave a low whistle.

She smiled and nodded at the piper.

The lithesome little girl with the long, curly red hair mesmerized, her movements fluid and seemingly perfect. Her toes pointed and her kilt swirled as she danced. Around and around she went, slowly, controlled, legs flashing, hands expressive.

When she finally stopped and curtsied deeply, Den clapped as loudly as everyone else.

Rob hurried out to her and picked her up, giving her a hug before kissing both of her cheeks.

She clung to him, blue eyes sparkling. They made quite a picture, the tall, rugged man in his red and black kilt, and the tiny redheaded girl with her dancing dimples.

Again, Den felt a stab of jealousy. What was the connection there? Would he spend his entire vacation sharing his old buddy with an entire island full of "folk" instead of the one-on-one conversations he'd looked forward to?

The next scheduled event was the storytelling and, sure enough, it was in that strange, lilting language. Elspeth was the speaker and her story seemed to go on and on—something about the great storm of 1921 and how it had changed the island forever, uprooting trees and lifting thatched roofs high into the air, allowing the pounding rain to ruin everything inside every cottage it touched, and requiring repairs that had lasted almost a year. Though Rob translated her words into English for Den, he never got interested. Life was for today, not the past.

After the storytelling came the part of the ceilidh that involved Den. He'd made an offhand comment to Maggie about his plans while Rob was in the shower. How could he refuse her earnest request? He was proud of Rob and all of his exploits in the war. But there was a snag. Den knew Rob would be upset by what was about to transpire—especially Den's part in it. He squared his shoulders. After the "two bonnie lasses" trick Rob had played on him, he had it coming. The musicians played a fanfare, and, when Maggie nodded at him, Den pushed his way out to the middle of the floor.

"Will Colonel Robert J. Savage please join me?" he shouted over the hubbub, shooting Rob a "gotcha" grin.

Chapter Forty-one

Den expected a glare, not the blank look on Rob's face. "Come on, Rob, everyone knows you're here."

There were a few laughs as Maggie pushed her husband forward.

"On ye go, Rob," that black-haired, blue-eyed young man shouted. "Better face the music."

Rob joined Den in the middle of the room, face grim, lips compressed. "What's all this?" he hissed.

Den ignored him. "Folk of Innisbraw, I have brought with me from America a few tokens of appreciation for one of their Air Forces heroes."

Rob turned to walk away.

Den grabbed his arm and held on for dear life.

Maggie appeared at his side. "Speak slowly, Den," she whispered into his ear. "Verra few of our folk speak English, so there will be a lot of translating into Scots and the Gaelic."

He waited until she had retaken her place at the edge of the crowd. "One of their reluctant heroes," he said to more laughter which gained momentum as those who didn't understand English were told what he had said.

Pausing after each sentence might work better.

"He can add these to all those medals he got from us and the Brits when he was flying P-47 fighters and B-17s." He reached into his jacket pocket and pulled out a leather case. He opened it and held up a red, white, and blue ribbon with a large gold star hanging from it. He turned so the crowd could see it, hearing a few oohs and aahs, then pinned it to Rob's black jacket. "This is the Silver Star with a bronze oak cluster, awarded for several instances of

278

distinguished gallantry in action against an enemy of the United States."

Rob squirmed, breath raspy.

Den pulled out two more oak leaf clusters, which he pinned to Rob's jacket. "These represent your second Distinguished Flying Cross and third Air Medal, which are awarded to the aviator who distinguishes himself by heroism or extraordinary achievement while participating in an aerial fight." When he pulled out the fourth oak leaf cluster, he could sense Rob was ready to bolt. He pinned it onto the jacket, took Rob's arm, and braced for Rob's inevitable attempt to escape. "This oak cluster denotes your third Purple Heart, awarded for injuries incurred during battle."

Rob's body tensed. His gaze darted toward the door.

"I expect a proper salute," Den said under his breath. "Don't you dare run." He dropped Rob's arm and stepped back, saluting smartly. "Congratulations, Colonel Savage."

Rob did not disappoint him. His salute was crisp and correct, but the look on his face gave Den pause. His buddy wasn't likely to forgive him for this. If there was one thing Rob Savage hated, it was to be called a hero. His pal would find a way to get even.

Everyone clapped and a few whistled. Graham and all of the young, ex-military lads in Rob's rescue crew stood at attention and saluted him as he made his way back to Maggie.

Tears streamed down her cheeks. She must have been part of arranging this, but he couldn't feel angry with her. She put her arms around him and gave him a hug.

He bent down and kissed her. "You're a sneaky one," he whispered in her ear. "You know I hate such things."

"Some things must be borne with dignity," she said, voice sweet as treacle. "The folk on Innisbraw deserve to see their heroes honoured. You never told me you already had one Distinguished Flying Cross, twa Air Medals, and twa Purple Hearts. Where are they?"

"I don't know. In storage somewhere, I suppose."

"And where was I when they were awarded to you?"

"I got the Air Medal and the first Purple Heart before we met, just for some shrapnel I picked up in my knee on a nasty mission. Hal gave me the other Purple Heart and the DFC and Air Medal when I was at Wing Headquarters one evening for the strike leading to that first crash."

"And you never told me?"

His eyebrows rose. "It's no' important, Maggie."

"Mebbe no' to you, but it is to me, and it will be to our bairns someday."

Rob rubbed the side of his nose. "I'd best go look for Robbie."

The look on Maggie's face assured him this conversation was far from over. "He's standing behind you."

He turned and there was Robbie, holding Den's hand and jabbering away in his usual mixture of Scots and the Gaelic.

Den looked flummoxed. "Who taught this kid to talk, anyway? I can't understand a word he says."

Rob snorted. "What did you expect, Den? That they come from the womb speaking American English?"

"I don't know. My head's reeling from trying to understand what these people are saying. How come I could understand Elspeth if she's some sort of elder, but I can barely make out a word or two that anyone else says?"

"Elspeth taught herself English. She has an ear for languages. She's the one who taught me Scots and the Gaelic."

"Well, what's next? Is the party over?"

"Hardly. The music will start again in a few minutes. We won't stay that long, but the ceilidh will go on far into the night."

"So the Scots like to party it up, huh?"

"They live difficult lives here with a lot of work and many hardships. When they get a chance to celebrate, they take it."

Den whistled. "No wonder everybody's in the party mood."

"Come on, find Fern and ask her for the next dance. Paddy McDonald and his lads have been practicing a special treat for our American visitor."

⁂

"I'm right here." Fern's voice.

Den turned and found her right behind him. "Well, are you

game? I don't know what we're getting into, but I'm willing if you are."

"I'm not sure what 'game' means, but I am willing."

The musicians took their places. A rugged-looking redhead pushed to the front of the platform. "Folks, the lads and I have a special treat for you, straight from America." He nodded and tapped his drum. The other musicians joined in.

Den couldn't believe what he was hearing. Who would ever think that Glenn Miller's "String of Pearls" could be played on the bagpipes, a weird-looking accordion, tin whistle, guitar, and drum? He held out his arm to Fern and they went out onto the dance floor. No one else joined them but Den didn't care. This was a tune he could dance to! He took Fern's hand and executed a few steps to familiarize her; then he really got down to it. He threw her out and pulled her back. Dancing his heart out, he twirled her under his arm, and she kept right up with him.

Her smile dazzled, her blue eyes twinkled, her black hair caught the overhead lights and sparkled.

Den was hooked. This was one chick he could dig.

When the dance ended, Fern collapsed into his arms, gasping for breath.

He hugged her, heart beating wildly.

The crowd clapped and hooted.

"That was fun," she panted. "Now that's what I call dancing."

"You were great. Where did you learn to dance like that?"

"You just taught me. Oh, Den, I haven't had so much fun in years."

Just be her friend, Rob had said. What would a friend do next? "How about a lemon skoosh? I'm so dry I'm spitting cotton."

"I'd luve one."

Fern let Den take her out on the dance floor for the next song, a romantic ballad.

They didn't talk or look around at the crowd, and she didn't pull back when Den tried to hold her a little closer.

The soft notes of the song touched her. She was lonely, but it was her own doing—always too busy to look for luve. Right now she would just relax and enjoy dancing with this enigmatic American. What harm could come from it?

Chapter Forty-two

Rob stared at John, eyes wide in disbelief. "But you said the X-rays showed nowt. Why do I have to wear that sling?"

John sighed. "I know you hate it, but X-rays can't show soft-tissue damage. I want that shoulder immobilized for twa weeks to see if the pain goes away. If it doesn't, you may be facing that surgery I talked to you about last year."

"I just pulled a muscle. Why are you making so much oot of it?"

The doctor flicked on the light behind the viewer and clipped an X-ray onto the screen. "On you come. I want to show you what your shoulder really looks like."

Rob got off the examining table and stood beside him.

"You see those three large, white objects?" John pointed. "Those are the metal plates I put in to piece together your shattered scapula. All the other sma'er ones are screws inserted to reattach your acromion—a slender bone at the back of the scapula—to the clavicle." He traced his finger over the bone at the top of Rob's chest as he talked. "I see no evidence that the screws have moved, and the plates look guid. Now look all at the grey area. That's soft tissue. There's no way I can look at this X-ray and see damage to tissue. If there is some, the muscle and tendons will no longer hold the shoulder where it belongs." He turned off the light. "You don't want to have that shoulder popping oot of joint. The pain is excruciating and I'll have the de'il's own time getting it back into place."

Defeated. "Twa weeks?"

"Aye. No longer, I promise. I'm expecting the pain to be gone by then, but if it's still painful to move your shoulder easily by that time, we'll have to talk about it further."

"Then let's get it over with. I've a heap of phone calls to make on the mornin to boat-fitting suppliers." Fifteen minutes later, Rob walked into the house.

Maggie and Den were seated at the table as she showed Den a bolt of cloth woven in a pattern Rinait had designed.

"Whoa," Den said when he saw the sling. "So you did hurt yourself, after all."

"Just a strained muscle." Rob kissed Maggie's cheek. "John couldn't find a thing wrong in the X-rays."

Maggie got up and hugged him. "How long do you have to wear the sling?"

"Twa weeks."

"In case there's soft-tissue damage."

"I had to marry a cannie Scots nurse."

"That thing looks uncomfortable as—as all get out." Den shook his head. "What are those straps for?" He pointed to a strap around the top of Rob's upper arm and another around his wrist, both connected to a wide web belt around his waist.

"They keep me from moving my arm away from my body, and you're right, it is uncomfortable. You'd be surprised how much you depend on your arm for balance."

"And you have to keep your elbow bent like that, even at night?"

"All the time. The only time I can take it off is to change sarks—shirts—and to shower." Rob took a chair next to Maggie. "What do you think of Maggie's weaving business? Pretty spectacular, isn't it?"

"This is awesome stuff. If it wasn't too warm to wear in San Diego, I'd like a sport coat made from it."

Rob eyed Den's dressy navy-blue jacket and slacks. "So, you decided to join us for kirk?"

"You said it yourself, bucko … 'when in Rome.'" Den checked his watch. "What time do we have to leave?"

"Just as soon as I change." Rob got up and headed for the bedroom.

Fern and Katie joined them for the walk to kirk.

Den pulled Robbie in the wagon, hoping to make a few points, but Rob insisted on carrying Annie over his right shoulder.

At first, Fern did not seem inclined to talk, but at the bottom of the hill, she caught up with Den and walked beside him. "So, what did you think of our ceilidh last night?" she asked in English, her smile open and friendly.

Den slowed his pace to keep step with her. "I had a good time." No wool-pulling—just the truth. "Especially when they played 'String of Pearls.'"

Her laugh made his pulse leap. "That was my favourite part too." She wore a lightweight sweater and matching wool skirt in a very flattering soft grey-blue. Her black hair flowed softly over her shoulders, highlights sparking in the sunlight.

If the setting were different, he'd love to sample that rosy mouth.

When they reached the kirk, Rob had to fend off a bevy of questions about his sling.

Den pulled him aside. "I hope I'm not too casually dressed," he said, looking around at the dark tweed suits the rest of the men wore.

"You're fine. As you can see, I'm still wearing my old Air Forces jacket and pants."

"Fill me in. Is this going to be in Scots or Gaelic? I don't want to be sitting when I should be standing or vice versa."

"You should understand most of the service. Hugh MacEwan, our minister, speaks good English. I'm sure he'll accommodate a visitor from America."

A portly, balding, middle-aged man came through the crowd, hand extended. "You must be Den Anderson," he said, shaking Den's hand. "I'm Hugh MacEwan. I tried to make your acquaintance last night, but every time I got close, someone whisked you off in another direction." For some reason, Hugh's English wasn't as heavily burred.

"Sorry about that. I was kind of at the mercy of the crowd."

285

"No apology necessary." Hugh turned to Rob, his brow creased. "I hope that sling is temporary."

"Twa weeks. Just a pulled muscle."

An elfin smile transformed that ordinary man with pudgy cheeks into a perfect picture of Santa Claus—minus the white hair and beard. "That's guid." He pulled out his pocket watch. "We'd best get inside. 'Tis almost time to start."

John joined them as they took their places in a pew.

Den looked around the sanctuary. There must be over two hundred people. He fidgeted. What was he doing here, anyway? He hadn't been inside a church since Rob dragged him to chapel at the Point.

Soon there were the usual prayers and hymns, all in what sounded like Gaelic, and then Hugh stepped forward to the lectern and began to talk. He spoke a few sentences in Gaelic, and then repeated them in English.

Would it be a sermon on sinning, or even worse, giving until it hurt? Nope. Hugh talked about the grace of God. He didn't lay a guilt trip on his congregation. His entire lesson concerned how blessed they were to have a Saviour who loved them deeply, no matter the state of their souls at that moment. "His love is unconditional," Hugh said. "It doesn't depend upon how loveable we are. It depends upon His personal essence. He is perfect Love, so He loves perfectly." After quoting scriptures to illustrate the point, he ended his lesson by reminding his flock to keep the lines of communication open between themselves and their Lord. "When you have sinned, confess it right then, don't wait. You are each your own priest. You don't have to share your sins with other folk, only your Saviour. Your sins have already been covered on the cross. God is always ready to forgive and to love you perfectly."

This was something new. The only God Den had heard about was a tyrannical shepherd, always ready to whip His flock into shape with some personal mishap or disaster—none of this "love" stuff.

Rob appeared to have been paying close attention throughout the whole service. While Den had graduated in the scholastic middle of his class at the Point, Rob was the third from the top and although

286

learning appeared to come easily to him, he still studied diligently, keeping up with each day's studies, never having to cram the night before a test like Den. Yet he and Rob had never discussed religion deeply. In fact, as close as they'd been, they had never delved deeply into any heavy subject. Their conversations had always concerned the present. At the Point, it was classes and, of course, a subject close to Den's heart—girls. At Edenoaks most of their conversations had involved one topic only—bombing missions.

Rob was not only a friend, he was a true hero. Why was Rob so interested in God? Den's buddy did not dally around with emotional clap-trap. There must be something interesting, or Rob wouldn't be wasting his time on it.

On the walk back to the house, Maggie and Fern busied themselves with the children and chattered about this subject and that, as good friends did. Rob pointed out objects to Robbie, giving them both their Scots and Gaelic names, waiting patiently until the lad said each word correctly.

Den meandered behind them all. He glanced at the sky.

Could there really be a God somewhere up there who cared about what happened here on earth—who loved every person unconditionally? The majority of people living on Innisbraw seemed to believe that, including Fern and Maggie. Both ladies had taken notes while the minister was talking and leafed through their Bibles, underlining verses.

He thought back on all the things he had done in his life—some good, some bad. Mostly a little of both, but always because it was what he had wanted to do at the time. Oh, he had his own set of morals. He never dated married women, or even flirted with them, and he always tried to tell the truth about important things. But he didn't write to his folks as often as he should, and he'd hurt a lot of people over the years with his irreverent tongue and warped sense of humor. How could God—if there really was one—love him?

Chapter Forty-three

The minute they reached the house, Rob pulled Maggie into the bedroom. "We've a date for a basket dinner, remember?"

Disappointment darkened her eyes. "But what about Den? We can't leave him alone."

"Och, I disremembered." He removed his sling and Sabbath clothes and reached for his denims, searching his mind for a solution. "Let's ask Fern and Katie to join us, too." He slipped a clean Jacobite shirt over his head. "We'll go down to the base of Innis Fell. There's no way I'm going to take anyone else to our special cove."

Violet flakes danced in her eyes. "That's a guid idea. Get some lemon skoosh and ale from Faither's cooling shed. You can pack it in ice from the refrigerator. I'll have Fern help me make something simple to take." She gave him an exuberant kiss. "We'll have a grand time."

"Let's ask your faither. I know he doesn't like the sand, but I think I can convince him to go by reminding him 'tis a chance to make up for all the time he's missed with the bairns."

She giggled. "'Tis sneaky, but 'twill most likely work. Lean over so I can tie these shirt laces."

John McGrath, who had often spoken of how he detested spending time anywhere near the sand, not only agreed to attend the picnic, he insisted on carrying Robbie down the steep path to the shore.

Since Rob's balance wasn't great with only one good arm, he grudgingly let Den carry Annie.

Maggie and Fern had made cheese toast and Scotch eggs, a delicious concoction of hard-boiled eggs covered with herbed sausage and fried to a golden brown. They rounded out the meal with a salad made of fresh greens from Maggie's garden and a basket filled with shortbread. Every bite disappeared.

After they ate, John rolled up his shirt sleeves and helped Robbie and Katie play fetch with Shep. The dog was in fine form, leaping great heights for the stick and dropping it in front of the children each time, blue eyes eager for praise.

Rob sat on the blanket with Maggie, basking in her closeness and the luxury of not having to jump up to rescue their son from some peril every few minutes.

Maggie suckled Annie, then laid her on her stomach on the blanket for a nap.

Rob watched their lass sleep, smiling at her innocence and sweetness. "She's so perfect. I don't think I've ever seen a bonnier lass."

"That's because there never has been one," Maggie said, smile fond. "She's so guid I sometimes think God must be missing one of His angels from heaven."

Den and Fern walked down to the dock to see the floatplane. Though difficult, Den adhered to Rob's advice. He kept the conversation light and amusing and restrained himself from touching Fern, though he was still dying to kiss those inviting lips. He entertained her with humorous stories of some of his experiences as a flight instructor, even telling her about the woman he had intended to steal away from her boyfriend, and how she had glared at him when he asked her to dinner, turned on her heel, and made her way to the office where she demanded to be given another instructor, resulting in Den receiving a severe—and admittedly humiliating—reprimand from the owner.

There was nothing girlish about Fern's laugh—it was throaty and very womanly.

Fern not only enjoyed herself, she was also changing her opinion of this American. At first she found him egotistical and shallow. Now she found he not only had a marvelous sense of humour, but he could also laugh at himself.

It had been so long since she'd spent any time alone with a man she did not know what to expect. If Den had been flirtatious or too attentive, she would have run the other way, but his casual attitude allowed her to be herself.

That evening, Den told Rob he would have to return the floatplane early the following morning. "I'd like to keep her the full month and a half but I'm not rolling in the long green stuff like you are." A grin deepened the creases at the sides of his eyes. "Why don't you come along? I know you can only use one arm now, but she's easy to control. I'll give you a little left-seat time."

The unexpected offer took Rob by such surprise he said the first thing that popped into his mind. "There's nowt—nothing—I'd like better, but I've got a full crew getting the shed ready for a lumber shipment, and I have a long list of supplies to order."

Maggie hugged his arm. "Go, luve. Graham can oversee the lads, and one day won't make that much difference with the orders. It will give you a chance to fly again. If you leave early enough, you can sail back with Malcolm on his post run."

Rob panicked. The work could wait, but that wasn't the real problem. What if flying still had a grip on his soul? Would one short flight open old wounds not completely healed? Why did Den have to mention it now, when Rob had fought so long and hard to bury the grief over being invalided out? He could not bear having it shred him to pieces again.

"Please, Rob," Maggie said when he hesitated. "Give yourself a day off. You can't miss an opportunity to fly."

He fought to control his racing heart. Maggie was surely remembering the times he had talked about being able to afford a floatplane someday. She had no idea it was only a dream that would never come true. And he couldn't let her know now.

Den poked him. "What's the matter? Don't trust your old buddy at the controls? I promise not to dump us in the drink."

Rob threw up his right hand. "All right, you twa, I give. But we'll have to leave early enough to catch Malcolm before 0600. He's no' expecting us."

Up late into the night, Rob prayed the Lord would help him get through this, that He would not allow the scar to open into a wound that even time could never heal. *Give me Your perfect peace, Faither. You know how much I want to fly again, but I'm afraid I won't be satisfied with only a few minutes.*

He awakened an hour before they had to leave and spent more minutes in prayer before getting up and putting the water on for coffee and tea. When he came out of the bathroom after taking his shower and shaving, Maggie and Den were both up. "Guid mornin. Sorry if I woke you."

She nestled against him. "You didn't, Annie did. Her schedule got all muddled up with the basket dinner yesterday."

Rob nodded at Den. "The bathing room's all yours. I didn't take a long shower, so there should be plenty of hot water."

"That's where I'm headed." Den swung his Dopp kit by the strap.

Maggie hugged Rob. "Och, luve, I know you'll have a grand time. Just relax and don't give a single thought to what you have to do on the morra."

"As always, you know me too well. I'll try to live for the moment, luve, 'tis a promise."

At 0445, Den turned the floatplane into the wind for takeoff. "Watch what I do. If I'm not mistaken, you've never flown a plane with pontoons."

Fears vanished and excitement grew like that of a bairn with a new toy. When the pontoons left the surface of the water, his stomach turned flips. No words could describe the feeling of being airborne again.

The sun rose out of the east, the brilliant orb cresting over the horizon like God spreading His grace and luve over the dark blue water. It was as though Rob had never been grounded.

Den eyed him warily.

"What? Did you expect me to act like a ground-pounder and throw up my hands in horror?"

Den's shoulders relaxed. "I wasn't sure. It's been a while since

291

you 'gazed at far horizons' from a cockpit."

"For Pete's sake, Den, it hasn't been that long."

"Well, you didn't seem too keen on coming. Maggie had to talk you into it."

Though Rob was much more open about his thoughts now, he had never shared them with Den.

Why no'? He's your best friend.

He forced his mouth to open and shared his grief at not being able to fly, how often he stared up into the sky, heart aching with a pain that never seemed to fade, and his sorrow and guilt at missing out on the last months of the war. He even told Den the real reason he had been hesitant about this flight—that it might renew his love for flying so much he would have to start the grieving process all over again.

Rob's outpouring stunned Den. He'd never given serious thought to how hard it had been for Rob to give it all up. What kind of friend did that make him? He remembered all the excited conversations the two had shared at the Point about someday being pilots. Shame burned his cheeks. This was the best friend he'd ever had, and he'd neglected to see his pain over not flying anymore.

There was a lump in his throat that was hard to talk around. "Want to take the controls?"

Rob grinned. "Do I!"

"Then she's all yours. It's a short flight but it'll give you a taste."

Rob placed his right hand on the yoke and his feet on the rudders. He closed his eyes for a second, overcome by a feeling of joy. There was little to do. The small plane almost flew herself. This was no sixty-three-thousand-pound bomber that had to be told what to do in no uncertain terms.

He made a couple of slow banks to the right before climbing and making a steep left bank to return to the correct heading. He felt as if he'd been flying for the past three years without interruption. He hadn't lost it after all—natural as breathing.

When they got closer, Rob reluctantly turned the controls back to Den. He wanted to land her but shouldn't. After all, this was a rental, and he had the use of only one arm.

"Well, bucko," Den said as they touched down, "how did it feel?"

Rob took a deep breath and let it out slowly. "It was as if I never stopped flying."

⁂

The two friends talked all the way back to Innisbraw on Malcolm MacNeill's trawler, the *Sea Rouk*. After discovering how much sailing Den had done in San Diego, Rob said, "I'll have to take you out on the *Maggie*. Give you a chance to at the helm."

"That's a lot bigger boat than the ones I've sailed."

"Don't worry," Rob countered with a wide grin. "She'll right herself if you capsize us."

Den gave him the evil eye. "I'm not that much of a novice. When can we go out?"

"How about tomorrow afternoon?"

"You're on."

⁂

That night, Maggie listened to Rob tell how it had felt to fly again.

He stumbled over the words at first, mind filled with so many images and emotions he had a difficult time describing them. Then the words flowed faster until they poured out effortlessly.

When he fell silent, she buried her face in the hollow of his throat, heart aching at the beauty he had described so vividly. "Then you must get a floatplane, Rob. You've put it off too long."

"Och, 'tis verra expensive and we don't have the silver now. Besides, I'm too busy with the boatworks to even think about taking time off for my own pleasure."

"No' pleasure, luve." She propped herself up on one elbow and gazed into his eyes. "Don't you understand? You were born to fly every bit as much as those golden eagles that nest high atop Heuch Fell."

He didn't look convinced.

"What if one of those you rescue needs medical tools Faither's

293

infirmary doesn't have—like a machine to measure brain waves? You could fly them to Edinburgh."

A spark of interest lit his eyes.

She laid her cheek against his chest. "As soon as you've paid for the twa new rescue boats, I want you to buy a floatplane—and I'll no' take no for an answer."

Chapter Forty-four

The sea was smooth as glass. Rob had a grand time showing off his boat, taking her through her paces at maximum speed and pointing out her agility and how quickly she responded to helm and screws. He turned the helm over to Den so he could familiarize himself with a large boat. "Hope you can do more than brag about all the sailing you've done."

Den whooped when he put the vessel into a tight turn. "I never believed a boat this size could be so agile in the sea. And talk about a smooth ride." Den hesitated to give control back to Rob when it came time to dock her. "This is one swell boat. I still can't believe you designed and built her."

"You should have seen me when it came time to put her in the water. I was shaking so hard I could barely stand up."

"Why?"

"I wasn't sure she'd float. Those air chambers were a new, untested concept. I could just see her keeling over and sinking at the shoreline."

"Yikes, what a thought."

"Exactly. And in front of everybody on the island."

Den snickered. "You may not be commanding an air group anymore, but you still live on the edge, bucko. There's no way I'd have taken this boat into rough enough waters to capsize her."

"I wasn't worried about that. Not until the engines quit."

"That when you hurt your shoulder?"

"Probably. I was holding onto the helm with my left hand while I tried to restart the engines with my right."

"One-handed in that rough water?"

"Without those engines, we were sunk. And I mean that

literally."

"Like I said, you still live on the edge."

When they docked, Den helped secure the ropes to the bollards. The last knot tied, Den looked back at the *Maggie*. "It's going to be dangerous making those rescues, isn't it?" He shook his head. "I've seen a few Pathé newsreels of the Coast Guard in the States saving men from sinking ships. You'll put your life on the line every time you go out."

"Och, they won't all be that difficult. Some will simply involve a tow, and others, medical emergencies. The only ones I'm concerned about are those around the skerries."

"The rocks in the middle of the ocean?"

"Aye. The currents are unpredictable there. I'm not looking forward to it. And our lads need to finish their medical training. Plus the electronics expert is teaching them the FFR."

Den nodded. "I noticed the radar antenna and screen. Pretty first class."

"We need it here. We get some really fantastic storms in these waters."

"I wish you could use a guy I met in San Diego. There isn't anything he doesn't know about radios and radar."

"Who is he? Maybe I've heard of him."

"I doubt it. He's an old B-17 radioman, name of Dale Taylor. He's the man you need as a partner. He'd have that equipment in top form."

"Dream on, Den. He's probably pulling down big bucks from some corporation."

"Not Dale. He works out of his garage. Never wanted to go the suit-and-tie route. Too independent."

"What about you? You ever think about going into partnership?"

"And give up flying?" Den rolled his eyes. "I only sail for fun, Rob. I'm a pilot. I live to fly—fly to live."

"Ever since that flight to Oban, Maggie's been after me to buy a floatplane. It would certainly cut down on the time we spend going to Scotland and back."

Den clapped him on the shoulder. "See, you're doing fine

without me. I'm too footloose and fancy free to settle down on an island. There's not enough excitement here to keep the old ticker pumping."

Pictures from the past paraded before Rob's eyes: a wrecked trawler being ground to pieces on the rocks, five fishermen lying dead on the sand; the bombing of the U-boat only kilometres from their shores, the landing of German troops armed with machine guns and untrained crofters with knives repelling it; the gales that lifted roofs and tore boats from their berths. "So you think island living is boring?" His laugh held no humour. "You might be surprised." Better lighten up before he ruined a fine day. "Come on, it's time for supper and I'm gleg as a gled. Which, to us, means starving."

Would Den ever settle down? Sounded unlikely, but there was nothing he'd like more than having Den as a partner. Though he came across as a playboy to casual acquaintances, the real Den was intelligent and loyal and could think on his feet. Besides, he was just enough of a joker that life would never be boring.

After the second week in the sling, Rob's shoulder no longer ached so John released him with a warning. "Don't tax that shoulder again. Every time you do, you risk the chance of another surgery."

Rob stopped by Angus's croft on the way to the shed early the next morning and asked him to help Den pick up some of the peats at the bog and transport them to Fern's croft. "I'll pay you. Then, if you've the time, you can help him learn to stack the peats."

Angus sucked on his pipe to keep it going. "I'll find the time and won't take a pence. With Fern helping John at the infirmary, 'tis an honour to add to her peats."

The following afternoon, Den arrived home for a very late supper, his new denims covered with peat-black, and a mood to match the colour. "Good gracious! That's the hardest work I've ever done. Why in—blue blazes—does each piece of that black stuff have to be stacked just so? It's all going to get wet when it rains, anyhow."

Rob's eyes narrowed. "If it's stacked right, only the outer peats will get rained on, and peat sheds water. Don't question what's worked for generations. Angus knows what he's doing."

Den threw his gloves on the bunker. "I still say it's a waste of good time. It'll all go up in smoke when it's burned, anyhow."

"That's the whole idea. If it does get a wee bit wet, it smokes and the smoke fills the whole house. You don't want Fern and Katie coughing for days on end this winter because you were too lazy to learn how to stack it properly."

Ah, his pal played dirty.

"I did it 'properly.' Even if it did take all day to learn how."

"You'll make a good islander, yet." Rob grinned broadly. "And just think how grateful Fern will be every time she lights a clean-burning fire in her stove or fireplace."

Yeah. That was a good thought. "Then it was worth it." Den headed up the stairs for a change of clothes so he could take his shower.

⁂

With Den going along to have an opportunity to see Fern, Rob and the lads finished their nightly medical training course and were given certificates of graduation by John when they all passed their final test.

The new mechanic and second coxswain, Neil MacLean, arrived from Harris and began work immediately. The electronics expert, John MacGregor, returned for four days. Den went along for the training, fascinated by anything to do with radios and radar. He couldn't believe how much he was enjoying his time on Innisbraw. Even having to walk everywhere no longer galled him.

He and Fern had developed a comfortable, friendly relationship, especially after all his hard work on her peat pile. He still wanted much more, found himself daydreaming about her, but he was afraid to rock the boat. And he was completely taken with Katie, even feeling jealous about the time she spent with Rob. Rob kept up his talk of a partnership, but Den still couldn't imagine himself in such a role.

He was a pilot, pure and simple. He flew to live and lived to fly.

298

The *Maggie* was certified "Ready for Duty" by the Royal National Lifeboat Institution on the twelfth of September. Rob proudly tacked the certificate up on the wall of the rescue boat's cabin.

Six new lads had been hired to help build the twa new boats: twa natives of Oban, one from the Isle of Mull, and the other three from a large boatyard in Glasgow. The siren was installed on Innis Fell and tested after ample warning that it was only a test. Eight families put their names on the list as volunteers to transport victims to the infirmary in their cairts, and the list was given to both Elspeth and Auntie Mairit.

A phone line was installed in Auntie Mairit's tiny cottage and Maggie spent an entire afternoon teaching her how to use the new telephone.

The lumber arrived and the men unloaded it, Den adding his back to the labour of cairting it to the shed and stacking it according to size. Only a few days later, the lumber was put to use as twa new keels took shape in the shed. Graham ran most of the shed operation, freeing Rob for his other duties, but he was still too busy to take much time off to spend with his family or Den.

To assuage his guilt over how little time he spent with his friend, Rob approached Den one afternoon about taking the *Maggie* out for one last spin before she settled into her role as a rescue boat. "You'll be leaving in a few days. What say we take her over to the skerries? I'll show you what they're like."

Den slapped his knee. "You're on, bucko."

They left the harbour at three in the afternoon, with hours of daylight left before what Rob called "the gloaming." As soon as they were in the Minch, Rob turned the prow south by south-west and handed the helm to Den. "Just keep plenty of room between us and the shore. There are some hidden rocks there, too."

Den nodded. "Gotcha." The thrill of speed at sea was pretty close to the thrill of speed in the sky. The boat was going the full eighteen knots and responded like a girl eager for her first kiss.

Rob pulled out a couple wetsuits and began putting one on.

"What's the matter? Don't trust me?"

"We're going to the skerries. 'Tis them I don't trust." Rob zipped his suit and held one out to Den. "I'll take the helm while you put this on."

"Aw, come on. You said this boat rights herself. I'll feel like an idiot wearing that thing."

Rob's lips compressed into a tight line. "Now, Den, or we don't go any further. This is Paddy McDonald's suit. It should fit you."

Den relinquished the helm and, after several minutes of tugging and muttered curses, managed to zip up the suit. Worse than an idiot. This rubber contraption was too tight and hot to wear in the cabin. He retook the helm.

"Just keep her on course. We're still a guid fifteen minutes away from the central skerries."

The radio squawked.

Rob flipped the switch to Receive.

"This is Innisbraw Control to the *Maggie*. Can you read me? Over."

He toggled the Broadcast button. "This is the *Maggie* to Innisbraw Control. What's up, Graham?"

"Rob, Maritime Distress just forwarded me a distress call from the central skerries. There's a sailboat in trouble there."

"Copy that, Graham. How many souls aboard?"

"Three. Twa American adults and one aulder bairn. They hit a rock, then lost power when they tried to back off with their engine."

Rob glanced at his watch. "Keep them on the radio, Graham. Tell them no', I repeat, no' to abandon ship. We should be there in about twelve minutes."

"Can you handle this, Rob, just the twa of you?"

"We'll do our best. Call me if anything changes. *Maggie*, oot."

"Will do. Don't do anything foolish, Rob. You can't be expected to save them all by yourself. Control, oot."

Rob turned to Den, eyes narrowed. "This is bad. I can't use the inflatable in that water, so you'll have to man the helm. I'll show you where to keep the *Maggie* so she won't get into trouble."

Den's stomach clenched. "Graham's right. You can't expect to save them all by yourself."

"I'm going to try. I'll get blankets, put three stretchers into the holders, and go out on deck to ready the ropes and ladders. Just keep her steady. I'll be right back."

Den's heart raced. This was no longer any fun. People's lives, his and Rob's included, depended upon his ability to keep the *Maggie* stable in pounding seas. Did he have the skill to do it? Why had he agreed to this trip?

Rob was back in a few minutes. "I can't use the transfer sling by myself, so I'll have to go into the water." He eyed Den's sweaty face. "Don't worry. You know I'm a strong swimmer. You spent enough time clocking me in the pool at the Point."

"But your shoulder."

"It'll be fine. Now give me the helm. I have to correct course west."

Rob turned the prow west and the twa diesels throbbed steadily.

Thank the Lord their new mechanic had given the engines a clean bill of health just the day before. Though Neil had assured him the problem he had experienced during the capsizing trial at Heuch Fell had been taken care of, Rob's unease grew. They were playing for keeps now, and they were all alone—no Barra lifeboat standing by to assist them.

He peered through the windscreen at the sea ahead.

Swells moderate. About right for this time of year.

He focused on the horizon and calmed his mind.

Lord, give me clear eyes and the strength to do this. Hold up the victims and help me make guid decisions, according to Your perfect will. In Jesus's name, amen.

Rob's lips moved but Den could hear no sound. The old bucko must have been talking to himself as he gazed out at the sea, probably psyching himself up.

Rob closed his eyes briefly.

Oh, praying. This situation must be even worse than he had imagined for his buddy to go that far.

The radio crackled. "Innisbraw Control to *Maggie*. Come in, *Maggie*."

Rob keyed the mike. "This is Rob, Graham. Any word?"

"Aye. The boat's breaking up. This is one cool man. He's got life jackets on all parties, and they won't go into the water until they have to. Over."

"Roger that. Tell him to tie the aulder bairn to one of the adults, preferably himself, and when they have to, jump as far away from the boat and rocks as they can. *Maggie*, oot."

"Will do. Godspeed, Rob. Control, oot."

Rob shifted the engines down and turned the helm. "There she is!" he shouted, pointing. "She's already on her side." He pulled the rope and a loud wail burst out over the water. He inched the *Maggie* forward, gaze darting from side to side.

They were so close to the churning, foaming water Den's throat felt like he'd swallowed splintered glass.

Huge sprays of water broke over the partially submerged rocks, tearing at the sailboat, which lay on its side. Even the sound of the wild surf couldn't drown out the grinding and screeching of wood and metal on rock.

Rob set the engines on idle and motioned Den to take the helm. "Put them into reverse and goose the engines if you start drifting closer to the rocks. Don't watch what I'm doing. Keep your eyes on the rocks. Confirm."

The familiar order calmed him. "Keep my eyes on the rocks, confirmed. Be careful," he called as Rob left the cabin. He chewed his lip.

Rob always put others' safety ahead of his own.

If Den believed in God, now would be the time to pray.

Rob scanned the churning water from the fantail.

There—three victims in the water, all fairly close together, and all wearing life jackets.

Praying for guidance, he tied one end of a large coil of rope around his waist and the other end to the railing. He pulled on his fins, jerked his hood up over his head, and climbed onto the railing. After taking another fix on the victims' positions, he jumped into the roiling sea.

Chapter Forty-five

Rob surfaced, rode a swell, and got another fix on the victims.

About forty-five metres straight ahead. Pounding waves surged and pulled at them.

He struck out, taking long, powerful strokes. He swam several minutes before getting another fix. *Had to hurry.*

The waves were pulling them toward the rocks.

He struck out again, making good headway until the sea rolled and swirled around him, interrupting his rhythm. He caught a mouthful of water and spit it out while conflicting currents pushed and pulled, making progress difficult.

A wave struck him—sucked him beneath the surface. His thigh brushed a rock as he struggled upward.

Fresh air! He gulped a breath and shook his head to clear his vision, treading water until he spotted the victims again.

They were being driven closer and closer to where the water crashed over the sharp rocks, spraying spume high into the air.

He swam as hard as he could, arms slicing through the water, tiring legs fluttering close together to keep him on course. At last! He reached out and took hold of a man's arm.

A young girl was next to the man, head thrown back to keep the seawater from dashing over her face as she clutched a rope tied between them.

"I'm a rescue swimmer!" he shouted in English. "I'm here to help you!"

The man grabbed his arm. "Save my wife. She's pregnant!"

Rob pulled him closer. "Take hold of the rope around my waist—it's tied to the boat," he yelled. "Pull in all the slack, then hang onto your lass and work your way back to the boat. Don't let go of that rope or pull against my end when I swim for your wife. Understand?"

The man nodded and took hold of the lifeline behind Rob.

Rob scanned the water for the woman. A churning wave caught him in the face and he swallowed more water. He choked and kept peering through the spume.

There! She was only a few metres ahead of him, but so close to the rocks.

He worked his way toward her, arms and legs leaden, vision impaired by the spume.

The surf tugged him closer to a large, jagged rock, its top just visible in the seething water.

He gave it everything he had until his hand touched something soft. He grabbed tightly as he shook the water from his face again. He had the woman by the shoulder.

She struggled to swim against the waves, but it was obvious she was exhausted.

"I'm a rescue swimmer!" he shouted. "Can you hold onto me?"

She shook her head, eyes wide with fear.

"Roll over on your back."

She hesitated.

Rob wrestled her onto her back. Holding onto a strap on her life jacket with his left hand, he began inching his way back toward the *Maggie*. He swallowed another mouthful of water and choked. A wave washed over his head. Couldn't make any progress. Pulling a victim through the heaving sea with only one arm was so slow. Gritting his teeth and kicking his legs harder, he pleaded to the Lord for strength as he swam blind against a strong current.

The shadow of a large wave loomed over them.

He held his breath and swam through it. So exhausted. How could he make it back to the boat?

A sudden image of Maggie flashed through his mind. "Come back to me, Rob." Her voice echoed in his ears.

He tightened his grip on the strap and concentrated on using every muscle in his right arm and legs, thrashing through the water with all of his might. He dove through another wave and took advantage of the height to shake his head and take a fix on the boat again.

The others were over halfway there. Water foamed at the prow as the *Maggie*'s screws turned. Den must be trying to get closer.

Be careful. Don't get too close to the crosscurrents or rocks.

Den gripped the helm and inched the boat closer to the rocks, frantically scanning the sea around them. Afraid to go any closer, he idled the engines and stood, looking through the windscreen for Rob's bright red wetsuit. He sat down with a grunt. Couldn't see a thing in that boiling sea with the mist spraying high over the rocks.

Where was Rob?

Forcing himself to remain seated, he fought every nerve in his body as they screamed to run outside for a quick look off the deck. But Rob had ordered him not to watch but to keep his eyes on the rocks. Just like during that last flight of the *Bonnie Maggie*. Rob had ordered Den to take the group home. If he'd been flying escort, he might have been able to talk Rob down, guide him to a safer landing spot.

Rob had to be all right. He had to be!

Only a vision of Maggie's bonnie face kept Rob going. He kicked his leaden legs as hard as he could for what seemed like hours. His left hand went numb and his thigh muscles burned. *Don't let them cramp, please, Lord.*

If only there was one more man on board the *Maggie* to pull in his lifeline.

His right hand collided with something. He opened his eyes.

The man, his lass at his side. They were only a few metres from the *Maggie*.

Thank Ye, Lord, thank Ye. They had all reached the *Maggie*.

Rob waved for them to follow him to the lower emergency boarding deck on the fantail where he'd tied his lifeline. Once on board, he retched again and again, seawater spewing from his mouth. The moment he could move again, Rob struggled to his feet, pulled down his hood, slipped off his flippers, and untied the lifeline from around his waist. "Into the cabin. Quickly." Och, his voice was raspy as a raven's.

The woman stumbled and sank to her knees.

Rob pulled her up and the twa men supported her weight between them while the lass held onto her faither's waist. They had to stop a few times while one or the other retched up seawater.

When they were inside, Rob shouted to Den, "Get us out of here. East by Northeast. Full speed." He grabbed the man's arm. "Strip your lass and wrap her in a blanket, then yourself. Hurry."

The man tried to help his wife first.

Rob shoved him away. While the man's instincts were perfectly natural, Rob was the one with the medical training. "See to your lass right now. I'll take care of your wife."

The girl leaned over and vomited again.

The woman knelt on the cabin floor, shivering violently.

Rob removed her life jacket and eyed the woman's swollen belly. Och, she was very biggen. He pulled her to her feet, supporting her body while he took off her sodden sweater and shirt and pulled down her skirt, willing his stiff fingers to obey. He grabbed a blanket and wrapped it around her as she doubled over, retching. "How far off the rocks are we?" he asked Den.

"Far enough to drop both anchors so I can help."

"Do it." Rob reached for another blanket and helped the woman onto a stretcher. He pulled her arms out of the blankets and rubbed them vigorously. "How far along are you?"

Her teeth chittered together. "A little over eight months."

He forced a smile. "That's good. Your baby should be fine."

Tears slipped down her cheeks.

"You'll be in a warm hospital bed in half an hour."

Sobs racked her body. "Th ... thank you," she cried.

Den stood at his side. "We're anchored fore and aft. Flukes are holding. What do you want me to do?"

"Make sure the lass is on a stretcher and pile the blankets on, then see that she's breathing all right." He rubbed the woman's arms briskly for several minutes, then reached for twa more blankets and pulled them over her before grabbing a stethoscope from its holder and listening to her lungs.

Miraculously, they sounded clear.

He moved the diaphragm to her belly and said another prayer of gratitude when it picked up the faint sounds of the unborn bairnie's heartbeat.

The man appeared at Rob's side and leaned over his wife. "How are you, Jill?"

She tried to smile. "Fine now."

"Lie down and get under some blankets," Rob ordered. "She's going to be all right."

"How's Brenna?" Jill asked.

"I'm sure she's fine. I'll check her now. Just lie there and rest." Rob took the stethoscope and moved over to the lass's stretcher. He listened to her lungs.

No water.

"How do you feel, Brenna?"

She cuddled down in the blankets. "My stomach's awful, but I'm getting warm now. I've never been so cold."

He pushed the hair back from her forehead. "How old are you?"

"Eleven."

"You're a very brave lass. You helped save your mother."

"I did? How?"

"By doing everything your faither told you to do. That way, I could spend all my time with her."

She smiled and closed her eyes.

Rob moved on to the man's stretcher and listened to his lungs, which sounded clear. "Are you getting warm?"

"Yes. Is Jill really going to be all right?"

Rob patted his arm. "She is. You're a lucky man. If we hadn't been close, we wouldn't have made it in time."

"That's what the man on the radio said." He took his arm out of the blankets and extended a shaking hand. "I'm Stewart—Stu Proctor."

Rob shook his hand. "Rob Savage. That fellow over there is Den Anderson, and you're aboard the *Maggie*, the Innisbraw Coastal Rescue Boat. She was just certified yesterday. You're our first rescue."

"We can't thank you enough. But if I may offer a suggestion … couldn't you use a larger crew?"

Rob grinned so hard his mouth went lopsided. "We'll usually carry a well-trained crew of six. Den's visiting from America and we were out for pleasure. You're lucky he knows how to operate this boat, or I couldn't have gone into the water after you."

Stu closed his eyes. "The Lord was watching over us."

"Aye, He was. And over us. You just—"

A loud grunt sent Rob back to Jill's side.

"I … I'm having a contraction." She gasped and grabbed his hand. "It's too early. My baby!"

Chapter Forty-six

A familiar dread chilled Rob's body. "You're far enough along for it to be born healthy." *Don't let me regret those words, Faither. Guide my thoughts and hands.*

Jill gasped again and drew up her legs as another contraction hit.

It was worse than he feared. Her water must have broken as he pulled her to the *Maggie*.

"Den, weigh both anchors and head for Innisbraw, full speed. Just keep away from the southern shore to avoid the rocks. Och, and get on the radio and have Graham alert the cairts and cuddies. We'll need two or three. Tell him to have John meet us at the dock. We have a woman in labour."

"Labor! You mean like having a baby—that kind of labor?"

"Aye. Do it." Rob glanced at his watch. "Jill, tell me when you have another contraction."

"I just did."

"You've had two?"

"Yes, I ... oh, here comes another."

Rob's dread grew. *No' again, Lord. Och, please, no' again.*

Stu came to her side, wrapped in his blankets. "Jill, no, you're not in labor yet. It's too early."

Rob took his arm. "Your little one has other plans. We'll no' make the hospital."

"What will we do?" Stu moaned. "I knew we shouldn't have taken this trip."

Stress triggered Rob's Scots. "Dinna worra. I helped birth my awn bairns. She'll do fine."

"But the baby."

Jill grunted and panted. "Oh, help me. I think it's coming."

"Hold your wife's hand," Rob said to Stu. "Raise your knees," he told Jill. He pulled the blankets up and positioned himself.

Another contraction racked her body. The baby's head crowned and Jill let out a loud cry as the head emerged.

Rob eased out one tiny shoulder, then the second. He caught the baby and held it up, running a finger between its lips.

Stu reeled. "It's a boy!"

The lad gasped and let out a reedy cry.

Rob placed him across Jill's stomach, then moved Stu's hand to cover the squirming bairnie. "Hold onto him. I have to cut the cord." He grabbed what he needed from the instrument cabinet, returned to Jill's side, and clamped the umbilical cord before using surgical scissors to sever it. Blankets were too large, so he placed a towel around the baby, wrapping it tight. He pressed several towels beneath Jill and put her lad in her arms before covering them both, tucking in the blankets.

She stared up at him through tear-filled eyes. "You're a doctor and a captain?"

"No, but I've had a bit of experience. My wife Maggie is like you. When it comes to birthing a bairnie, she doesn't waste time."

Stu rested his head against Rob's arm. "We can't thank you enough. There just aren't words."

Jill cradled her now-sleeping, new son against her chest, a tiny smile tilting her lips as she dozed. When he made his way over to Brenna's stretcher, he found her fast asleep, respirations normal. He nodded at Stu. "Better lay down for a while. We'll dock in about twenty minutes." He unzipped his wetsuit halfway and took his arms out, peeling it down to his waist. His muscles were so tired, even his hands shook. He went forward and collapsed into the coxswain's seat, blowing out a long breath.

Den's stare penetrated his foggy mind.

"What's the matter?"

"All those scars. You look like some animal caught you for breakfast, then spit you out half-eaten."

"Och, I'd better put my shirt on. I usually cover them up."

"No way. You stay right there." Den ran his fingers through tousled hair. "I don't see how you did it. You saved three people, bucko. Three! Oh—I forgot the baby. Make that four."

"I never could have done it without your help, or Stu's."

"Don't give me your usual line. Aren't you ever going to learn when a simple 'I guess I did' will be enough?"

Rob put his head back against the seat and closed his eyes. He rested for a long time, taking deep breaths, thanking God silently for all of His help and praying that the family had not suffered any ill effects from being in the sea for so long.

⚓

Den eyed his friend anxiously. He'd probably hurt that shoulder again and he looked wiped out. Not only had he spent all that time getting to the people in the water and then towing a pregnant woman through those conflicting waves, he'd actually delivered the baby. Where had he learned how to do that?

And all those scars.

The truth of how much pain Rob had gone through finally hit him as if he'd been gut-punched.

"You'll have to take her in for me," Rob mumbled. "I don't have anything left."

"Talk me through it, then." Den swiped a hand across his stinging eyes. "We're almost at the mouth of the harbor. Want me to hit the horn as we enter?"

"Aye. Three pulls of the rope. About three-quarters of the way to the dock, cut to low so you can manoeuvre. Just be sure to signal any other boats you see."

"Gotcha." Den eased the *Maggie* up to her berth.

John rushed into the cabin and stopped short of Jill's stretcher, a smile tilting his beard. "Well, I shouldn't be dumfoondert, but I am." He looked around.

Rob slumped in his seat, head back, eyes closed.

John rushed to him. "Are you hurt, lad?"

Rob opened his eyes. "Just spent."

"Are you certain?" John took his wrist.

Rob pulled away. "You'd better check the others. I think they're all right, but Jill—the mither—needs a guid examination,

312

and the laddie, too. I'm no' a doctor."

John patted his shoulder. "So you had to deliver another bairnie. You're in the wrong profession, Rob. You'd make a fine obstetrician."

Rob exhaled loudly. "In your dreams, John."

Den sat back, dazed. Another bairnie?

Maggie rushed through the cabin door. A sharp pain pierced her chest at the sight of Rob. So pale. He must be injured. She dashed to his side, went to her knees, and clasped his hand. "I'm here, Rob. Where are you hurting?"

His hand trembled. "Nowhere, luve. Just spent."

She eyed him closely. "Are you certain? You're shaking."

"Biddy certain. After everyone's on their way to the infirmary, I'll get dressed and we can go. I just need to fauld my fit a while."

She looked up at Den. "Is he really all right?"

"He says he is, but he was in that water, swimming against those waves, for a long, long time. If it were me, I'd have to be carried out after something like that." He chuckled.

"What's so funny?"

"All that and he delivered a baby, too. I don't know how you folk did it, Maggie, but this island sure hit the jackpot when Rob Savage came ashore."

She rested her head in Rob's lap. "You don't have to tell me that, or any of our folk. 'Tis why we treasure him so."

Den and Alec both insisted on helping Rob into the back of Alec's cairt.

"Should we stop at the infirmary?" Alec asked Maggie.

"No need. Just take us home. All he needs is a guid long rest."

Den climbed onto the bench. Alec clucked to his cuddy, and the cairt moved off at a sedate pace.

Rob leaned his head against the side railing. If one more person asked how he felt, he would explode. Maggie cuddled against him and he put his arm around her, kissing her hair.

"Do you hurt anywhere at all, Rob?"

No' again! But this was his Maggie. She had a right to ask. "No place special. I feel every muscle in my body. As much as I've practiced with my crew, I had no idea it would be so hard pulling a victim in against the current using only one arm. I need to work on building up my endurance."

"How about your left shoulder?"

"Doesn't hurt any more than my right."

She smoothed a lock of hair back from his forehead. "We're almost home. Then you can go straight to bed."

"I need to shower the salt off first."

"Wouldn't a bath be better than a shower?"

"I'm afraid to lie down unless I'm in bed. I'll never get up again."

"Then a shower it will be."

Rob climbed down from the cairt, waving a hand at Alec. He couldn't walk fast, but at least he didn't limp. A chuckle tickled his chest. Both legs felt so weak, how could he know which one to favour?

Maggie turned the shower heater on. "I'll get the bed covers pulled back. You stand in front of the fire." When she came back out of the bedroom, she asked, "Are you cold?"

"No' with my wetsuit on. The warm just feels guid. Where are the bairns?"

"Flora has them at her cottage."

Den eyed Rob. "Want me to stay in the bathroom with you? You look like you're out on your feet."

"I'm just going to wash the salt off, then hit the sack."

"How about a big glass of that good peaty water? Or did you have your fill in the drink?"

"Sounds good. But one isn't enough. My mouth feels like cotton wadding." He gulped down three glasses of water before the shower was ready.

Maggie peeled off his wetsuit and helped him shower. Rob hadn't seemed so exhausted since his run one and a half times around the island in the rain storm the year before. She waited until he soaped and rinsed his hair before helping him from the shower

314

and toweling him dry. "The bed is ready."

He leaned against the wall and pulled up his boxers.

Och, so tired, he couldn't even stand alone.

She led him through the living room into their bedroom, offering her thanks to God for bringing him home safely.

"Coorie doon wi' me, lass." He collapsed onto the bed.

She pulled up the cover, took off her shoes, and spooned her body close while running her lips over his bare shoulder.

"You saved me, Maggie."

"What do you mean?"

Seconds later, he was asleep.

Chapter Forty-seven

When Rob awakened, he lay still for a moment, savoring the feel of Maggie's body pressed against his. He stretched his arms above his head. Didn't hurt, not even the left shoulder. *Thank Ye again, Lord, for holding us all up with Your mighty hand—and for giving me the strength to do what You willed. Continue to guide me, to help me to make guid decisions when I'm overwhelmed by the power of the sea. Give Maggie Your courage when hers falters. And be with the souls saved. In Jesus's name.* He kissed Maggie's shoulder.

After he was dressed and ready for the day, he took inventory of his body. His legs and arms were tired but they didn't hurt, and the tremors that had plagued him after he left the water were gone. He put some broken peats in the stove and filled the coffee pot and tea kettle with water, then stirred the embers in the fireplace and added more peats while Maggie sat in front of the fire suckling Annie. Looking at his bonnie wee lassie brought a stab of concern. "I hope that new bairnie is all right."

Maggie wrinkled her nose. "It sounds like I'm no' so different after all. That woman couldn't have laboured verra long."

He kissed the top of her head. "She didn't. I'll admit to being flummoxed when she had her first contraction, but after that it was all so familiar I felt like I was on autopilot. I'd like to go over to the infirmary and see how they are this mornin."

"Wait till I finish feeding Annie and get Robbie up, fed, and dressed. I want to go with you."

Den came down the stairs, holding Katie's hand. "Guess who I found on the rug by my bed this morning?"

Maggie's hand flew to her mouth. "Och, I disremembered Fern had to work this mornin. I didn't hear her bring you in, Katie, lass."

Katie tugged at her nightgown, studying the floor. "Mither said we had to be real quiet, so I sneaked upstairs, but Den was sleeping in my bed. I just laid down and went back to sleep." She looked at Den, eyes wide. "Did I do a bad thing?"

Den patted her shoulder. "A bonnie girl like you? I don't believe you've done a bad thing in your life." He winked at Rob and Maggie.

The dimples deepened in Katie's cheeks. "Good. I'll go get dressed. I brought all my claes—clothes."

The moment she skipped up the stairs, Den's gaze pinned Rob. "How do you feel?"

"Grand. But how about you? It wasn't easy keeping the *Maggie* steady in those waters."

Den rolled his eyes. "A lot easier than being *in* those waters, bucko. How's the shoulder?"

"Which one? They both feel good."

"So you don't hurt anyplace?"

"Only my stomach."

Maggie gasped and Den frowned.

"I'm gleg as a gled."

Maggie giggled. "There are fresh scones in the kitchen press, luve, and clotted cream in the refrigerator. I'll fix you a proper breakfast when we get back from the infirmary."

Heading for the kitchen, Den talked over his shoulder. "I could use something to eat, too. You're spoiling me, Maggie. I haven't had anything but coffee in the morning since the Air Forces, but thinking about your scones is making my stomach growl."

"If you're really hungry, I can fix you some brose when I've finished nursing Annie. I need to make it for Robbie anyway."

"Brose? What's that?"

"Oatmeal," Rob said, "only creamier."

"Oatmeal?" Den grimaced. "No, thanks. I'm only hungry, not starving like you, though I would like to tag along and see the Proctors. They're real pioneer stock."

"Pioneer stock?" Maggie asked.

"Yeah. What I mean is, they were strong and did what they had

317

to, no matter how hard. Just like the pioneer people who settled our West."

⚜

Jill was nursing her newborn when they arrived at the infirmary, so Rob and Den waited while Maggie sought out her faither. Fern brought Stu and Brenna to the foyer.

Brenna dashed in ahead of her faither. She was a fresh-faced lass with a long, dark blonde braid, a sprinkle of freckles on her nose, and soft grey eyes. She wore a sweater and skirt that were too large, and her feet were covered with heavy woolen socks. Her appearance belied the past twenty-four hours' events. She threw her arms around Rob and hugged him tightly.

"Let the man breathe," Stu said with an embarrassed grin.

She dropped her arms and smiled up at Rob. "Is this your son and daughter? They're cute."

Rob returned her smile. "Thank ye, lass, they are indeed. The lad is Robbie and the lass is Wee Annie."

She wrinkled her nose, just like Maggie. "Wee Annie. I like that name."

Stu wore ordinary clothes, obviously donated by one of the island's men, and stood about six feet tall. Slim, but his short-sleeved shirt revealed well-toned arms, and he moved with the grace of a natural athlete. His brown hair was cut short and he was freshly shaved—obviously a man who believed in good grooming.

"How do you feel?" Rob asked.

"Fine. How about you?"

"Very good," Rob said. "How's Jill?"

"That woman amazes me. Her only complaint is how thirsty she is. Here she spent over an hour in the ocean yesterday, and she's drinking water like she's been in the desert."

"The salt water dehydrates you. That, plus nursing, and she's bound to be thirstier than usual."

"You sound like you're an expert on the subject."

"Personal experience. I about drank the tap dry last een, and Maggie's always thirsty when she has a bairnie—baby—to nurse." Stu's hand felt warm in Rob's as they shook.

"I keep saying this, but there's no way we can ever thank you

318

enough for all you did yesterday. You saved our lives."

"The Lord was with us all."

"He certainly was." Stu gripped Den's hand. "I want to offer our thanks to you. You handled that boat like a pro. If I'd been that good, we never would have gotten into so much trouble."

"Den Anderson, a fellow American."

"What happened?" Rob asked. "Walk me through it."

Stu blew out a long breath. "We rented the sailboat in Oban. Took her through the sound, then into the Atlantic. Didn't have any trouble till our return trip."

"Didn't they warn you about the skerries when you rented the boat?"

"Skerries?"

"The rocks you hit. They just pop up out of the sea from nowhere. They're a real menace in the seas south of us."

"They didn't say a word about any rocks so far out in the Atlantic, just told me to avoid sailing too close to any of the islands because of submerged rocks around their shores."

Instant anger fueled Rob's words. "Eejits! They deserved to lose their boat."

"I might have made it if my engine hadn't stalled. I was able to back off the rocks a good twenty-five yards before we lost power, but the waves just carried us right back. And that was the beginning of the end."

"You sound like you've had some experience sailing," Den said.

"Grew up in California. Been sailing since I was a kid, but I really screwed up royally this time."

Rob clapped his shoulder. "Well, it's all over now. And you've a fine new lad to show for the experience."

"That's my biggest mistake. I'm a CPA for a large accounting firm in San Diego and I won this trip at this year's Christmas raffle. We should have waited until next year to claim it, but we hadn't been anyplace for so long, we decided to take the chance. Brenna was born almost two weeks late so we thought we had plenty of time. I really blew it."

Den grinned. "I'm from San Diego. Teach flying at a private airstrip there."

"Small world. Who would have thought we'd meet a fellow San Diegan on an island in Scotland?" He laughed and led them to the large room which had once been Rob's. "Jill's anxious to see you and show off our son."

Maggie sat on a chair next to Jill's bed, holding the Proctor's bairnie. "He's such a braw lad," she said to Rob after she had been introduced to Stu and Brenna. "He reminds me of our Robbie."

"I had the same thought. Even though he came a bit early, he was a lot larger than our Wee Annie when she was birthed." Rob could see where Brenna got her wholesomeness. With her face shiny from soap and water and her dark blonde hair tied back with a ribbon, Jill did not look old enough to have an eleven-year-old.

She held out her hand to Rob. "I want to thank you from the bottom of my heart for saving our lives and helping our little one into the world."

Maggie poked Rob with her elbow.

"You're most welcome," he said, squirming inside.

"Have you told Rob what we're naming our son?" Jill asked her husband.

"I wanted you to do the honors."

Maggie handed the bairnie back to Jill.

"Come closer," Jill said to Rob. "I would like you to meet Christopher Rob Proctor."

He picked up the newborn and cradled him close. "I'm honoured."

"It's the very least we could do." She choked over the words. "None of us would even be here if it weren't for your bravery. We'll call him Chris, after his grandfather, but Rob will be a tribute to the man who saved his life."

Stu cleared his throat. "We had a visit from your minister last night. He brought us clothes and toilet articles donated by the people here on Innisbraw. He said you're going to christen your boat tomorrow after church—kirk, I believe he called it. We'd like to be there if that's okay."

"We'd be honoured to have you," Rob said.

Fern came into the room carrying a large bouquet of flowers. "These are from Elspeth NicAllister's garden." She set the vase on the bedside table. "She had Angus deliver them with her best wishes."

"Oh, Fern, they're beautiful," Jill said. "But who is Elspeth?"

"She's our Island Elder. She's over one hundred one years old and still tends her garden every day."

"Oh, my. How thoughtful. Please thank her for us."

"I will." Fern smiled at Rob. "I see you've met your namesake again."

"I have."

"Isn't he a braw lad?"

"He is that." Rob placed the bairnie in Jill's arms. "We'd better be going. After all you've been through, you need your rest."

"Not until I've had a chance to thank Den." She held out her hand and Den stepped up to her bedside. "Thank you for holding the boat so steady," she said, clasping his hand. "I still don't see how you did it in that sea."

Den's face flushed. "I guess Rob would say God had a hand in it."

Jill smiled. "Of course He did."

Fern walked with them out to the front entry. She smiled up at Den. "I hear you'll be leaving us next Tuesday."

"Yep. Time to get back to the old grind."

"I hope we can visit a while before you go."

She sounded so sincere, Den's heart pounded. He swallowed. "Maybe we could drop in at the howff Monday night. If you're free, that is."

Fern's smile warmed him. "It sounds like fun." She raised her hand. "See you at kirk on the morra."

Rob looked at Maggie, his right eyebrow raised.

She nodded.

"Why don't you and Katie come to supper this een. I'm thinking we have some celebrating to do."

"Aren't you too tired? That was quite an ordeal."

321

"I've never felt better."

"Then we'll be there. Guid-bye now."

Den tried to act nonchalant, but he was grinning on the inside as they walked back to the house. He still had a day to score.

Shame made him cringe inside. Fern was too nice a woman to think of that way.

He hoped she'd at least kiss him good-bye. His heart raced at the thought, then fell like a stone.

Good-bye sounded so final.

⚓

Fern was delighted to be present at the festive dinner. John, Elspeth, and Hugh were also there. After the table had been cleared and the dishes were soaking, they all had questions about the rescue.

"Alec called and told me you were very tired after it was all over," Elspeth said to Rob. "Are you going to be asking too much of your rescue crew when the next shout comes in?"

"Och, it was because there was nobody on deck to help pull me in. That would have made a huge difference."

"But how could you pull in three at one time, and one very biggen?" Hugh asked.

Rob described how Stu and Brenna had reached the *Maggie* on their own by using his rope. "The outcome could have been tragic if he hadn't been so strong."

Hugh's elfin grin lit up his face. "I'm thinking our Lord knew just who was going to be in harm's way when you faced your first shout. 'Tis just another example of His luve and omnipotence."

Den's cheeks flamed. "You mean God made that boat ground herself on the rocks? That doesn't sound like love to me. They could have all drowned."

"I didn't mean that God caused the accident. Just that He foresaw what was going to happen and made sure Rob and you were in a position to help. Remember, He holds each believer in His hands and knows the instant he or she will be called home into His presence."

"You mean He told Rob to ask me out for a sail yesterday afternoon and at exactly the right time to be close enough to help?"

Rob leaned forward in his chair. "I didn't hear a voice in my

322

ear, if that's what you're thinking, Den. But I pray constantly to be doing what He wants, and I'm convinced the Holy Spirit is the one responsible for us being in that exact spot at that exact time. I'm thinking if you asked Stu and Jill, they'd agree."

Den shook his head, got up, and refilled his coffee mug.

Fern stared at her hands, good mood shattered. Either Den wasn't a Christian, or he was a very immature one. Did she still want to go to the howff with him?

But it should be all right. He was leaving for America the next morning, and she would never see him again.

John broke the uncomfortable silence. "I want you all to know that Jill and her bairnie are in fine shape. All that laddie needed was a bath. The same could really be said for his mother."

"It's a good thing he wasn't born while you were still in the sea, Uncle Rob," Katie exclaimed.

"Och, that's the truth. That would have been a rare fankle—och, a real problem."

Maggie got up and brought both the coffee pot and teapot to the table. "I've shortbread and a clootie pudding. Who's ready?"

Den took his seat, hand shooting up. "Put me down for the clootie pudding, especially if you have some of that clotted cream for the top."

The sun sparkled off the turquoise water near the shore and brightened the colours of wildflower petals fluttering in the light breeze. Maggie bounced Annie on her hip, and cast a loving smile at her Rob. *Thank Ye for such a bonnie day, Faither, and especially for placing a need in every heart to attend the christening of Rob's rescue boat.*

Angus's cairt parked on the path with Elspeth and Auntie Mairit perched on the bench, watching over the heads of the throng of people crowding the pier and shore.

The rescue crew and the lads who had helped build the boat, as well as Hugh, Graham and Rinait, Fern and Katie, Den, and the Proctors all clustered around her family on the dock, faces wreathed with smiles, cheeks bright with excitement. Malcolm, Mark, and

Tormad stood a little apart, as though embarrassed by Rob's recognition for their help in designing the boat. Robbie rode Rob's shoulders and Katie, Den's.

Hugh pressed Rob's arm and stepped to the front, raising his hands for silence. The sun glinted off his eyeglasses and highlighted his rosy, cherubic cheeks.

Rob leaned close to the Proctors so he could translate Hugh's Gaelic into English.

Fern leaned toward Den to do the same.

"Good people of Innisbraw," Hugh said. "This is a solemn occasion. For the first time ever, our island is blessed with her own rescue boat. Never again will our brave fishermen have to face an angry sea without help nearby. Never again will strangers who venture into our waters perish because there is no Innisbraw Coastal Rescue Service. Because of the dream of us all and the work of one man, Rob Savage, this has all come to pass."

The folk clapped and whistled.

Hugh waited a moment before raising his hands again. "There is a very fitting Salm for this occasion. Here in Scotland we call it the 'Traveler's Salm.' I would like to read it to you now." He took out his worn Bible and opened it. "'I will lift up mine eyes unto the mountains: from whence shall my help come? My help cometh from the Lord, which made heaven and earth. He will not suffer thy foot to be moved: He that keepeth thee will not slumber. Behold, He that keepeth Israel shall neither slumber nor sleep. The Lord is thy keeper: the Lord is thy shade upon thy right hand. The sun shall not smite thee by day, nor the moon by night. The Lord shall keep thee from all evil; He shall keep thy soul. The Lord shall keep thy going out and thy coming in, from this time forth and forevermore.'"

Tears blurred Maggie's vision. *Let me remember Your promise when there's another shout, Faither.*

Hugh closed his Bible. "Let us bow our heads for a word of prayer."

A rustle whispered through the crowd as heads dipped.

"Our most merciful Heavenly Faither, we come gratefully before Your throne, knowing that You have blessed this endeavour since its beginning. We thank You for Your faithfulness in providing Your servant Rob with all he needed to fulfill his promise to us. We are humbled by the rescue of the Proctor family and by the safe delivery of their son. Your hand was holding Rob up as he went into the water and again as he helped in their baby's birth, just as Your hand was on the helm as Den held the boat steady. You provided courage and stamina to Stewart and Jill and Brenna. We will be eternally grateful."

Rob's warm hand closed over Maggie's.

"Continue to bless this endeavour. Give our lads courage and clear minds. Give our Rob wisdom as he makes decisions on how to bring about successful rescues. Help our medical team as they minister to those in need. We thank You, we glorify You. In the name of Jesus Christ, our Saviour, we pray. Amen."

Rob lowered Robbie into John's arms, and Maggie handed a sleeping Annie to Fern.

Tears swam in his eyes as Rob placed a brown bottle tied with white ribbon into Maggie's hands. "We don't have champagne," he announced in a loud voice. "We'd rather use our own ale, brewed here on these shores."

A roar erupted.

He waited until it died down before leading Maggie to the rescue boat's prow. "I know you can't reach the verra front, luve," he whispered. "Just hit her along that board, right there."

Maggie nodded and raised the bottle. Loud and clear so all could hear, she said, "I christen you *Maggie.*" She swung the bottle.

It bounced off without breaking.

She laughed and grabbed Rob's sleeve. "Help me. I'm no' strong enough."

He grinned as he placed his hand over hers. "Just relax and let me do the swinging." He brought his arm back and thrust it forward with a powerful arc.

The bottle smashed into pieces, spraying ale over those nearby.

The folk of Innisbraw voiced their approval as Graham activated the boat's siren with three loud wails. It had finally come to pass. The Innisbraw Coastal Rescue Boat, the *Maggie,* was officially in service.

Chapter Forty-eight

Nervous sweat beaded Den's forehead as he changed his shirt for the third time. Fern and Katie would be at the house in a few minutes. He hadn't felt this discombobulated before a date since high school. He'd even nicked himself shaving. He took off the small piece of toilet tissue and examined his chin in the dresser mirror. Good, it barely showed. He blew on his hands and rubbed them briskly together.

This was it—he'd leave for home tomorrow morning.

He sat down on the bed, stomach in knots. What was so different about Fern that she had him feeling like some addlepated adolescent? She was beautiful, but he had dated a lot of beautiful women over the years. She was intelligent, but so were many of the women he'd gone out with. She was natural—

Ah, there was a huge difference. She wore no face paint. Her clothes were never clingy or screamed, "Look at me, baby!" or had those ridiculous padded shoulders most women wore in the States. She wore blouses or sweaters and skirts. Her hair fell in natural waves to kiss her shoulders, not frizzed into tight curls. No elaborate pompadour, just an occasional wide ribbon like the one she'd worn to the kaylee. And the scent she always wore—light, sweet, slightly spicy, never overwhelming or cloying.

He got up and paced. Fern would never be willing to leave Innisbraw, nor would he feel right asking her to. She had a good job at the infirmary, one she seemed to enjoy, and she was an island girl, born and bred. And there was Katie, the bright, bubbly little girl with enormous blue eyes, hair that sparkled in the sunlight like newly minted pennies, deep dimples in her rosy cheeks. He loved that little girl.

And her mother?

He groaned and smacked his fist into his palm. How should he know? He'd never even kissed her, for Pete's sake. He knew he felt more strongly attracted to her than any other woman he'd ever met, but was that love? He shrugged into his sport coat.

Voices echoed downstairs.

He combed his hair one last time and descended the stairs, heart in his throat.

Katie sat in Rob's lap in front of the fire, her arms around his neck.

Another stab of jealousy. What was happening to him?

Fern and Maggie were in the kitchen, laughing at Robbie's attempts to do a somersault.

Fern turned and looked at him as he walked through the living room, her smile so warm, so welcoming, his knees felt weak.

Get a grip. Tomorrow, it's "I'll be seeing you."

"Hi," he said. "You ready to dance the night away?" Voice shaking like a pimple-faced teen on his first date.

"More than ready." She was wearing the same pale blue outfit she had worn to the kaylee, and her blue eyes sparkled as she took his elbow. "Don't let Katie pester you into more than one story," she called to Rob.

He waved. "Have fun, you two." As Den opened the front door, Rob's voice dropped an octave. "I expect Fern home at a decent hour."

Den turned and gave him the evil eye. "Yes, Father."

Fern was so nervous she fought to steady her breathing. She had already decided she had no business prying into Den's spiritual beliefs. If he wasn't leaving so soon, that would be another matter, but on the morra's mornin, he began his journey back to America.

Would he ever return? Or would he forget her the moment another woman caught his fancy? Tears stung her eyes. She swallowed, refusing to allow them to fall. She would just be herself and enjoy their last evening together, as hard as that might be. She forced a smile when his hand gripped her elbow as they made their way to the gate. "You and Rob act more like brothers than friends."

Den unlatched the gate and ushered her through. "I guess that's because Rob's the closest I ever got to having a brother." He gave a self-deprecating laugh. "I grew up in a household dominated by sisters—three of them. And to make things even worse, I was the baby of the family."

"Oh, poor you."

He continued to hold her elbow as they started down the path. So comforting, that.

"How about you?" he asked. "Sisters? Brothers?"

"Just one sister. We were never very close. She's a lot older than I am."

They chatted about their families until they reached the howff. The musicians were tuning up as they walked in the door.

Paddy McDonald raised an arm. "Here's one of our heroes, then! Free drinks all around."

Den's grin fell away.

The room was crowded. So much for a quiet evening.

Go with the flow, man. "What's your pleasure?" he asked Fern.

"An ale, please."

His gaze swept the room. Only one unoccupied table, but it was off in a corner by itself. Maybe there was a God, and He was smiling on them after all. He seated Fern and fetched two ales.

Paddy approached, wearing an obviously mock funereal expression on his florid face. "'Tis a sad, sad day tomorrow, for you'll be leavin'. Can't we do somethin' to convince you to stay?"

Den grimaced. "Have to make a living, Paddy."

"Oh, what a shame, and me thinkin' you were one of those rich Americans." The Irishman turned his attention to Fern. "You're a sight to behold, you are. What's your pleasure for the first dance?"

No hesitation. "I'm thinking an easy strathspey. I want to teach Den at least one Scots dance before he leaves."

Den's heart leaped. She was willing to teach him a true native dance.

"A strathspey it is." Paddy nodded. "You'll notice we have a fiddler now. We not only got a mechanic and second coxswain, but

Neil's a grand fiddler. Enjoy."

Den took a swig of ale and pulled out Fern's chair. "Don't expect too much. Remember, I'm a novice strathspey dancer."

"'Tis easy. Just a gliding step with only a small skip—no leaping about. They're playing 'Sandy O'er the Lea.' It's a two-couple dance so just watch me and the other couple and you'll learn it in no time." She took his right hand and pulled it around her back, lacing her fingers through his. "We start this dance side by side. Just watch my feet and hands."

The small dance floor quickly filled and another couple approached them. As they danced, whenever he took Fern's small hand in his, he felt a thrill. He didn't know the other couple dancing with them, but they showed a great deal of patience as they crossed hands and changed positions on the floor. They circled the room several times before the song ended and Den escorted her back to their table. "That was great," he said, surprised by how much he meant it.

Her smile made his breath catch. "You could hold your own, no matter the step. You're the best dancer I've ever seen."

This is why Rob squirmed when he was complimented. "Thank you, but you're forgetting one thing. A perfect partner can make any dancer look good."

It was Fern's turn to look embarrassed. Her cheeks bloomed deep red when he held out her chair.

As the night went on, she showed him several reels. He couldn't remember ever having a better time. This woman loved to dance. As time passed, he realized how much he would miss her.

"I suppose we should be heading home," she said after finishing her ale. "I hate to keep Maggie and Rob up too late, and you have an early boat to catch in the morning."

Not *that* early. But he couldn't act like a spoiled brat. "I guess you're right. Let's have one more dance before we leave."

Paddy banged on his bodhrán for attention. "I think you'll all enjoy our next dance, even though you'll be watchin', no' dancin'. Come on Fern and Den. Show these folks again how it's done in America."

329

The musicians launched into "String of Pearls." Den and Fern danced as though they had been partners for years. She wriggled her hips as he tossed her out and drew her back and spun her under his arm time and time again.

The crowd clapped and whistled.

When the song ended, she collapsed into his arms, gasping for breath.

Here she was, right where he had wanted her almost from the moment they met, and all he felt was an unfamiliar tenderness. He held her close, savoring the feel of her slim body close to his.

She looked up at him, eyes wide.

He bent down and kissed her cheek. Her cheek, for Pete's sake!

She smiled and reached up to kiss his.

"Thank you for a fantastic dance." Impossible to keep the regret out of his voice.

"I enjoyed it more than you'll ever know."

It seemed perfectly natural for them to hold hands on the walk up the hill. They took their time. Not much breeze now, just a light breath on his cheeks. The half-light cast soft shadows across the path in front of them.

Fern looked as though she were on the verge of tears.

He, too, ached with deep regret. He had to leave tomorrow, but he didn't want to go. He glanced over at Fern and she gave him a fleeting smile. That same feeling of tenderness washed over him, but he didn't try to fight it this time. He couldn't. He cared for this woman—deeply. He'd miss her so much, just the thought of leaving her made his eyes burn.

When they reached Rob and Maggie's front entry, he could no longer control himself. He pulled Fern into his arms and kissed her. She tasted exactly the way he had known she would, warm and womanly. He breathed in her fragrance, heart pounding. "I'm going to miss you, Fern," he whispered. "Terribly."

She looked up at him, tears misting her eyes. "I'll miss you, too. Terribly."

He kissed her again.

She caressed the sides of his face with her fingertips.

Her lips felt so soft beneath his. He tilted her chin up with his fingers and kissed it, then brought her hands up and kissed each of them softly. "I don't want to go, but I have to."

She blinked away tears. "I know. You have a life in America, and I a life on Innisbraw."

He couldn't suppress a groan. "I can't give up flying, Fern. It's been my life since I was a kid."

"I know. I wouldn't ask you to."

"But I'll be back someday." He recognized how hollow the words sounded.

"I hope so." Tears trickled down her cheeks.

He wiped them away with trembling fingers. "I will."

Fern had a difficult time falling asleep. Den's kiss had awakened something deep inside her she had thought long dead. She turned over and punched the pillow before lying down and sighing deeply. It felt so right, so comforting to be in his arms. *Och, Faither, I should never have gone to the howff with him. It makes this so much harder.* Tears wet her pillow. *I want someone to luve, Lord. But it can't be an unbeliever, and I know that. Please give me the strength to go on with my life and see all the blessings You have in store for me and my Katie.*

Fern was not at the dock to see Den off.

Rob thought his buddy looked disappointed. When it came time to board, he clasped Den's shoulder. "Don't wait so long to visit next time. Life's too short."

"I won't. I know you can't get away from all your commitments, so I won't even ask you to come to San Diego."

"Come back, Den. There will always be a home for you here."

"I know." Den punched his shoulder. "Watch those rescues, bucko. You'll have a crew to back you up, but I also know the risks you take to save others. Don't put your life on the line. You mean too much to too many people ... including me."

He gripped Den's hand. "Write to us. I promise to answer."

"Will do. Take care." Den picked up his bag and walked up the gangplank.

Sim stowed the gangplank as Rob untied the mooring lines and tossed them aboard.

Rob stood on the dock until the *Sea Rouk* was only a small speck far out on the Minch. Disappointment weakened his bones. He'd hoped Den would promise to return and take him up on that partnership. But that would mean giving up flying—something Den would never do. He stared out at the sea, shoulders bowed.

When would he ever see Den again? Mebbe in a year or twa for another short visit?

In the meantime, he would be too busy with the boatworks and shouts to miss his best friend very often. But there would be nights when he would relive their time together on Innisbraw.

He turned and shambled off the dock and down the pier. When he passed the infirmary, he saw her—his Maggie—waiting on their entry. His steps quickened, his spirits buoyed by the thought of holding her body close and hearing her soft words of comfort.

The End

Acknowledgments

I have been fortunate to have read many books published about the Royal National Lifeboat Institute which gave me invaluable information into the types of lifeboats they used during this time period.

And once again, my thanks to Paddy MacKinnon and her hospitality. Though she has moved from the Isle of Barra to Alfreton, England to be closer to her grandchildren, she is still a fount of information and knowledge about the Outer Hebrides Islands of Scotland. She also provides me with warm hugs, funny anecdotes, a lovely place to stay, and gourmet meals when I finish my holiday every summer in Scotland.

Also, thanks once again to Christina Tarabochia, my editor, who's saved my bacon time after time.

The origins of electricity and telephone service to the Outer Hebrides have been simplified and the dates changed to fit the storyline. Any mistakes are mine alone, but thank you to Kristen Johnson, John Ashcraft, Andrea Cox, and Tami Engle for attempting to find them all.

Remember, Innisbraw is a fictional island. You'll only find it on the map of my imagination.

Dianne fell in love with writing at the age of five. Because her father was a barnstorming pilot, she was bitten early by the "flying bug" as well. She attended the University of California, Santa Barbara, and met and married the man God had prepared for her—an aeronautical engineer. After their five children were in school, she burned the midnight oil and wrote three novels, all published by Zebra Press. When her husband died, only three years after he retired, she felt drawn to visit the Outer Hebrides Isles of Scotland, where her husband's clan (MacDonalds) and her own clan (Galbraiths) originated. Many yearly trips, gallons of tea, too little sleep, and a burst of insight birthed her *Thistle Series*.

PUBLISHER'S NOTE: Dianne, born August 1933, lived joyfully despite dealing with terminal cancer and died in August 2013, a mere week before the release date for the first book of this series, *Broken Wings*. Everyone involved with the production of the six books in the series has been blessed beyond measure to be part of giving readers a chance to meet Rob and Maggie and visit the beautiful, fictional isle of Innisbraw.

Leave a message for her family and sign up to hear the latest about her books at www.ashberrylane.com/dianneprice or www.facebook.com/authordianneprice.

Glossary

All words are Scots, unless otherwise noted.

APC: headache medicine.
auld: old.

baffies: bedroom slippers.
bairn: child.
bairnie: baby.
bed sit: small place to rent.
ben: mountain.
biddy certain: very sure.
biggen: pregnant.
blether: talk, visit. (In the plural, nonsense.)
blootered: very drunk.
blowsterie: windy, gusty, boasting.
bodhrán: Gaelic (pronounced *bo-rahn*), one-sided drum.
bonnie: beautiful.
bowf: a dog's bark.
brae: hillside.
braw: handsome, a pleasing sight.
bree: soup or broth.
breeks: pants or trousers.
brogans: tough, ankle-high shoes.
brose: creamy oat porridge, soaked overnight.
bunker: counter, like in a kitchen.
bunnet: a flat cap.
burn: small stream.
buttery: biscuit made with butter.

cairt: cart pulled by a horse.
cannie: shrewd, expert, skillful, or lucky.
casting peat: slicing off pieces of peat, digging peat used for
    fuel.
cat's lick: wash hands and face, short wash-up.
ceilidh: Gaelic (pronounced *kay-lee*), party with music, dancing,

sharing of news.

chappit: knocked, bruised.

chaumer: parlour or gathering room.

clootie: dumpling, pudding dessert served with clotted cream.

coo: cow.

coo gang: pen for cows.

coorie doun: nestle together, back to front, spoon.

croft: piece of land.

crofter: farmer, or one who owns a croft used for agriculture.

cuddy: small, shaggy horse, usually used to pull a cart.

cutty: clay pipe.

daft: insane.

digester: UK, septic tank.

disremember: forget.

dreich: dreary, dull, grey, usually describing weather.

dumfoondert: confused.

dunt: a blow, or to deliver a blow.

eejit: idiot, fool.

een: evening, can be written e'en.

entry: porch, passage into house.

face flannel: UK, washcloth.

faither: father.

fauld yer fit: rest, sit down.

fankle: disorder, entanglement.

fash: worry, vex.

fell: mountain or hill.

FFR: Fitted For Radio.

flag: piece of stone used as floor of a cottage.

girse: grass.

gleg as a gled: starving, keen as an eagle.

gloaming: twilight.

gobsmacked: astonished.

grandbairn: grandchild.

guid: good.

haddie: haddock, white-meated fish.
handsel: gift, usually handmade for a special occasion, like
    marriage.
hap: knitted blanket, afghan.
haud yer wheesht: hold your tongue.
hippen: diaper.
Hogmanay: New Year's Eve.
howff: pub.
hoy: greeting.

incomer: outsider who comes to live on island.
infirmary: UK, hospital.
in the scud: naked.
Irisher: Irishman or woman.

jawbox: kitchen sink.
joint: UK, roast.

keek: look at, peek.
ken: know, understand.
kirk: church.
kittled up: excited, enlivened.

lang-nebbit: prying, nosy.
lemon skoosh: sparkling lemonade.
louring: dark, black, heavy clouds or sky.

machair: Gaelic (pronounced *ma-K-er*), alluvial plain, unique to
    Outer Hebrides.
mebbe: maybe.
medicaments: UK, medicine.
merrit: married.
midden: dirty, messy, untidy place.
Minch: arm of the Atlantic between Outer Hebrides and Scotland.
mither: mother.

natter: chat, talk, often nag.
neeps: turnips.
ned: hooligan.
Nevermass: an event which never happens.
no': not.
nowt: nothing.

owt: anything.

partan: common crab.
piece: snack, usually a small sandwich or buttery.
pishing: hard rain, usually used by men.
plowtering: splashing, playing in water.
polis: police.
pottle: pot full.
press: cabinet.

reeky: smelly, sometimes refers to smoke.
redd: clean, organize, tidy (up).

sark: shirt.
Sassenach: English person.
Sellotape: UK, clear, one-sided tape, like American Scotch
    tape.
shilpit: skinny.
Siobhan: Gaelic (pronounced *Shi-vahn)*, woman's name.
skail: heavy, driving wind.
skellum: little imp or misbehaving child.
skite one's lug: box on the ears.
slaisterin: slobby.
sleeperie: sleepy.
sma': small.
snell: cold, if wind, usually from the north.
sook: to suck.
strathspey: regal, gliding dance.

tablet: UK, vanilla fudge.
tatties: potatoes.
the day: today.
the morra: tomorrow.
tick: a second in time.
trews: leggings, tight pants, worn by a male.
turns: jobs, chores.
twa: two.

verra: very.

watterie: toilet.
whinging: complaining.
whummled: overturned, knocked down.

BROKEN Wings

THE Thistle SERIES
Book One

DIANNE PRICE

He lives to fly—until a piece of flak changes his life forever.

A tragic childhood has turned American Air Forces Colonel Rob Savage into an outwardly indifferent loner who is afraid to give his heart to anyone. RAF nurse Maggie McGrath has always dreamed of falling in love and settling down in a thatched cottage to raise a croftful of bairns, but the war has taken her far from Innisbraw, her tiny Scots island home.

Hitler's bloody quest to conquer Europe seems far away when Rob and Maggie are sent to an infirmary on Innisbraw to begin his rehabilitation from disabling injuries. Yet they find themselves caught in a battle between Rob's past, God's plan, and the evil some islanders harbor in their souls.

Which will triumph?

ASHBERRY LANE
ASHBERRYLANE.COM

Wing
AND A
Prayer
DIANNE PRICE

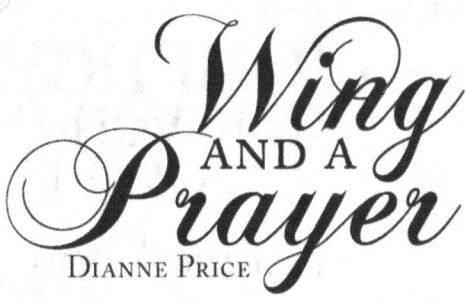

Confronting death isn't the
most difficult challenge he will face.

When Colonel Rob Savage
recovers enough from a near-
death accident to resume
command of the demoralized
Heavy Bomber Group at
Edenoaks Air Base in England,
he faces many challenges. As
Rob labors to make his group
best in Wing again, his bride,
Maggie, works long, exhausting
hours as an RAF nurse, all the
while fearing for Rob's safety
during bombing missions.

The unthinkable happens. Rob and Maggie return to their
Scots island of Innisbraw, battling to keep alive their dreams
for the future. Rationing, blackouts, and the threat of
German U-boat invasions conspire against the newlyweds.

Can Rob and Maggie cleave to their faith in God through
such hardships and trials as the devastating war goes on
and on and on?

ASHBERRY
LANE
ASHBERRYLANE.COM

The Journey of Eleven Moons

Bonnie Leon

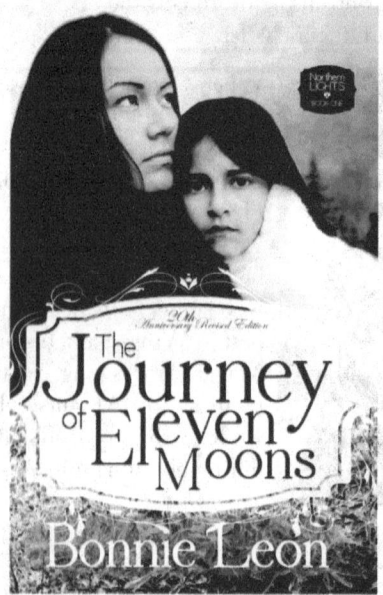

A successful walrus hunt means Anna and her beloved Kinauquak will soon be joined in marriage. But before they can seal their promise to one another, a tsunami wipes their village from the rugged shore … everyone except Anna and her little sister, Iya, who are left alone to face the Alaskan wilderness.

A stranger, a Civil War veteran with golden hair and blue eyes, wanders the untamed Aleutian Islands. He offers help, but can Anna trust him or his God? And if she doesn't, how will she and Iya survive?

ASHBERRY
LANE
ASHBERRYLANE.COM

On the Threshold

Sherrie Ashcraft &
Christina Berry Tarabochia

Suzanne ~
a mother with a
long-held secret

Tony ~
a police officer with
something to prove

Beth ~
a daughter with a
storybook future

When all they love
is lost, what's worth
living for?

Ashberry
Lane
ASHBERRYLANE.COM

www.ingramcontent.com/pod-product-compliance
Lightning Source LLC
Chambersburg PA
CBHW011757010726
47497CB00013B/3245